CONVENTION

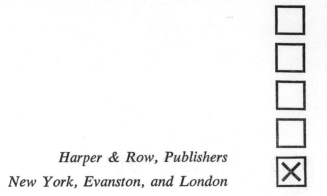

Harper & Row, Publishers
New York, Evanston, and London

Books by Fletcher Knebel and Charles W. Bailey II

CONVENTION

SEVEN DAYS IN MAY

NO HIGH GROUND

CONVENTION

By FLETCHER KNEBEL

and CHARLES W. BAILEY II

D-O

To our good friends, the professional politicians, all of whom—and none of whom—appear in this book.

CONVENTION

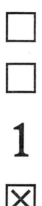

1

Archie DuPage opened the door, but a blast of trumpets rang down the corridor and drove him back inside the hotel room.

California, here we come!

Around the corner and down the hall trooped one of the amateur bands already plaguing the convention like trilling locusts. First came an enormous poppy, state flower of California, held high by a youth in gilt pants and jacket. Next pranced a drum majorette, attired in a strapless golden costume that began at mid-breast and ended at mid-thigh. Behind her, in single file, marched a dozen young musicians of both sexes, all shimmering in golden garments, all playing instruments of high decibel potential. The racket caromed off the walls and burst through the open doorway of suite 2306.

Archie winced and closed the door, but the noise pursued him through the cracks and over the transom.

California, here we come!
Bryan Roberts, he's the one!

Six female voices set the tempo, then the trumpets and trombones joined in, and by the time the marchers reached the Royal Skyway suite, the sound was deafening. Most of the group passed the door without recognition, but the last noisemaker, a lad belaboring a bass drum, paused long enough to shout:

"Don't worry in there. Roberts will take you for vice-president!"

The clamor dwindled gradually as the band turned the next corner, but it left some casualties. As Archie peered out again, a door down the hall was jerked open and a man wearing only pajama pants shuffled sleepily into the corridor. He rubbed a patch of graying hair on his chest and looked at his wrist watch. The man, who was a minor functionary in the headquarters, saw Archie's protruding head, then shook his own.

"Not even ten o'clock yet, for Chrissake," he grumbled in Archie's direction, "and already the nuts are at it. Thank God for our side. At least Charlie Manchester don't have so many lunatic bands."

The complainant retreated into his sanctuary and Archie went back to the sitting room of suite 2306 to see what was detaining the others. As usual, it was the telephone.

The candidate was speaking into the white phone, one of three on the desk. Secretary of the Treasury Charles B.

Manchester held his tall frame erect and his blue lightweight suit showed the sharp creases of morning. Two other aides stood beside him, somewhat impatiently. The day had just begun in Manchester-for-President headquarters, but already Archie sensed the quiver of disrupted schedules.

"That's very thoughtful of you, Mr. President," Manchester was saying. He toyed with the telephone cord and his tone was one of respectful affability. "Well, I hope it doesn't blow the tube on your set. It's a little early in the day for statesmanship on television. . . . Don't worry about that. The farm issue won't be mentioned. . . . I know, I know. . . . Again, thank you, Mr. President. I certainly feel better for your call. . . . Good-by, sir."

Manchester grinned at his three assistants as he hung up. "The old fox. He pretended he wanted to wish me well before the press conference, but he was really worried about the farm thing. Afraid I'd get trapped. All right, let's go."

The four men filed out of the suite, Manchester in the lead. He did not seem to be moving fast, but the others had to hurry to keep up with his long, easy strides. Archie noted how straight the candidate held himself and involuntarily squared his own shoulders to correct his youthful slouch.

Charles Manchester's figure would have looked trim in any group and his carriage made him appear taller than six feet. He strode along with an air of casual confidence, and only a hand tugging at an ear lobe told Archie that the candidate was preoccupied. Archie guessed that Manchester was thinking ahead to the press conference and the unpredictable questions that would be coming.

Obie O'Connell was concerned with the recent past, not the

future, and he was grouchy as he hurried his tubby body in a rolling gait beside his candidate. "That damn California song," he complained, "uses itself up quicker than anything since Taft and his 'Four-Leaf Clover' in '52."

"I like it," Manchester said. "It's got zing."

O'Connell massaged his puffy face. "You haven't seen enough conventions, Charlie," he said. "The first time, you love everything."

Louis Cohen edged between the candidate and the manager. Cohen, the "issues man" who taught political science at Princeton, had a face that seemed molded in a perpetual frown. His thin features appeared frail under the heavy frame of his glasses and he looked more unhappy than usual.

"Mr. Secretary," he said, "the President is right about the farm program. You really can't go into it now. It'll be a month before we have that study group paper—even if you're nominated."

"What do you mean 'if,' Louis?" asked Manchester. He beamed down at his little professor as they walked along. Archie DuPage marveled that a man could look so radiantly confident so early in the day. "We'll win," said Manchester, "on the first ballot."

"The last ballot," O'Connell corrected. "You always win on the last ballot."

"The last ballot," Manchester agreed, and he grinned again.

They were approaching the elevators, but DuPage steered Manchester away with a hand on his elbow. "Let's take a service elevator," he said. "The Hilton may have fourteen elevators, but they started skipping floors yesterday. It'll be murder by Monday."

The service elevator contained a laundry cart. A white-coated employee held the cart with one hand while he worked to dislodge a piece of food from a molar with the other.

"Good morning," said Manchester, "I'm Charles Manchester."

"I know," replied the service man. He said it flatly, as though celebrated personages were a routine fixture in his world.

"And your name?" asked the candidate.

The man was startled. "Joe," he said. "Joe Greimer."

"Democrat?" asked Manchester.

The hotel employee nodded, abruptly ceasing his toothpick labors in embarrassment.

"That's a pity," said Manchester. "You really ought to give the Republican program a hearing, Mr. Greimer. If union men would only—"

"I'm getting off here," said the employee. The elevator had stopped at the fourteenth floor. Manchester, however, moved slightly and the man found his exit blocked.

The candidate's full attention was focused on the stranger. He asked the man how much he made and how many children he had. Under the questioning, the laundry worker's look of apathy was replaced by one of surprised pleasure. The others could feel the warmth of the connection being soldered between Joe Greimer and the Secretary of the Treasury. Archie whispered to O'Connell: "Wouldn't you love to have a picture of this?" O'Connell nodded. "If we could only get him two minutes with every voter in the country," he replied, "it would be a landslide." Louis Cohen looked at his watch. "He's going to be late," he protested.

Manchester finally stepped aside and the laundry man left, pushing his cart of soiled linen. Joe Greimer was smiling and he winked at Archie. "Some guy," he said with a flick of his head toward Manchester.

As the elevator descended the rest of the way to the mezzanine floor, Archie thought about his candidate. This sudden concentration on a person—any person—was no political trick. Manchester did it time and again, though frequently such a meeting would riddle his schedule. He seemed to have a compulsion for involvement with strangers. He disliked crowds, as Archie knew only too well, and so he broke them into tiny fragments. When he spoke, he spoke to the individual. In conversation, he became absorbed in the thoughts and problems of the other person. Charles Manchester, Archie had decided long ago, was a walking person-to-person program.

And how *could* Manchester lose the nomination? Big, cheerful, smart, compassionate, a leader with the magnetism that marked a winner—he was all of these. Above all, Archie thought, he looked like a winner, and what this Republican convention wanted most was a winner in November.

The victory four years ago had whetted the party's appetite. President Stuart's ill-health dampened hopes for a few months, but since he'd stepped aside and anointed Manchester as his successor, the party felt good again. Well, perhaps "anointed" wasn't quite right. Stuart merely declined to comment when Senator Floberg of Iowa, the Senate leader, said he understood that if the President were a delegate to the convention he'd cast his vote for Manchester. But that was enough. The party knew that Manchester was Stuart's choice. Privately, the evidence was even more solid. The President had called three times since their arrival in Chicago on Thursday.

As of this Saturday morning, August 12, with the convention due to open Monday, the challenge of Governor Bryan Roberts of California was somewhat less than frightening. A candidate needed 655 votes to win the nomination; count as he would, giving Roberts two thirds of the doubtfuls, Archie DuPage could reach a grand total of no more than 450 for the Californian. Manchester had almost 200 pledged votes from the primaries and another 500 hitched as securely as anything could be in politics.

Archie ran his fingers through his curly black hair and congratulated himself on his political acumen. A Yale graduate with a public relations office in his home city of Rochester, he had done some publicity chores in the Stuart campaign. He moved his one-man firm to Washington with the advent of the new Republican administration. When Manchester entered the Stuart administration as Under Secretary of the Treasury, fresh from the bank in Cincinnati, Archie persisted until he landed a public information job with this newcomer to politics. When Manchester moved up to the cabinet a year later, Archie went with him. He admired Charles Manchester's intelligence, his quick adaptibility to the alien forum of politics, his humor, his easy grace, his confidence, his courage. If he were to fault his boss at all, it would be for his frankness. Sometimes the Secretary blurted out the truth when silence would have served him better. But what a guy! Manchester was made for the White House, and Archie, thirty-three, hankered for a seat of his own in that place of power.

The miscellaneous clamor of a convention—"a drunken cocktail party mated to an iron foundry," O'Connell called it —enveloped them as they stepped out of the elevator. A young girl, recognizing Manchester, shrieked and jabbed him in the stomach with an autograph book. The Secretary scrawled his high, looping signature and gave her a private smile. In a booth labeled "Have a Coke—With Manchester OR Roberts," another girl in a starched white uniform waved wildly. A crowd came from nowhere, pressing around the candidate with the flushed and aimless pleasure of unexpected proximity. O'Connell scowled and beckoned to a Chicago policeman nearby, and soon the four men from 2306 were burrowing through the gathering throng, Manchester sandwiched between the officer and O'Connell while Cohen and DuPage struggled to stay with them.

Manchester walked into the high-ceilinged Grand Ballroom, with its shimmering crystal chandeliers, at 9:58 A.M., on time despite his chats with the President and the laundryman. The buzz of conversation increased as the Secretary smiled, nodded and mouthed an inaudible "hello" to several newspapermen in the front row. Four television cameras focused on him and a shoving mob of still photographers began shouting indistinguishable and conflicting orders at him. His three aides sat down on the platform as Manchester stepped to the lectern and, precisely at 10 A.M., held up his hands for silence. The relative quiet that ensued was pierced by a shout from the rear of the room, where a few dozen gate-crashing spectators had gathered.

"The Man! The Man! The Man Who? Man-ches-ter!"

Manchester grinned and held his palms out in a muffling gesture.

"I appreciate the enthusiasm," he said, "but I'd ask the partisans to—uh—quench their ardor for the next half hour. This time belongs to the press, and it has its job to do. All right, ladies and gentlemen, I'm at your disposal. If you'd be good enough to state your name and affiliation—I'm sure your employers won't mind the publicity."

The opening laugh was friendly. The stenotypist recorded it in muted clicks on his keyboard as Manchester palmed the side of his head, where the neatly combed black hair was streaked with gray, and nodded to the first questioner.

"Corson, Associated Press. Mr. Secretary, some of your backers are talking about a first-ballot victory. Do you agree?"

Manchester moved his shoulders forward as he grasped the lectern, and a smile again softened the rather sharp lines of his lightly tanned face. "You must be telepathic. My mentor, Mr. O'Connell, informed me only five minutes ago—and I quote him—'you always win on the *last* ballot.' " A second laugh, heavier this time, rolled from the four hundred newsmen. "Obie insists that at a convention it's always done that way. Since he's my only manager, I think I'd better not fall out with him before the roll is called on Thursday."

"Why aren't Mrs. Manchester and the children with you?" The question erupted unbidden in a southern accent from a large, blonde woman in the front row.

"I'm afraid I didn't get the name, Mrs. Oliver." This time the laugh was a roar and Archie DuPage glowed. This thing was starting well. "Independent Alliance, isn't it?" Manchester added. The female journalist nodded in triumph, happy for the personal plug on all four networks.

"Well," Manchester went on, concentrating on Mrs. Oliver as though she were the only person in the room, "there's really no mystery. My wife is at our place on Lake Winnipesaukee in New Hampshire, baby-sitting for our granddaughter, Amy. If I should be nominated—with, I hope, the help of the New

Hampshire delegation—Mrs. Manchester will fly here after the balloting. We just felt that the convention atmosphere was a bit too hectic for family life."

"What about the children?" Mrs. Oliver was not ready to yield the spotlight.

"Jake and Martha really aren't children, you know," replied Manchester. "Jake is rather new on his first job with a bank in San Francisco, and like most banks it takes a dim view of its young men plunging into politics in full view of the depositors. Martha's husband Ed is at sea with the Navy, so Martha's with her mother and the baby at Lake Winnipesaukee. I think that about takes care of the Manchester family. Let's just say that if you want to see my wife next week, you might ask any delegates you see to vote for me."

All right, all right, Archie thought. That's about enough humor, Mr. Candidate. You're not running for toastmaster. Remember what happened to Adlai. As if he had heard the plea, Manchester dropped the easy smile and looked seriously at the crowd of newsmen.

"Carl Johnson, Des Moines *Register*. Mr. Secretary, the latest Iowa poll shows that only thirty per cent of the farmers in our state favor the Stuart administration farm program. Do you have something new in mind?"

Manchester nodded. He could imagine President Stuart sitting before the television set in the oval office at the White House, and he yearned fleetingly to say exactly what he thought—that the Stuart farm program was a shambles and would have to be abandoned. But he had been warned by the President and by Louis Cohen. He frowned as he spoke.

"I haven't seen that particular poll, but I would wager that

even those who oppose the program would agree that the
President has tried in good faith to find a sensible solution for
what seems a perennial problem in this country. I might say
it's one problem we're lucky to have, really. But the program
does have shortcomings. The President recognizes that and
I recognize it. We have a task force at work, and by Labor
Day at the latest the Republican party will have a sound
program ready for American agriculture. It will be fiscally
reasonable and it will be calculated to do the job. Until then,
I can assure you and our farm people that it's a problem
uppermost in my mind."

The press conference settled down to serious, if not always
significant inquiry. Roberts was claiming Nebraska. Was that
justified? No. Would Manchester debate Senator Hendrickson,
the Democratic nominee, on television? Of course. Was he
being briefed by the CIA on intelligence matters? Not yet,
but of course as a member of the National Security Council (a
dig at Roberts, whose Sacramento statehouse was a continent
away from such pinnacles of government) he kept abreast of
all major developments.

Did he favor deficit financing? No. Pay-as-you-go was the
basis of his fiscal thinking. Why had he become a candidate?
Because he found he enjoyed the challenges of government
and the greatest challenges were those of the Presidency—and
because he thought he could make a contribution to his
country. Manchester said this slowly and carefully, and he
knew it rang true, because he meant it. He had thought about
it many, many times.

Would he lower the social security retirement age? Take
sides between Israel and the United Arab Republic? Cut

foreign aid? Meet with the Canadian prime minister? Ask statehood for Puerto Rico? The questions came like a barrage and he faced the fire with only an occasional sidestep. Manchester glanced once at Archie and found him looking quite content.

An elderly man stood up in the middle of the room. His voice did not carry, and there was a pause while a hand microphone was passed to him.

"Thank you. Calvin Burroughs of the Burroughs newspapers, Mr. Secretary. There have been speculative stories out of Washington to the effect that you favor a substantial cut in defense spending. To my best recollection, you have not stated your views publicly. Could you do so now?"

"I'd be happy to, Mr. Burroughs," Manchester answered. He paused a moment, selecting his words, although he knew in general what he wanted to say. "This country has carried an enormous defense burden ever since World War II. We shall have to continue major outlays in this area. The Soviet Union has met us part way in reducing some of the tensions, it is true, but it would be foolhardy to think that the long cold war is over for good. And then, of course, we have the steadily growing menace of Red China. So we have to maintain a large and alert defense establishment. But with that understood, we must recognize that a new element has entered the situation in the last few years. The United States today has enough nuclear weapons, and can deliver them, not only to eradicate Russia from the face of the earth, but literally to erase civilization itself. In short, the question now arises—do we need more? My mind is open on the question, but I must say I approach it in the negative. I would have to be shown that we needed more nuclear warheads, or delivery systems, than we now possess. Does that answer your question?"

Burroughs had stayed on his feet through the answer. Now he raised the little microphone again. Archie glanced at O'Connell. The manager's chubby face was tensed.

"In part, yes, sir," replied Burroughs. "But it leads straight off to the obvious question. As you know, there are a number of big contracts pending of the kind you mention, ones that won't go into production for some time yet."

"I'm aware of that, and I know that as a metropolitan publisher, Mr. Burroughs, you are perhaps even more familiar with them." Manchester spoke carefully. "I don't think it would be proper for me to comment on existing plans, except to say that if I am nominated and elected, I would want to re-examine each one in some detail."

A man in the second row stood up quickly. "Corson again, AP. Does that mean a hold-down on all new weapons systems?"

"No, I didn't say that." Manchester stroked the back of his head. Archie noticed it; it was a familiar sign that the Secretary was troubled. "There are weapons systems and weapons systems. For instance, the Navy is working on a hydrofoil warship that would be able to travel at upwards of sixty knots even in a heavy sea. That kind of advance we must always encourage, and with considerable funding, if necessary. I am referring to weapons systems which would do nothing more than deliver a great nuclear load a second or two faster."

Questioners were on their feet all over the room. The pack was alerted. O'Connell now wore a frown almost as deep as that normally carried by Louis Cohen.

"McIntosh, *New York Times*. Are you implying, sir, apart from the delivery systems, that the United States already has a large enough arsenal of nuclear weapons?"

"I am," said Manchester, "within certain well-defined limits. If we discover a really new principle, or method of explosion, why, of course, I would favor its development. But merely the piling up of more existing weapons, no. I'm against that."

The buzz of conversation in the room rose to a steady hum. Chairs scraped as more reporters got to their feet. Questions now followed one another like quickening raindrops in a summer shower.

"What weapons systems now under consideration do you have in mind, Mr. Secretary?"

"I would not want to particularize. That would require expert study."

"But you mean, sir, you won't give the green light to a new delivery system of the type you mentioned?"

" 'Won't' is pretty final. I would be most cautious, put it that way."

"There is one major contract for a delivery system that's just been let, Mr. Secretary, for the Daphne missile, and we've been given a ten-billion-dollar figure on it. What about that?"

"That contract was approved by the Secretary of Defense and by the President."

"Well, as Secretary of the Treasury, Mr. Manchester, do *you* approve it?"

"I'm not here as Secretary of the Treasury. I'm here as an individual and as a candidate for the Republican nomination for President."

"Does that mean you do not approve of the Daphne contract?"

"I think my answers indicate my feeling."

"So, if you are elected, you'd re-examine the Daphne contract too?"

"Now, let's understand just what we're talking about. The Daphne contract was let several months ago. It will require a year of preliminary design work. While this is expensive by personal standards, no substantial commitment of funds will be necessary for another year yet."

"Does that mean, Mr. Secretary, that Daphne would be re-examined?"

"Well, yes. All such matters would be, as I said."

Two reporters near the door ran from the room. One caught his pocket on a doorknob as he went and the sound of ripping cloth cut through the rising medley of noise in the hall. Archie DuPage left his chair and whispered to Manchester. The candidate shook his head and turned back to the microphones.

"Let me try to put this matter in perspective," he said, "since I seem to have touched your news sensibilities. This country, according to the last official figures of the Joint Committee on Atomic Energy of the Congress, has ninety thousand nuclear warheads or bombs in stockpile. If they were detonated at one time, it's a question whether any human being would survive anywhere on the globe. All I'm saying is that enough is enough.

"The same thing applies to the long-range delivery systems. We have several dozen, from Atlas to Minuteman to Polaris. Here again, to be absolutely candid about it, enough is enough. Now, as I understand the argument for the Daphne, it would cut the delivery time from our launching pads to Moscow by about twelve seconds. When we talk about spending ten billion dollars to shave twelve seconds off the time required to bury humanity, I think it has some of the elements of sheer idiocy."

"What was that last word, sir? Idiocy?"

"Well, perhaps idiocy—that was the word, yes—is too strong but, gentlemen, I do feel strongly on this subject."

O'Connell groaned softly. Later, seeing a shot of himself at that instant on filmed television, he was shocked by his own stricken look. Professor Cohen cracked his knuckles. Archie DuPage felt uneasy, but didn't quite know why. A pang in his stomach reminded him, for the first time that day, of his ulcer.

"Mr. Secretary, Universal Forge has announced the hiring of ten thousand new employees to handle the Daphne contract. Would they be laid off?"

"I wouldn't have any comment, one way or the other, about Universal Forge's operations. I'm merely giving you my candid views on something that I think is vital to this country—and to the world."

"Sir, are you willing to make your argument that 'enough's enough' an issue between you and Governor Roberts?"

"Oh, I would think the Governor would feel much as I do. The sentiments of the opposition are something else again. We'll just have to wait and see what Senator Hendrickson and the Democrats have to say."

"Thank you, Mr. Secretary!"

These final words—shouted by a wire-service reporter as he broke for the door—turned the press conference into a tangle of heads and arms as newsmen pushed their way to the exits. The band of partisans in the rear melted away after another explosion of joy for the candidate. A policeman again escorted the Manchester group toward the service elevator, and as they crossed the mezzanine floor, Archie thought he could sense a new excitement. Laughing women jumped to get a look at the candidate over the heads of those who pressed closer. The whole floor seemed to be a forest of curious faces, all seeking a look at Manchester. Burroughs, the publisher, was shoved against the Secretary.

"Excuse me, Mr. Secretary," he said. "But I think you've made a convention out of this tea party."

"Apparently so." Manchester's brief smile suggested that he was not quite sure what Burroughs meant.

In the shelter of the service elevator, O'Connell slumped against the wall of the car and began kneading his face again.

"Honesty, honesty," he said with a heavy sigh. "It causes a hell of a lot more trouble in politics than corruption."

Manchester looked puzzled. "You think I went too far, Obie?"

"Far?" O'Connell's pale eyes darted from the candidate to DuPage to Cohen. "I don't know about the distance. All I know is that when you've got a nomination sewed up you don't usually throw out a big surprise all of a sudden."

"What do you think, Archie?" asked Manchester.

Archie took a deep breath. "As always, boss, I admire your candor and what you said was great. But the timing? I'm not sure President Stuart—"

Manchester interrupted, clenching his fists in frustration. "Dammit, I can't keep my mouth shut on every important issue. I'm willing to cover up for the President on something like the farm problem, and I can go along on a lot for the sake of keeping people happy, but I'm not Stuart's patsy. It may not be so smart, but on something as important as this I'm going to be my own man."

He stopped abruptly, as if apologizing for his outburst. Archie, rebuked by Manchester's unexpected anger, remained silent, but Cohen, his dark face brooding, offered: "It's high time it was said, but I'm not sure it had to be said today."

O'Connell looked balefully at Manchester. "The time to have popped off like that," he said, "would have been Thursday—right after the last ballot."

2

Six men sat silently in suite 901 of the Sheraton-Blackstone, across Balbo Street from the Conrad Hilton but also fronting on Michigan Avenue. Breakfast debris was strewn across the tabletops: emptied glasses marked by wavering lines of dried tomato juice, two silver coffee pots, forlorn chunks of scrambled eggs, leftover toast, and on one plate three untouched strips of bacon, dusted with the ashes of a cigarette that had been stubbed out in their midst.

A young man crossed the room to the television set and turned it off. The last image on the screen was that of Charles Manchester, pushing his way through a crowd while a white placard—"The Man? The Man Who? Manchester!"—jiggled up and down in the background. The scene contracted swiftly to a white spot in the center of the screen, then faded out.

No one spoke for a moment. The eyes of five men moved naturally toward a high-backed armchair directly facing the television set. In it sat the sixth, huge in a yellow terrycloth bathrobe, his legs stretched out in front of him. The bare feet were as enormous as every other part of him. He wasn't smiling, but his face had a cast of good humor, as though he were about to laugh aloud. It was a full face, so rounded that the two folds under his eyes twinkled with little beads of sweat.

"Well, Bin, what do you think?" It was Carl Fleischer, the Roberts campaign manager, a man whose smoked glasses, shiny gray summer suits, and pocket-sized leather pill case were familiar trademarks in Republican politics.

Governor Bryan Roberts crossed his legs, a process somewhat akin to the shifting of heavy machinery. He gazed at the blank television screen as though seeking some insight from the vanished picture of his rival.

"I think . . . No, let's go around the room first," he said. "I'd like to hear from the experts. Davey?"

The young press secretary cocked his head and thought a moment.

"It looks to me," he said, "like Manchester stumbled into something that will appeal to the country. But whether President Stuart will like it is something else. After all, Stuart approved the Daphne contract."

"I agree on Stuart," said Fleischer. The manager jerked his shoulders back as he spoke. "But I'm not so sure Manchester has hold of anything good. Nobody will know for certain whether the people like his ideas or not before the voting Thursday. And there's a lot of missile work going on in this country. Maybe some delegates to this convention are wonder-

ing right now whether Manchester hurt them in the pocketbook."

Roberts nodded to Roger Abbott, a tall man whose bald
head was relieved only by a half dozen strands of colorless hair
meticulously arranged across the top. He was the Republican
state chairman of Kansas, a position he had held almost as
long as he had worn the yellow bow ties that were his unvary-
ing custom. He was now functioning as Roberts' convention
floor manager, a task second in importance only to that of
Carl Fleischer.

"Nobody who's come as far as fast as Charlie Manchester
does things by accident," he said. "My hunch is that he discussed this with Fred Stuart at the White House before he
came out here. Next thing we'll be getting a story out of
Washington saying Manchester has the President's full backing. I think you ought to be damn careful what you say for a
couple of hours."

The two other convention aides of the California Governor
gave opinions that went over the same ground. The staff men
looked again at the candidate. As he sat in the full morning
sunlight, his freshly shaved cheeks shone. A ring on his right
little finger sparkled as he tapped the arm of his chair, the
metal circle pressed into the flesh as though he had put it on at
birth and the finger had grown around it.

Every exposed portion of his flesh bespoke good living.
"Bryan Roberts lives it up—up two pounds at every meal,"
one comedian had said, and the country had chuckled.
Governor Bryan Roberts of California, with 240 pounds
clinging to his big frame, was for his countrymen a symbol of
the good life. You'll know we're in trouble when Bin starts to

diet, they said. More important politically, they viewed him with affection, and Bin Roberts reciprocated the feeling.

"Charlie Manchester said what he believed." Roberts' voice was deep, thoroughly friendly. He shifted heavily in his chair. "He had this atom and missile thing on his mind, and when Cal Burroughs pulled the cork with a question, it just flowed out. The Secretary is very frank. Too frank for his own good. But it was no trick, Roger."

A girl with reddish hair, wearing a large gilded "Bryan Roberts" button on her bosom, opened the door tentatively. She wore the harassed expression of all convention secretaries.

"There are about fifty newspaper fellows out there, Governor," she said. "They want to know what your stand is on the Daphne missile contract."

The press man waved her off. "No press conference, sweetie," he said, then looked to Roberts for confirmation. "Right, Governor?"

"No press conference," Roberts agreed. "But tell them we may have some kind of short statement in a half hour or so."

"Yes, sir," the red-haired girl said, and left.

"Let's be damn careful about shooting too quick," Carl Fleischer warned. A reflection of the room in miniature shimmered in his dark glasses as he reached into the side pocket of his jacket and fiddled with his pill case. "Maybe Manchester has put his foot in his mouth—and we don't want to jump in after it."

"But the Governor's got to say something," the press secretary protested. "He can't just pretend missiles don't exist."

"Of course we'll say something," Roberts said. The big

smile, by now familiar to all America, spread across his face, slowly rearranging its mass as it went. "Charlie touched my vulnerable point with that crack about his being on the National Security Council, but he gave us a nice opening too. It seems to me our pitch should be that vital issues like this one ought to be decided in the—well, the high councils of government, coolly and deliberately, and not in the heat of party conventions."

"Well, let's at least begin by saying a good word for Manchester's intentions," Abbott said. His yellow bow tie moved up and down with his prominent Adam's apple. "We've got to watch out that we don't start off this convention being tagged as anti-peace, or warmongers, or something. Believe me, in Kansas there's a lot of peace sentiment right now."

Fleischer shook his head. "Look, the pocketbook is what's going to count in this convention," he said. "Who knows? There may be a lot of uncommitted delegates from districts that have defense plants in them. Let's not start by throwing away any ammunition they may have handed us."

Roberts nodded. "You're both right. Now listen, Roger, write this down and let's see how it sounds." He eyed the ceiling and chewed on his lower lip. "Quote. Every American realizes the necessity for an impregnable defense—uh—structure. The militant expansion policies of the Soviet Union permit no relaxation of our guard, regardless of the high cost in taxation. . . . Let's see now . . . oh, yes. . . . Whether any particular weapons system is adequate to the task assigned to it is always a matter for continuous study and appraisal. But the place for such appraisal is in the National Security Council and other high councils of government, not in the heat and clamor of a party convention. Unquote. How's that?"

"I'd knock out that business about taxation," Abbott said. "Why remind everybody about taxes? This is August, not April."

Fleischer twitched his shoulders. "Manchester goofed, if you ask me, when he made that 'idiot' crack. He said something about Daphne having the elements of idiocy. The papers will pick it up and some people are going to get mad. We ought to work it in."

"Well, maybe," Abbott said, "but let's get it straight, if we're going to say anything about it. Did we have anybody monitoring that press conference?"

Fleischer nodded, went to the desk behind Roberts, and picked up one of several phones on it. The line was part of a special system linking all key people in the Roberts-for-President organization in a half dozen hotels and in McCormick Place, the convention hall.

"Get me the transcription room," he said. Then: "Henry? This is Carl. Read me back that 'idiocy' stuff from Manchester's press conference, will you? Yeah, it's near the end somewhere. . . . Okay. . . . Hey, go slower. I'm taking it down."

When he finished, Fleischer turned back to the group and read: " 'When we talk about spending ten billion dollars to shave twelve seconds off the time required to bury humanity, I think it has some of the elements of sheer idiocy.' "

Abbott said quickly: "So do I, and so will a lot of people. I'd skip it. Let other people argue about it."

"Wait a minute," Roberts said. "Manchester is mixing up

two completely different things. The idea of Daphne is not to bury humanity. It's to hit Russia faster than any other missile would. That's the trouble with the Secretary's famous candor—it comes out so fast it sometimes gives the wrong impression. And that's his weak point as a Republican candidate. This is going to be a close election, and if Manchester blundered just once, the Democrats would take him. Hendrickson's a pretty smooth article."

"Let's forget Hendrickson," said Fleischer curtly. "We've got to win the nomination first. But let's work on this 'idiocy' bit. Manchester's vulnerable there, regardless of whether he's right or wrong on the whole idea."

"Yes," mused Roberts, "there ought to be a way."

The room fell silent while the candidate went back to inspecting the ceiling. You've got to hand it to this guy, Fleischer thought. Fifty newspapermen hollering outside and he takes his time, just as though he had a month to decide. He can take the pressure, and that's worth plenty in this crazy business. Fleischer recalled how Roberts had once knocked heads together in a West Coast airlines strike, refusing to let anybody out of the room until he had an agreement. He may be fat as hell, he thought, but he's not flabby above the ears.

"How about this?" Roberts asked. "Quote. Whether any improved weapons system is worth the price and the sacrifice is a matter for mature and deliberate study. Nothing is solved by questioning the intellectual capacity of those championing the new weapon. The place for appraisal and the place for decision is in the National Security Council and the other high councils of government, not in the heat and clamor of a party convention. Unquote."

"You've got 'council' in there twice," said the press secretary. "How about making it 'organs' the second time?"

"Organs sounds sexually suggestive," said a man sitting on the window ledge. They all looked at the Stanford professor who had spoken only once since breakfast, and they laughed. "No organs, please," he insisted.

"Okay, no organs," Roberts agreed. "Let's just make it 'in the National Security Council and the White House.' "

"Bin, please take out that word 'sacrifice' too," urged Fleischer. "You're supposed to be the candidate of the abundant life. We aren't running on sacrifice this year."

Roberts grinned. "Sold. Sacrifice is sacrificed. Now read it back with the changes, Roger."

The Kansan's Adam's apple bobbed as he read aloud, a trifle pompously, as though his audience were the world— which it soon would be.

"Only one suggestion," said the Stanford professor when Abbott had concluded. "Make it 'Communist Russia' instead of 'Soviet Union.' More impact in this context."

"All right," Roberts said. "I like that better."

"I still don't like the line about 'intellectual capacity,' " Abbott said. "I don't see where we gain anything picking a fight over words with Manchester."

"No, I want that in there," insisted Roberts. "A lot of people around this convention are going to be thinking that Charlie Manchester went too far when he didn't have to to make his point, and they'll be wondering whether he'd do it again. I want them to know I think that too. It raises a question about Manchester's basic qualifications as a candidate and as a President. All right, Davey, go feed the animals."

"I'll get a question on the 'intellectual capacity' line," said the press aide. "They'll want to know if you're referring to Manchester's idiocy crack."

"Tell them the statement speaks for itself," Roberts said, "but it's all right to say that if you were writing the story, that's the way you'd write it."

Abbott poured new coffee around as the press secretary left. Roberts dropped two lumps of sugar in his cup, then added cream until the color of the mixture thinned out to a soft beige. The phone rang. Fleischer, answering, slid his smoked glasses up and down the ridge of his nose as he listened.

"That was the labor section," he reported. "Gus Maguire just called in. Wants to talk to us. You suppose Manchester has got him upset?"

They all knew whom he meant. Gus Maguire was the president of the Missile and Aerospace Workers' Union, fifth largest labor organization in the country.

"If that's it, it could be a break," Fleischer continued. He picked up the private-hookup phone. "Give me the card room. . . . Art? I want to know how many delegates are members of the missile workers' union. What? No, never mind the alternates for now. Yeah, I'll wait."

When Fleischer turned back from the phone, after only a short wait, he held up a slip of paper with some numbers written on it. "Thirty-three delegates are members of Maguire's outfit. They come from seventeen states, but most of them are from California and six other states."

Roberts' smile was one of admiration. "That's a pretty good setup we've got."

"Best I've ever seen," said Fleischer. "It shows you what

can be done when a kook like Art Segunda decides to improve on the old system."

Abbott ran a flat hand over his lonely strands of hair. "Missile workers in the California delegation won't help us much, even if Maguire's call means something. If you don't have your own state already, Bin, we might as well throw in the towel now."

"Don't worry about California," said Roberts. "It's solid—all 92 votes."

Fleischer looked at his watch, took the pill case from his pocket and selected a capsule from the green rack. He took a glass of water from the coffee table, gulped the pill and washed it down with water. Roberts observed this operation with an amused expression.

"Pills, pills," scoffed the Governor. "Carl, you don't live right."

But Fleischer seemed buoyed by the process of medication and he returned to the subject. "I'd like to know what that call from Maguire means," he said.

"The man is full of surprises," said the Stanford professor. "Remember when he took the missile workers away from the Democrats four years ago? And recently he's been saying some nice things about Manchester."

"I know," said Fleischer. "If we could get him to switch to our side, it could be big for us."

"Thirty-three votes," said Abbott skeptically, "assuming he could get his boys a hundred per cent."

"That I'd bet on," replied Fleischer. The manager studied his sheet of paper again. "Four of those missile union members are on the Pennsylvania delegation."

"I'm pretty sure that must be the Pittsburgh area," said Abbott. "Universal Forge has a big fabricating plant there for nose cones and heat shields."

"That's right," added the Stanford professor, "it's the biggest missile facility under one roof in the country."

Roberts fingered the band of flesh under his chin. "Let's stay away from Pennsylvania," he said. "Ben Wilcox thinks the delegation is his personal property. He'd accuse us of poaching and we'd never get a look-in there."

Fleischer nodded agreement. "I didn't mean we ought to work on those four people. Actually, I've never figured Pennsylvania in any tally since we got into this thing. Wilcox is going for Manchester at the last minute, no matter what we do, so why the hell should we give him the satisfaction of making a play for him?"

"The way I see it," said Abbott unhappily, "we can't win without the Governor of Pennsylvania, but if we win with him, he'll be an unholy nuisance for four years."

"Cheer up," Fleischer suggested. "Wilcox won't be governor for four more years."

Roberts held up a hand. "Never mind that now. Give me the morning line, Carl. Where do we stand compared to yesterday?" The candidate studied a long state-by-state tally sheet as his manager rattled off figures.

"We've got a loss of one state and two other delegates since yesterday," Fleischer reported. "Missouri caucused in St. Louis last night before they came up here and went for Manchester. If we get a couple out of there we're lucky. Also one delegate in Illinois and one in Kentucky announced for Manchester. So I make it 410 sure for him, including 197 pledged or instructed by primaries. We've got 278 sure, including the 92 in California. But I figure another 180 delegates leaning to Manchester, which puts him close to the nomination. Even with our leaners, we're only around 375, which is not quite enough to be nominated dogcatcher in this convention."

"So we need a miracle passed?" asked Roberts.

"So we need a miracle," Fleischer echoed.

The manager reached over and took the tally sheet from Roberts, walked to a wastebasket, and tore the sheet into little shreds. The scraps fluttered down like a quiet snowfall.

"That score card is as out of date as last year's World Series," he said. He adjusted his dark glasses, jerked at his belt and kicked the wastebasket for emphasis. "It could be a whole new convention since Manchester's press conference. But who knows? Come on, Roger, we got work to do."

Roberts heaved himself out of his easy chair. "I better get dressed," he said.

Fleischer, Abbott and the two other strategists left the Governor's suite and walked down the headquarters corridor. Through open doors on either side came the rattle of typewriters, the mingled protests of unanswered telephones, and the flash of white shirts as men moved about in a seeming chaos of convention chores.

The lobby fronting directly on the ninth-floor elevator entrance was a thicket of heads, shoulders and arms. Newspapermen dusted cigarette ash over the thick carpeting. Four mobile television cameras were in operation, the cameramen sweating and shouting. One newsman, trying to squeeze closer to the Roberts spokesman, tripped in a tangle of cables. His curses rose above the general din.

"Goddammit, RBC doesn't own this convention!" he yelled at the cameraman, who replied in the standard language of the ancient convention war between the media: "Your head, your head—it's blocking my picture! You some kind of nut or something?"

The press secretary stood on a brocaded chair. The Blackstone would have to repair it after the convention, along with unnumbered carpets, draperies and tables fouled in the quadrennial process of selecting a leader for the greatest democracy on earth.

"Read it just one more time, Davey," ordered a voice which seemed to emerge from somewhere in the elevator shaft.

"Every American realizes the necessity—"

"Slower, please!"

"That 'please' is the first civilized word I've heard this morning," said the Roberts press spokesman.

"Can the compliments, Davey. Just read the damn thing."

"You're blocking my picture again!" screamed the cameraman. The offender turned and solemnly raised his hand in a gesture he hoped the Federal Communications Commission would consider obscene.

It took five minutes to reread the brief statement of Governor Bryan Roberts.

"Does that line about questioning the 'intellectual capacity' of people refer to Manchester's 'idiocy' remark?" The question was a shout. So was another: "Yeah, is that supposed to be a rebuke to Manchester, or what?"

The press secretary smiled, pleased that he had anticipated the questioners.

"Now, ladies and gentlemen, the Governor's statement speaks for itself," he said. "But if I were writing it, I would assume that the sentence about questioning the 'intellectual capacity' of those championing new weapons does represent the opinion of Governor Roberts that Mr. Manchester's remark about 'idiocy' was uncalled for."

"You mean he thinks Manchester insulted the intelligence of a lot of people."

"Governor Roberts thinks the remark was uncalled for, period."

"Why, Davey?" Another yell from the back of the crowd.

"I'm sorry, I can't answer any more questions. The statement speaks for itself."

"Just for guidance, Davey, does he mean—"

The spokesman waved his arms in a gesture of finality and got down off the chair. "Interpret it yourself, gentlemen," he said.

A stampede began for the phones in the Roberts headquarters press room, a converted suite down the hall. A woman wailed, fell against the wall, and gazed sadly down at the crushed toe of her new blue pumps.

One group of reporters moved in a body to the elevators. Others headed for the stairway and nine long flights downward. The outraged cameraman fussed over his equipment, still reviling the unknown reporter who spoiled two seconds of filmed history forever.

In the bedroom of suite 901, Bryan Roberts emerged from the shower, toweling vigorously. He stepped into his size 46 shorts and looked out at the sunlight glistening on Lake Michigan and flashing from the windshields and roofs of the cars on the outer drive.

I can't explain it, he thought, but I can feel it. Charlie

Manchester has stubbed his toe and the odds on his being nominated have shortened.

He thoughts dissolved, as they often did, into a series of imagined scenes. Bryan Roberts tended to think in pictures instead of words, to see even abstract ideas as graphs or charts. Now it was sparkling montage: the roar of thousands of people. . . . Two great arms stretched out in response. . . . His wife at his side, blinking under the arc lights. . . . The cry of the chairman: "Delegates, ladies and gentlemen, I give you the next President of the. . . ."

Roberts shook his head as if to clear it, stood unsmiling a moment, then walked to the telephone beside the oversized bed.

"Operator, see if you can locate Mr. Mark Davidson for me. He's either in a hotel here in the city or else he's in Los Angeles. D-a-v-i-d-s-o-n. He's president of the Universal Forge Corporation."

3

The train rushed northward through the flat corn lands of Illinois, carrying the 56 delegates and 56 alternates of the Texas delegation, plus a motley supporting chorus of relatives, friends, newspapermen, lobbyists and miscellaneous merrymakers. Seen from the windows of the Convention Special, the corn rows flicked past like long, green fingers. The soil, blacker than coal two months ago, now lay bleached by the August sun. The metronomic regularity of the plantings, broken only by an occasional cluster of farm buildings or grove of trees, could lull a passenger to sleep.

But not on this train. A cowbell jangled, and up the center aisle of the dining car came a short, beet-faced man wearing a ten-gallon white sombrero. Gold letters on a crimson hat-band proclaimed him a "Longhorn Republican." He lurched, as much from his obvious cargo of whisky as from the sway of the train, and had to steady himself with a hand on a tabletop. When he did so, he grinned helplessly. Whichever hand happened to be free swung the cowbell. It clanged busily.

In the middle of the diner, he took a brave stance, fumbled in his shirt pocket, and gravely studied a slip of paper he found there.

"Results of the official unofficial Texas poll!" he bellowed, to no one in particular. "All 56 delegates voting. For ol' Bin Roberts, God love every pound of 'im, seventeen. For Manchester, twenty-eight. No choice, eleven. These results certified by the Texas Livestock Breeders Association—which is pourin' free bourbon three cars back."

He eddied toward a table where two women sat and spoke to the older of the two, a woman with a gleaming coiffure. "Howdy, Grace, you doll you. Prettiest politician north of Brownsville."

The woman smiled and gestured him onward with a flutter of her hand. "Tell it to the next car, Sam," she said. "They're dying for news."

"You're right, Gracie," he said. His face was happy, though vacant. "I've got eight cars to make before sundown."

He proceeded through the diner, falling back slightly with the jerks of the train, but bending his shoulders manfully to the task. He rattled the bell one last time before disappearing. The younger of the two women leaned across the table. "Who was *that*, Mother?" she asked.

The answer was lost in a flourish of music. Up the aisle, in single file, came a college band dressed in white leather chaps, purple bandannas and yellow shirts with the map of Texas printed on their backs. It was several minutes before the last bars of the "Yellow Rose of Texas" faded into the next car, giving way again to the quiet, rocking rhythm of wheels on rails.

"That," said the older woman, "before I was so rudely interrupted, was just Sam, the delegation's clown and town crier. He's harmless for about three more drinks. Then he's a pest."

She was a handsome woman with silver-white hair swept upward above a high, uncreased forehead and eyes so deeply blue as to be almost purple. She took a final bite of ground beefsteak and speared the last green leaf on her salad plate, then eyed with evident distaste the remains of a club sandwich and a thick chocolate milk shake across the table.

"You better lay off that rich gunk, dearie. If you keep that up, you'll wake up Friday and find the girdle doesn't slip on so easy over your slim little fanny."

There was both affection and amusement in the look returned by the younger woman. They understood each other, these two, even though their differences were more apparent than their similarities.

Mrs. Grace Orcott, at forty-eight, was tall and elegant, her skin a smooth white. She was carefully groomed, expensively but conservatively dressed. Seen across a room, she might have been thought aloof, even arrogant; but across a table or over a cup of coffee—the way those who knew her as Republican national committeewoman from Texas saw her most often— there was a disarming honesty in her face and in her talk that banished such thoughts at once.

Kay Orcott was quite another person. At twenty-four

there was little in her appearance, except for the color of her eyes, to suggest that she was the daughter of her luncheon companion. She was much shorter and wore her hair in a close-cut brown tangle that bore no resemblance to her mother's exquisitely tended head. Kay's face was cheerfully sunburnt, with a spatter of freckles spilling across her thin, slightly prominent nose. Now she pouted fleetingly.

"Oh, mother, for goodness' sake," she said. "I haven't gained an ounce since I left college. Stop worrying about me getting fat. I don't have to diet and I'll—"

"Get married when I'm good and ready." Her mother finished the line and they both laughed. "I know the refrain, dear, but you've never been to a national convention before. You don't sleep, so you eat—and drink—all the time to keep up your energy, and when you get home, the scales scream at you. And if you forget what you're eating, before you know it you'll think you have rocks in your stomach. Things get pretty tense at these parties."

"Well, maybe so, but I don't see how they're going to be very tense at this one," Kay said. "I mean, I guess I'm for Roberts, like you, Mother, even if he doesn't look like much, but . . ."

"Let Bin Roberts be a lesson to you, and don't let your figure go," said Grace Orcott, grinning at her daughter.

"No, stop it, Mother. I mean, I don't see how experienced political people like you think he can be nominated. I mean, did you see that St. Louis paper they put on the train this morning? It looks to me like Secretary Manchester has it all fixed up."

Mrs. Orcott gave her daughter a you-think-you're-so-smart

look as she pulled a cigarette from her bag. Kay lit it for her, cupping the match in her tanned right hand.

"I swear, Kay," said Grace Orcott, "you do that just like your father."

"He taught me, silly. Don't change the subject. I mean, how can Governor Roberts win?"

"I saw the paper. As a matter of fact, the *Globe-Democrat* gave a pretty accurate rundown. Of course, Roberts is way behind in pledges right now. The point is they aren't voting now. They're voting Thursday."

Grace Orcott had been committed to Roberts for six weeks. She believed, quite simply, that experience counted in politics. She herself had been a doorbell-ringing precinct chairman in Dallas ever since the exhilarating days when Eisenhower first made life worth living for Texas Republicans. Charles Manchester, she said time and again, just didn't have the political seasoning; a banker turned mid-term cabinet officer simply couldn't qualify. Bin Roberts, with twenty-five years in elective office, a veteran campaigner, did. Period. That was it so far as Grace Orcott was concerned, and it was enough to put her on Roberts' convention team as a regional floor whip, responsible for four southwestern states. In her own state of Texas, many delegates looked favorably on Manchester because of his conservative fiscal views, but Republican conventions did not permit states to be bound as units. Each delegate could vote as a free agent and Grace Orcott intended to get as many as she could for Roberts before the roll call on Thursday.

"Oh, I know that, Mother," argued Kay, "but Manchester has twice as many votes as Roberts already."

"You mean he has twice as many pledges." Mrs. Orcott's tone was that of a schoolteacher with a slow, if willing, student. "That doesn't mean he'll have twice as many votes five days from now. A lot can happen."

"Like what?"

"Like Charles Manchester could get into a row with the leaders or something. Or Bin Roberts might personally charm the delegates by twos and threes, the way Wendell Willkie did in 1940 before you were born. As a matter of fact . . ." Her voice trailed off and she turned to the window, gazing across the sea of green toward the horizon. Absorbed in thought, she stubbed out her cigarette automatically.

"As a matter of fact," she resumed, "I hope Manchester doesn't decide to see delegates in intimate little groups. I understand he can be quite a charmer himself."

"But," Kay insisted, "I can't see that you said anything, really. I mean, Manchester seems to be so far ahead. So what could change it?"

"I have to admit, dearie, that he's way ahead right now. But don't forget, he's new to politics. Crazy things happen at conventions. When things get tense, well, we'll see. . . . I know this: A veteran like Bin Roberts will take it in stride. As for Manchester, we'll just have to wait and see."

"You're just trying to whistle up some hope for your candidate, Mother," said Kay. "I don't think you think he has a chance."

Grace Orcott laughed. "Honey, if I didn't think he had a chance I'd never have declared for him. Just take my word for it. Things are more complicated at a convention than you think. Now tell me, have you figured out how to have a good time and also get the best spot on the corral fence, so you can cut out a good-looking man if he comes along?"

"Oh, stop that phony cowboy talk, Mother. It makes you

sound absurd." Kay pulled a printed schedule from her purse. "But I am going to have some fun while you connive. I thought I'd start tonight with this Young Republican dance at the Edgewater Beach. Want to come along . . . Slim?"

"No, thanks." Her mother laughed as she got up from the table. "But it's a good idea for you. Just pin on your Roberts button and look fetching."

The steward, smiling, held the door open and they were out in the vestibule with its iron clamor of wheels and couplings. Grace Orcott had to raise her voice to be heard.

"And don't waste all your time on the kids. See if you can find a delegate or two to work on."

They swayed into the adjoining Pullman and all was quiet again. When they reached their compartment, Kay picked up the thread of their talk.

"Make up your mind, Mom," she said. "Do you want me to marry the man—or just convert him to Roberts?"

"Why, both, of course."

"All right, Mom. Now let's forget it for a while, okay? I'll get married when I'm good and ready." Kay settled herself on the green plush seat, picked up a book and opened it with a flourish that clearly signaled her intention to discuss the subject no further.

Her mother watched her for a moment, then dismissed the matter with a sigh and turned to her own work. The compartment was quiet for the next hour as Kay kept her face buried in the half-read novel. Grace Orcott worked over a sheaf of delegate lists while they sped toward Lake Michigan.

Later the train slowed as it entered the maze of railroad yards, and then they were climbing down to the platform of the Illinois Central station. A short, happy man waved a snow-white sombrero at waiting photographers and turned to a radio newsman holding a microphone toward him.

"Texas," he cried, "has come to Chicago to help nominate the next President of the United States!"

*   *   *

Mrs. Charles B. Manchester snorted as she snapped off the little transistor radio and leaned back in her canvas beach chair.

"God, a whole week of that nonsense!" She mimicked the bray of the Texas happiness man. "Tayx-us ez come t' Chicawguh..."

The wife of the leading candidate for the Republican presidential nomination sat by a sunny cove on the shore of Lake Winnipesaukee in New Hampshire. Behind her the white pines came down almost to the little rim of sand which edged the water. She lay back in the chair in a bathing suit and sunglasses, her face and body so arranged as to catch every possible ray of sun. From time to time she turned her head to watch a three-year-old girl puddling in the wet sand. This was Julia Manchester's afternoon duty: minding her granddaughter Amy so her daughter Martha could have an hour of peace and quiet, to rest or read or write to her Navy husband.

"Amy! Don't go out so far. Sail your pretty boat over here by Grammy."

There was nothing tentative about the command. Julia Manchester was not a tentative woman. "Competent" was the word often used to describe her at first meeting. Her voice was low-pitched and a little rough; she said what she thought, and generally she thought before she spoke. She had confessed, more than once, that Washington was the city for her—the only one in which she'd lived where men were willing to talk seriously with a woman about ideas and events. She liked it that way.

But those who dismissed her as merely competent missed the woman. She was short and chunky, her pepper-and-salt hair trimmed in a casual feather cut, her skin darkened with the kind of tan that comes from spending part of every winter in the West Indies and most of every summer in the northern sun. She seemed somewhat masculine in the rather severely tailored clothes she favored for town; but anyone who saw her, as now in a bathing suit, or riding in a pair of jodhpurs, would know this was a complete woman. Her body was still full and firm, her legs trim. Friends in the Virginia horse country gave her their own accolade—"a fine figger of a woman."

Amy approached, sprinkling sand impartially on both of her grandmother's legs. "Gramp coming see Amy?"

"Maybe next week, honey," said Julia Manchester. "He's awful busy now."

Amy absorbed the intelligence, frowned momentarily, then skipped back to her sandpile and toy sailboat.

Julia could not get her mind off the press conference she had watched that morning and the scattering of radio commentary that had followed it. Charlie saying what he thinks again . . . that's fine for bankers, but sometimes not so good for politicians. . . . Politicians? . . . She smiled. Charlie Manchester, Politician. . . . Thank God, he isn't slippery. I couldn't stand that, for President or anything else. I do admire the honesty and I know he believes it. . . .

How many nights has he talked to me about it? Five? Ten? But it would be nice if his sense of timing were, well, better developed. I know he's right, but maybe people don't take time to think at a convention. God, to hear some women talk about it, you don't have time to go to the toilet—even if you've remembered to carry dimes in your purse. . . . Well, Charlie said it and that's it. Anyway, he always succeeds at whatever he tries. Maybe he's got a charmed life. . . .

Julia looked over at Amy, and the sight of the little girl set her mind wandering again. I wonder when Jake and Patsy will make grandparents of us again? We don't hear much from Jake. . . . I suppose he's busy enough, getting his feet under him at the bank. . . . It's an odd business for him to go into. He's so independent and he's such a loner, you wouldn't think he'd take to it, even if Charlie hadn't been a banker. The way Jake always fought with his father, you'd never have expected him to set foot in a bank. . . . I sometimes think I was happiest at Jake's wedding because I knew then I was finally getting out from between them. . . .

And if Charlie is nominated, it's going to be hard on Jake. They can't try to drag Jake into the campaign. . . . He won't do Charlie any good and God knows it wouldn't do Jake any good. But he won't be able to keep Patsy out of it. . . . Thank God Jake found her. She's a nice girl and awfully good for him too. . . .

Amy, exploring the beach, spied the front page of a Boston paper discarded by her grandmother. It included a large photograph of the Secretary of the Treasury arriving in Chicago.

"There Gramp!" She stamped a wet foot on the image and pointed in triumph. "There Gramp picture!"

"Yes, baby, that's the great man, all right." Julia glanced again at the picture, and a rush of other images followed, like turning pages in an album: Charlie when he graduated from Michigan. Charlie's look of embarrassed pride the morning after Jake was born. Charlie on the cover of *Time* magazine the week after he announced for President. The cover showed him cooking fish over a campfire, and it bore the caption, CANDIDATE MANCHESTER: *It's Hard to Think in Cities*. And now his future was to be decided in a city convention, far from the woods and the open waters where he liked to sort out his thoughts. . . . Obie O'Connell and Archie, she thought, you be good to that man. He needs others at times, more than he knows.

Then she grasped Amy firmly by the hand. "Time to go up now, baby, and see Mama." Together woman and child walked slowly up the path through the brown pine needles to the house.

* * *

"Well, what do you think of the family statesman now?"

Jake Manchester snapped off the television set and threw the question across the room to his wife. The candidate's son had just watched the press conference, rebroadcast for West Coast viewers who were still in bed when it occurred two time zones away in Chicago. Thanks to this courtesy by the networks, Jake and Patsy had been able to see it as they ate a late Saturday breakfast in their cliff-hung apartment above San Francisco Bay.

"I think he was just wonderful, that's what I think of him!" Patsy Manchester said it with such emphasis that she bounced a little on the couch as the words came out. She pushed her chin, no less determined for the dimple that softened its line, toward her husband.

Jake Manchester shrugged and turned to look out the big picture window that was standard equipment in their section of Tiburon, a little town plastered against the steeply rising hills across the bay from the city. Below him he could see patches of white canvas on the choppy water stretching toward Angel Island. The weekend sailors were out, as he himself hoped soon to be, whitecaps or no.

"Wow!" Patsy wriggled and stretched out flat on the couch. "He was great. I can see us right now, visiting them—in the *White* House!"

She lay back, hands behind her head, one sandal dangling as she swung a foot in the air. Jake never could get over her enthusiasm. She was so eager that she seemed forever breathless, so physically cheerful that she seemed always about to burst from her clothes. Which wouldn't be a bad idea, he mused, summoning from very recent memory the image of Patsy unclad. But she was elsewhere now. Though today she wore a frayed shirt and a pair of blue jeans that had long since shrunk beyond the point of public propriety, her mind was obviously on silken evening gowns, long white gloves and candlelit state dinners. Her eyes rolled as she talked gaily of visiting famous in-laws.

His face reflected no such buoyancy. John K. Manchester somewhat resembled his father, with the same black hair, the same handsome, sharp features and the same lightly tanned skin. He had some of the same mannerisms; a way of tilting his head when talking to someone he liked, a habit of tugging at an ear lobe when immersed in thought. But Jake had his mother's frame: he was short and square-cut, at five-feet-eight barely an inch taller than Patsy. There was also something of his mother's brusque tone in his reply now.

"I'm not so sure how great he was, Patsy. He sure picked a helluva place to talk about defense policy—and to toss off something that could change the whole setup. Jesus! He always sounds so sure of everything!"

"Well, I should hope he'd feel sure about *that*." Patsy was sitting upright now. "Maybe you don't ever think about an atomic war, but I do. He couldn't be righter—enough's enough!"

"Oh, dammit now, I'm not talking about that," Jake replied. "It's just that he stands there and talks about 'idiocy' like he was telling some developer back home that his plans for a new shopping center were no good."

Patsy started to speak, but Jake waved her down. "Oh, he's a helluva smart guy, I know—you and everybody else always tell me so—but he's not talking about some bunch of two-bit borrowers now. We've got a lot of pretty smart military men and some pretty big industrial people who won't agree with him, I bet. And the President of the United States, how about him? The *present* one, I mean."

Patsy began to pick up the breakfast plates and cups. She said nothing, but she bustled a bit more than necessary and Jake knew why.

"I'm sorry, sweetheart." He intercepted her on the way to the kitchen and slipped both arms around her from behind. "I don't mean to drag you into my family fights with the Old Man."

She wriggled and, when he held on, put her sandal down hard on his bare toes. He grunted, but didn't let go.

"Okay," she said, "you're forgiven. But you better turn me loose if we're going sailing this morning. I want to be back in time for the next installment from the smoke-filled rooms of Chicago."

Patsy took a step toward the kitchen, then turned to face her husband. One tail of the old shirt hung out over her blue jeans. Her face was as bright as a canary at sunup, and Jake knew instantly that some new idea had seized her.

"Jake," she said. "Let's fly to Chicago!"

"Chicago! Good God, kid, I've got to go to work Monday. You know that."

"Oh, the bank." She screwed up her face in mock disgust. "But I bet they'd let you off to see your father nominated for President."

"Maybe," he said, "but the bank is only half of it. In case you hadn't noticed, the candidate didn't invite us."

"But you know he'd be tickled silly to have us there, Jake."

"You maybe," he said. "Me I'm not so sure about."

She folded her arms. "Oh, come off it, Jake. You know he thinks you're the greatest."

"Patsy, we're not going. It's his show. Not mine. That's final."

Her mood of elation had passed.

"Well, it was a good idea," she said. "It would have been fun to get in there and help. I feel kind of useless, two thousand miles away."

4

Archie DuPage and Obie O'Connell consulted a list as they stood on the sidewalk outside the Hilton.

A breeze came off the lake to play tag with the pools of heat still lingering on the pavement. The blur of evening was settling on the city and the first lights winked from the canyon wall stretching north along Michigan Avenue. Both men looked crisp in starched shirts and dinner jackets, but they were already sweating under the fresh linen. Archie looked gratefully toward Lake Michigan.

"Thank God for small favors," he said. "At least we've got a breeze."

Obie O'Connell inspected his moist fingers with distaste. A man sweats at conventions even when they air-condition the sidewalks, he thought.

"Nervous tension, Obie," Archie suggested.

"Yeah," replied O'Connell without enthusiasm. Archie was a nice kid, but these psychiatrist types made him feel undressed. He pointed at the list.

"You take the mayor's cocktail party for delegates, like I said, and I'll take the national committee buffet. That's the break I get for being older. At the mayor's, they'll have ninety gate-crashers for every delegate. I'll go on to the Nebraska and Idaho dinners—Cohen's making the New Jersey banquet —and you take the Young Republican dance. Then I'll see you at eleven at the Chicago Club with the finance committee."

Archie squinted at the list. "How long is the Secretary supposed to spend there with the fat cats?"

"We'll have only twenty minutes before Roberts and his crew arrive. So let's be sure to get to the club a couple of minutes before eleven. We gotta make time at that one."

"What do you really think, Obie?"

"Like I said this morning, we're . . ."

O'Connell's opinion was lost in a sudden collision of sound. From the Blackstone, up the avenue, came one of Roberts' golden bands, a drum-and-bugle corps composed exclusively of girls in shimmering shorts and spangled halters and led by a tall, bright blonde majorette. At the same time an all-male banjo band from Cincinnati marched around the far corner of the Hilton. They were dressed in blue satin coveralls and a wild man led them, smashing at the empty air with a tambourine. "California, here we come," clashed with "Beautiful Ohio," while unorganized pedestrians fell away like peas from a knife. The golden girls came on down the avenue until the two bands faced each other, still playing at full volume, in front of the Hilton entrance.

O'Connell sighed and pushed Archie into a taxi. "You take this one," he ordered. Then, leaning his barrel-shaped body toward the window, he added: "Like I said this morning, that was a big surprise he threw out at that damnfool press conference. But we still win easy on the last ballot, kid."

Archie grinned and made a circle with thumb and forefinger. "On the last ballot, Obie. See you around."

As Archie's cab slowed for a red light just north of the Tribune Tower, a metallic braying filled Michigan Avenue and echoed from building walls in dissonant waves. A sound truck carrying a roughly lettered, homemade sign, "The People Want Manchester," was parked against the curb. A man in a dirty polo shirt, Vandyke beard and uncombed hair sat behind the wheel. His mouth was close to a hand microphone and from the truck's loudspeakers came a jumble of sentiments:

"Why do the poor people want Manchester, folks? Same reason the rich people want him. Charles Bedford Manchester stands for every American. He wants what you want and he has the brains to give it to you. He's a family man. Charles Bedford Manchester has lived with the same wife for twenty-eight years. He's a religious man, folks. Every Sunday morning you can see him at the little Episcopal church which overlooks the hills of Cincinnati, folks . . ."

Archie cringed as the inanities tumbled over one another in a brassy cascade, each new announcement fighting for precedence with those which bounced back from the walls of nearby office buildings. He made a mental note to call the Chicago police inspector in charge of the convention detail and beseech him to deny the public streets to this unknown bearded fool. For all Archie knew, some smooth operator in the Roberts camp might have hired the fellow. The cab driver, monitoring his face in the rear-view mirror, said: "Takes all kinds of nuts to make a convention, don't it, Mac?"

The mayor's reception for convention delegates was already at full pitch when Archie arrived at the Drake. A crowd of curiosity seekers lined the corridor leading to the ballroom. Young girls, intent on seeing a celebrity, pointed at him and giggled as he stepped into the glare of the inevitable flood-lights. Then, remembering, he elbowed his way to a phone booth, consulted his pocket memorandum book and called police headquarters. The inspector was brimming with sympathy and promised to send a squad car over right away to chase the sound truck and the bearded barker off the streets. Archie, happy with at least one small accomplishment, picked a path through the sticky crush of bodies to the ballroom.

The sight and sound dismayed him. Two thousand men and women covered the floor as though they were living fixtures, deprived of either means or desire to move. Each person held to his square foot of floor space with a look of glazed belligerency. Off to one side a bedraggled line weaved toward a swarthy little man with a mustache, the Democratic mayor of Chicago. He wore an expression of weary horror, as if appalled at the number of Republicans surrounding him. Archie plunged into the bosom of the mob, aiming in a generally northerly direction toward the long bar against the windows.

He reached his goal many minutes later, bearing the scars of combat. The right side of his pleated shirt was damp with spilt martini, a smear of lipstick stained one sleeve, and a mere scraggle of thread on his lapel showed where his Manchester button had once been. Archie ordered a Scotch highball, squared his shoulders and looked about him. Time to go to work.

A dumpy woman with a jeweled Roberts pin on the shoulder strap of her gown clinked a glass against his. Archie's memory streaked off in zigzag fashion, searching frantically for a name. Gloss? Glass? Glutz? He was sure it began with a "G." Wyoming, Montana, some place out west. A state treasurer—or was she a state senator? He wished he had taken the time to acquire Obie O'Connell's patented name-plus-face technique. He smiled nevertheless.

"Hi, there," he said cheerfully. "Surprised to see you here with the hoi polloi."

She obviously appreciated the compliment, but was unwilling to let him off the memory hook without playing him a while first. "I'll let you call me Martha if I don't have to call you Mr. DuPage," she said.

Winds of relief rippled through Archie. Sure. Mrs. Martha Gloss, a state senator from Wyoming and a minion in the Roberts forces.

"How goes the battle, Martha? Has the Governor got any votes in Wyoming yet besides yours?"

Mrs. Gloss dropped her party manner and moved her lips closer to his ear. Archie bent forward to hear her over the hubbub.

"Your man shook some people this morning," she said. "I've always thought a lot of him, I have. Even if I'm for Bin Roberts. But the Secretary raised an issue I'm not sure belongs in a convention."

Archie ran his fingers through his curly black hair and moved quickly to the ramparts. "Martha, the Secretary is a man of integrity. He feels deeply that we're sliding toward disaster without really thinking about it. He said it. He means it, and he'll say it again."

"Oh, don't pretend, Archie," she said. "I listened to that press conference and it was plain as the nose on your face that he got sucked into it. He didn't intend to say any such thing. Now, admit it, between us."

"There's nothing to admit," said Archie, maintaining his smile but suddenly feeling on the defensive. "This has been on his mind since long before he became a candidate. If the world is going to be blown up, at least it shouldn't be done by the sheer momentum of more and more weapons."

"Oh, come off it, Archie," she said, flourishing her highball. "Enough's enough."

The phrase annoyed him. Since entering the Drake he had overheard it several times in snatches of conversation. And he thought he'd heard the term employed derisively, much as Mrs. Gloss had just used it. A catchphrase turned back on its inventor could be damaging in politics. Archie felt a quick intestinal pang as his ulcer protested—was it the taste of the mayor's cheap whisky or the foretaste of trouble? He set the glass back on the bar and inched away.

"How we doin', Archie?" The questioner's watery, evasive eyes darted over DuPage's shoulder toward somebody behind him. This one Archie knew. He was a delegate whom Archie had met during the Indiana primary campaign and who now represented an elected vote for the Secretary. In token of his status, he wore a big badge which read, "Pledged to Manchester—And Proud Of It."

"You tell me," Archie replied. "I'm just scouting tonight."

"The man sure dropped a blockbuster this morning," said the delegate, his eyes roving restlessly to every face but Archie's. "Guess he knows what he's doing, but he's got some of the troops shook up. It's all right with me. If you don't drop an issue into a convention, it can be duller'n dishwater. I ought to know. This is my sixth."

Archie promptly decided that the Hoosier had given the matter little, if any, thought. Still he prodded. "What do you mean, shook up?"

"Aw, some of the fellows don't like it and some do," the delegate explained. "A couple of our boys have missile plants in their districts. They're not sure what it would mean for jobs and all. Anyhow, people are arguing about it."

As Archie moved, a yard or two at a time, he discovered the truth of this observation. Manchester's press conference was the chief topic of discussion. A woman from Nevada, a Roberts delegate, said it sounded to her as though Manchester had stubbed his toe. A Manchester regional leader from New England said the Secretary struck a responsive chord in that area. A Negro ward leader from Cleveland, in the solid Manchester state of Ohio, said he'd heard that some members of the Missile Workers' Union weren't too happy about Manchester's remarks. A Florida delegate joked that he was sticking with Manchester even if he did own a little piece of an electronics plant near Tampa; at least the Secretary was a pay-as-you-go man on federal finances and we could sure use some of *that* for a change. By the time Archie DuPage got back to the ballroom entrance nearly two hours later he was worried. What did all this ferment mean?

He picked up a new Manchester button from a girl at a card

table in the lobby, walked down the street to a drugstore and tried to assess what he had heard while he ate a cheeseburger and drank two glasses of milk.

The cab ride along Lake Shore Drive to the next stop made him feel good. The breeze off the lake had stiffened and stars marked the blue-black sky with brilliant pinpricks of light. The driver was silent, and for the first time in two days Archie could feel alone, away from the hundreds of milling human bodies and the drone of their voices.

Then he was fumbling for change at the Edgewater Beach Hotel, and suddenly aware of a bright surge of laughter. He had arrived at the second stop on his schedule, the dance for delegates under thirty-five sponsored by the Young Republican National Federation. Archie smoothed his shirt front and entered the hotel.

Two bands held forth in different ballrooms, and as Archie joined the couples sauntering from one to the other he guessed that neither Manchester nor Roberts would win so much as an alternate's pledge at the Edgewater Beach this Saturday night. Except for the campaign buttons and the elephant-shaped nameplates, it might have been a college house-party dance. Almost unconsciously Archie exaggerated his usual campus slouch and slowed his long legs to a casual lope. He grinned as he thought of his reaction. What had they once called Harold Stassen—the veteran youth leader? That was Archie DuPage: the aging youth leader. He entered the room with the less maniacal brand of music and stood against the mirrored wall. A medley of colored spotlights swept slowly around, catching the sequins on a skirt or momentarily painting a face blue or orange. The crowd of dancers was humming an old favorite.

Every star above
Knows the one I love.
Sweet Sue, it's you.

Archie wondered just what O'Connell expected him to do here—cut in on one of the gliding young couples and start lecturing about Manchester and the balanced budget? He pulled a cigarette from his pocket and began searching for his lighter. He couldn't find it. As he fumbled from one pocket to another, he noticed a girl standing nearby, grinning at his predicament.

"Allow me, sir." Her voice was low. A cupped hand, quite small and quite tanned, held a match to his cigarette. He inhaled instinctively, then looked up in surprise.

"Where did you learn to do that?" he asked.

"Do what?"

The girl stood just a bit higher than his shoulder. Her brown hair was close-cut in a kind of planned tangle. Her eyes were . . . purple, he guessed. Her nose was so straight and thin that it made him want to laugh: it seemed something apart, sort of lonely. She wore a green dress of subdued hue, which made the big golden Roberts button at her waist look slightly ridiculous. Archie smiled and, for the first time in his many meetings that night, it was no effort.

"Cup your hand for a match," he answered.

"That's so the match won't go out," she said.

"I know, but only men do it that way."

She smiled too, and again her smile seemed to mock him a bit.

"Here," he went on, "give me a match and I'll show you." He struck a match and held it out unshielded between thumb and forefinger. An eddy of air snuffed it out.

"See?" she said. "If you hold it that way, it goes out."

"I know. That's the way women hold matches. What I asked you was where you learned to do it the right way."

"My father taught me when I began to smoke. He said if I insisted on ruining my health, at least I ought to learn to do it right."

"I suppose women don't think it's dainty to do it that way."

"I'm dainty," she protested. "That's the only thing I do like a man. Except drive a car. I drive just as unsafely as a man."

"You are also talking to a strange man," Archie said. "That's unsafe too, as any father can tell you."

"But I like your curly hair. It's cute. You can't keep it combed, can you?"

"This is the silliest conversation I've had in weeks," Archie said. "Come on, let's dance."

She held herself just right. She didn't melt or cling, but neither did she hold herself prudishly away. She just danced comfortably close. She didn't sing the song, either, or watch the other couples, or pull him toward the band. Archie began to think of her as the most sensible girl he'd met since he left Washington two—or was it two hundred?—days ago.

When the music stopped, he led her to the bar. She took a Scotch and water, and said nothing when he ordered plain water.

"What's your name?" he asked.

"Kay. Kay Orcott. I guess I should have picked up a nameplate to help the strange men I talk to. I'm from Dallas with the big D. What's yours?"

"Mother called me Archibald, but no one else is allowed to. It's Archie. Archie DuPage. I'm from Rochester. The R isn't very big. Then Yale and public relations. But right now I'm from Washington, where I work for the Secretary of the Treasury, Mr. Manchester. He's out here running for President."

My God, DuPage, you're really running off at the mouth, he thought. Who turned you on?

"I'm for Roberts," said Kay Orcott. "I mean, my mother is, so I guess I am. She's a wheeler-and-dealer in the Texas delegation."

"You mean Grace Orcott, the national committeewoman?"

"Yes. Isn't she pretty?"

"You're more fun."

"Well, I'm younger and I'm not married either."

"What do you mean, either?" Archie asked.

"I mean, you're not either." She peered at him over the top of her glass. "If you had been, I wouldn't have lit your cigarette for you."

"How do you know I'm not?"

"Because you don't have that responsible married look."

"I think I'm as responsible as the next guy."

"No, you're not. The next guy is married."

"Look," said Archie, "this is all very Noel Coward, but we're not getting anywhere with it. Are you like this all the time, or has the convention got you already?"

"I like you," she said.

They sat down and talked—with no more questions. They danced again. They sat and talked, about everything except the convention, and when Archie looked at his watch again, it was 10:35.

"I'm due at a meeting at eleven," he said, "but I'll be through in half an hour. You want to go somewhere? Chicago never closes."

"I'd like that," she said without either hesitation or haste. "We're staying at the Ambassador East. Would you like to call me when you get through?"

"Eleven-forty-five, okay?"

She nodded. Archie hurried out to the cab stand. He'd forgotten about the nagging protests of his ulcer.

It was a cool cab ride to the Chicago Club, a solid building of restrained architecture at the corner of Michigan Avenue and Van Buren Street. A uniformed doorman stopped Archie just inside the entrance and asked for his name. He received it with an air of wary suspicion. "Mr. Colby's party," explained Archie. "Ah, yes," said the doorman with a flicker of respect. "You'll find it in room 100. Take the elevator to the fifth floor, if you will, sir."

Archie followed the pointed finger to the elevators. He looked curiously about him as he waited for a car. The Chicago Club bespoke money, influence, position—and a century of occupancy. The walls were canvas-covered, their yellowish, dark-bordered panels smudged with the patina of age. At the head of a broad stairway, its handrail glistening with polished brass trim, hung a full-length portrait of a dour old gentleman. The gilt frame was aged to a dusty bronze and the colors of the painting had darkened with the years.

By contrast, the elevator car was quite modern, its walls elegantly upholstered with tan leather and adorned with the club's crest. At the fifth floor, Archie made his way to room 100. Stanton Colby, the Chicago broker who headed the Republican National Finance Committee, greeted him affably at the door.

"Room 100 is one of our inner clubs, Mr. DuPage," he

said. "We pride ourselves on being a small but beneficent monarchy."

Men in dinner jackets stood in huddles or sat at ease in chairs scattered around the comfortable living room. The buzz of conversation and the clink of ice in glasses blended quietly. Archie felt compelled to apologize for the moist spot on his shirt.

"The mayor's reception," he explained with a gesture toward his damp linen. "They spilled as much as they drank."

Colby's ruddy face crinkled as though he were sighting a clay pigeon on the skeet range where he found his principal recreation. "The mayor would like to sabotage us," he said. "He's . . . Ah, here's the Secretary now."

The room hushed. Some fifty members of the finance committee or the "Five Thousand Club"—those who had contributed $5,000 or more to the Republican party in this campaign year—turned toward the door. Secretary of the Treasury Charles Manchester stepped into the room, trailed by Obie O'Connell. Manchester's smile glowed as he greeted Colby.

"Hello, Stanton," he said. "How's your shooting eye? Still sharp as ever?"

The Secretary moved briskly around the room, calling men by their first names, grasping an elbow, occasionally asking after the health of a wife. Archie watched his candidate with a feeling of pride. Manchester's black hair, springy and full, was neatly combed. In his dinner jacket, the Secretary was tall and trim, with no bulge at the waist. The flush of the outdoors was on his face and occasionally, with a special friend, he tilted his head while chatting—a sure sign of inward pleasure.

Manchester was easy, assured, confident. These men were his
kind. He had known some of them long before he entered
politics; he shared their interests, their backgrounds, some of
their prejudices. He was rewarded with glances of approval—
mingled with some awe, for a banker who essayed elective
politics was something rare in their clan.

O'Connell faded away from the candidate and sought shelter beside Archie. "He's at home now, back among the WASP
elite," Obie whispered as he rubbed a pudgy jowl. "I bet I'm
the only Catholic in the room."

Archie grinned. "This is where all good white Anglo-Saxon
Protestants go when they die, Obie."

"If they can get past the doorman," rasped O'Connell.

Colby held up his hands for silence. "This is candidates'
night," he said, "and the Secretary has graciously given us a
half hour from his busy schedule . . ."

"Some of you have already paid for a full hour," Manchester quipped. A friendly chuckle ran around the room.

"This is very informal," continued Colby. "I suggest that
you take seats where you can find them and we'll let the Secretary hold forth for a couple of minutes. Then he's open for
questions. We must conclude by eleven-thirty, because Governor Roberts is due then. Needless to say, anything said here is
in the family and not for publication. That goes for you, too,
Jim." He winked at a lanky man occupying a chair against the
wall, the owner of a string of solidly Republican newspapers.
"All right, C.B., the floor's yours."

Manchester turned a chair around and sat down, folding
his arms on the back rest.

"I'm not going to make a speech," he said. "You'll be hear-

ing plenty of oratory before Thursday. I just want to emphasize again what most of you already know, that if I'm
nominated—and elected—the country will have an administration that believes in fiscal prudence. There won't be any
planned deficits—or unplanned ones, either, if I can help it.
Still, you mustn't expect the millennium. After four years of
helping President Stuart struggle against the terrific spending
pressures in this country, I can assure you that it's a daily fight
just to keep even. But I plan to do better than that, now that I
know the ropes, and come up with a surplus or two. That's my
little talk, gentlemen. Fire away."

The first question came almost before he had finished, from
a man who inspected the ash on his cigar as he spoke. "C.B.,
I think the question on everybody's mind is whether you intended to state your views on missile contracts this morning at
the press conference, or whether you were . . . well, trapped
into it?"

"To be perfectly frank about it," Manchester replied, "I had
not planned to state my views just then. But I decided a long
time ago to make a hold-down on new weapons systems a part
of my program. So the subject was not a new one to me, and
I meant every word I said this morning."

"Then you will cancel the Daphne contract if you're
elected?" The question came from the publisher.

"I will make it the subject of a searching study by the best-
qualified people I can find, Jim. But as I indicated, and as I
have no hesitation in telling you, the Defense Department
would have to come up with some spectacular new data to
convince me we should spend upward of ten billion dollars to
gain twelve seconds to Moscow. On the evidence now available, I'd cancel it."

"But Mr. Secretary." It was a voice halfway back in the room, carrying a thin edge of protest in its tone. "Aren't you in danger of winding up with a lot of obsolete weapons?"

"Not in the least." Manchester shot the answer back. "Any promising new weapon would get the green light. What I'm talking about are these small refinements that cost billions and don't improve our defense establishment by the width of a gnat's eye."

"Why can't you cut back on welfare," suggested a man with a face as benign as a full moon, "and waste, and those meddling regulatory agencies, instead of taking it out on defense?"

Manchester hammered gently on the back of his chair with the edge of his hand. "We'll run a taut ship on *all* civilian expenditures, but you know you can cut to the bone there without saving enough to run the Defense Department for a week. The Pentagon is fifty-five billion a year."

"C.B.," said Colby, "we all admire your candor and I'm sure you'd want us to be just as frank with you. Before you arrived, we'd been discussing this thing. To put it bluntly, a lot of men in this room think your program could wreck—or at least badly upset—the economy if you're not careful."

Manchester sat in the chair a moment without answering, his face reddening under the tan. Then he reached into his inner breast pocket and pulled out a silver cigar case. Archie recognized the movement, a delaying tactic when the Secretary felt his temper rising. Manchester lit a thin panatela cigar and blew a fat smoke ring toward the chandelier overhead. The doughnut of smoke wavered lazily as it almost, but not quite, reached a crystal lobe. Manchester watched the smoke ring until it dissolved, then swung his chair out from under

him and stood up. The easy smile was gone as he looked at
Colby.

"That's the real issue, isn't it, Stan?" he asked. "It isn't defense or national security or our ability to cope with Russia at
all. It's the jobs and the payrolls and, let's face it, gentlemen,
in this room it's the profits."

He set the cigar aside on an ashtray, but still held the light
chair with one hand, thumping it gently on the floor. "Well,
to me these things are secondary. They have to be secondary.
We're riding a runaway fire engine, and we've got to get control of it again before it's too late."

"Mr. Secretary . . ." someone interrupted.

"Excuse me," Manchester continued, "but I'd like to complete my thought. Gentlemen, I wish security would allow me
to itemize just what we have stored away in our nuclear lock-
ers. It's simply fantastic. Maybe I can get the idea across with
some figures that have been published already.

"We've got forty Polaris submarines, each carrying sixteen
missiles. That's a total of six hundred and forty, and each of
them has a warhead many times more powerful than the bomb
that killed a hundred thousand people at Hiroshima. Next, we
have over eight hundred Minuteman missiles in hardened silos,
and each of them is as powerful as a Polaris. Set that against
the fact that there are only about a hundred and fifty cities in
Russia with more than a hundred thousand population."

Manchester let go of the chair and paced back and forth,
the force of his argument sweeping him along.

"As I said this morning, the Joint Committee listed a total
of ninety thousand warheads—ninety *thousand*—ranging in
power from one thousand pounds of TNT equivalent to . . .
well, to almost one hundred million tons. And we've got

twenty different delivery systems to put them on target.

"Honestly, gentlemen, when you consider all that, I think it's an insult to the human race itself to talk about the economy in the same breath with that kind of destructive force. This is an urgent matter—in a way, the most urgent moral dilemma facing mankind today. I'm not ordinarily much of a praying man, but I'm dead-earnest when I say I think the Lord would want us to make this His cause."

Manchester's face was now flushed with exertion and emotion. He paused a moment, then aimed a pointing finger at the moon-faced man.

"Look, we're flirting with the survival of the world," he said. "I'm not exaggerating. You men in this room direct the biggest corporations in the United States. You're the ones—the *only* ones, really—who can help stop this crazy business that is slowly dragging us to the edge of oblivion. You have the power to do something about it, and I hope you'll join me and help me in a . . . well, I know the word has been cheapened by politics, but this *is* a crusade, really. And you can't come along if you're going to insist on thinking first and only of payrolls and profits."

Manchester stopped abruptly, straightened the chair and sat down again. He retrieved his cigar and studied the lengthening ash a moment. "Well, I guess that's it, Stan."

In the stillness of the room the scrape of his chair had sounded like a bulldozer tearing the pavement off a street. Archie looked anxiously from face to face as the seconds ticked by. Then one man in the rear began to applaud, tentatively. The clapping was taken up by a number of others, only to die out slowly in embarrassment. Perhaps a third of them had joined in. The rest sat stolid, their faces blank above the black and white of their evening clothes. Colby stood up nervously.

"Thanks, C.B.," he said. "I know all of us . . . appreciate your coming here at this late hour." He was groping for words. "And we admire you for speaking straight from the shoulder, whatsoever . . . however much some may differ. I know we're all proud that a man of your caliber is seeking the Presidency." He finished haltingly. "I'm sure we all wish you luck."

Manchester shook a few hands. O'Connell nodded to several men from whom he had solicited party funds over the years. Then Manchester and his aides were out of the room and headed for the elevator. Halfway down the hall, they encountered the opposition: Roberts, his great bulk swaying slightly as he walked, and Carl Fleischer, all but hidden behind his chief.

"Charlie." Roberts greeted Manchester with outstretched hand. "Can a country boy from the West survive that den of lions in there?"

"You have nothing to fear from that crowd," said Manchester. His hand, not a small one, was lost in Roberts' grasp. The two men continued to pump hands as they measured each other.

"I don't know," Roberts said. "They're your kind, Charlie. Bankers and brokers—not a bookie in the house."

Manchester smiled. The two candidates released each other's hands, the pleasantries ended and the clumps of rival warriors moved on. As the Manchester trio stood at the elevator, they could hear a sprinkling of applause when Roberts entered the room they had just left.

"Bastards," growled O'Connell.

"I sermonized," said Manchester, almost as if apologizing. "Nobody likes the preacher to aim too close to home."

An official convention limousine, one of dozens lent to prominent party figures by the city's automobile dealers, waited at the curb. They climbed in and told the college-boy volunteer driver to head for the Hilton.

"By that reaction," Manchester said, "maybe we're in for some trouble after all. Most of those fellows have been friendly to me right from the start, last winter."

"All the fun went out of the game when you told them that the economy came second," Archie said.

"Profits," corrected Manchester, "not the total economy. That's not involved. But two out of three men in that room have a finger in the defense pie. They're the ones who didn't applaud. Colby underwrites big aerospace issues. Galsworthy's company has magnesium and exotic metals contracts. The Mercantile Manhattan—that's Harrison's bank—is up to its eyeballs in financing missile works. I could name them all."

As they got out at the Hilton, Archie remembered. "I've got an appointment," he said to Manchester. "You don't mind, do you? I'll see you at breakfast."

"Not at all," said Manchester, smiling. "Ladies first, always."

"Well, her mother's a national committeewoman," said Archie. "That makes it business."

"Mother!" scoffed O'Connell. "Broads you date at midnight don't have mothers. Stay off the sauce, kid. It's still five days till the last ballot."

O'Connell bought an early edition of the Sunday Chicago *Sun-Times*. He and Manchester started to scan the front page, but a black-rimmed box in the center drew their eyes. They read together for a minute, then lowered the paper and stared at each other.

"That's not good, Obie," said Manchester.

"It's murder," said O'Connell.

The short news story read:

> MOSCOW, Aug. 12 (AP)—Pravda will praise Secretary Charles B. Manchester's missile stand in its morning edition, the Soviet news agency TASS announced tonight.
>
> TASS said a Pravda editorial, to be displayed on the front page, will hail Manchester as a "peace fighter" and as a "foe of the imperialistic-militaristic ruling circles in the United States." The Soviet organ, which reflects official Russian policy, will quote excerpts from Manchester's Saturday press conference and say his remarks "clearly indicate his fitness" for the Presidency.

"Well, that's an embrace I could have done without," said Manchester.

"It figures," said O'Connell, "but I thought they'd take a couple of days before tagging you as the Commie candidate."

"Communist candidate?" Manchester looked startled.

"Sure," said O'Connell. "That's what you'll be as soon as Carl Fleischer sees the story."

They were walking through the lobby now, and O'Connell noted two newspapermen bearing down on them. He hurried Manchester through the service doors and into the shelter of a freight elevator. As they rode up, they both reread the bulletin from Moscow.

"We don't need that story," said O'Connell, pawing his plump cheeks. "We don't need that damn story at all."

Archie called Kay from the lobby of the Ambassador East and she came down promptly from her room.

"You're five minutes late," she said. "Is Manchester safe at home yet?"

"He's probably in bed," Archie replied. "It was a little cool out for our side tonight. Tomorrow is another day. Pump Room okay?"

She shook her head. "Half the Texas delegation is in there. Let's go some place quieter. How about The Buttery at the Ambassador West?"

The Buttery proved to be less than placid. Late diners crowded the tables and several celebrating Republicans waved at Archie. The headwaiter found them a wall table in the cocktail area and this time, amid the clatter of a convention Saturday night, they talked politics. Kay said her mother thought the Secretary had erred in raising the missile issue, and Archie, trying to rebut the premise, found himself telling her about Manchester's performance at the Chicago Club. He remembered the precise phrases used by his candidate, for Manchester's spontaneous "sermon" had touched him. He was proud to be working for the man and now he wanted desperately to help him win.

"Why, that's a beautiful speech," Kay said. "It's really wonderful. It's too bad the little people can't hear it."

"Little people?"

"Like me," she said. "I'm little people. We don't understand these things when they talk in stuffy generalities, but the way he puts it, we can."

"You can't vote," said Archie. "And I'm not working any more tonight."

"But we vote in November," she said. "Don't you see? If you're the big public relations man, you ought to figure out some way to get all of us for your man."

"That's for the campaign," he said, "not the convention. Anyway, it's kind of late. The voting's Thursday."

Kay vetoed Archie's suggestion of another night club visit and suggested instead that they go for a walk. They walked to the drive, crossed it and strolled along the lakeside. The waves drove against the concrete breakwater with a steady, echoing beat. The stars were not so bright now and off to the east, over the lake, a cloud bank cloaked the horizon. Their talk drifted away from politics to childhood, parents, ambitions, likes and dislikes; the small credentials of people seeking visas for more than a brief stay. Finally she stopped and faced him.

"Now, I think it's time you kissed me," she said.

He did, tentatively, his hands on her shoulders, and then less tentatively, both arms around her as she reached up to hold him. The embrace was one of seeking and yet of withholding, but for Archie, the convention suddenly dissolved into lips, cheeks, hair and a pulsing warmth.

There was a tiny clink on the sidewalk and she put one hand to the side of her head, then pushed him away.

"My earring, dammit," she said. "Come on, help me find it."

They crawled about, laughing and bumping shoulders. He dared her to light a match in the breeze. She did, but it quickly flared out and they were left in the darkness. Finally his knee felt something hard and he held the earring up triumphantly.

They kissed again and this time there was a knowing and a softness. They grinned at each other, sharing the knowledge of mutual pleasure. Archie tapped her nose.

"It's a funny thing, that nose, Kay." He kissed it lightly.

They walked, hand in hand, back from the lake. It was 3 A.M. when he delivered her to the door of the Ambassador East.

"Tomorrow night?" he asked.

"Or whenever you can," she agreed. "And, Archie, don't forget us ordinary people, huh?"

He fell sound asleep in the taxi before it turned south on Michigan Avenue.

"Here you are, Mac." Archie looked groggily at the bulk of the Conrad Hilton, facing the equally imposing mass of the Blackstone across Balbo Street. Five long, hot days ahead until they called the roll of the states for the first ballot.

5

A few minutes after Archie DuPage fell into his hotel-room bed, a short, dapper man wearing a narrow-brimmed straw hat walked briskly to the reservation desk at the O'Hare Inn near Chicago's airport, some twenty miles northwest of the Loop.

This new arrival on the rim of the convention city was trailed by a bellboy who carried a hand-tooled leather dispatch case. The initials "M.D." were stamped in gold under the handle.

"Good morning, Mr. Davidson," said the desk clerk, smiling and inclining his head an inch or two. "The company suite?"

The arriving guest nodded and scrawled his name on a registration card.

"No calls, please," he said, "and I'd appreciate it if you didn't list me with the switchboard girl. Actually, I'm here for only three hours or so and I need the sleep."

"Certainly, Mr. Davidson," said the clerk. He handed a key to the bellboy. "Mr. Davidson goes to 205."

Inside the suite Mark Davidson handed the bellboy a crisp dollar bill and nodded at the wide grin he received in exchange. When the boy left, he took an electric razor from the dispatch case, ran it briefly over his jaw and then carefully washed his hands and face.

He checked himself in the mirror, straightening his tie and smoothing out an all-but invisible wrinkle on one sleeve of his gray summer-weight suit. He took a quart bottle of tomato juice out of the refrigerator and poured a tall glass full. He pulled a sheaf of typewritten papers from his dispatch case, turned on a floor lamp and settled into an armchair. The president of Universal Forge Corporation obviously had no intention of going to bed, despite his remarks to the desk clerk.

In a few minutes there was a single light tap on the door. Davidson crossed the room hurriedly and opened the door.

"You're punctual, Gus," he said, closing the door quickly behind the man who had entered. Davidson looked at his watch. It was 3:47.

"Almost time for Mass," replied the newcomer. He smiled thinly as Davidson extended his hand.

"No handshake, please, Mark. Remember, I'm a man of my word."

"That I'll testify to," said Davidson. "Hang up your coat?"

As the two men hung their suit jackets on hangers and fussed with such auxiliary preparations as transferring articles from coat to pants pockets, each once again thought of his strange relationship to the other.

They were almost of an age. Arthur G. Maguire, head of the Missile and Aerospace Workers' Union, was forty-six; Davidson was forty-seven. Both were sons of middle-class families. Both had earned master's degrees, Davidson at the Harvard Business School, Maguire at Columbia. Both were prosperous. Davidson made $100,000 a year plus bonuses, stock options and a liberal expense account. Maguire's union paid him a $60,000 salary, plus a handsome pension plan and an expense account fully as elastic as Davidson's. Both were bandbox dressers and regular weekend golfers.

Both were also tireless workers who had built empires. Davidson's management genius had strung together a bewildering series of mergers and purchases until finally Universal Forge dominated the welter of Pentagon missile and space contracts. It was the nation's third largest corporation and still growing, its stock the shiniest of the glamour issues on the market.

Maguire was no less astute. Spurning strong-arm tactics, profanity and liquor, he had moved surely and coldly ahead, raiding a union here, absorbing another there, always keeping his eye on the flaming rockets that were both the nation's military muscle and its springboard to outer space. He was the cream of the new manager class of organized labor; newspapers called him "the Ivy League boss." Now his Missile and Aerospace Workers' Union was the nation's fifth largest and bidding to become the giant of them all. Like Mark Davidson, Gus Maguire could not stand to be second—in anything.

The wary respect they had for each other grew from the

fact that they had once clashed head on, and each had been forced to settle for less than victory. They had matched guile and power in a bitter, 27-week strike, and neither had won. Davidson yielded less in wages and hours than Maguire demanded, but he had to give more than he wanted, to avoid losing several new defense contracts because of the shutdown. Maguire put his members into the highest skilled-labor pay bracket in the nation, but it would take them a decade, even with strike fund benefits and the new hourly rates, to make up the lost pay envelopes. To protect his own position, Maguire —with Davidson's advance knowledge and assent—accused the Uniforge president of "double-cross" and swore he would not shake his hand again until the four-year contract expired. He had honored the vow, for Maguire, like Davidson, kept his promises.

Now they sat facing each other in the glow of the single lamp, drinking tomato juice while Chicago slept. Their preliminary talk had been so brief that a stranger would have thought them unfriendly, but no such thought entered their minds. Davidson squared the sheaf of papers.

"Gus," he said, "you know that Manchester press conference was completely unacceptable. It means our bread and butter."

"My bread. Your butter, Mark," said Maguire. His coat was off, but he left his tie and collar neatly clasped by a silver pin.

"Honest to God, it shocked hell out of me," Davidson said. "I had no idea he was going to say anything like that. Were you surprised?"

"I was. You know I haven't announced for anyone, but I've said a few nice things about him. He's the President's man, and we've gotten a fair shake from the Stuart administration."

"So have we," mused Davidson. "I just don't get it. I can't believe Stuart wants to cut back on the big delivery systems. If he does, why would he have gone ahead with Daphne?"

Maguire shrugged. "I don't think there's any mystery about it, Mark. I think Manchester is one of those sincere guys who just says what he believes. They can be the worst kind, especially when they're wrong. And Manchester's dead wrong."

"He's dead wrong and he could be dangerous for the country," said Davidson. He pointed to two Sunday papers he'd brought from the airport. "Why, the Communists are already praising the hell out of him."

Maguire glanced at the headlines. These were final editions and the story from Moscow ran a full column now in both papers. "I know," he said. "I heard it in the car radio coming out. That'll hurt Manchester in this convention."

"How can it be fanned along?" asked Davidson.

"A thing like that takes care of itself. You just make sure that everybody has heard it. If a guy hasn't, you tell him."

"Regardless of the Communist reaction, Manchester's position could be dangerous," said Davidson. "He could wreck our whole defense structure."

"Do you really believe that?" Maguire's question was sharp.

"Well, maybe not 'wreck' exactly. But it could play unshirted hell with . . . with the industry."

"And specifically with Uniforge?"

Davidson inspected the labor leader over the rim of his glass. Then his eyes fell to the tomato juce as he swished it about.

"I know what you're thinking," he said after a pause. "I

thought that through on the plane. Sure, I guess my response is from self-interest, just like yours, I suppose. But who is Charlie Manchester to change everything at the drop of a sentence? This thing is too big, there's too much involved for the country, to go barging off on a tangent all of a sudden."

Maguire's smile was slow and friendly. "I understand," he said. "I guess we've both been going through the moral bit. You can run yourself through hoops till you're dizzy. But the fact is that Manchester is taking a dangerous tack. It may be okay, but also it could be disastrous. Who knows? So, in that sense, right now in this convention, like I said, Manchester is dead wrong."

They looked at each other uneasily a moment. Ethics was not a familiar subject of exchange for these two hard bargainers. Then Davidson grinned.

"Okay," he said. He looked like a man happy to be rid of an unwanted burden.

"Good," said Maguire crisply. "I've been thinking about what we ought to do, and I guess you have too."

"I have. You go first."

"Well, first off, anything said in this room stays in this room, right?"

"Of course."

"Then," Maguire continued, "I think we've got to make up our minds right now to beat Manchester. He looked like a shoo-in twenty-four hours ago, but now there's a chance he can be taken if we work it right. And you can do a lot more than I can."

"Can I?" Davidson stirred his tomato juice idly with a finger.

"Yes, you can, Mark. I've got thirty-three union delegates

in that convention, and every one of them will go for Roberts. But that's not going to help much, because some of them are already on his side, like the four in the California delegation. Sure, they can swing some other union men, but there aren't many of those. I keep reminding myself that this isn't a Democratic convention. So it boils down to maybe twenty-five to fifty votes that I can pick up, net. That's chicken feed in this game."

Davidson had been listening intently. "So it's up to me?" he asked, and Maguire nodded. The missile maker took over. "I've been thinking along the same lines, Gus. Happily, if you'll pardon the word, labor doesn't cut much ice at a Republican convention. But business does. I bet that Daphne contract alone means money in the pockets of three-four hundred delegates, one way or another."

"Add the stockholders, and the bankers, and the chambers of commerce," said Maguire, "and pretty soon you'd have the whole ball of wax, if you only knew how to figure it."

Davidson took an envelope from his pocket. "Here's a for-instance I was doodling with on the plane. This happens to be a delegate from New Jersey, a fellow I know about through business connections. Now, take a look at this."

He put the envelope on the coffee table and elaborately smoothed out the wrinkles.

"He's a lawyer from Newark. He's unpledged, but it's no secret he admires Manchester. Okay. But he also happens to be a partner in a big law firm, and the firm's best client is Ogleby & Sampson, the electronics outfit. Right now, ninety per cent of O & S production is a little gadget about as big as a goose-pimple." Davidson measured a tiny space with thumb

and forefinger. "That little gadget is part of the inertial guidance system in every single missile made in this country. O & S
is a supplier for all the major missile makers, including us. So
suppose somebody in my shop calls Jerry Sampson and asks
him to call this delegate's law firm?"

"That's what I had in mind," Maguire said. "Manchester
would never know what hit him."

"There's only one trouble," Davidson said. He tapped his
wrist watch with a finger.

Maguire nodded in assent. "Yeah, time. And manpower. It
would take a whole army of snoopers to dig up that kind of
stuff between now and Thursday. And it would have to be by
Wednesday, too; you got to get to them at least one day before
the voting."

"That's the big hurdle, all right," said Davidson, "but maybe
it won't be so tough."

"What do you mean?"

Davidson smiled. "I got a call from Bryan Roberts."

"Oh?" This time Maguire smiled. "You get the big man. I
called in there to the Roberts outfit today and talked to the
labor section. But we're on the same wavelength."

"Roberts got me at our main office in L.A. I'd just finished
watching Manchester on TV. And, brother, was I boiling."

"What did he want?" Maquire asked.

"Oh, he sparred around for a minute or two. Asked me what
I thought of Manchester's missile statement. He read me what
he was putting out. Sounded pretty good for our side."

"Yeah," said Maguire. "I read it in the afternoon paper."

"Then he said if any of his friends—apparently he considers me one of them, which I had just become when he

called—if any of his friends wanted to help in any way, why, they, the Roberts people, had a pretty good file on the delegates. 'Pretty thorough' was the way he put it."

Maguire was unimpressed. "Oh, hell, every decent campaign organization has a card file of delegates. But it wouldn't do us much good. They just have districts, primary stands, friends in the organization, that kind of thing."

"Still," said Davidson, "I think we ought to see what they've got."

"Well, I'll see what I can nose out later in the morning," Maguire said. "I can talk to their labor man. Since my call yesterday, he knows I'm ready to do whatever I can."

"In the meantime," suggested Davidson, "let's sit down with this delegate list and see what we can come up with on our own. Between us, we ought to be able to wrap up some pretty good leads on a fair number of delegates. What do you say?"

Maguire stood up and stretched. "I'm for it. But let's get something to eat first. My stomach is yelling at me. How about calling room service for some bacon and eggs?"

"No, sir." Davidson shook his head. "I'm not opening that door until you leave. But you won't go hungry. There's food in the icebox and I'll be the chef."

So the president of the nation's third largest corporation fried eggs and brewed coffee for the president of the nation's fifth largest labor union—an act which Maguire thought fittingly symbolized their relative standing in the American economic kingdom. They ate at the coffee table with the list of delegates and alternates to the Thirtieth Republican National Convention between them. Davidson scratched notes on the margins as they ran down the names of 1,308 delegates, state by state.

"Kilgore, Henry. Connecticut."

"Never heard of him," Maguire mumbled through a mouthful of toast.

"Samuelson, Jacob. Connecticut."

"Nope."

"Me neither. Delaware: Flaherty, Mrs. Edward."

"Hold it," Maguire said. "Flaherty. . . . Yes, I know her husband. He has a big trucking outfit. The Teamsters tried to organize his drivers once. Didn't make it. I knew him at Columbia. Same class."

"Any credit problems?"

"Could be. He's always expanding. Better check."

On they went, calling the roll. Every tenth or twelfth name would yield valuable information, sometimes from the company president, sometimes from the labor leader, sometimes from both. In Maryland, Davidson spotted the vice-president of a salvage company which had an exclusive arrangement with a Uniforge subcontractor. In the Missouri delegation, Davidson called off the name of Hubert Germaine.

"You should know him," said Maguire. "He's sales manager for Vitrionics in St. Louis."

"Vitrionics is one of our subcontractors, I think," said Davidson.

"I happen to know it is. Maybe we should switch jobs, Mark —and salaries."

"Okay," said Davidson, "I'll talk to Germaine myself."

Daylight came as they labored down the list. Davidson pulled back the draw curtains, opened the windows and heated more coffee. They went back to work.

It was almost eight o'clock when Davidson read off the last name, that of a Virgin Islands delegate unknown to either of them. The missile president had covered his list with the names of people, banks, corporations, union officials, even churches. He threw down his pencil.

"If we know what's good for us, you were never in this room, and if anybody says you were, I'll deny it. As a matter of fact, I wasn't here either. I'm going downtown and check in at the Executive House. Call me there as soon as you get some word on what the Roberts people have in their delegate file, will you, Gus?"

"Okay," said Maguire. "I'm at the Congress when you need me." His eyes were heavy, but he was awake enough to grin and shake his head when Davidson extended his hand again.

"I forgot, Gus," said Davidson, withdrawing his hand. "You're a man of your word."

"Our man Roberts isn't in such bad shape," said Maguire, stretching his arms and flexing his shoulders. "At least he doesn't have the Kremlin around his neck."

The company president opened the door and peered both ways down the corridor. "Okay," he said. The union president slipped out and walked rapidly down the hall.

6

Calvin Burroughs pushed away the room-service breakfast table and settled in a corner of the couch to read the Sunday papers. He still wore pajamas and a purple silk dressing gown, although he had shaved and his gray hair was neatly combed.

Burroughs read with the double vision of a successful newspaper publisher, skimming through the news and at the same time comparing the judgment of his own editors with that of their rivals. Saturday's preconvention developments in Chicago dominated all the front pages, exiling to the inside columns such ordinarily prominent items as the mid-air collision of two private planes, the divorce of a thrice-married member of the international jet set, and the drowning of a Florida man who fell out of his boat when the tarpon he'd hooked leaped in. Manchester and Daphne monopolized the big type today.

The Chicago *Sun-Times* had a three-deck headline:

Manchester Nixes
$10 Billion
Missile Contract

The *Tribune* said:

Moscow Hails Manchester's
Stand On Missile Warheads

The *New York Times* headlines read:

Manchester Says
He Would Cut
Defense Funds

Burroughs had air-mail editions of two of his own papers. "Manchester: No New H-Bombs Or Missiles" was the way the St. Louis *Herald* put it. The New Orleans *Globe* banner, eight columns wide, said:

Manchester Calls Daphne Missile "Idiocy"

A subordinate headline added:

Reds Laud Manchester
As "Imperialism" Foe

Burroughs made a mental note to call his New Orleans editor and compliment him. He thought the *Globe* had best caught the explosive possibilities of Manchester's press conference. And the publisher had decided before he went to bed early that morning that the possibilities were, indeed, explosive.

He finished with the papers, slipped off his robe and went to a desk across the room. He carefully inserted a cigarette in his ivory holder, rolled two sheets of paper into a portable typewriter and began pecking swiftly with his two index fingers:

(Burroughs—Monday column)

Burroughs News Service
Convention Bureau
Conrad Hilton Hotel

STRICTLY POLITICS
By Calvin Burroughs

CHICAGO—Mountebanks and statesmen, golden girls and hustlers, college boys and precinct pols are thronging Michigan Avenue on the eve of the opening of the 30th Republican National Convention.

This is one that should be all over—including the shouting —before it begins, with Treasury Secretary Charles B. Manchester drafting his acceptance speech while he waits for the delegates to nominate him on the first ballot at about 2 p.m. Thursday.

But it's not going to be that way, for Manchester astonished his handlers by winding up and swinging at his own chin yesterday even before the first bell. It may not turn out to be a knockout punch, but it's already clear that no contestant in a sporting event has done so much for his opponent since Roy Riegels ran the wrong way in the Rose Bowl in 1929.

With that much of his weekly political column completed, Burroughs sat back and stared at the paper. He had done much the same thing every Sunday morning for two decades. The

publisher's weekly commentary went to all of his eight metropolitan dailies. Though he was a Republican who had bolted
his party only once (for Kennedy against Nixon in 1960),
Burroughs prided himself on the impartiality of his column.
He tried to come up each week with an exclusive story or a
choice morsel of political gossip, Democratic or Republican,
and he did well enough so that politicians of both parties
made his column "must" reading. He took special pride in
the dispatch he filed on the eve of each national nominating
convention. Three or four times he had called the exact ticket
when it wasn't easy, and once he even named the vice-presidential nominee before the presidential candidate himself was
aware of the identity of his running mate.

Now Burroughs smoked a second cigarette and frowned.
What exactly did that press conference mean? He walked to
the window, watched the noon sun sparkling on the lake, saw
a freighter trailing smoke on the horizon. He sat down again
before the typewriter, but almost as quickly got up again and
wandered back to the window. Finally he consulted a mimeo-
graphed convention telephone list and called the Morrison
Hotel.

"Governor Wilcox of Pennsylvania, please. . . . Is he there?
This is Calvin Burroughs of the Burroughs Newspapers.
Thank you. . . . Governor? Hello, this is Cal Burroughs. . . .
Fine, thanks, and yourself? . . . I wonder if you'd be kind
enough to let me pick your brains for a couple of minutes. . . .
Thanks."

Burroughs slipped into his formal interviewing style, the
one he found went best with second-drawer politicians.

"Governor," he said, "let me come straight to the point. I

need your guidance, off the record. Did Secretary Manchester change this convention yesterday?"

"This for your column, Cal?"

"Yes, but of course not for attribution, Governor."

"I understand. That's a fine column, Cal. I read it every week."

"Thank you, Governor."

"Well, if we're talking in complete confidence, I don't mind telling you the way I see it. Number one, Charlie did the party a disfavor. He may be right in his diagnosis of our defense problem, but I'm beginning to wonder about that since these stories this morning out of Moscow. Have you seen them?"

"Yes, I have," said Burroughs.

"If the Communists like his line, you can be sure a lot of delegates won't. Anyway, why in God's name bring up that kind of an issue now? That's the sort of thing a new President ought to unwrap in a special message to Congress sometime next spring—after a full discussion with the leaders."

"Didn't anybody know about this in advance?" asked Burroughs.

"Not a soul so far as I can tell. I'd give my right arm to hear what Fred Stuart's saying about it in the White House right now. The whole thing indicates to me . . . well, it raises a question about Charlie Manchester. A Republican President has got to be a team player, Cal. Eisenhower was a team man, and so is Stuart, and they both gave us pretty good government."

"So where does that leave you, Governor?"

"Cal, you know I'm here as Pennsylvania's favorite son. But you and I are realists. I just wanted to hold our votes and make them count. There was a lot of sentiment for Manchester in my delegation last week. We might even have gone for Charlie on the first ballot."

"And now?" the publisher asked.

"Now I think maybe I'll sit tight. I'm not sure, of course, but Pennsylvania may want to vote for me on the first ballot. Maybe more."

"You mean Manchester's no longer a sure thing?"

"He's still the leader, of course, Cal," said Wilcox, "but things can change. You've heard the same reports I have since that press conference."

"Any heat from the missile people?"

"Not yet." Wilcox paused. "Not yet. But the day is young, Cal, a lot younger than you and I."

Burroughs thanked the Governor, hung up the phone and went back to his typewriter. The two-finger tattoo resumed:

It's not generally recognized yet, but it's a fact that at his press conference Manchester, who came to town looking like a sure winner, managed to throw the nomination into question. Right now, this has the makings of the closest G.O.P. nomination contest since the Eisenhower-Taft fight in 1952.

Moscow's blessing may no longer be the kiss of death it once was, since rank-and-file politicians have become more sophisticated in their reactions to Kremlin propaganda. Still, Pravda's quick applause for Manchester's missile stand will hurt the Secretary, perhaps severely in some delegations.

One fact is indicative of the new trend: It's learned on reliable authority that Gov. Benjamin Wilcox of Pennsylvania has hardened his position in the last 24 hours. It had been assumed that after an appropriately coy but brief courtship, Wilcox would hand his 64 delegate votes to Manchester and get a kiss blown his way by President Stuart. Now Wilcox may sit out the first ballot in anticipation of a deadlock which conceivably could kill off both Manchester and Gov. Bryan Roberts and throw the nomination to a third man—and the only third man of any stature here is Benjamin Wilcox.

Wilcox is not alone in his new caution, nor is his attitude dictated solely by the possibility of personal gain. Many Republican leaders believe that Manchester may or may not be right on the issue of nuclear defense, but they are unhappy at his raising of the question now. Among political professionals, an error in timing is rated a cardinal sin—comparable to Communism, pornography and going back on your word. In the White House, they reason, timing is the essence of success— and a man who blunders into an issue is not to be trusted.

Burroughs pecked out another line and a half, then crossed it out and started the new paragraph over. Again he stopped and ran a line of x's through his words. He began to fidget once more, returning to the window for another long look at Lake Michigan. The freighter was hull-down now and the smudge from its smoke was much fainter.

Finally the publisher went to the phone.

"Operator, I want to speak to General Wesley Shaw, S-h-a-w, in Santa Barbara, California, please. I don't have the number. . . . Person to person, yes."

Burroughs tucked the phone between his head and shoulder so he could fit another cigarette into the holder while he waited for the call to go through.

"Hello, Wes? Cal Burroughs calling. . . . Yes, I'm in Chicago. That's why I wanted to talk to you. Have you got a few minutes?"

Burroughs pulled a chair under himself and sat down.

"I imagine you've read about the press conference that Secretary Manchester had here yesterday."

The voice that came back was brisk. Burroughs could

visualize his friend sitting in the souvenir-cluttered study of his California home, the morning sun highlighting the bald head that seemed three sizes too big for his face, a smile cleaving the cheerful homeliness of that face and tightening the network of old-pilot's wrinkles around his eyes. General Wesley Shaw was certainly the least handsome man ever to head the Air Force—but no military man in years had been more respected by his subordinates or more popular with the country.

"Oh, hell, yes, Cal," he said. "Matter of fact, I watched the whole thing on television."

"I didn't know you retired Air Force types were so interested in politics," Burroughs joked. "You always told me when you were chief of staff that you never paid any attention to it."

"Well, now that I'm retired, I'm allowed to. I do have one vote, you know."

Burroughs chuckled. "I suspect you'd have a lot more than one, Wes, if you could ever be persuaded to open your mouth in public."

"It's not for lack of opportunity that I haven't, Cal. But you know when I agreed to go on the Uniforge board, I made them promise there wouldn't be any of that, and Mark Davidson has been as good as his word."

"In that case, Wes, I certainly wouldn't try to drag you into it." Burroughs tilted his chair back, his feet hooked around its legs. "But I did want to ask your opinion on the substance of what Manchester said yesterday."

"What do you mean?"

"I mean, does his argument hold water? I don't know anything about missiles, but you do, and you know quite a bit about the Daphne in particular."

"I don't know how much of it I can talk about, though."

Burroughs brought the chair down on all four legs with a thump. "I don't want you to get into anything classified, Wes. But, in general, is Manchester right when he talks about Daphne being simply a relatively minor improvement on existing weapons?"

"Yes, I guess so." Shaw was thinking as he spoke, and his first words were tentative. Then he added, more assuredly: "Yes, that's about right. It's a better bird—and I don't say that because it's ours, either—it's quite a bit better. But it isn't anything revolutionary. There aren't any breakthroughs involved."

"Do you think Manchester's right, then?"

"You know, Cal, I'm afraid he is, although judging by the morning paper, that looks like it puts me in bed with the Reds."

"That bouquet from Moscow could be expected," remarked Burroughs.

"Sure. They even praised me once. If we made policy by trying to take the reverse of the Communist line, we'd wind up in knots. Look, it may sound like high treason coming from a fellow who spent years trying to pry more money out of Congress for the Air Force, but I think Manchester's right. Somebody's got to get control of that spending or we *will* wind up with an economy that's so hitched to defense we can't do anything about it. And I guess this is as good a place to blow the whistle as any."

Burroughs was scribbling notes on the desk blotter. "Well,

would canceling the Daphne leave a big gap in our defenses, maybe five years from now?"

"Nope," the General said quickly. "It's not that kind of thing. There won't be a gap if this isn't built. Of course, we've got to keep up the research work—that's the only way you make the quantum jumps—but it can be done in the laboratory, or at least on a smaller scale. You don't have to spend ten billion bucks to get answers to questions."

Burroughs switched subjects. "But wouldn't cancellation be pretty rough on Universal Forge?"

Shaw grunted. "I suppose I don't sound like a very loyal director of Uniforge, do I? But look, Cal, this is a pretty big outfit, and we're diversified all over the place. We've got plenty of contracts and there are more where those came from. I don't think my stock is in danger."

"I'm sure it isn't. . . . One thing, though: Have you heard anything around Uniforge about Manchester's statement?"

"No, I haven't. But it's the weekend and everything is shut down, and I don't get into the office too often anyway. But I haven't heard from Mark or anyone else. The company steers pretty clear of politics, as a rule."

"I know, Wes, but I have a feeling this may be different."

"I hope not," said Shaw. "Defense contractors have no business messing in politics, and I think Davidson and the other officers know that as well as I."

"If you hear anything, will you let me know? I'm staying at the Hilton."

Shaw agreed and the two men, friends of more than a decade's standing, chatted on for a few minutes about families and friends. When they finished, Burroughs went directly to his typewriter and picked up where he had stopped with the sentence about "a man who blunders into an issue is not to be trusted."

This leads to a second question being asked around Chicago today. Did Manchester blunder into advocating the cancellation of Daphne or did he intend all along to make it an issue? The pros think it was an accident; the amateurs think he did it on purpose.

Either way, the politically untried Secretary of the Treasury has tipped over a basket of eels, for the Daphne contract touches some of the most sensitive pocketbook nerves in the country—employment, business profits, banks, schools, local tax revenues, the very economic existence of whole cities and towns. In brief, Manchester has pointed a knife at the entire political-industrial defense complex which has provided a livelihood for millions—and great profits for thousands—in the past 30 years.

But whatever the forces involved, and whatever the wisdom of his timing, the country is indebted to Manchester for bringing the issue into the open. It is an important one. There is strong reason to believe that the Daphne contract wouldn't add much to the over-all strength of American defenses. And there is every reason to believe that the more general issue—controlling defense spending—is one of the central questions of our time. The country needs to know more about these things, and open discussion is the only way to learn. Certainly the country has a right to know how a candidate for President feels on these issues.

Also, it may develop that Moscow's flash reaction reflects more substance than propaganda. Russia, no less than the United States, feels the burden of defense production; and the Communist hierarchy is sensitive to pressures from its people, who are weary of the arms race and its denial of the consumer comforts they have been promised for so many years.

All of which, unfortunately, won't have much influence on the decision to be made here in the next five days. Manchester has certainly upset the calm preconvention mood of his party, and there's no telling what will happen now. Certainly there will be heavy pressures on the delegates. Manchester will have his hands full holding onto his supporters in the face of what is sure to be a renewed—and much strengthened—challenge from Bryan Roberts.

(end)

Burroughs read through the copy, penciling in a word here and there. Then he dressed and headed for the elevators, the story tucked in his pocket. The convention traffic jam was routine now, and he found himself crammed into an elevator against a bountiful, if somewhat elderly, bosom. The tip of a Manchester pennant, held by a man in a Daniel Boone costume, threatened his nose, and he had to arch his neck stiffly to avoid the pennant. The operator, her freshly painted face already strained, made a tentative stop at the eighth floor. But she closed the doors again when a voice from the rear of the car boomed, "No! Enough's enough!" The occupants all laughed.

A cacophony of teleprinters, typewriters and television sounds assailed Burroughs' ears as he entered the basement exhibition hall which had been turned into a huge press room. Heavy black curtains separated the convention work spaces of the nation's major newspapers, wire services and networks. In a center area, where a lectern and microphones faced several hundred chairs, a dozen reporters took notes while one of Bryan Roberts' assistants read off the Governor's schedule for the day.

Calvin Burroughs stepped into the curtained cubicle of the Burroughs Newspapers and handed his copy to a wiry, shirt-sleeved man sitting at a littered table.

"Anything new?" Burroughs asked.

"The UPI ticker has a speculative story that Mark Davidson of Universal Forge may have flown to Chicago from Los Angeles last night," his desk man replied. "We're trying to check it."

"Hank," the publisher said, "this thing is turning into a convention. I think—"

He was interrupted by the bell on the United Press International's convention news service teleprinter. It rang five times. Both men bent over the machine to read:

UPI Convention 23
     Chicago—A dispute over defense policy today threatened to stir up a major fight at the Republican convention.
     The defense subcommittee of the platform committee was called into an emergency session at 2 p.m. (CDT). The hastily summoned meeting, according to G.O.P. platform writers, was provoked by Treasury Secretary Charles B. Manchester's blockbuster press conference yesterday, when he labeled the new Daphne missile "idiocy."
     The defense plank had been completed and adopted Friday by unanimous vote, but Manchester's stand against new missile contracts broke the seal of agreement.
     Subcommittee Chairman Frank R. Doyle of Arkansas, a Manchester backer, issued the call for the meeting despite protests by supporters of Gov. Bryan Roberts. The call was for a secret session, but word quickly spread among delegates.
     GR127PCDT

Calvin Burroughs grinned. "See what I mean?" he said. "I think we've got a real convention on our hands."

*   *   *

Bryan Roberts sat in his Blackstone suite with his two top lieutenants in their daily strategy session. The Governor, filling his favorite armchair, listened as Carl Fleischer made his point again.

"Our pitch in the defense subcommittee is simple," reiterated the manager as he fingered his smoked glasses. "We're satisfied as is. We don't want a word changed. Right?"

"Not a comma," agreed Roberts. "It calls for a strong defense establishment, and that's our position."

Roger Abbott smoothed the lonely strands on his shiny head. "I think they're making a mistake," he said. "My guess is the subcommittee won't want to get into this missile hassle."

"I agree," said Fleischer, "but I think this is the committee chairman's doing. Obie O'Connell is too smart to get the committee all riled up unless he has the votes. And he doesn't. This just happens to be one committee where we've got an edge."

"I hope you're right," said Roberts. "I wouldn't want to lose the first test vote in the convention."

"We won't lose. Don't worry." Fleischer leaned forward and tapped the Governor's knee. "But there's another place, Bin, where we can really make some hay. This story out of Moscow is a natural for us. I want to play it for all it's worth."

"What do you mean?" asked Roberts.

Fleischer pulled a sheet of paper from his pocket and handed it to Roberts. "I just tried out some wording for a handbill," he said. "I'd like to get the boys to put one of these under the door of every delegate's room."

Roberts heaved himself out of his chair. He stood in the center of the room and pulled at the flesh on his neck in the gap left by his open shirt collar. A frown creased his forehead as he studied the paper. Fleischer's penciled words read:

WHY DO THE COMMUNISTS WANT MANCHESTER?
WITHIN A FEW HOURS OF SECRETARY MANCHESTER'S AS-
TONISHING PRESS CONFERENCE, PRAVDA, OFFICIAL ORGAN OF
THE KREMLIN, HAILED MANCHESTER AS A HERO. BEFORE YOU
VOTE FOR A MAN WHO WOULD TEAR DOWN AMERICA'S DE-
FENSES, READ WHAT THE COMMUNISTS SAY ABOUT HIM. HERE
IS THE EXACT TEXT AS DISTRIBUTED BY TASS, THE SOVIET NEWS
AGENCY.

"Then we just print the text out of the newspapers," said Fleischer when he noted that Roberts had finished reading. "We don't have to sign the leaflet."

Governor Roberts did not reply. He walked to a window and looked down at the side street where hundreds of persons were crossing between the Hilton and the Blackstone. On a sidewalk two men were unfurling a long paper streamer which, when stretched out, implored: "Win With Bin—A Square Shooter." The California Governor's big body cast a broad shadow in the room as the early afternoon sun beat against him.

He turned to Fleischer and shook his head.

"No, Carl," he said. "We're not going to do or say a thing about that *Pravda* editorial."

"Why not, for God's sake?" exploded Abbott.

"Because, Roger, you and I and Carl know that there isn't an ounce of pro-Communism in Charlie Manchester's whole makeup. This thing would be a smear on a loyal American and I'm not going to do it—and you aren't either."

Fleischer lowered his head under the reprimand. "Bin," said the manager defensively, "the whole convention is going to be talking about this anyway and I was just suggesting we help it along."

"Let them talk," said Roberts. "That we can't help. But I don't intend to hang a Red tag on Charlie Manchester and I don't want anybody even hinting at it around this headquarters. He may win the nomination. I hope not, but he may. And if he does, I'm going to support him. I don't want any Republican candidate going before this country with Communist mud all over him."

"He's already got some, if you ask me," said Fleischer.

Roberts flared up at his manager. "Well, we're not adding to it. That's final." He stood silent a moment, then rekeyed his voice to his normal conversational level. "What else have we got?"

*   *   *

The Sunday papers were strewn over the floor of the apartment in Tiburon. Patsy Manchester was down on her knees and elbows, reading the text of the Russian editorial again. She wore her jeans and old shirt, but also a gray cashmere sweater. Fog enveloped Tiburon like a wet sheet and the air was chill. The "little winter" of August lay upon the San Francisco Bay area.

"The dirty Communists," Patsy yelped. "Why do they have to stick their nose in everything?"

Jake lay on the sofa, his sneaker-shod feet propped on the back of the upholstery. He yawned and stretched.

"You could bet they would the minute Dad sounded off at the press conference," he said. "The opening was wide as a barn door."

Patsy swung around to face him and sat with her legs crossed under her. "But if those old poops in the Kremlin really agree with C.B., why would they praise him? They must know that would hurt him. What are they, dumb or something?"

"I'm no Kremlinologist, honey," he said. "If you tried to follow all their dodging and weaving, you'd go nuts. All I say is that it proves what I was trying to tell you yesterday. Dad picked a lousy time to pop off on missiles."

"You don't think he's in real trouble, do you, Jake?" Her voice was plaintive. "I just couldn't stand that."

"Maybe he is and maybe he isn't. If he is, maybe for once the great man will need some help." He picked up a Sunday supplement and began reading it, and so did not see Patsy when she grimaced and stuck her tongue out at him.

7

Manchester, who disliked air conditioning, had turned off the machine in the sitting room of the Royal Skyway suite and thrown two windows wide open. The night air freshened the room. Off in the dark void of the lake, a ship's lights twinkled. From Michigan Avenue, far below, came the faint rumble of Sunday night traffic.

The shirt-sleeved candidate thumped the arm of his easy chair. His tanned face was ruddy with temper, and his voice reflected the strain in the room.

"I can't run on that platform," Manchester insisted. "It's as simple as that. This isn't a question of politics, Obie. It's a question of honesty."

The three aides sitting with him were silent for a moment.

Louis Cohen slumped on a couch. Obie O'Connell's pudgy face bore a look of impatience. Archie, down on the floor with a mess of papers around him, scratched his head absently. His scalp itched, as it always did when he was short of sleep.

They already had settled their tactics in response to Moscow's unwelcome intrusion into their plans. Cohen had argued for a formal statement by the candidate, but Manchester said flatly he wouldn't dignify the *Pravda* editorial with comment. In the end, it was decided that Archie would issue a short statement over his own name as press secretary: "The Russian government's heavyhanded attempt to interfere in this convention will be greeted by Republican delegates with the ridicule it deserves. Secretary Manchester regards the *Pravda* editorial as propaganda unworthy of comment." O'Connell feared this would fail to repair the damage caused by the Sunday headlines, but agreed it probably was the best they could do.

Now they were dealing with the formal action of the platform subcommittee on defense, and finding the candidate obdurate and unyielding. They had been locked in dispute for an hour.

"Look, Charlie, let me lay it on the line once and for all," O'Connell said wearily. "You're on the spot. We tried to change that plank in the defense subcommittee this afternoon. We lost. If you appeal to the full platform committee, you'll lose again. If you appeal again to the convention floor, you'll get a shellacking that could kill you. I'll say it's simple—like one, two, three strikes you're out."

"If I don't fight it," Manchester snapped, "I'm a fourflusher who doesn't mean what he says."

Obie dismissed the objection with a wave of his hand. "I didn't ask you to say it in the first place—but never mind that. What we got to do now is cut our losses the best we can. You won't cut 'em if you stand and fight on this one."

"I'm ready to take this to the floor," Manchester insisted.

Louis Cohen, his normally pessimistic face turned morose, disagreed again. "Believe me, Mr. Secretary, there's no sentiment anywhere in this convention to change the language of that defense plank," he said. "I agree with Obie. We can't do it."

Cohen had carried the Manchester banner into the session of the subcommittee earlier that day. The fifteen-man group, charged with drafting the defense plank for the Republican platform, called three witnesses—Cohen; a Roberts brain truster; and Graham Reddig, President Stuart's special counsel and emissary to the convention. Reddig offered some innocuous wording about the need for "continuing reappraisal of all weapons systems," suggesting it could cover everybody's position. Cohen, for Manchester, proposed a new sentence saying that "only those new systems that offer a clear advance in military technology" should be added to the armed forces. The Roberts man said happily that his candidate liked the plank just the way it was. After two hours of wrangling, the subcommittee voted 9 to 6 to leave its draft unchanged, and the evening radio and TV news programs trumpeted a "setback" for Manchester.

"Can't you fellows understand that this is a matter of principle?" Manchester persisted, hunching forward on the edge of his armchair and holding his hands out toward his aides. "That language needs to be changed."

"Look, they didn't go for it in the committee," Obie said. "If you risk a floor fight and lose, you're dead. Then you don't have to worry about running on anybody's plank, that's for sure."

"But I don't propose to lose, Obie." Manchester said it as though the announcement assured the result.

O'Connell's voice went up half an octave. God, it was hard to tell these amateurs anything. "Charlie, that's the way conventions are, believe me. You can't work this thing on a flow chart. In '52, the minute the Eisenhowers won that fair play gimmick on the floor the Tafts were dead. The delegates are looking for the winner. In a convention, if you can't win a fight, you don't fight."

"Obie's right, Mr. Secretary," said Cohen. "Convention psychology rests on a fragile base. Break one leg of it and your lead can collapse."

"What do you think, Archie?" Manchester asked.

Archie ducked. He offered his opinion only when he felt confidence in its value. This was his first convention, while O'Connell's experience stretched back through half a dozen. "I just don't know, boss," he said.

"Let me give you an example of the way things are going," said O'Connell, pressing his point. "Two or three times tonight I heard people complaining about 'the width of a gnat's eye.' Remember you told the Five Thousand Club last night that the Daphne wouldn't increase our defenses by 'the width of a gnat's eye'?"

Manchester came to his feet, his face flushed clear down to his collar. "By God!" he exploded. "That was all supposed to be off the record!"

O'Connell was unmoved. "So somebody leaked," he said. "Rich men gossip too, Charlie. Anyway, these guys claimed you were getting a little smart-alecky, talking like that."

The Secretary glared at his manager. "Smart-alecky?" He almost shouted it. Then he calmed himself and went on: "Good God, Obie, it's just an expression, a figure of speech, that's all."

"I know, I know," O'Connell explained, "but when they start quoting you like that—and bitching about it—look out."

"What's the matter with you, Archie?" asked Manchester. His press secretary had snapped his fingers, then risen from his chair.

"I think I just remembered something," Archie said. "Excuse me a minute."

Archie went down the hall to his own makeshift office and pulled the telephone out from under the papers littering his desk. He dialed the Ambassador East and asked for Kay Orcott's room.

"Hi, you," she answered brightly. "I'm curled up in bed reading a love story. Do you like love, Archie?"

"Not at the moment." It came out snappish and he didn't mind. "Listen, Kay, did you tell anyone about Manchester's talk at the Chicago Club? Remember my telling you about it last night?"

There was a pause. "Sure," she said, her voice low and composed, "and don't bark at me. I told Mother. The way you put it, Manchester's little speech was wonderful, and I wanted her to understand that too."

"Jesus, Kay," Archie yelped, "this is a fight, not a college seminar! Your mother works for Roberts, I work for Manchester. They're fighting for the Presidency. You know, that big white house in Washington?"

"But, Archie—"

"But, nothing. Your mother spread the word that Manchester said the Daphne wasn't worth 'the width of a gnat's eye.' You told her that, too, didn't you?"

"Yes, but what has that got to do—"

"Just that they're murdering him with it, that's all."

Now Kay's tone grew sharper, too. "But that's what he believes, isn't it? . . . Well, isn't it?"

"Sure he believes it. But that's the kind of quote people can twist and make a guy look . . . well . . . arrogant."

"Well," she said, "I'm sorry, Archie, but I can't see that it's as awful as all that. If I were you, I'd be worrying more about that story from Moscow."

"Let me be the judge of that," he said. "But that's not the point, Kay. If I tell you something in confidence, you ought to respect it."

Kay bridled. "Is that today's lecture, Mr. Morals Teacher?"

Archie stabbed a letter opener into the mound of jumbled papers on the desk and tried to restrain his voice. "Dammit, it's not a lecture, Kay, it's an order. From now on, don't go telling your mother what I say—or anyone else, either."

"Okay, I promise." Her voice was small and distant. "I'm sorry, Archie. I am. But I'm just one of the amateurs, and we don't know all the rules, I guess."

Archie softened. "I didn't mean to blow my stack, Kay. It's just that it's getting down to the clutch now, and it looks like my guy's got one strike on him."

"Am I going to see you tonight?"

"Can't," he replied. "We've still got a lot to do." He was in no mood for Kay—or any other woman. The pang in his stomach was back, and he reminded himself to buy a bottle of sleeping pills at the drugstore. "Tomorrow sometime."

"Oh, don't call us, we'll call you?" She sounded brittle.

"No, no, don't take it that way. Look, let's make it definite. You come over here to the headquarters in the morning." He tried to lighten his voice. "One look at you and I'll be ready to rush back into battle."

"You make me sound like some kind of battery charger." She giggled. "But it's nice. Okay, I'll come over in the morning. G'night, Archie."

He put the phone down and sat for a moment, smiling as he thought of a man and woman bumping each other as they crawled around in the dark, looking for a lost earring.

Manchester was standing in the center of the sitting room when Archie returned. The candidate was fingering an ear lobe and listening intently to Louis Cohen.

". . . and it would be perfectly proper, Mr. Secretary," Cohen was saying. "A statement by you would make it clear you aren't backing down an inch, but you won't have to prove anything with delegate votes."

"I don't know, Louis," Manchester said. "I still think it looks like evasion . . . but maybe it would do. See what Archie thinks of it."

"Archie's got something else on his mind," the press secretary said. He briefly recounted how the "width of a gnat's eye" had become public property.

Manchester grinned affectionately at him, and Archie thought it was a measure of the man's stature that the mistakes of others were so seldom a subject of criticism by him. Perhaps it was because he had so much confidence in his own ability to straighten out almost any mess that others got him into. Whatever the reason for this tendency to forgive and forget instantly, it forged links of loyalty as strong as iron.

Obie O'Connell was less charitable. "Christ," he said, "that's what you get for trying to impress a dame by talking politics. And I wouldn't trust any kid of Grace Orcott's as far as I could—"

One of the volunteer workers came into the room with a newspaper. It was so fresh they could smell the ink across the room.

"Here's the early edition of the *Tribune*," she said. "I thought you'd like to see it right away."

Manchester's remark of the night before was public property now, spread across page one in an eight-column streamer: "Manchester: Daphne Not Worth 'Gnat's Eye.' "

The four men bunched together to read the story, which the *Tribune* was at pains to tag as exclusive. It recounted, with reasonable accuracy, the gist of the Secretary's talk to the Five Thousand Club. Archie's stomach complained again.

"We need that like a hole in the head," growled Obie.

"We're exaggerating," Manchester said with a tone of finality. "The phrase won't hurt us except with people who are against us anyway." The subject was dismissed—forever, as far as Charles Manchester was concerned. O'Connell shook his head in obvious disgust, but said no more about it.

"Archie," said Manchester, "Louis has suggested something he thinks might get us around this platform thing. He thinks I should issue a statement merely saying that I reserve the right to interpret the defense plank my own way if I'm nominated. I think it may have some merit. What about you?"

Archie thought a moment as he ran his fingers through his short tangle of black hair. "Fine," he said. "If it's worded right, it could get you off the hook."

"Nothing takes us off the hook now," objected O'Connell. "But it's the best deal yet."

"How about this?" offered Cohen, who had been scribbling on the back of a room-service menu. "Statement under the Secretary's name: 'I subscribe wholeheartedly to the defense plank as drafted by the resolutions committee. I reserve the right, of course, to interpret it for myself if nominated by this convention. I propose to maintain our strategic forces un-diminished, but I do not propose to build weapons systems that do not enhance our capabilities.' "

Manchester walked over to one of the windows as Cohen read, and he remained thus, his back to the others, for several minutes. Occasionally he palmed the back of his neck—the familiar sign that he had not yet made up his mind.

Charles Manchester was not aware of this, nor in fact of anything but the debate he was conducting with himself. How can I compromise this thing, he thought, when I started it myself? Maybe I'm not very smart as a politician, but I know I'm right on this, and I'm glad I said it. Why not stand on it and tell them all to go right straight to hell in a handcart if they don't like it? If I give in on this now, how much harder is it going to be if I do win the nomination and try to start all over again a second time? Once you give up the initiative it's so hard to get moving again—especially against the kind of pressures involved here. I might get to be President and never

again have the kind of leverage I've got here in the convention.

But don't forget, he reminded himself, that you might
never get to be President if you stand on it now and lose.
Didn't you tell yourself when you first went to Washington
that compromise was going to be required—that government
was the art of the possible, that you had to do the best you
could with what you had at hand at a given moment? If you
compromise now, you may get to be President; and if you get
to be President, you may be able to do something about this
—instead of just talking about it to people who won't listen.
How far did you get on the Daphne with Fred Stuart? What
makes you think you'd do better with any other President—
except yourself? And let's be honest about it, too, since you're
so well known for your candor: You want to be President,
period. And wouldn't it be foolish to throw away all the work
—especially with all those delegates committed to you already?

Manchester swung around abruptly. "Would you read that
again, please, Louis?" He listened, his head cocked to one
side. "All right. The idea's fine. Now let's work on the wording
a little."

Archie felt the tension drain from him like water sinking
into the sand of a beach. Cohen grinned in relief at the acceptance of his proposal. The two of them huddled with Manchester over the draft, but O'Connell remained seated by
himself. "You do the words," he said. "I'll do the votes." The
others worked for fifteen minutes, and then Manchester stood
up and stretched. He took off his little half-round reading
glasses and tucked them into his pocket.

"I'll stand on that," he said. "Release it any way you want, Archie. And now, gentlemen, let's call it a night. I'm going to bed." As far as the candidate was concerned, the matter was closed, and he was not going to waste time and energy worrying about it further.

Archie found two girls still on duty in the headquarters workroom. Their fresh, bright appearance in the middle of the night appalled him, with his own thirty-three years seeming all at once as ancient as the New Hampshire mountains he had climbed as a boy. He commandeered one of the girls to cut the mimeograph stencil, but both insisted on helping. They oohed and aahed over the statement and chattered away as though they were at a sorority slumber party instead of a political convention.

Armed with 300 copies, Archie started for the basement press room. There were only a few stragglers, flushed and teetering with alcoholic benevolence, in the corridors now, and he was able to get a regular passenger elevator within seconds. Downstairs it was different; although it was almost 1 A.M., the press area still throbbed with activity. Archie thumbtacked one copy of the statement on the huge bulletin board devoted to news releases and left a stack on the table. Then he made the rounds of the curtained cubicles, delivering the statement to a desk man or, if a bureau was closed for the night, leaving a copy in a typewriter.

Calvin Burroughs was still up and still immaculate, his brown summer suit as neatly creased as though a valet had just pressed it. The publisher was chatting with one of his reporters when Archie entered their workroom.

Burroughs read the statement over the shoulder of the reporter, then turned to Archie.

"Got a minute?" he asked. He inserted a cigarette in the ivory holder and drew Archie aside. "This means your boss isn't going to fight."

"What do you mean?" said Archie with a touch of belligerence. "That's a fighting statement. He isn't retreating an inch."

"He isn't risking a floor fight, either."

"He doesn't have to," Archie protested. "There's nothing wrong with the plank, if you read it our way."

"That's not what your people were saying this afternoon," Burroughs reminded him quietly. "They tried to change the wording and got voted down."

"That was several eons ago, Mr. Burroughs," said Archie, and indeed he felt that it was. Sunday afternoon already seemed as outdated as the Piltdown man. "More to the point, what do you think of the Secretary's position?"

Burroughs flicked an ash on the floor and studied his old holder. "I think he's a man who's taken a very courageous position—and I think it may cost him the nomination."

"Are you serious?" Archie was shocked, hearing for the first time a neutral judgment that the weapons issue was more than a troublesome tactical problem—that it could, in fact, lead to complete disaster for Manchester.

"I'm very serious. Do you realize that both Davidson of Uniforge and Gus Maguire of the Missile Workers are out to get your man? We've found out they're both here working for Roberts, and by tomorrow night every arms maker in the country is going to be putting the squeeze on the delegates."

"That's hard to believe," said Archie.

"Let's hope I'm wrong," said Burroughs, "but don't underestimate the vigor of the reflexes where the pocketbook is involved."

"How about you personally, Mr. Burroughs? Do you agree with the boss?"

Burroughs studied Archie for a moment. "Yes, I do. I gave it a great deal of thought today." He spoke slowly, then smiled. "You can tell the Secretary that at least he made one newspaper publisher think. Manchester is right. We're going to have to draw the line someday. Unfortunately, I'm afraid he's ahead of his time right now."

"But if you've come around to his way of thinking," asked Archie, "why shouldn't others?"

"There's not enough time." Burroughs waved the cigarette holder. "The delegates don't have time to think before Thursday. All they can do is react."

Archie went to bed depressed. Not until he had put on his pajamas, swallowed a sleeping pill and butted out a nest in the pillow for his head did his mood lighten. Then, dozing off, he thought of a small, sunburnt girl with a splash of freckles across her nose. He fell asleep wondering whether she was in bed too.

If Kay was in bed, Obie O'Connell definitely was not. At that moment, he was sitting on a high stool at the circular bar in the Pick-Congress Hotel. Before him rested an unusual drink, a daiquiri on the rocks, and within him a tempest raged.

Dammit, they had just about blown his months of hard work. His mind trundled back over the weary preconvention campaign circuit. He saw again the great, gracious living room of the Manchester house, high on the Virginia palisades above the Potomac, the room where he'd agreed to be Manchester's campaign manager . . . the grubby restaurant in Little Rock where he had sold Manchester to the leader who was to head the Arkansas delegation . . . the all-night conference in Sacramento with Carl Fleischer, when he'd argued Roberts' manager out of entering the New Hampshire primary—and in return had agreed Manchester wouldn't enter the Oregon primary. Pure bluff; they couldn't have coaxed Obie into Oregon with a $10,000 bill . . . the endless procession of chicken-and-peas banquets . . . the slow recruiting of the campaign staff, and the day he had to bounce one of his oldest friends in politics when he found he'd been pocketing half the campaign contributions in his state . . . the decision to take the primary route—which Manchester at first opposed— and the eventual harvest of 197 delegate votes by doing it . . . the nights on the airplane which crumpled his suits and ruined his digestion.

Obie had traveled 75,000 miles for Charles Manchester in less than a year—and now, one goddam blooper at a press conference and they were in deep, deep trouble. Why, oh, why, couldn't the amateurs shut up until the pros told them it was time to talk? Not a bad guy, Charlie Manchester, in fact a great guy in his own way, but about as much sense of timing as a broken cuckoo clock. And that statement? O'Connell shuddered involuntarily. Manchester's real trouble was his sublime self-confidence. He was a guy who'd always got all the breaks. It's hard to talk sense to that kind.

O'Connell rapped his glass, now empty, on the bar. "One more of the same," he said to the bartender. That's right, he thought in answer to the barkeep's glance, a grown man drinking daiquiris—and on the rocks yet. Obie wasn't supposed to drink. "If you don't get that blood pressure down," his doctor had said, "you'll erupt like a volcano one day." So

he had been on the wagon for three months, so dry he'd dream
at night of Scotch rushing out of a faucet and splashing into a
glass. But after what's happened in the last thirty-six hours,
he told himself, one little mild drink would bring his blood
pressure down, not up. A daiquiri? Right. Mildest of the mild.
And the place to drink it? The Congress bar, where the
political pros came to compare notes after midnight.

"Obie, move that fat can of yours. You're taking up two
seats." A bulky man with silky blond hair shoved O'Connell's
leg aside and took the stool next to him. A short, slighter man
who wore a hearing aid slid into the seat beyond him.

"Hi, Monty. What's the word from Meen-ee-saw-ta?" said
O'Connell, trying to make his nasal Irish intonation sound
Scandinavian. "I see you got your banker with you. Hi, Bones,
you're just in time to pick up the check."

Montcalm Andersen, so named because his father admired
the French general who had defended Quebec, was an in-
fluential member of the Minnesota delegation. He had almost
—but not quite—committed himself to Manchester in private
talk with Obie, and he appeared on O'Connell's delegate tally
sheet as "probable." The second man, Wilfred Cramer, was no
delegate, but he was one of the most famous mercenaries in the
party. Though currently on the payroll of the Rocky Mountain
Conference of Republican State Chairmen, he had labored for
a half dozen candidates over the years and was primarily a
bag man. He knew where money could be raised quickly in
emergencies, and no questions asked. No one objected if a
reasonable amount stuck to Bones Cramer's fingers in the
process, for a man of his talents was expected to live well and
be a good provider. It was almost a reflex reaction for him to

reach down the bar, as he now did, and pull the check toward him. Bones Cramer reputedly was neutral in the Manchester-Roberts fight, but O'Connell often consulted him. Cramer's sources of information were infinite, and their friendship was an old one. Indeed, some of the Roberts workers wondered whether O'Connell had a private understanding with Cramer during the convention.

"There's lots of word from Minnesota," Andersen said. "Your man has got the boys all upset."

Bones leaned closer and adjusted his hearing aid. His pale cheeks had deep central hollows, as though a glacier had once crossed his face and left its mark. "Upset isn't the word for it, Obie," he said. "I hear there's hell to pay in some states."

O'Connell knew exactly what they were talking about, but he played it dumb in the hope of extracting a maximum of useful information. "What's got who upset?" he said.

"Ahh, knock it off, Obie," said Cramer. "We're talking about that missile crap, what else?"

"So what's wrong with my candidate on that? He makes a statement of his views. It's a free country. Is he supposed to go around like a clam all week?"

"If he'd clammed up yesterday on that question, he'd have the nomination in the bag," Andersen said. "Now, who knows?"

"Come off it, Monty," said Obie, taking a cut at his drink. "We start off with three hundred more votes than Roberts and go from there. It's easy."

"If you think it's going to be easy," Cramer said, "let me tell you something." He lowered his voice to a whisper—a feat of skill for a man with a hearing aid. "I was just talking to a

Colorado delegate. He tells me he got a long-distance call from his banker at home, asking him to vote for Roberts. He wondered why—then he gets to thinking, and the biggest plant in town is working on a Uniforge subcontract. When Daphne gets tooled up, it figures to get a bigger one."

"Oh, what the hell," protested O'Connell, with more conviction than he felt. "Somebody is always calling somebody. I don't see how that cuts much ice."

"Okay, I'll give you one from Minnesota," said Andersen. "We got a bunch of new electronics plants up on the Iron Range. Two delegates from up there got called today by Gus Maguire. He makes a big pitch for Roberts."

"They members of his union, or what?" asked O'Connell.

"Yeah," replied Andersen. "At least, one of them is. The other belongs to some other union. Electricians, I think."

"So Davidson and Maguire are working for Roberts," said O'Connell. "Bin can have those guys. We've got bigger men working for Manchester."

"Like who, for instance?" asked Andersen.

O'Connell tilted his glass and drained off the liquid, savoring the tart blend of rum and lime juice. You're on the wagon for three months, he thought, and it doesn't take much to make you feel good. He motioned the bartender toward his glass.

"Oh, just take Dun & Bradstreet," he said, "and run through it alphabetically. Every other name in there is for Manchester."

"*Was* for Manchester," corrected Bones Cramer. "I hear he laid an egg with the Five Thousand Club last night."

"Face it, Obie, your man's got troubles," Andersen said.

"It isn't so much whether he's right or wrong. It's the timing—popping off like that, kind of offhand almost, two days before the convention starts. And already the Communists are getting into the act."

O'Connell's defenses against *Pravda* had already been prepared. "If the Commies try to mess up my man with hearts and flowers," he said, "that means they really want Roberts. Am I right? Jesus, let's not be played for suckers."

Cramer nodded. "You can live with the Moscow endorsement," he said, "but shaking up the delegates with threats to knock off the Daphne contract is something else again."

The first draught of the third drink was inside O'Connell now and he felt much, much better, again in command of a situation which for a time had him boiling helplessly. He leaned nearer to his two barmates.

"Listen, you guys aren't taking that missile stuff seriously, are you?" he asked. "My guy is a smart operator. He's trying to make an issue, liven up a dead convention. Now he's got everybody stirred up and hopping. That's bad, for Christ's sake?"

"You saying he doesn't mean it?" Cramer showed skepticism.

"I mean it's just talk, convention talk," said Obie. "He gets in the White House, gives the Daphne the big study and then puts out a long, technical report saying we need it and he's going ahead with it."

"You mean he's planning it that way?" It was Andersen's turn to be skeptical. "Somehow that doesn't sound like Charles Bedford Manchester."

O'Connell felt a vast relief. Play it shrewd now, Obie, he

thought, and we'll pull this thing right out of the fire. When a situation starts falling apart, a manager has a duty to put it together again. His voice was edged with guile now, its volume just above a whisper. He felt slick as a newly skinned hickory stick.

"I'm telling you," he said, "this whole thing is strategy, and damn carefully thought out, too. Louis Cohen is no lightweight." That's no lie, he thought, surprised as Louis might be to hear it in that connection.

"Let's come clean," Andersen suggested. "Are you saying that if he's elected, Manchester won't cancel the Daphne contract?"

"I am." O'Connell looked him in the eye as he said it.

"Can I quote Manchester on it?"

"Oh, act your age, Monty." O'Connell hoped his words didn't sound loose, and he tried to bite them off crisply. "You know we can't do that. But you can quote *me* privately as saying Manchester won't do anything to interefere with a good healthy missile industry in this country."

"That's not the same thing," said Cramer.

"Okay, Bones. You can quote me—off the record, now, dammit—as saying that Manchester intends to go ahead with the Daphne."

"Has the man authorized you to peddle this line?" asked Andersen.

"He has," said O'Connell flatly, cutting his last line to the riverbank as he swirled out into the rapids. Well, he thought, we might have different ideas about who "the man" is.

Bones Cramer speculated as he played with the dial on his

hearing aid. "You put it that way, it makes some sense. You pick up the peace vote, a lot of women delegates—they love that stuff. Still, it's risky, Obie. Those missile people got an awful lot of dough." He spoke the last words in a tone of profound respect.

"Ah, leave it to me," said Obie. "The Manchesters have landed and the situation is well in hand."

Bones Cramer paid the check without protest, but O'Connell remained after the other two left and had one more for the road—the road being the two blocks on Michigan Avenue between the Congress and the Hilton. He felt sound of body and peaceful of soul; everything was buttoned up for the night and it was time for bed.

He strolled down the sidewalk, breathing deeply of the night air. Above him the sky arched in a blue-black dome, thousands of bright dots pinning it to the infinity beyond. But Obie O'Connell was not a man to gaze at stars; he kept his eyes on finite things, in this case his feet as they moved with unaccustomed lightness toward his hotel.

A manager, he thought, has to do what he has to do, and what the candidate doesn't know won't hurt him. Didn't Abe Lincoln's managers go behind his back and get the big Pennsylvania delegation by promising to put that crook Simon Cameron in the cabinet? They did. And if they hadn't made deals like that, there'd never have been a Gettysburg Address. Didn't Dewey's men get Indiana by promising the vice-presidential nomination to Charlie Halleck in 1948? They did. And did Halleck get it? He did not. And was anybody sore? Maybe Halleck—but no one else. No, a manager has to have room to maneuver, even if he has to make the room himself.

What the candidate doesn't know will never, never hurt him.

There was almost a lilt to the phrase and it swung tunefully in O'Connell's head. By the time he reached the bank of Hilton elevators he was whistling.

Obie O'Connell slept soundly that night, and there were no dreams of Scotch pouring from a faucet. Daiquiri on the rocks was a nice, safe drink.

8

The helicopter settled onto the south lawn like a broken-winged heron. It roared and clattered, the gusts from its big overhead rotor tearing at the magnolia trees and bending the shrubs and flowers in the rose garden.

A dozen men—Secret Service agents, White House policemen and newspapermen—stood clear of the furious little windstorm until the racket died away. Then they moved forward toward the dark-green Marine helicopter and waited for the President of the United States to alight. It was 9:30 A.M. on the second Monday in August, and Frederick Stuart was returning from his customary summer weekend at Camp David, the presidential retreat in the Catoctin Mountains of Maryland.

Stuart climbed down from the aircraft, placing his feet
carefully on the steel rungs of the short ladder and holding
onto the handrail. He wore no hat, and a person seeing him
thus for the first time would note that his hair was all white
now. He was a tall man, but his shoulders were stooped and
his frame seemed spare inside a gray summer suit, as though
the shrinking of extreme old age had set in. Fred Stuart was
sixty-six, but he seemed a decade older. The hepatitis that
struck him the previous year had wasted his body, if not his
spirit, and had stolen the luster from his eyes. As he walked
slowly across the carpet of grass, his appearance was ample
explanation of his decision not to run for a second term.

The White House reporters closed about him respectfully,
their manner bespeaking deference both for his office and
for his age. All summer the President and the newsmen had
operated under a gentleman's agreement: they would not follow him to Camp David and in return he agreed to chat
with them "for guidance only" each Monday morning when
the 'copter set him down a few yards from his oval office.

"Good morning, Mr. President. How was the weather up
there?"

"Fine. Bright and sunny all weekend, wasn't it, Bill?"
Stuart turned for confirmation to an army brigadier general,
his military aide, who stood quietly at his elbow holding the
President's dispatch case. The officer nodded.

"Do you have any reaction to what's going on in Chicago,
Mr. President?"

Stuart smiled. "It looks as if we'll have a pretty lively show
out there before they're through, doesn't it?"

The senior White House newsman, a stocky middle-aged

man with a rasping voice, stepped closer. "Specifically, Mr. President, we wondered what you thought about your man's press conference statement on missiles Saturday morning."

"We're under the usual rules, I suppose," Stuart said warily. Several of the reporters this morning were unfamiliar, substitutes for first-line regulars who had been assigned to the convention. "No attribution—for guidance only?" The newsmen nodded.

"Well," the President said, "that choice of words—'your man,' I think you said—doesn't quite fit the situation. The White House isn't raising a finger to influence the party's choice of a candidate."

"But, Mr. President," protested one of the reporters, "Senator Floberg quoted you two months ago as telling him you favored Manchester, and you didn't knock it down."

"That's true." Stuart seemed weary already, though the morning sun was only now beginning to touch the water in the big south fountain and the grass in the shadow of the mansion was still moist with dew. "Charlie Manchester is a member of my cabinet, and a friend. Under the circumstances, it would be natural for me to vote for him if I were a delegate. But that's a long way from trying to dictate to the convention."

"Do you approve of Manchester's proposed hold-down on missile contracts, Mr. President?"

"Frankly, I'm not sure just what is involved or exactly what the Secretary has in mind," said Stuart. "I just lay in the sun up on the mountain, and I haven't been in touch with Chicago at all. I suspect Charlie will be calling me before too long."

"You do plan to talk to him, then, sir?"

"I would think he would call, yes." Stuart took several

tentative steps toward his office, as though to end the interview.

But the reporters moved with him. "Can you tell us, Mr. President, were you surprised by what he said?"

"Surprised?" Stuart stopped to answer. "Surprised? Yes, I suspect I was surprised. I didn't expect just that kind of ending to his press conference. We had . . . well, let's just leave it at that."

"Thank you, Mr. President."

Fred Stuart walked slowly through the rose garden, pausing several times to inspect the marigolds and zinnias that had been moved into the beds to provide midsummer bloom. The reporters trooped off to the press room, conferring noisily about what they had just heard and what they could do with it under the "south lawn ground rules," as they called their agreement on the Monday-morning talks. The helicopter started with a roar, rose in a wild rush of wind, and swung southward over the traffic curving past the iron fence at the foot of the grounds.

Inside his office, Stuart sank gratefully into his swivel chair and silently cursed the fact that even briefly sustained exertion still seemed to tire him. He eyed the stack of papers neatly squared on the corner of his desk, but made no move to touch it. His mind was on Chicago.

He buzzed for his secretary and she hopped in, fragile and bright as a chickadee, and greeted him in the piping, cheerful voice that never varied.

"Get me Graham out in Chicago, please, Susie. And have them send over a little coffee, will you?"

Graham Reddig, the White House special counsel and private presidential envoy to the Republican national convention, was on the phone within a couple of minutes.

"What's going on out there, Graham?" Stuart asked. "All I know is what I read in the papers."

"In a nutshell, Mr. President, Manchester has set the convention on its ear." Reddig prided himself on terse, graphic reports, skillfully capsuled for an aging President. "The Roberts people are spreading the word that the Secretary double-crossed you. Naturally, everyone out here is interested in your reaction."

Stuart asked about the platform. Reddig described his unsuccessful effort to insert in the defense plank an innocuous sentence which would encompass all views. The plank, he reported, would remain as is. Manchester had ducked a floor fight, but announced he would interpret the plank his own way. In brief, the Secretary of the Treasury was challenging administration policy.

"Of course," Stuart said, "you and I both know Charlie has had this thing stuck in his craw for some time, but I'm frankly annoyed that he didn't talk to me about it before he sprang it. I had no warning at all. Did he discuss it with you, Graham?"

"No, sir, he didn't. At first I assumed he'd talked to you, but then I sensed that there hadn't been any communication on it."

"What baffles me," Stuart continued, his voice spiked with irritation, "is that he didn't mention it Saturday morning. We talked about the farm problem just before the press conference, but he never said a word about defense."

"The missile people, particularly Uniforge, are working on

the delegates," Reddig reported. "So is Maguire's union. They're putting on the heat for Roberts."

"Gus Maguire? I thought he was for Manchester."

"I think he was," said the counsel, "but yesterday I got reports that he's working with Mark Davidson to put over Roberts."

"I don't like the sound of that," said Stuart.

"No, sir."

The President paused as he thought for a moment. "It's the union that bothers me most," he said. "I worked pretty hard—hell, I broke my back—to get Maguire away from the Democrats last time. Now this Manchester press conference may jeopardize the whole thing."

"Well," comforted Reddig, "I expect that if Maguire goes all out for Roberts, he'll have to stay with us in November."

"Not if Manchester gets the nomination, he won't." Stuart's temperature was rising slightly as he talked. "Maguire would switch to Hendrickson without batting an eye."

"Of course you know about the Moscow endorsement, Mr. President?"

"Yes," said Stuart. "What's the reaction to it out there?"

"Naturally it's hurting Manchester with a lot of delegates, although I must say some people are beginning to wonder this morning what the Kremlin's real purpose is."

"I just don't like the idea of a Republican candidate being blessed by the Communists." Stuart laughed, a single derisive snort. "It's messy, whatever it means. And, of course, it wouldn't have happened if Charlie had kept quiet on this missile thing."

"Any orders, Mr. President?"

"No, just keep me in touch, Graham. I suppose Charlie will be calling me before long. I'm anxious to hear what his explanation is. Right now, I don't like the looks of it at all."

Stuart replaced the phone and made a triangle of his fingers under his chin. He stared at the curved wall of his office and tried to remember just what Manchester had said about defense policy in recent months. The Secretary, he recalled, had opposed the Daphne contract in the National Security Council, but there had been no formal written objection from him —as often happened in major policy disagreements. Several casual references at cabinet meetings, yes. And one rather lengthy discussion after a small dinner at the White House in the spring. If he remembered correctly, they hadn't been far apart, either. Both the President and Manchester thought the services were spending too much on new weapons systems that didn't promise real advances, and that something ought to be done—eventually. But to pop a thing like that at a convention!

Stuart's mind wandered down the long trail of conventions he had known: the churning mobs in the aisles during demonstrations, the harsh cackle of voices in all-night meetings; the time he slept, fully clothed, on a desk top from 5 to 7 A.M. after one such session; the frantic day when he was picked for vice-president at breakfast and dumped by the leaders before noon; the night four years ago when he arrived at the convention hall after his own nomination and felt, rather than heard, the waves of noise washing over him like great swells on the open sea. He rested his head against the back of his chair and closed his eyes.

When his secretary came quietly into the room a few minutes later with his coffee, an old man with sunken cheeks was asleep at his desk. He opened his eyes and looked at her inquiringly.

"Did Secretary Manchester call?"

She shook her head. The President sighed and reached for the stack of papers on the corner of his desk.

9

The door bore the legend "No Admittance" in fresh black paint on its galvanized-iron sheathing. It stood at the top of a flight of rickety stairs, which in turn were reached through a narrow entry where sullen gray paint flaked off the door-jamb and a layer of grime covered the transom window above. The entrance was squeezed between a pawnshop and an establishment called the Tropic Isle, where window placards announced that Celeste, Ginger, Kashmir and "Turquoise, the Tropic Bombshell" removed their clothes in continuous rotation each night from ten o'clock on. The entrance that led to the stairway was on Clark Street, five blocks west and eight income brackets down from the Conrad Hilton.

Grace Orcott tiptoed up the worn flight of stairs, careful

not to catch a spike heel in one of the holes that were imperfectly patched with cracked strips of linoleum. An aroma of stale beer, laced with cheap disinfectant, stabbed into her nostrils. She was thankful for the three friends with her; the Ambassador East was never like this. A man ahead of her rang the bell beside the galvanized-iron door with the "No Admittance" sign. It was promptly opened by a short, bustling, red-haired man. His sleeves were rolled up and another patch of red hair showed at the open neck of his shirt.

"Come in, come in," he said. "Let's see, you're four? Good. That means everybody's here."

A surprisingly trim suite of offices opened out behind the door. The walls were freshly painted, new soundproofing material lined the ceiling, and desks were spaced around the rooms. Young girls, as eager and buoyant as those manning all the convention secretarial warrens, clicked about the office or hammered on typewriters. Against one wall, three girls sat beside telephones at an almost bare table.

"I'm Art Segunda," said the red-haired man in a cheery voice, "the only redheaded Latino in the whole convention. I'm boss of this funhouse, and I'm Oscar's keeper."

Ten men and two women—the convention floor managers for Governor Bryan Roberts of California—stood in a rather formal semicircle around him. They had been summoned to the decrepit address on Clark Street, late this Monday morning, for a briefing on the research and reporting services available to help them round up votes among the delegates.

Segunda, an effervescent extrovert who had long deplored the traditional reticence of his fellow mathematicians, rubbed his hands together and beamed. "Well," he began, "I guess the best way to begin is to show you just what Oscar can do for you."

"And who, may I ask, is Oscar?" said Grace Orcott. She patted her gleaming hair, as if to reassure herself that it was still there after the perilous voyage to Clark Street.

"Oscar isn't a who," Segunda said, "he's a what. But before I go any further, one caution to all of you. This office is classified, to use the government's phrase. What we do here is just what managers of candidates have done for decades: keep track of the delegates. The difference is that instead of doing it with a card file, we do it with Oscar. We have kept news of this office out of the press, because efficiency frightens some people and Oscar is very, very efficient. Do I make myself clear?"

Roger Abbott, who as chief of the Roberts floor managers had called the others to this meeting, nodded and gestured at the group. His bald head shone above a fresh yellow bow tie as he spoke to Segunda.

"Don't worry, Art, this is all in the family," he said. "I thought my people should understand just what you can do for them for the price of a ten-cent phone call."

"Right," said Segunda cheerily. "So! So much for the security lecture. Now, let's follow the process."

He led them toward the long table where the three girls sat. All three smiled at the visitors. "These girls take down any request you may make," Segunda explained. "They also jot down new information on delegates that may be coming in —in light of changing conditions, and so forth."

He swept his arm toward other tables where young women were typing busily. "These girls over here type up the information which Oscar needs, and also the questions we want to ask him. The cards they make are then taken over here . . ."

Segunda ushered his visitors into another room where a large black machine with a hooded top was being operated by a young man in a sports shirt. "This is Mr. Weimer, a graduate student at Cal Tech, where I teach," Segunda said. "He helped me work up the programing and information retrieval for this system. He translates information and questions into the code language which Oscar understands, and transfers it onto punched tape, which is what Oscar eats. He is, in short, both the input and the output man for Oscar."

Segunda shepherded the group through a door into a room that was bare except for a three-section metal cabinet, modestly adorned with colored dials, and an adjoining device that looked something like a teletype printer.

"That's Oscar!" he announced proudly.

The group gazed at the cabinet with the blank expression displayed by all laymen when they are first ushered into the presence of one of the more recondite miracles of science.

"That's the five-oh-seven," said Segunda, "the loveliest, liveliest little portable computer ever built." He caressed the smooth gray side of the machine. "Its memory can store twenty billion separate items, far more than we'll ever need for this job, and it can spit out information at the rate of seventy lines a minute on the printer here." He pointed to the machine that resembled a teletypewriter.

"Very interesting," said one of the spectators, "but just what exactly does it do for us in this convention?"

"All right." Segunda perched on a window sill. Chairs were brought in for the women. "What does the ordinary file of convention delegates contain? Usually it's a shoe box with a bunch of cards arranged alphabetically by states. You get the delegate's name, address, place of business, preference for the nomination, and who's supposed to be keeping tabs on him. Am I right? Some lists were a little more sophisticated, as I understand those of the Dewey people in '48 and the Kennedys in '60 were. But basically, while you might have some more information on the cards, that's about it.

"Now, Oscar here is a brand-new breed of convention animal." Segunda was warming to his love. "He knows just about everything any mortal could want to find out about a delegate. In his memory is stored the delegate's home, church, family, bank, job, best friends, likes and dislikes, his views on candidates, issues and life in general. And we can extract that information in a hurry. Let me show you. Somebody ask a question about the delegates—anything."

"How many are women?" asked Grace Orcott.

Segunda called to the man in the next room: "Weimer, let me have an instruction on the number of women delegates."

The shirt-sleeved young man, his face solemn and intent, came into the room almost immediately with a short length of punched paper tape, which he fed into a slot in the cabinet. He twisted a dial and pushed a button. Instantly the printer coughed out a line; Segunda tore off the yellow paper and held it up.

"Four hundred and thirty-seven out of one thousand three hundred and eight," he announced. "Now, let's carry that a little further and ask Oscar how many of those women are married, what the average age is and which delegation has the most women and how many."

Weimer punched out more tape and repeated the feeding process. The printer discharged several lines of figures on the yellow paper, then promptly subsided. Segunda read off the figures.

"Four hundred and twelve of them married. Hmm. That means only twenty-five gals in the market for men. Average age of all women delegates: forty-three. I would have guessed it was higher. Delegation with the most women: New York, with thirty-eight. Of course, we didn't ask Oscar which state had the highest *percentage* of women delegates. He could tell us that, too."

"But what use is that stuff?" asked one man. Judging from the expressions of his colleagues, he was voicing a collective skepticism.

Segunda smiled, a trifle patronizingly, and gestured toward Roger Abbott. "Mr. Abbott asked us Friday how many delegates earned less than ten thousand a year. We got him the answer while he held the phone. Three-seventy-five, wasn't it, Roger? About what you'd expect at a Republican convention. You'll have to ask him why he wanted it."

Abbott nodded approvingly. "There was a discussion of the position we ought to take on the tax reform plank in the platform," he explained, "and we wondered how many of the voting delegates would be affected by any change in the lower income brackets."

"Hell, you could have guessed that one without a machine," offered the skeptical man.

Segunda walked over to the computer. "That's probably true," he said, "but I defy anyone to guess the answers we came up with yesterday morning. First we were asked to find out how many delegates had Universal Forge plants in their districts, and to list their names. Obviously a result of the Manchester press conference. Then the names of delegates who had Uniforge subcontracts in their districts, and finally the names of delegates who had missile work of *any* kind going on in their districts. Now, that took a little time, because we had to process quite a bit of input data, but we got the program tapes fed into Oscar in about two hours, hit the start button—and, bingo, there were your answers."

"Where'd you get the list of Uniforge contracts and subcontracts?" Segunda was asked.

"I don't know." He shrugged. "I suppose the company passed it along. All I know is that Carl Fleischer sent a boy over with the list. But here's the important thing." Segunda tapped the computer with his knuckles. "When we got through, Carl not only had all the names of delegates with missile business in their home towns but he had a rundown on a lot of auxiliary information to make that data useful to him."

"I don't get you," said one of the floor managers.

"The names of civic leaders, friends, bankers in the delegate's district," Segunda said. "That kind of thing. A way of approaching the delegate, I guess. I don't know about that. That's your business. I just look after Oscar."

Grace Orcott stepped over and inspected the knobs and dials on the computer. They told her absolutely nothing. "Can you make it come up with something I already know about?" she said. "You know, just to see how accurate it is."

"Sure," said Segunda. "Well, how about you? You're a delegate. Let's see what Oscar knows about you, Mrs. . . ."

"Orcott," she said, "Grace Orcott, of Texas."

Abbott protested. "Oh, I don't know that we want to go into that, Art. Some of that data is a bit, well, confidential, if you know what I mean, not for use by anyone, really. We're pretty careful how we use the computer."

But Grace Orcott was intrigued now, and Segunda was anxious to show off his machine's skills. "I tell you," he said, "we'll just run out Mrs. Orcott and let her have the print-out as a memento."

"That's fine," said Grace. She watched while the serious young man punched a tape and inserted it, then pressed what Segunda had called the "start button." The printer chattered briefly, and Segunda handed her the printer copy without reading it. She ran her eye quickly down the list of facts about herself, then stuffed the paper into her handbag.

"Very thorough," she said. "And very accurate."

The visitors departed in little groups of three and four, a few minutes apart. Roger Abbott said they would attract less notice that way. Grace Orcott thought the precaution pointless; if a newspaperman saw any one of them coming out of that shabby building, the questions would be endless.

She walked to the Hilton and took a little table in the cocktail lounge, where she was to meet Kay for a preluncheon drink. She took the wrinkled sheet of yellow teleprinter paper from her handbag and spread it out on the table. She lit a cigarette as she read it over again.

Orcott, Grace. Her age, marital status, the list of her close friends, her church, her bank, her credit rating, her husband's business ("Genl Contractor"), the family's annual income ("$38,000"). All very accurate.

The next line dealt with her home address—in a most unusual way:

"Res 8365 Lyman Blvd/Dallas/1st trust/Reliable Savings

& Loan/Dallas/Initial $15,000/Pd down to $4,300."

I don't think I like that, she thought. And I know damn well George wouldn't like it. What was that kind of information doing under her name in that machine? It made her feel a bit undressed, as though someone had snatched away her gloves, shoes and earrings.

But the last item on the list, the one that had jumped up at her when she stood next to Oscar reading it for the first time, made her feel completely naked.

"Children/1/Katherine born 29 Feb 48/2/George Jr born 4 May 50 Died 8 May 50."

Maybe someone could explain why they need to know how big our mortgage is, Grace thought angrily, but they'll never be able to tell me why they needed to know we had a baby son who never came home from the hospital with me. . . .

She shook herself hard, stuffed the yellow sheet back into her purse, and used her handkerchief. Don't let it throw you, Gracie, she thought. You wanted to play politics with the big boys. And you have to admit Mr. Segunda's machine is a lot better than that messy precinct card file you used to keep on the closet shelf at home. You have to move with the times, and if it's good for Bin Roberts it's good for the party.

Still, it was a little ridiculous—and a whole lot too private. Grace Orcott promised herself to talk to Carl Fleischer about it the next time she had a chance. She really didn't like it a bit. Not one little bit.

10

It was midafternoon Monday when the last of the 64 Pennsylvania delegates entered the conference suite at the Morrison Hotel under maximum security precautions. The precautions consisted of four hulking, gray-uniformed state troopers, guarding the two doors of this temporary temple of the democratic process.

Governor Benjamin Wilcox had employed his own Pennsylvania state police as doorkeepers today because he believed the mission of the caucus was almost sublime: to help nominate the most capable living Republican for the most powerful office in the world. At most, Pennsylvania sought the deciding voice in that selection. At the least, it hoped guesswork would place it on the side of the winner, thereby ensuring a little patronage and a few extra federal projects should the Republican candidate triumph in November.

Governor Wilcox assayed his own role in this convention in much the same way that a woman of means looked forward to a visit to Tiffany's. In brief, he felt he couldn't lose. And if he showed the rare judgment of which he believed himself capable, he just might walk out with the finest jewel of all. As a modest man—and Wilcox held himself to be essentially humble with respect to his own talents—he knew that he was not of the cut of Presidents. Of course the convention could go further and do worse and probably would, as the saying went, but Wilcox knew his own limitations. A responsible, capable cabinet officer, of course. A good, sturdy vice-president, yes. But President? Well, if fate should saddle him with that awful responsibility, he would get down on bended knee, pray for guidance, do his duty and, when all was said and done, do it a damn sight better than some he could mention, including James Buchanan, the only native Pennsylvanian in the lot.

Thus the presidential nomination was but an outside hope, albeit a few watts brighter than it had been Saturday morning. But Ben Wilcox figured that if he played his cards adroitly he could be the kingmaker of the convention and thus become the second most powerful Republican in the country. He had hand-picked the delegation. At least 57 of the 64 delegates would do his bidding, and perhaps one or two more. Wilcox had settled on his strategy some weeks ago: he would wait until the opportune time—not at the last minute, but almost—and then throw Pennsylvania's big bloc of votes to Manchester. His reward might be the vice-presidency, or a potent voice in party councils for the duration of the Manchester administration. At any rate, his would be the shining convention hour, eclipsing in radiance even that of Manchester himself.

Wilcox had decided on this strategy because he believed that only Manchester had a chance of winning. But now, on Monday, two days after Manchester's "enough's enough," the situation had changed. Now Bryan Roberts had a chance, and the prospect of throwing Pennsylvania to Roberts—who needed it desperately—was infinitely more alluring. If Wilcox could put Roberts across at the crucial moment, the world would indeed be his. You want to be Ambassador to Italy, Secretary of Defense, Commissioner of Internal Revenue? "Clear it with Ben." A dinner invitation to the White House, a re-hearing before the FCC, a special mission to Europe? "Clear it with Ben."

But could Roberts make it—even with Pennsylvania? In fact, could either Roberts or Manchester make it? The situation was becoming less and less predictable, more and more hazardous. Ben Wilcox, sitting in the chairman's seat behind the lectern, decided this was the time to stall. He cleared his throat twice and rapped the gavel.

Even with the state police outside, the security of the caucus was something less than maximum. A dozen reporters had discovered a back hall with two more doors opening into the conference room. While their less imaginative colleagues kept the troopers occupied, they shared the work in the hallway. At each door, two reporters lay prone, their ears jammed against the crack above the doorsill. Others sat in a semicircle with notebooks, ready to take whispered dictation from the eavesdroppers. One individualist stacked up three wooden banquet tables and listened through a dusty air vent.

The Philadelphia *Bulletin* did not stoop to such tactics. It didn't have to. A delegate from Philadelphia who privately loathed the Governor had agreed to report everything said at the caucus to the *Bulletin*'s statehouse reporter. The delegate-agent sat in the back of the room with a tiny concealed microphone in his tie clasp and a tape recorder in his pocket. He smiled blissfully at everything said up front.

Ben Wilcox's head was crowned with a stand of bushy black hair that looked as though it would crackle with static electricity at the first touch of a comb. His prominent jawbone was shadowed by the roots of a heavy beard. His shoulders hunched forward and his eyes never wavered from the point of focus. He failed to smile as he rapped his gavel for the third time.

"As you all know," he began, "this caucus was scheduled at the time of our last meeting three weeks ago in Harrisburg. At that meeting, responding to the wishes of the delegation, I agreed to let my name be presented to the convention as Pennsylvania's favorite son. It was well understood that this was simply a device to hold the delegation together as a harmonious group and make our influence felt when the time comes. I firmly believe, as I know many of you do, that we should not lose that unanimity of purpose as we deliberate this afternoon. I now invite discussion from the floor."

The inevitable period of silence followed. Then a tall man with a weather-hardened face stood up in the middle of the room. It was Joseph Rohrbaugh, Speaker of the Pennsylvania House. A prosperous York County farmer, he had long been a confidant of the Governor and his chief political lieutenant.

"I think it's obvious to all of us," he said, "that the situation has changed greatly in the last forty-eight hours. Secretary Manchester is still the leading candidate, but a strong contest is developing and I'm not at all sure he can win on the first ballot now. So I think it would be a great mistake to take any final action today. Therefore, at the proper time, I will move that the Governor's name be placed in nomination and that further action be withheld until another caucus just before the balloting Thursday afternoon."

"Can it be assumed that the Speaker is also voicing the sentiments of the Governor?" asked a delegate. A ripple of laughter played through the room, for the Speaker and the Governor always spoke as one, usually after lengthy consultation. Wilcox's brooding eyes fixed the questioner in mild reproof. He did not join the laughter, nor did he deign to comment.

A bulky man raised his hand and got a nod from Wilcox. "Simmons, Pittsburgh," he said. "For myself and three other members of the Missile and Aerospace Workers, I just want to say we're against Manchester." A number of people applauded. "We think Pennsylvania should be for Governor Roberts. Maybe we shouldn't vote today, but when we do, it ought to be Roberts."

Another delegate asked caustically: "Is Mr. Simmons saying that he and his colleagues wouldn't abide by the majority wishes of the delegation?"

Simmons jumped up again. "No, dammit, I didn't say that. I'm just telling you how we feel. We're with Governor Wilcox right down the line, of course, but if the delegation decides to go with Manchester . . . well, I don't know about the other guys, but it would sure stick in my throat, and I don't mean maybe."

A man in the front row, wearing a conservatively tailored suit, removed his glasses as he got up and turned to face the group. He was recognized as the Philadelphia broker who was spokesman for the little Main Line contingent.

"Candor, I believe," he said, "would lead any of us to say that Secretary Manchester's prospects are not quite so . . . ah . . . effulgent as they were a few days ago. Personally, I have always admired the Secretary, as I'm sure the Governor has. On the broad range of issues, Mr. Manchester speaks as a middle-of-the-road Republican and comes pretty close to what we want in our candidate. I would add, however, that some people think he raised an extraneous issue Saturday. Under the circumstances, I think we should proceed with caution. Therefore I'm prepared to second the Speaker's motion."

A slight Negro woman, a sociology teacher at Swarthmore College, got to her feet. "I really think we ought to have a little discussion of that issue," she said. "I'm not sure it's extraneous, and I think a lot of people are worried about it."

A delegate said: "With all due respect to Mrs. Potter, and we do respect her as an eminent educator and a loyal Republican, if members of her race are worried, about eighty per cent of them are worrying as Democrats."

Mrs. Potter grinned as she stood up again amid laughter. "It's never too late to be saved," she said. She made an enfolding gesture, as though gathering the wayward to her bosom. "We hope to make them repent and return to the fold in November."

"If you can do that," the skeptic shot back, "we can pick a candidate blindfolded. Whoever he is, he'll win in a landslide."

Mrs. Potter was persistent. "Let's not get sidetracked now," she argued. "I think Secretary Manchester spoke logically and with great common sense."

One or two delegates applauded, but the approval proved to be less than contagious. The Main Line broker spoke again. "I agree that Mr. Manchester raised a very serious question of public policy," he said. "But when I said 'extraneous' I meant outside the proper purview of this convention. As Governor Roberts indicated, that kind of thing belongs in the National Security Council. It's a little naïve to think that the heat of a nominating convention can throw any very helpful light on the situation."

"He means Manchester's timing stinks." It was a delegate blanketed in cigar smoke who spoke without standing. "And it sure did. Now he's got the Communists for him. And it's a sorry day, if you ask me, when a leading Republican becomes the fair-haired boy of Moscow."

"But I'm sure Mr. Manchester thought the delegates had a right to know exactly how he felt," said Mrs. Potter, "and I think he ought to be commended for speaking out, Communists or no Communists."

The delegate shrouded in cigar smoke stood up now. "Let's talk common sense," he said. "We want a winner in November. I happen to think Manchester is probably right in the long run, but in the short run—meaning the campaign—he'll get murdered on that issue. This election could be close. We can't afford to nominate a man who'll start out with a handicap.

Why, he'd be on the defensive from now till November. It's as simple as that."

The discussion went on for an hour. Mrs. Potter had her way, for the debate revolved around the substantive issue of building more nuclear weapons and missiles. One delegate thought a hold-down on new missiles might hinder the peaceful exploration of space. Another asked if it were true that Mark Davidson of Uniforge was in Chicago working for Roberts. Another said that if Manchester had his way, four more cities in southwestern Pennsylvania would become depressed areas. Finally the Speaker of the House rose again.

"I think I see a consensus," Rohrbaugh said. "It seems to me that this delegation, while applauding Secretary Manchester's intentions, is not at all sure that he should have spoken when he did. Further, that it would be a grave mistake for Pennsylvania to show its hand today. Therefore, Mr. Chairman, I now move that we present the name of our Governor for President, and that we adjourn and caucus again at McCormick Place before the first ballot on Thursday."

"Second the motion."

"You've heard the motion and the second," intoned Wilcox. "Are you ready to vote?"

"Just a minute." The delegate inside the cloud of cigar smoke had a booming voice. "Before we vote, let's put it on the line what we're doing. This convention has been turned inside out all of a sudden, and if we play it right we have a chance to nominate the ablest administrator in the country, a man of judgment, foresight and wisdom—the great Governor of Pennsylvania!"

Cheers mingled with applause. A flicker of a smile appeared

on Wilcox's dark jaw, but he erased it as quickly as he slammed down his gavel. "Enough's enough," he said. "All in favor of the motion say 'aye.' " A chorus replied. "Opposed, 'no.' " There were none. "This delegation will caucus again about one-thirty Thursday afternoon off the convention floor at McCormick Place. Meeting adjourned."

The Pennsylvania delegates filed out between the state troopers. The man with the fancy tie clasp searched for the political reporter of the Philadelphia *Bulletin*. In the back hallway, reporters got up, brushed their clothes, and hastily copied the notes of those who had taken dictation from them. The word spread into the lobby of the Morrison and then into the street, to be carried like a torch to the Hilton and the Blackstone: another setback for Manchester. The big Pennsylvania delegation, thought ready to go for him, was holding tight. The name of Ben Wilcox would be placed in nomination as a favorite son.

In the lobby of the Morrison, where they had been waiting anxiously but helplessly, the managers of the two major candidates met at a drinking fountain. Carl Fleischer, Roberts' man, had just swallowed one of his pastel-colored pills. He peered at Obie O'Connell's plump and sweating face through his dark glasses and smiled.

"Tough luck, Obie," he said cheerfully. "You can't win 'em all, and you better start getting used to the idea."

O'Connell stared back without expression, but silently he cursed Ben Wilcox. Things may not turn out the way they seem to be going now, he thought, but conventions are like icebergs in reverse: what counts is what's showing on the surface.

"That was no loss," he said, but his voice lacked conviction. "We'll get Pennsylvania Thursday. You know these guys with the kingmaker complex."

Fleischer put his mouth to O'Connell's ear. "Frankly, the guy who gets Wilcox is buying himself four years of trouble."

"You're telling me."

"By the way, Obie, I hear you're telling delegates that Manchester didn't mean it when he said he'd cancel the Daphne." Fleischer's tone was casual, but his eyes were alert behind the smoked glasses.

"That's not what he said, Carl." Obie's reply was evasive, but he felt better. Much better. His plan was working, taking hold, as he had known it would. Fleischer wouldn't have brought it up unless he was hurting. "And you can hear anything you want around a convention, I guess."

Fleischer grasped O'Connell's elbow and pulled him through a service entrance door. "Obie," he said, "let me talk to you away from these damn newspapermen."

They stood in a dark hallway beside several trash cans. O'Connell toyed with a long-handled broom while Fleischer took off his dark glasses and began polishing them carefully with his breast-pocket handkerchief.

"I want to make you a good deal, Obie," he said.

"Shoot." O'Connell was wary.

"It's that messy credentials business," Fleischer said. "Those two outfits have been screaming and hollering for a week and the committee is sick of it. They're ready to dump the whole thing onto the floor."

O'Connell needed no further explanation. For a week, the credentials committee of the convention had been trying to settle a contest between two rival Mississippi delegations, one solidly for Manchester, the other for Roberts. At stake were the state's 13 convention votes. Two separate Republican conventions had been held in Mississippi, with each claiming to be the legitimate party conclave. Each named a full slate of delegates and sent them to Chicago. They traded insults and charges before the credentials committee, which listened to endless hints about promised postmasterships, folding money passed in dark doorways, and offers to pay delegate expenses. The barrage of claims and counterclaims left the committee alternately weak with laughter and rigid with frustration at its inability to find (or fabricate) a rational basis for decision.

"What you got in mind?" asked O'Connell. He mopped his forehead. There was no air conditioning in this part of the hotel.

"Let's split Mississippi," suggested Fleischer. He placed his hands on the lapels of O'Connell's jacket. His manner was that of a man about to bequeath a large sum to charity, and Obie's spiritual guard instantly tightened.

"How we gonna split thirteen votes?" he asked. "You know there's no fractional voting, Carl."

"Look," Fleischer said, "if the committee sends this thing to the floor and the whole convention votes, you're liable to lose."

"So are you," countered O'Connell.

"Let's face it, Obie. If you lose, it will hurt you bad. If we lose, we can take it. We're on the upswing."

"Says who?" O'Connell snorted.

"The credentials committee report comes up Tuesday night before they read the platform. You're the front-runners. You can't afford to lose a floor fight on TV. In second place, we could roll with it. You know that, for God's sake."

O'Connell had indeed reached the same conclusion a full twenty-four hours earlier. In fact, he had been ready to deal all day, but had resisted the temptation to call Fleischer, hoping—for bargaining purposes—that the Roberts manager would make the first approach.

"I don't say I buy that, Carl," Obie said, "but I'm willing to be reasonable with you." He tried his opening offer. "We'll take eight and you take five."

Fleischer let go of O'Connell's lapels and fell back a step in mock horror.

"You've got to be kidding," he said, his voice brimful of shock and sorrow. "Eight-to-five Manchester? When your boom is leaking air like a peanut whistle? Let's be sane, Obie."

"So what do *you* say, pal?"

"We take the eight," Fleischer said matter-of-factly. "You take the five."

"My God," said O'Connell. It was his turn to feign injury. "What do you take me for—the guy who hands out the foreign aid?"

"Obie." Fleischer dropped all the banter and warmth from his voice. "If you let this go to the floor, you don't stand to lose thirteen votes. You stand to blow the nomination."

O'Connell eyed his opponent without flinching. "No deal," he said. But he made no move to leave, and Fleischer could see the rejection was not final.

"Listen, Obie," said the Roberts manager, "let me tell you something in confidence. You owe us one. Bin Roberts has already let you fellows off the hook."

Fleischer described the scene in Roberts' sitting room Sunday afternoon when Fleischer proposed to circulate a handbill stressing Moscow's pleasure with Manchester.

O'Connell was unimpressed. "So your man refuses to go for your dirty tricks," he said. "That makes him a humanitarian?"

"That's not the point." Fleischer tapped a finger on O'Connell's chest. "Suppose I dropped a little hint somewhere—and somebody else began distributing handbills all over the place."

"You're a blackmailer, Carl." O'Connell said it without resentment. The tubby manager stood for a moment, his eyes measuring Fleischer for signs of pliability.

"Okay, Carl," he said. "So you got to have your pound of flesh. I'll make you a deal you don't deserve. Seven for us, six for you."

"Split the difference," Fleischer countered. "Seven for Roberts, six for Manchester."

O'Connell knew the psychological dangers of accepting. The news tickers would chatter: *Manchester loses credentials fight*. The word would spread poisonously among the delegates: another break for Roberts, another setback for Manchester. A small thing, but it was like another drop on the forehead in the Chinese water torture.

However, if he refused, the consequences could be calamitous. If the convention seated the entire delegation that was for Roberts—and, by a hair, it appeared to have the better claim—the psychological blow would be much worse than the mere loss of 13 votes. The fact was that Carl Fleischer had him by the short hairs. Better to take a little defeat now, and hope the convention would forget it, than to risk a disastrous rout on the floor before millions of television viewers.

As he had reminded Manchester the night before in a different context, look what happened to Taft in 1952.

"You're a louse, Fleischer," he said with a sigh, "but you got yourself a deal." He held out his hand. "Can I take a charity deduction for this on my tax return?"

They shook hands. "Let's both call the credentials chairman," suggested Fleischer.

"We got to," O'Connell replied. "God knows he wouldn't believe you without an affidavit from me."

The two men, smiling now, re-entered the lobby. They laughed when Fleischer offered to put up the dime for the pay phone. "Seven to six," said O'Connell. "You bought yourself one ten-cent vote."

An hour later the lesser of Obie's two fears was confirmed by the United Press International's convention news wire:

UPI Convention 47

Chicago—Manchester forces suffered a second reverse Monday afternoon when Gov. Bryan Roberts of California won a majority of the disputed Mississippi delegation.

The credentials committee, awarding seven seats to Roberts and six to Treasury Secretary Charles B. Manchester, acted an hour after the big Pennsylvania delegation dealt Manchester a more significant blow by refusing to endorse his candidacy.

The Keystone state's 64 delegates voted unanimously to offer Gov. Benjamin Wilcox as the state's favorite son Wednesday night and to withhold a final decision until just prior to the Thursday balloting.

EDW536PCDT

11

The crowd churned and eddied like steers in a stockyard. Mc-Cormick Place, Chicago's vast convention hall, was already choked with people, but it swallowed a stream of late arrivals from the taxis and buses that clogged Lake Shore Drive for blocks. More than fifteen thousand people already stood or sat in the hall; soon it would be packed to capacity.

A haze of smoke lay upon the delegate and alternate sections on the floor and drifted up past the banked tiers of spectator seats. The aisles were jammed with seemingly aimless wanderers. A muffled roar, like that of a distant waterfall, gave evidence of the merger of thousands of voices. Above the delegates, a huge hanging platform supported a cargo of cameras and cameramen and a tangle of television cables. On the floor, on either side of the central platform, the clicking of typewriters in the press sections provided metallic orchestration for the ragged human chorus. From the press benches, individuals on the floor appeared no more distinctive than ants in the throng, which had already developed a sound, an odor and a collective will of its own.

Archie DuPage leaned across the bunting-draped rail that marked the box-seat area reserved for privileged guests. Kay Orcott had a front seat in this V.I.P. section.

"Isn't it exciting, Archie?" She hugged herself by way of illustration.

"Nothing happens here tonight except talk," he said. "I'll see you up at 2306 after the session, okay?" She nodded and Archie elbowed his way back into the crowd, heading toward the first of nearly two dozen delegates whom Obie O'Connell had instructed him to see that evening.

Roger Abbott, the Roberts floor boss, stood by the Massachusetts standard, arguing with a portly delegate. On the platform, Carl Fleischer sat in a padded swivel chair and studied a list of names. In an identical chair on the other side of the platform, Obie O'Connell spoke in a low voice into a telephone which linked him with a dozen key Manchester leaders on the floor. Halfway back in the center aisle, immaculate in a freshly pressed suit, Gus Maguire of the Missile Workers spoke earnestly to another man while passing elbows shoved him first one way, then another. Maguire wore a beribboned badge with the words "Official Messenger" on the brass holder.

The minute hand of the clock over the platform clicked up to eight o'clock. It was nine in the East, six on the Pacific Coast: starting time for the convention. In millions of living rooms, rumpus rooms, bedrooms and barrooms, people settled down around television sets.

"Delegates will clear the aisles!"

The injunction, repeated at half-minute intervals, had no effect at all. The twisting streams of people continued their snail-like progress toward unknown destinations.

Joseph Terhune of Wisconsin, chairman of the Republican National Committee, stood at the podium at the end of the platform ramp. His white mane and craggy features gave him the appearance of a ship's captain on a flying bridge. He slammed his gavel once, twice, then set up a steady hammering on the special block installed for the purpose. Its hollow resonance carried the sound of the gavel through the vast hall, but to no avail. Terhune surrendered to the inevitable and plunged ahead.

"The thirtieth convention of the Republican party," he intoned, "will come to order! The party of Lincoln, Theodore Roosevelt, Eisenhower and Stuart is met here to nominate the next President of the United States!"

A roar of approval—the first of hundreds that would fill the convention hall—greeted this traditional forecast of the November election results. Terhune drove on.

"The world-famous soprano, a star of the Metropolitan Opera," he cried, "Miss Emily Bond, will now lead us in singing 'The Star-Spangled Banner.' "

A statuesque blonde, her milk-white skin contrasting vividly with a shimmering black gown, pealed forth the anthem. The high notes soared for the roof, battling for supremacy with the music of the unseen organ. Miss Bond lost; the organ finished triumphantly, its bass pipes rumbling on for almost a whole bar after smothering her final notes.

Now Frederick Cardinal Fitzsimmons, Catholic archbishop of the Chicago diocese, came to the lectern. Alone on the end of the ramp, he delivered his invocation one word at a time to thwart the echoes of the public-address amplifiers.

"In the name of the Father, and of the Son, and of the Holy Ghost, Amen," he began. "Almighty God, giver of light and truth, knowledge and compassion, we beseech Thee to shed Thy Grace upon these Thy children gathered here; to sustain them as they take up their awful responsibilities; and to guide them as they seek the path of prudence and wisdom."

Both O'Connell and Fleischer leaned forward nervously to catch the slow phrases and dissect them for hidden bias. When the Cardinal finished, they leaned back and grinned at each other. His Eminence had been satisfyingly neutral in the intra-party battle, and the final words of his invocation pleased almost everyone in the convention hall. They sounded a wee bit anti-Democratic, and if God was ever going to be on the side of the Republican party, this was a good year for it.

After the prayer, minor business—cut to the bone to avoid boring the television audience—occupied the convention for a few minutes. While Terhune disposed of the routine minutiae, Carl Fleischer went to the rear of the platform at the request of a group of newspapermen. Soon thirty reporters were clustered around him as he munched a hot dog and drank a Coca-Cola from the bottle at a refreshment stand.

"Carl," a reporter asked, "what's your reaction to Manchester's statement reserving the right to interpret the defense plank?"

"It was his only out," replied Fleischer. He took another bite of hot dog, his smoked glasses jiggling with the workings of his jaw. "He couldn't win on the floor, so he took a powder. It shows they're on the skids."

"But," protested one newsman, "candidates have done that

before. Alton Parker wrote his own gold plank at the Democratic convention in 1904."

There is one erudite scholar of political lore in every convention crowd, but Fleischer knew his history too. "That was after Judge Parker was nominated. This is different. If Manchester had the convention with him, he would have taken it to the floor and jammed it down our throats."

"What do you personally think of his missile argument, Mr. Fleischer?"

The manager stuffed the last extra bit of bread into his mouth and wiped the mustard off his upper lip. "I count noses, not nose cones," he said. The reporters chuckled; they liked a candidate's handlers to sound hard-boiled. It livened up their copy and gave them a feeling of being privy to the inner mechanics of the political process.

"Seriously," Fleischer went on, "I stand with Governor Roberts. The place to settle big issues like that is the White House, not McCormick Place."

"How do you figure it as of tonight, Carl?"

"Bin Roberts is going to be nominated," the manager said flatly. He aimed a finger at his questioner. "The whole mood of this convention is changing. I've picked up fifty pledges today that I know of, and half of them—at least—are switches from Manchester. Let's face it, fellows, the Secretary goofed. He goofed badly."

"Did you and Obie make a deal on that Mississippi thing, Carl," he was asked, "or was it done in the credentials committee?"

Fleischer smiled dryly. "Obie and I had a little talk this afternoon—about a lot of things. Let's just say we won that

Mississippi fight, and won it big. Last week I didn't figure
to get one delegate out of that bucket of catfish."

Out on the floor, next to the Kansas standard, Gus Maguire
knelt beside Roger Abbott's aisle seat. He showed him a list
and ran his finger down the names.

"We're going to get nine out of ten of the union men in
this hall," Maguire said. "I've already seen damn near every
one of them and they're all scared of Manchester. The Teamsters don't like it. Neither do the Machinists."

Abbott's Adam's apple moved as he whispered: "What
about Davidson? How's he doing? We got a lot more stockholders than union members in this convention."

"I just talked to Mark," replied Maguire. He was bumped
from behind and he paused to wipe the grime from his knee
with his clean handkerchief. "He says he's doing as well as I
am. He's got a couple of big banks putting on the heat. We
can win this one, Roger."

Abbott fiddled with his bow tie and shook his head. "We
can if nobody worries about sleep between now and Thursday."

"I can make it on two hours a night," said Maguire with a
grin. "This is a tea party compared with a union convention."

Private conversations all over the hall were smothered by a
bellow from the platform. Terhune had surrendered the gavel
for the time being. (He would return shortly as permanent
chairman, by mutual desire of both Manchester and Roberts
camps.) The temporary chairman, the Governor of Kentucky,
had launched into his keynote speech. His arms were thrown
wide as he waved them like the blades of a windmill. Sweat
beaded his forehead and his cheeks glowed. The audience

didn't know it, but already Governor Jim Bob Cole was soaking wet from neck to waist, though he had spoken less than three sentences.

"Just two weeks ago," he shouted, "this great hospitable city of Chicago was host to a political party which once shed glory and renown on this beloved land of our forefathers." There were scattered boos. "But, oh, my friends and my countrymen, how the mighty have fallen. That party which once gave us pride would now give us charity. That party which once gave us self-reliance would now give us handouts. That party which once would have all Americans walk as men would now have us crawl as children. Nay, as babes—with their bureaucrats in Washington as the baby-sitters. That party which gave us Jefferson and Jackson would now give us"—he shook his head and held his arms out with an exaggerated shrug of the shoulders–"Hendrickson."

"Pour it on, Jim Bob!" The plea rang shrill from the Kentucky delegation. Governor Cole smiled, paused, then shifted to a more conversational tone.

"My friends and my countrymen," he said, leaning forward confidentially, "I'm just a small-town boy from a little place beside a muddy creek. It's called Big Swallow. Big Swallow, Kentucky, and we're proud of it. It's not big. You could put the whole of Big Swallow in one section of this great hall and have five rows left over. There's no swallows, either. We've got jay birds and crows and buzzards, but no swallows. We've got a hundred eighty-seven folks in Big Swallow—when I'm home and when my Uncle Paul isn't over to Louisville philanderin'.

"But my friends and my countrymen, every soul in Big Swallow watched that other convention on television. And you know how they felt? I'll tell you how they felt. They felt ashamed. Shame . . . shame . . . shame, deep in their loins and deep in their hearts. They asked to be addressed as mature Americans, but they were talked down to like runny-nosed kids. Yes, sir, the smart-aleck professors of the Democrat party talked down to them and told them they didn't have to work for a living . . . didn't have to pay for what they bought . . . didn't have to send men to Washington who knew a nickel from a dollar.

"Oh, my friends and my countrymen, it was the professors talking. The professors of sociology, of psychology, of meteorology. Of every blessed ology in this whole wide world. Yes, sir, every blessed ology—except the good old Doxology. But Big Swallow knows better, my friends and my countrymen, and in November the whole wide country will show it knows better too."

He paused again as the hall roared. The tension of his intimate moral lecture showed under the arms of his white linen suit, where damp splotches were beginning to spread. Then he raised his arms like a camp-meeting preacher calling the sinners to confession.

"Will America let the baby-sitters get away with it?"

"No!" boomed thousands of voices in the hall.

"Will the little professors of the big ologies rule this land?"

"No—oo!" The chorus was taken up by the spectator tiers.

"Will we send a President to Washington who doesn't know a nickel from a dollar—and a Democrat dollar at that?"

"No–oo—oo!"

Jim Bob Cole held up his hands as though to still the multitudes.

"No," he said, "we will not. We will not, because this nation faces its most crucial choice of this century. As we look about the world tonight from this blessed land of plenty, we see the eyes of our allies—and our enemies, too—fastened upon this nation and upon this great convention. They are watching to see how America decides. They are asking, just as millions of Americans are asking: will the choice be bravery and self-reliance—or timidity and submission? Will the choice be the individual—or the state? Will it be fiscal sanity—or the everlasting *in*sanity of the federal credit card? . . ."

*   *   *

In the third-floor apartment in Tiburon, California, Jake Manchester removed the martini glass from its precarious balancing place on his chest, swung his feet down and got up from the couch where he had been lying. He stepped to the television set and snapped it off, then faced out the wide, full-length picture window overlooking the bay. It was still daylight, but the sun was slipping close to the Pacific. Across the bay in Berkeley, on the east shore, thousands of windows sparkled in reflection of the sunset, like myriad diamonds suddenly sprung from the ground.

"And just when," asked Patsy, "did we start turning off the TV without consulting our roommate?" She was curled in an easy chair with her feet tucked under a billowing flowered cotton skirt.

"He's a cornball." Jake spoke flatly, without turning around. His stocky, square-cut frame was silhouetted against the brightness outside. He took another drink as he gazed out the window. Over the shoulder of Angel Island, almost directly to the south, the sunset bathed the hills of San Francisco.

"Well, he's part of the greatest show on earth," Patsy said, tossing her blonde hair, "and I don't intend to miss any part of it."

"Come off it, Pats," he said. "You know they won't do anything tonight. As soon as the great orator from Big Swallow runs out of gas, they all quit and go back to their hotels." He turned and slumped down on the couch again, one leg hooked over a pillow.

His wife uncurled in the chair and eyed him over the rim of her glass. She was always "Patsy" to him except in moments of stress. Then, for some reason, he invariably called her "Pats."

"Anything wrong, dear?" she asked.

"Wrong? No. Why should there be anything wrong?"

That proved it. If there weren't something wrong, he would have made up something—to tease her.

"Jake Manchester, you have said just about fourteen words since you came home an hour ago. You're being icky."

"How could I talk with that guy braying at me?"

"According to your ideas, he was talking sense. Fiscal integrity and all that jazz."

Jake shrugged. "Yeah, I guess so, but why does he have to bring in all that corn? 'Uncle Paul philanderin' over to Louisville,' for God's sake!"

"But if we left the set on," she argued tangentially, "we'd get the commentary and see how our dad is doing."

"You're beginning to sound like he was more your father than mine. I'm Manchester, remember? You're the one who married me."

"Well, you've been treating him for the last couple of days like he was an in-law." She came to the couch and nestled beside him. "Jake, C.B. isn't doing so hot, is he?"

He reached out to the coffee table to pick up his drink, and when he sat back he was an inch or two farther away from Patsy. "Well, what did you expect? A lot of people don't agree with him. Is everybody supposed to roll over and quit thinking when Charles B. Manchester speaks?"

"And are you one of those people who don't agree with him, Jake?"

"No, I don't say that." Jake frowned and twisted his ear lobe, reminding Pasty again that he looked just like his father when he was concentrating on something. "It's just that he issues, well, a kind of ukase, like a czar or something, when there are an awful lot of things that have to be considered. The defense of the country, the jobs, the investments . . ."

Patsy grunted. "Ugh! That again. He said we have ninety thousand atomic bombs and oodles of missiles, enough to blow up the world. What more do you want?"

"I'll tell you what I want," he said. "I want to know why Governor Roberts is so wrong when he says that's the kind of question to be settled in Washington, not at some Roman circus of a convention."

"Jake!" She put down her drink and squeezed away into the far corner of the couch. "This is a *democracy,* remember? A leader is supposed to let the people know what he believes."

He didn't answer, but merely drained his glass and looked inquiringly at hers. She shook her head. He went to the kitchen and this time mixed a martini-on-the-rocks that filled an entire highball glass. She grimaced when she saw it.

"Oh, big banker's drinking night." When he failed to answer, she tried once more. "Come on, Jake, what happened at the office? You're going to tell me sooner or later."

He gave her a rueful half-smile. "I guess I'm not such a big banker, Pats. At least J.R. didn't treat me that way this afternoon."

At the Bradbury Commercial National Bank, where Jake had been working for two years as an assistant in the trust department, "J.R." was James R. Duggan, assistant to the president in charge of personnel, public relations and a weird assortment of miscellany known only to the ranking officers of the institution. Jake had gone into banking reluctantly— almost against his will—and had taken this job only because his father buoyantly insisted and greased the ways for him. Now he had to admit to himself that he really rather liked the complexities of banking and was beginning to think that someday he'd master the business.

"J.R. called you on the carpet?" Patsy asked.

"Carpet? No, nothing like that." Jake pulled his ear again. "It was worse, in a way. He called me in and offered me a cigar. Then he began to talk about Dad's statement on missiles. Asked me what I thought of it."

"What did you tell him?"

"Same thing I told you. I'm not so sure about it, but it didn't seem like the right place or time to bring it up."

"Always the loyal son," she needled.

He disagreed. "Candor, darling, candor—it's the family trait, remember? Anyway, he said Bradbury holds two hundred million of Uniforge paper. He talked a lot about Uniforge's role in the economy of the West and California in particular, and he said when they get tooled up for Daphne it can mean a hundred thousand new jobs west of the Rockies."

He stopped and she asked coldly: "Is that all he said?"

"Nope." Jake took another gulp of his drink. "He talked about a bank's responsibilities to its customers, and he said there were all kinds of ways of helping a customer over . . . well, difficult periods. Inevitably—I think that's the word he used—a bank has to keep an eye on politics, because so many big decisions are made there. He said he realized my close relationship to the leading candidate."

"That's putting it mildly," Patsy interjected.

Jake didn't smile. "And he said because of that he realized it was a delicate area, and all, but he wondered how I felt personally."

"And?"

"And so, well, I said just because he's my old man I don't always agree with him, and . . ." Jake kept his eyes on his hands as he talked. "Gee, Pats, I told him the same things I told you just now."

"Don't you want your father to be President?"

"Well, I'm not so sure," Jake said. He glanced at his wife, saw the storm warnings and hurried on, as if trying to escape. "Anyway, J.R. said he thought I might know some delegates who . . ." His voice faltered.

"Who *what?*"

"Who . . . dammit, I'm trying to remember what he said, so will you lay off, please? . . . who might be interested in hearing the other side, he said."

"You mean who might switch to Roberts, that's what you mean." Her tone was icy.

"No, no, not that at all." Now Jake showed a touch of anger. "But for God's sake, Pats, if what J.R. says is true, and this thing Dad jumped on is . . . I don't say he's wrong, actually, but a convention is sure one hell of a place to bring it up."

"Okay, I get the picture." She sat up straight in her corner now, her arms folded stiffly across the high belt of her skirt. Two pink spots appeared on her cheeks. "You said you'd call some delegates."

"Oh, Christ, Pats, I didn't do anything like that. I said I only know one delegate myself, a fellow from business school, and I didn't say I'd call him."

"I see. You just gave him the name, that's all."

"I didn't tell him anything."

"So I suppose he asked you to call Jim Steadall? That's who it is, isn't it?"

"Yes, it's Jim. He's a delegate from Massachusetts. But he didn't ask me to call, and he didn't ask the name. He just said he thought it was too bad Dad had raised the issue at just this time, and he thought everybody had a responsibility to clear the air as to what was involved."

"Especially everybody who wants to get ahead at the Bradbury Commercial National Bank."

"Oh, Goddammit, Pats *no!*" She paid no attention to him, but flounced off the couch and disappeared into the kitchen. When she came out again, she had a martini—her second—in her hand. She stood before him with her legs planted defiantly.

"Jake," she said, "that is the most disgusting, crawly story I've ever heard. Did you lean over the desk and punch him in the nose?"

"No," he growled. "Are you crazy? He didn't ask me to do anything."

"Maybe not, but you know and I know what he was angling

for. What kind of man are you turning into? Your boss practically orders you to go out and work against your own father—"

"That's a lie."

"That's the plain truth, no matter how he glossed it over or how you try to wiggle out of it. And you didn't do a thing, not one damn thing."

"What do you want me to do? Resign?"

"You bet I do." Her voice rose dangerously. "You should have stuffed your ID card, or whatever that miserable little bank gives you, right down his throat and walked out."

"God, you're brave when you get a drink in your hand," he said. He made no effort to keep the snarl out of his voice.

"Don't talk about drinks to me. You had to get half stiff before you had the courage to tell me about it." She looked him over deliberately from feet to head. "I'm beginning to wonder just what kind of a man I married."

"Goddammit, you listen to me!" He stood up and glared at her.

"Don't you dare swear at me, Jake Manchester!" She was screaming now.

"I'm not swearing at you. But I've had a bellyful of your fine moral lecture. I didn't do anything to hurt my father. I didn't give anyone any information. I haven't called any delegates."

"You just acted like a worm, that's all," she said bitterly.

"Patsy!" It was a plea—the one that usually served to end a brief spat. But she refused to respond.

"Go on," she taunted. "Go call your friend Steadall. Go ahead. Tell him he ought to vote for blowing up the world and for insanity and for Roberts. Go ahead. Call him. The whole world's sick already, so why not you too?"

Tears ran down her cheeks in broad trickles. She cried out once and ran down the hall, her sandals slapping erratically on the old wooden floors. Jake heard the door to the guest bedroom slam, and when he went to it a moment later he could hear her sobbing.

"Patsy," he said, "I'm sorry. Please open the door, honey."

There was no answer. He heard her come across the room, but instead of opening the door she threw the bolt. Patsy Manchester had locked herself in.

Jake sat for almost two hours on the little balcony which hung out in front of their apartment. He sipped at the long martini and he watched the twilight crumble into night. Fog rolled in from the sea, blotting out Raccoon Strait below him and Angel Island beyond it. Far behind the island, where the lights of San Francisco glittered on a clear night, only a dull glow showed. Jake's mood was black as the night.

He thought of the time when, as a small boy, he had set a tin pan in front of of a board fence and thrown a baseball, trying to pitch strikes over the pan. His aim was hopeless, and he sprayed the fence with his pitches. Then his father came up behind him, took the ball and threw three straight strikes. "Control, that's all it takes, Jake," the man had said. Never since that time had he been completely at ease in his father's presence. He recognized the symptom for what it was: envy. Charles Manchester did everything right, usually the first time, always with the appearance of effortless instinct. But it didn't help any to pinpoint the emotion. Sure, Patsy was right. He should have told J.R. to go to hell and walked out. That's what his father would have done. Well, why hadn't he? Because he didn't react fast enough, for one thing, and he wasn't quite sure what was being suggested to him, for another—not until he'd got home and thought about it during that damnfool speech. So he wasn't all the heel Patsy thought. And, anyway, how did he know his father was right this time? After all, he wasn't omniscient. He wasn't God.

His drink was gone now and he shivered in the damp air. Jake got his old golf jacket and a battered rain hat out of the closet and went for a walk. Coming out of the apartment house, he turned right along Paradise Drive, past the old two-story-high stone tower, crossed the railroad tracks and wandered down Main Street to the one-block commercial center. There was a burst of music and laughter as someone opened the door at Sam's Place, but otherwise the street was silent. Turning back, he walked up the hill past the homes above. Their owners were all in bed now and he was alone with the mist and the far-off cries of a sea gull. By the time he let himself back into the apartment two hours later, he felt much better.

He looked at the telephone, a bright yellow "color-coordinated" instrument which Patsy had chosen. It rested in a wall niche in the dining alcove. After a moment, he picked it up.

"Operator, I want to talk person-to-person to a Mr. James Steadall in Chicago. He's a delegate to the Republican convention, and he'll be staying at the same hotel with the Massachusetts delegation."

12

Archie saw them first as he stepped out of the limousine ahead of Charles Manchester. He motioned toward the group and said to the candidate: "I don't think you better hang around here, boss."

Back and forth in front of the hotel paraded two dozen pickets carrying homemade signs on long poles. The legends were printed in awkward, wavering letters. "Vote For Disarmament: Vote Manchester!" . . . "Down With Daphne" . . . "12 Seconds to Burial" . . . "Humanity First—Roberts Second." An old man with gray hair which brushed his shoulders in long, dirty coils carried a small statue of Christ on the cross. He wore a sandwich-board sign which read, "Thou Shalt Not Crucify Mankind on a Nuclear Cross." Behind him marched two little children, a boy and a girl, each carrying an American flag in one hand and a United Nations flag in the other.

Manchester paused as he stepped to the curb and stared at the marchers with a puzzled frown. As he did so, a woman threw herself at his feet and clutched his legs. On her knees, she looked up at him wordlessly and adoringly. As Manchester struggled to free himself, two photographers standing by the picket line snapped his picture. The look on Manchester's face, during the fraction of a second it required to record the image on film, was one of uncomprehending fright.

His facial composure returned immediately. He jerked first one leg and then the other free and, clutching Archie's elbow, started across the sidewalk toward the hotel entrance. But the disheveled band of pickets pressed about him, shouting encouragement. One man shoved his sign at Manchester and demanded an autograph. The woman who had thrown herself on the sidewalk ran after him and grabbed his coattail. One of the children clutched at his sleeve, leaving a smear of chocolate.

"Faster, boss," whispered Archie, towing the candidate behind him and bruising his way forward like a fullback. Even inside the hotel they were not safe. The pickets shoved through the door behind them, shrieking and swinging their placards, as the beleaguered candidate and his aide tried to slip out of sight and get a service elevator. A Chicago policeman, at a nod from Archie, barred the peace partisans from the service door.

Inside the elevator, Manchester tried to wipe the chocolate off his sleeve. "What in the name of all that's holy," he asked, "was that bunch? Where did they come from?"

Archie shook his head. "Nuts. Peace nuts," he said. He noticed a tear in his pants leg and felt the familiar pang of protest in his stomach. "Somebody should have warned us they were there. We could have come in the side entrance."

"But why should they pick on me?" asked Manchester, genuinely puzzled.

"You're the new prince of peace, it says here," explained Archie in disgust.

"How could my position be distorted by anyone into anything that could appeal to those people? I'm not for disarmament, for God's sake."

"You will be—in the afternoon papers."

"What do you mean?"

"Two wire-service photographers snapped you just as that crazy old dame hit you with the flying tackle."

"Can't you get it killed?" asked Manchester.

"You know better than that, boss." Archie's tone was one of aggrieved professional reproof. "At a convention, anything goes."

The two men walked in silence to suite 2306. So far, Tuesday morning had been all bad, Archie thought—and the balloting was now little more than forty-eight hours away. The breakfast with the Maine delegation at the Executive House had got off to a limp start and quickly turned sour when a delegate asked what President Stuart's position was on Manchester's "interpretation" of the defense plank. The Secretary answered honestly that he'd been "out of touch" with the White House on the matter. Under prodding, he conceded that he had not talked with Stuart since before the Saturday press conference.

Archie could see the look of knowing cynicism on the faces of several delegates: So old Fred Stuart is cooling off on his man, huh? The session ended with the coffee and the atmosphere equally cold. Not even the genuine friendliness of the Maine chairman, an old friend of Manchester's, helped much. The ride back to the Hilton was cheerless—and then those picket zombies. Peace, thought Archie, it's frightful.

In the living room of his suite, Manchester peeled off his jacket and dropped it carelessly on a chair. He paced restlessly around, his face flushed with irritation.

"I just can't understand it," he said. "Nothing I ever said should attract that kind of extremist fringe. And where on earth did they come from?"

"Who knows?" Archie shrugged. "A bunch of loonies."

"They're not insane," Manchester said glumly. "They're just misguided zealots who completely misunderstood what I've been saying."

"Well," said Archie reluctantly, "a lot of misguided delegates apparently don't understand it much better." He tapped his wrist watch. "Look, the Pennsylvania delegation will be here in a couple of minutes, in case you want to use the john or anything right now."

When the men and women of the Pennsylvania delegation filed in, Manchester stood by the door to greet each one with a handshake and a smile. He was pleased at the number of names he recalled without difficulty; he had never been much good at matching names and faces, but when he became a candidate he decided he must master the skill, and set about it with the same vigor he applied to every task in life.

"Good morning, Mrs. Potter," he said as he shook the

hand of the college professor. He had met her only once, after a speech in Philadelphia weeks ago.

Helena Potter gave his hand an extra squeeze. "Stick by your guns, Mr. Secretary. You're right."

Manchester waved the delegates to seats as a crew of volunteer workers set up extra chairs. Archie noted unhappily that not many extras were needed. He counted only 45 of the 128—delegates and alternates—who had been invited to meet the candidate. Governor Wilcox was not there, but Archie really had not expected him, for political protocol would hardly allow a bona fide favorite son to call on a leading contender. If you wanted to see Ben Wilcox at this convention, you called on him. But at least Wilcox's chief lieutenant— Joseph Rohrbaugh, the Speaker of the Pennyslvania House —was present. He sat with a blank face as Manchester moved to the center of the room.

The Treasury Secretary's face was without expression, but his mood was bleak. I wonder where the rest of them are, he thought. This isn't much of a turnout. Maybe some of the others started to come up here and saw those poor fools out on the sidewalk and changed their minds. He looked around at the delegates. There wasn't much warmth in their attitude; they seemed almost to be waiting for him to prove himself. Well, that's what he was here for. He folded his shirt-sleeved arms, picked out one man in the corner of the room as a focus for his words, and started to go over the same old ground once more. Maybe this time he could make them understand.

"It's no secret to any of you," he began, "that my stand on new nuclear warheads and long-range delivery systems has created considerable controversy in this convention. I believe that's a healthy thing for the party. We must always be willing to discuss and debate any vital issue, regardless of whether or not we differ on it. My position is quite clear, and I won't bore you by restating it.

"But I would like to set the record straight on one or two things, because some people seem to have a misapprehension about what I said and some others, I'm afraid, are intentionally distorting my remarks for their own purposes. Now, first, it cannot be argued by any stretch of the imagination that I'm tinkering with the safety of the country. I am not, and will not. I want us to have the strongest military force in the world. If I'm nominated and elected, I'll spend every cent that's needed to keep up the strength we've built up under recent administrations—of both parties.

"Second, these scare stories about how I'd wreck the missile and aircraft industries are pure, unadulterated nonsense. For one thing, there isn't any question about carrying out all of the present plane contracts. As for the missile industry, you've got to remember the space program, on which we've made so much progress and which has challenged man's imagination like nothing since Columbus. We're already spending billions every year to reach out to the planets, and we shall continue to do so."

Manchester fingered his ear and stepped closer to the group. "Now, specifically, let's take Universal Forge. This company is very heavily into the space effort. It's true that if the Daphne war missile—and I stress *war* missile—were canceled, Uniforge would expand less rapidly than planned. But that's a far cry from saying the company would be destroyed.

"So, really, I'm trying to call attention to a relatively small, but tremendously expensive and I believe wasteful, area of defense production. I'm simply saying—and I intend to go right on saying it—that we have no business stockpiling weapons that don't really improve our defense posture. I'm sorry if I didn't get my point across on Saturday. I hope I've made it clear now."

Manchester stopped abruptly and stood there, his chest moving slightly with the exertion of his speech. Several delegates applauded, but most seemed unimpressed. Manchester glanced around, then asked: "Any questions?"

A dapper little man, whom Archie recognized as the boss of one of the few Republican wards in Philadelphia, stood up. "Mr. Secretary," he asked, "if we could come back to earth for a moment, how are you going to treat us on federal jobs? President Stuart hasn't given Pennsylvania much except the back of his hand."

Manchester joined in the burst of laughter, thankful that the tension had been punctured. "Pennsylvania," he said, "is a big Republican state, and the Commonwealth and its governor will be treated accordingly. That's a promise." This time there was hearty applause. "But, Mr. Giovanni," he added, pointing at the ward leader, "it's a violation of the corrupt practices act to promise anything of value to win an election, so let's just leave it in generalities. You can be assured your state won't be forgotten."

"Of course, Mr. Secretary," interjected Archie, "that's a two-way street."

"Yes, indeed," Manchester said in mock solemnity, and when they laughed again, Archie began to feel a little better. But the atmosphere of good will was short-lived.

"Mr. Manchester," said a heavy-set delegate, "you said at your press conference"—he waved a newspaper clipping—"that the Daphne would only cut the flight time from our bases to Russia by about twelve seconds. Now, Mr. Davidson of Uniforge says that's the *minimum* time that could be saved, and that it could be as much as two minutes. What do you say to that?"

Spots of color came into Manchester's tanned cheeks. "He's arguing about the difference between twelve seconds and a hundred and twenty seconds, and that's just quibbling in my book. I stand on the statement that this missile system gives no promise—*no* promise—of improving our defense capability. That's what I meant by 'enough's enough.' "

"What about that editorial in *Pravda?*" asked another delegate curtly.

"Yes, what about it?" echoed Manchester without irritation. "Just what does it mean? Certainly, if the Communists really wanted me nominated, the last thing they'd do is say something nice about me. But what their devious game is, I'm sure I don't know. At any rate, I hope no delegate in a Republican convention is going to be so gullible as to pay any attention to what the Reds say."

Speaker Rohrbaugh cocked his head and eyed Manchester appraisingly, as he might one of the black Angus steers on his farm at home. "Mr. Secretary," he said, "I'm going to ask a blunt question, since we're in private and there aren't any reporters here, and I hope it won't give offense."

Manchester nodded. "Please do."

"The story is going around," Rohrbaugh said deliberately, "that you have indicated privately you have no intention of putting a hold-down on bombs and missiles—that you only raised the issue to liven up the convention and, well, cater to the peace vote."

"That's a deliberate lie!" Manchester fired the charge at his questioner. "And, frankly, I do take offense at it. I think you're questioning my integrity, sir."

The Pennsylvanian, hardened in the cut-and-thrust of state-house politics, held Manchester's angry stare with his own eyes. "I accept your word, Mr. Secretary, but I wanted to hear it from you."

"Well, where did you hear such outrageous nonsense?" blazed Manchester. He stepped directly in front of Rohrbaugh. Archie had never seen him so angry.

"I have it on very good authority that your manager has been spreading the word that you didn't mean what you said." Governor Wilcox's man spoke calmly enough despite Manchester's sudden belligerency.

"I don't believe it for a minute," Manchester rasped. "I just don't believe it. Mr. O'Connell is an honorable man."

"Then you'd better issue some kind of statement," the Speaker suggested quietly. "A lot of delegates are hearing that you're privately repudiating your public statements, and they're calling you a welcher."

"A *what?*" Manchester almost shouted. He trembled as though making a physical effort to keep from striking the Pennsylvanian.

"Simmer down," said Rohrbaugh, his farmer's face still impassive. "I said 'welcher,' but it's not my choice of words, Mr. Secretary, I'm just telling you what other people are saying. I'm trying to be helpful."

Manchester glared at him without replying. In the embarrassed silence, several delegates near the door stood up, and in a moment the entire group was filing out of the room. Helena Potter remained behind, her black, kindly face reflecting sympathy and personal hurt.

"I don't blame you for getting mad, Mr. Secretary," she said. "I think the Speaker's action was inexcusable."

Manchester took her hand and patted it. "Thanks, Helena," he said, "if you don't mind my calling you that. It's been a long time since any man said anything like that to me."

"Cheer up," she said. "I think you've done a wonderful thing for our country."

Manchester was silent, but only until she had followed the other delegates out and the door closed behind her. Then he exploded again.

"Where's Obie?"

Archie shook his head. "I don't know."

"Well, get him. Right now."

"Yes, sir." He turned to leave, but Manchester stopped him.

"Wait a minute," the candidate said. "Do you know anything about this?"

"Not a thing, boss. It was as much of a surprise to me as—"

"Get me Obie!" Manchester interrupted. "Find him. I don't care if you have to call every hotel in Chicago."

13

Charles Manchester pulled on his suit coat very slowly and carefully, as though physical deliberation might help him control his temper. Never since his days as a Michigan halfback had he felt such a desire to hit someone. He should have struck the Pennsylvania Speaker for his audacity. Accusing him—in front of forty people—of being a liar!

Manchester's body was still trembling, but his mind began to move directly again. Benjamin Wilcox was obviously lost to him; if this were not the case, the Governor's henchman would never have dared address him so rudely. Had Rohrbaugh really been seeking information, he would have brought the matter up in private, where it would have been a legitimate inquiry. But what *had* Obie done? Could he possibly have lied in some cheap political intrigue? He better have a good answer when he arrived. . . . The thought fired his anger again. Manchester flexed his fingers, then walked to the window and stared out. He needed some movement to release the pressure.

The white telephone rang. Its bell was louder and more insistent than those of the two other phones flanking it. Manchester looked at it for a moment without quite accepting its summons. The direct line to the White House had not so much as murmured in three days—not since Saturday morning, before the press conference. He lifted the instrument slowly.

"Is the Secretary there?" It was Susie, President Stuart's secretary.

"Yes," Manchester said. "I'm on the phone."

"Charlie." The flat, resigned tone was characteristic of Fred Stuart in recent months.

"Yes, Mr. President," said Manchester. "It's good to hear from you. How are you feeling?"

"No better, no worse, Charlie, but thanks anyway. Have you got a few free minutes?"

"Certainly, Mr. President, as much as you like. You know that, sir."

"Charlie, let me be frank with you." The voice might be tired and old, but the tone was no less positive for that. "I don't like the sound of things I hear from out there. I thought you'd have called me by now—by way of explanation."

"Mr. President," said Manchester, choosing his words carefully, "I didn't think it was my place to call. I am a candidate, you know, sir, and I felt that determination should rest with you."

"Well, could you give me an explanation of this missile

thing? I'm sure the press reports can't be accurate."

"I think they are, Mr. President, from what I've seen at this end. And there's really not much to explain. I made my statement last Saturday and I'm standing by it, word for word, despite some shabby gossip to the contrary out here."

"Charlie," said the voice from the White House, "I don't like it. You realize, don't you, that you've challenged the judgment of an administration of which you're a part. I made the final decision on the Daphne contract after a pretty full discussion, as I recall."

"Yes, sir, and I dissented, too, if you'll recall, Mr. President," Manchester replied. "Of course, naturally I went along after the decision was made."

"But you're not going along now, Charlie." The voice had a plaintive note.

"Mr. President, I thought it was my duty to let the country know where I stand on one of the important questions facing it. I'm sorry if that puts us at odds, but really, Mr. President, as you know it's one of only a very, very few matters on which we differ."

"Charlie, I don't question your sincerity or your right to differ with me." Stuart's tone hardened. "But I can challenge your political judgment. That kind of thing has no business in a convention. You're splitting the party just when we need unity for the campaign."

"But it had to be said, Fred." Manchester was so intent that he dropped the formal form of address without thinking. "Otherwise I couldn't live with myself."

"A thing like that should have been talked out with the leaders first," insisted Stuart. "It should have been talked out with me. Charlie, that wasn't an act of team play."

Oh, the hell with team play, thought Manchester, this is too important for that. He had to fight the impulse to say exactly that, oath and all. "I'm sorry you see it that way, Mr. President."

"I've worked out a little statement, Charlie. I think it would clear the air for all of us."

Manchester was wary. "Yes, sir?"

"It's quite short, and I believe it would do the trick without compromising you in any way," Stuart said. "Listen. This would be a statement by you, and it goes like this: 'If nominated by the Republican convention, I propose to name a conference of scientific experts for the purpose of surveying the whole weapons and delivery systems field. The committee would be asked to make a definitive report several months from now. Until that time, my own views on the matter, which are already well known, would be held in abeyance.' That's all there is to it, Charlie."

That's plenty, thought Manchester. It's brief and clear— and it would compromise my stand. He played for time. "Mr. President, would you be kind enough to read that back slowly while I make a few notes here?"

"Sure, Charlie." The President repeated it, phrase by phrase. Then there was silence for a few moments before Manchester spoke again.

"I could subscribe to that, Mr. President, provided the last sentence were changed."

"What do you have in mind?" This time it was the man in the White House who was wary.

"Something like this," Manchester said. "Of course, this

is off the top of my head and, if you agree generally, we could smooth out the language: 'The guidelines for the committee study would be those I have already outlined, namely, whether this nation should commit further large sums of money to new weapons systems which may, in effect, duplicate those already in being.' "

The President spoke at once. "Charlie, that's not the same thing at all. You're just reinforcing your own opinion. What I'm anxious for you to do, for the sake of the party, is to withhold it—to provide time for a breathing spell, so to speak."

"But, Mr. President, I can't do that. I see this as one of the major issues in the campaign, assuming that Senator Hendrickson and the Democrats choose to contest the viewpoint."

"That's exactly what I'd hate to see," said Stuart. His voice had an edge to it now. "That could tear the country apart, Charlie. That kind of thing should be settled here—in the White House—without heat or rancor, and with plenty of solid scientific opinion."

"I don't regard this as essentially a scientific question at all," Manchester protested. "It's a question of national policy in which the people should have a voice."

"That leaves us about a hundred and eighty degrees apart, Charlie." The President spoke with finality.

"I'm afraid it does, Mr. President. But, as I said before, there are a hundred other things on which we're together."

"On this one, Charlie, I'm afraid I'm going to have to make my position clear."

"I understand, Mr. President." Manchester felt as though a great rock at his side had turned to powder, leaving him nothing to lean on. Had he been leaning on it? He wasn't sure, but what might have supported him was dissolving—rapidly.

"This has nothing to do with my personal regard for you, Charlie." The President followed the ritual of sincerity, but the words meant nothing.

"Nor mine for you, sir."

"This all could have been avoided," Stuart said wearily and somewhat remotely, "if you had talked to me about this before you went to Chicago."

"I won't take issue with you on that, Mr. President."

"Well. . . Good luck, Charlie."

"Good-by, Mr. President."

Fred Stuart turned his swivel chair and faced the long French windows overlooking the rose garden. The August heat smothered Washington and the broad, shiny leaves of the magnolias drooped without luster. The midday sun struck down mercilessly. The President sat and thought, as still and wilted as the flowers in the garden outside.

Then he turned back to his desk, picked up a pen and began to write on a memo pad which bore the seal of his office. He scratched out several words and wrote above them. Once he smiled faintly, thinking of the historian who would come across this slip someday in the Stuart papers. Could he re-create the emotions of the writer—frustration, disappointment, sadness? That was the essence of it: sadness. Manchester, a great man in many ways, had shown a fatal weakness. Of what value courage, intelligence and integrity in this oval office in the west wing, if a man lacked political antennae? He'd be mired in woe before the last of his inaugural address trailed into memory. Bin Roberts, for all his girth and his—well—lack of depth, would understand that. There was no perfect man for this job, but some were more fitted than others.

President Stuart sighed and reached for his buzzer.

"Marty," he said to his press secretary, "call the boys in. I've got a little statement for them."

In a few minutes six reporters stood in a semicircle around his desk. Three of them Stuart had never seen until the previous morning; most of the top Washington correspondents were in Chicago, he realized, to chronicle the crowning of a new king. For the dying king, there were summer-replacement courtiers. Stuart smiled sympathetically. We're all second-stringers here now, he thought.

"Gentlemen," he said, "I've been fretting about your curiosity yesterday morning when you asked for my reaction to the developments in Chicago. Curiosity is a laudable virtue, and I was remiss in not rewarding it on the spot."

The reporters grinned and as one man produced notebooks and pencils from their pockets.

"So I have a short statement here," the President continued. "I'll read it slowly: 'Delegates to the Republican National Convention have a solemn duty to select the man best fitted to carry the standard of this old and proud party. Each delegate should reach his own decision on his own, without outside pressure or influence. That is the American way.

" 'I am not a delegate. If I were a delegate, I would resent any effort at dictation, from whatever source. If I were a delegate, I would exercise my own judgment. The White House has no official choice. The decision is up to the delegates, as free and independent men and women.'

"That's all, gentlemen," the President concluded.

A reporter looked up from his hurried scribbling. "But, Mr. President, yesterday you told us that if you were a delegate it would be natural for you to vote for Manchester."

Stuart nodded—reluctantly, it seemed. "From here on," he said, "it'll have to be off the record. For background only. Yesterday I was not in possession of the full facts from Chicago. Today I am."

"But, sir, you've let Senator Floberg's statement stand for two months—the one where he said you were for Manchester."

Stuart jabbed at the corner of his desk blotter with an ivory letter opener, a gift from the prime minister of India. "That's right. But I think it's obvious that the situation in Chicago in the last few days has changed a lot of attitudes."

"Would you still vote for Manchester if you were a delegate?" The questioner watched Stuart's face closely for reaction.

"I am not a delegate." Stuart kept his face blank. "Therefore, the question is academic."

"But this will be interpreted as meaning you're turning your back on Manchester."

"I can't control the interpretations. I'd merely point out that my statement says no such thing. It says that the choice at this convention is up to the delegates."

"Mr. President, have you talked to Manchester about this?"

"I talked to Secretary Manchester today," Stuart replied. "I can't go into the conversation."

"How about Roberts, sir?"

Stuart thought for a moment, then shook his head. "No, I haven't talked to the Governor in some time."

The newsmen prodded and pried for a few more minutes. Their only reward was a compliment. "Gentlemen," the President said with a smile, "as Lyndon Johnson used to say, you ought to get A for effort."

"Thank you, Mr. President." The brief press conference was over. The reporters walked swiftly to the door of the President's office, then broke into a clattering run in the hall and raced for the press room. One man skidded into the drinking fountain, unable to make the sharp turn on the waxed floors.

*   *   *

Manchester was standing by a window in the Royal Skyway suite a few minutes later when Archie brought him a yellow sheet torn from a news ticker.

UPI Convention 67
Bulletin—Stuart Dumps Manchester

There was an empty space on the page, and then another item:

UPI Convention 68
  Washington—President Stuart this afternoon abruptly canceled his support of Treasury Secretary Charles B. Manchester and threw the Republican presidential nomination open to the "free and independent" choice of the delegates.
  His action bolstered the swiftly rising hopes of Gov. Bryan Roberts of California and dealt another blow to the sagging Manchester forces.
                    (Text follows)
  EDW225PCDT

Archie ran his fingers through his curly black hair. He felt the prickles of fatigue on his scalp. His eyes were gritty. Four hours' sleep wasn't enough—especially three nights running.

"That's rough, boss," he said.

"I expected it," Manchester said. "Fred called me a while ago. He wanted me to back down. I wouldn't."

Archie tried to put a lilt into his voice. "So we've got to win it on our own. We can do it."

"Of course we can," Manchester said. His confidence was obviously genuine. "But there's the other thing to settle first. Did you find Obie?"

"He's on his way up."

"When he gets here, send him right in. But you'd better stay outside. I want to see Obie alone."

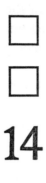

14

Obie O'Connell gestured toward the torn piece of yellow ticker copy on the coffee table.

"That's bad trouble, Charlie," he said glumly.

Manchester seated himself on the sofa and motioned O'Connell to the nearest easy chair. Watching the manager massage his round cheeks, the candidate himself felt the twinges of weariness for the first time. What a man needs at a political convention, he thought, is some kind of portable sleep machine. He shook the thought off.

"That's not what I want to talk to you about, Obie. There's something more important."

O'Connell eyed him with frank curiosity. "What the hell could be more important than that right now?"

"Obie," said Manchester slowly, "the Speaker of the Pennsylvania House stood here this morning and called me a liar. He said you're quoting me as saying I didn't really mean it on the missile thing."

"Where'd he get that?" O'Connell did not look directly at Manchester.

"He didn't say. 'Reliable authority,' or some such. Obie, *have* you said anything like that?"

O'Connell leaned forward, his elbows on his knees. The whites of his eyes showed flecks of red and the pouches underneath were fat little balls. "Look, Charlie, your press conference put us on the spot. By Sunday night we were in rough shape—and it's getting worse instead of better."

"Obie, I want an answer." Manchester's eyes fixed on O'Connell's. The manager's wavered. "Did you tell anyone, at any time, that I did not mean what I said Saturday?"

O'Connell twisted in the big chair. "Well, yes, sort of, that is. Look, Charlie, it kind of slipped out. Sunday night I had a couple of drinks."

The manager went on to recount his meeting at the Pick-Congress bar with the Minnesota chairman and Bones Cramer. Manchester listened, much in the manner of a ship's captain hearing an offending sailor describe what happened after "a couple of beers."

"So," O'Connell concluded, "I was just trying to start a backfire. At the time, it seemed like a great idea. A manager has to do what he can. But I haven't said a word like that since Sunday night. Charlie, I'm sorry."

Manchester could feel his anger seeping away as O'Connell talked. After all, he mused, Obie was trying to cover up for a mistake that he thinks I made. When he responded, he spoke gently. "Well, I'd better put out some kind of statement reaffirming my stand. Then I think you ought to get Cramer and that Minnesota man up here and we'll just tell them the truth. The same goes, I should think, for the Speaker."

O'Connell shook his head. "Please let me handle this my way, Charlie. I'll tell Cramer and the others, but not up here—in front of you."

"Why not?"

"Okay, so call it face, or something." O'Connell's mouth set stubbornly. "I've been in this game twenty-five years, Charlie. I can't bring old pals up here and confess like some kid in front of the teacher."

"That's the way I want it," insisted Manchester. "I don't want a single iota of doubt about where I stand. I want to tell them myself—and I want you here when I do it."

O'Connell stood up. "Charlie, that's playing it like an amateur. People like Andersen and Bones wouldn't understand it at all. I'm really not worrying about me so much as about you. They won't like you for it."

"My integrity has been questioned," said Manchester. Now he felt the anger come pounding back. "It's been a long time since any man called me a liar."

"Integrity!" scoffed O'Connell. "You're a candidate, Charlie, and you're taking a licking. This is one helluva time to be worrying about integrity."

Manchester rose and the two men faced each other. "As a manager," Manchester said acidly, "I would think you'd find that particular item salable in this convention. There doesn't seem to be too much of it around here right now."

"I'm not your manager, Charlie, I'm just another one of your errand boys—like Archie. A manager is supposed to *run* a campaign. He's got to have some leeway to operate. Take that Mississippi deal. I suppose you didn't like that either."

"I haven't questioned that at all," Manchester replied. "I just assumed you did the best you could."

"Well, that's something," O'Connell said grudgingly. "Look, Charlie, I really am sorry about Sunday night."

"I know you are, Obie. All I ask is that we settle this thing right now before it goes any further."

"But you want to settle it your way, Charlie, not my way." O'Connell thrust a finger at the lapel of Manchester's coat. "You've got to start relying on your manager—if it isn't too late already. Your little red wagon is falling apart."

"I don't see it that way."

"Yes, you do. You just won't admit it." O'Connell's voice rose. "You've lost the President. You've lost on the defense plank. You've lost Pennsylvania. Since Saturday you've lost damn near a hundred delegates. I had to make a bad deal on Mississippi. Charlie, the boat is leaking like a sieve. Unless a rescue team turns up pretty quick, you're sunk."

"Then you refuse to bring Cramer and the others up here and tell them the truth?"

O'Connell ignored the demand. He pulled a folded paper from his coat pocket and shook it at Manchester. "See that list? There are ninety-two names on it. Every one is a delegate who used to be for you and has gone over to Roberts since Saturday noon. There'll be plenty more if we keep on this way. But if you give me a green light, I can bring some of them back."

"How?"

"That's my business." O'Connell was curt.

"With deals I wouldn't make myself, Obie?" asked Manchester disdainfully.

"With plain common sense." A flush of anger spread over O'Connell's pudgy cheeks. "Jesus, Charlie, even Lincoln wouldn't have been nominated if his managers had obeyed his orders. Go down the list of the big ones, Wilson, Roosevelt, Eisenhower. You think they put the reins on their managers the way you're doing? It's crazy. Roberts and his guys are playing it rough. In the close ones, you got to have room to operate."

"This is entirely different," objected Manchester. "In this case, it's a simple question of whether or not I'm a liar. If I were, I wouldn't deserve the nomination."

"If I can't take care of it my way," said O'Connell sourly, "the ball game's over."

"You mean you're quitting?"

"If I've got to play your rules, yes."

"No, you're not." Manchester's face hardened. "You're fired."

O'Connell stood silent for a moment, studying Manchester. His lips moved as though he were about to speak, but he merely lifted his hands, let them fall and turned toward the door.

Again the anger in Manchester ebbed swiftly, to be replaced this time by a weary sadness. His mind ran back over the months since he'd first met this simple, friendly man who had done so much for him. Obie, even more than Archie, had become a part of him, a working part which moved in

CONVENTION
harmony with the whole of him. He felt dismembered, as though a surgeon had obeyed a sudden command to amputate a limb.

O'Connell paused at the door and looked at Manchester without animosity. "Charlie, I got a lotta friends in this convention. You'll do yourself less harm if you don't announce that I've been fired. Just say I've been carted off to the hospital with a sudden attack—like moral leprosy, or something."

"Obie!" Manchester came striding toward him.

"Nope," said O'Connell, waving him off. "No postscripts, please. They get sloppy." He was already through the door and closing it behind him as he spoke.

When Archie entered the room a few minutes later, Manchester was slumped in the easy chair O'Connell had recently vacated. He seemed now less a candidate for high office than a tourist who had tired of sightseeing and realized he was a stranger in an alien city.

"Obie tells me he's out," said Archie.

Manchester nodded. He described the exchange hurriedly, as though reluctant to dwell on painful memories.

Archie felt hope draining from him, and his ulcer throbbed. Less than forty-eight hours to go—and no Obie! Who could take over? Who knew what to do Thursday? Never mind Thursday. Who knew what to do right now? His thoughts whirled and skittered like leaves in a cold November wind. It was an effort to focus on the immediate problems.

"Well, Obie's right," he said at last. "We can't say he was fired. I'll say he's in the hospital. Under an assumed name, I guess, but I don't think there's much chance the newspapers will swallow that one."

Manchester made no protest, though the thought occurred to him that he was now temporizing with the truth when only a few minutes ago he had dismissed a manager for doing the same thing. Of course, he assured himself, the two cases were not on the same level at all. A little white lie could hardly be compared with a question of personal probity on an issue that concerned all mankind. But the parallel nagged at the corners of his mind nonetheless. Obie O'Connell was gone, but he had left an unwanted ethical bequest.

"Who's our new manager?" asked Archie.

"You are." Manchester said it as if it were a fact long known to all.

"*Me?*" Archie stared at his employer in total disbelief. "Look, boss, I don't know the first thing about running a convention campaign. My God, this is the first one I've ever been to."

"You can learn." Manchester smiled wanly. "In fact, we've both got a lot to learn, it seems. Seriously, Archie, I trust you, and that's the main thing right now. You can get plenty of advice on details from the floor managers."

Archie felt as though the ceiling had collapsed on him and he were standing amid a pile of rubble, wondering how to rebuild—and with what. He wasn't a carpenter, he didn't know how to plaster, and to top it all he had an ulcer which was suddenly screaming for relief. Just what should he do next? Archie stood in the center of the room. He had never felt so helpless and unstrung.

One of the volunteer workers stepped brightly into the room. Her smile was radiant and her two-way Manchester button— you saw a picture or a slogan, depending on the angle of sight—shimmered above one breast. She looks as cheerful, thought Archie, as if she was about to lead the grand march at the Inaugural Ball.

"Senator Floberg is here and would like to see you if it's convenient, Mr. Secretary," she said.

"Of course. Send him right in." Manchester brightened, not so much at the appearance of the pretty girl as at the mention of the caller's name. Boise Floberg of Iowa, Republican leader of the United States Senate, had been one of the first recruits to the Manchester candidacy. He was a slow-mannered man with a comfortable, rough-cut face and unhurried speech. His advice was always sound, and Manchester had taken to him from his first days in Washington.

Floberg crossed the room and shook hands with Manchester. Archie made a move toward the door, but Floberg beckoned him back. "No secrets here, Archie," he said.

A lock of sandy hair fell loosely over the senator's forehead. He had the look of the soil about him, from this cowlick to his large freckled hands. He owned hundreds of acres of Iowa corn land, as his father had before him.

Manchester offered Floberg a chair, but the senator declined. All three men remained standing, a bit awkwardly.

"I'm here on a mission that I don't enjoy, Charlie," said the Republican leader.

"Oh." Manchester's eyebrows lifted.

"Yes. This is one of those things where it would have been easier to phone or send you a note. But I don't play that way, Charlie. You've got a right to hear it straight from me."

"Bad news, Boise?"

Floberg nodded. "Charlie, I'm going to switch to Bin Roberts."

Manchester looked as though he had been slapped across the mouth. He stood stunned for a moment, and when he did speak, it was in a small, remote voice.

"Why?" he asked.

"Yes, why?" Floberg frowned. "I didn't get much sleep last night, Charlie, and after I saw Fred Stuart's statement a little while ago I guessed that he didn't either."

The senator paused. "Charlie, that 'why' would be self-evident to the President and myself, as old as we are at this game. But we're the ones who should be asking you why. Why would you say a thing like you did at that press conference without consulting us? Why would you split your own party without talking with your friends first? Why would you suddenly try to take the whole country down a completely new path without any notice? Why?"

The series of questions gave Manchester time to recover. He thrust his hands into the side pockets of his suit coat. He looked down at the senator, for he was slightly taller.

"Boise, that's not fair. It's not at all fair. I've discussed this thing with you at least twice that I can remember, and I thought we were in some measure of agreement. As for the President, I couldn't have been more explicit in my views. I dissented vigorously when the Daphne contract was awarded."

"I know that." Floberg waved his hand in dismissal. "But you completely ignored us when you got out here and decided to sound off on it. You gave us no warning whatsoever. Good Lord, Charlie, we were in your corner as solidly as any two men could be in politics. Why didn't you talk to me about it first?"

"All right, charge it up as a neophyte's mistake," Manchester conceded. "But is it such a crime? I was asked a legitimate question and I gave an honest answer."

"But if you'd talked this over first with the leaders, the people who'd gone out on the limb for you, we could have arranged something for the next session of Congress—a study, a commission, anything."

"And kept the issue out of the campaign?" Manchester snapped.

"Of course," said Floberg. "That kind of issue is awfully complicated. It's really for the technical people to argue about. It hasn't much business in a campaign—and certainly none at all in a convention."

"I disagree with you," said Manchester. "This is a question for the people. It's their life and their death. It's too important to leave to the scientists."

"Well, I disagree with *you,* Mr. Secretary, one hundred per cent. That's why I'm switching to Roberts."

Manchester advanced a step closer to Floberg. "Tell me, Boise, has either Mark Davidson or Gus Maguire talked to you?"

Floberg's jaw tightened. "I don't like the implication in that question, Mr. Secretary. I think you'd better withdraw it."

"If you asked *me* that, I'd answer it," said Manchester doggedly. Now he was angry again.

"I understand," said Floberg slowly, "that you almost bit one delegate's head off this morning when he implied that you really didn't mean what you said. Now you seem to be challenging my integrity."

The set of Manchester's face softened perceptibly. He had the look of an abruptly chastened man. "I apologize, Boise,

you're right," he said. "The question—and the implication—
was out of bounds."

"I accept the apology, Mr. Secretary," said Floberg stiffly.
"But for whatever it's worth to him, I'm going to vote Thursday for Bryan Roberts."

Manchester tried to end with a pleasantry, but his spirit
wasn't in it. "Until now, Boise," he said with a weak smile,
"I've always admired your judgment. And I think you used to
respect mine. At least we can part as friends."

The two men shook hands, as embarrassed as was Archie,
standing off to one side. With a slight bow—exasperatingly
formal, thought Archie—the Senate leader turned and left.

Archie slipped out with him. "Do you have to make a public
announcement of your . . . uh . . . switch, Senator?"

"I intend to, yes."

"Could I talk you into holding off until Thursday?" Archie
jerked his head toward the room they had just left. "They're
rocking the man pretty hard today. If you could . . ."

"As a favor to you, Archie," said Floberg, dropping a
friendly hand on the press secretary's shoulder. "And to Obie.
This is pretty rough on you fellows, too, seeing six months of
hard work going down the drain."

"Well, Obie . . ." Archie began, but the senator was already
walking out past the row of desks where the bright college
girls sat and smiled.

As Archie turned to re-enter the sitting room, one of the
volunteers hurried ahead of him, carrying the late editions of
the afternoon papers. The staff had orders from Manchester
to deliver copies of each edition to him as soon as they reached
the newsstand in the lobby. Archie caught a glimpse of one

headline and tried to stop the girl, but she was already half-way across the room toward the candidate.

Manchester spread out the papers on the coffee table. The Chicago *Daily News* proclaimed, in its top headline: "Manchester Drive Crumbles." The *American* had a double-deck banner: "President Dumps Manchester as Roberts Soars on Missile Issue."

Manchester rubbed the back of his head. Archie saw the deep disappointment in his eyes as he skimmed the political stories covering the front pages. The Treasury Secretary leaned back on the sofa. His face seemed drained and tired, without even a glimmer of the enthusiasm and zest which always shone from Manchester like a trademark.

"Don't tell me you're leaving, too, Archie," he said dryly. "I'd cut my throat—if I could find anybody to lend me a razor blade."

"Boss, we've still got about forty-five hours. We're going to fight."

"Go down fighting, huh?" The candidate spoke sardonically, and it occurred to Archie that he sounded more like Obie O'Connell than Charles B. Manchester.

"What have I got next on the schedule?" asked Manchester a moment later.

"Nothing till seven," Archie said. "Then you've got about two hours' work. We've got three delegations scheduled to come up."

"Cancel them," ordered Manchester. "I'm dead-tired."

"But, boss . . ."

"I'll fight tomorrow." Manchester managed a smile. "But not tonight. Tonight I want to be left alone. The wounded knight alone in his castle. Pull up the drawbridge over the moat, Archie."

When Archie left, the candidate was standing with a hand again rubbing the back of his neck. He stared moodily down at the newspapers which chronicled his undoing. Archie closed the door softly.

Back at his own cluttered desk, the new manager thought a minute and then placed a long-distance call to a cottage on Lake Winnipesaukee in New Hampshire. Ten minutes passed before Julia Manchester came to the phone. She held the receiver with a towel while water dripped from her bathing suit onto the floor, and she listened quietly as Archie DuPage told of the day's reverses.

"So," he concluded, "if you could get out here, I think maybe it would—"

"Don't worry," she interrupted in her husky, abrupt voice. "I'll be there tonight if I have to charter my own plane."

15

It was nine o'clock before the resolutions committee chairman finished reading the platform in a high, hurried singsong. No more than half the delegates were in McCormick Place for the convention's second session, and those who had come were bored. Even a series of illustrations projected on a big screen —designed to show the television audience that the G.O.P. had the heart of Florence Nightingale, the wisdom of Solomon and the thriftiness of Ben Franklin—failed to lighten the tedium.

There were gaps in the spectator tiers as well as on the floor, and the auditorium yawned like an open mouth with a third of its teeth missing. Approval of the platform was a foregone conclusion, as was the fact that the evening's only

speech—Joe Terhune's address as permanent chairman—
would be less than electric. The party, from President Stuart
to precinct captains, loved Terhune; but the party also had
listened for thirty years as he struggled to rise above platitudes,
and it knew the platitudes would win every time. Few wanted
to suffer with him through another defeat.

The committee chairman intoned the last sentence of the
platform and Terhune, his hair snow-white under the arc
lights, brought his gavel down thankfully.

"Do I hear a motion to adopt the report of the committee
on resolutions?" he suggested.

"I so move," cried a voice from the floor.

"Second the motion."

A tall, bald man wearing a yellow bow tie spoke from the
microphone at the Kansas standard.

"Mr. Chairman, Roger Abbott, chairman of the Kansas
delegation, speaking. May I ask, has a motion been filed with
the chair to amend the language of the defense plank?"

"The chair has received no such motion," replied Terhune.

"Thank you, Mr. Chairman," said Abbott, his Adam's
apple bobbing in rhythm with his speech. "I thought, in view
of the great outcry here in the last few days, that a move
might be made this evening to reverse the resolutions committee. I am pleased there will be no such effort. If there had
been, I'm sure it would have been overwhelmingly defeated on
this floor."

Cheers mingled with a few boos, but both were good-
natured. The convention was in no mood for a brannigan
tonight, and it shouted its approval of the platform without
further discussion. Few delegates would ever refer to it again.

After a few preliminaries, Joe Terhune cleared his throat, planted his hands firmly on the upper corners of the rostrum, glanced at the teleprompter and began.

"Fellow delegates to this convention, and fellow Americans: Never before in the history of our beloved nation has a great party assembled in such a critical period . . ." Terhune's sonorous and totally anticipated phrases began to roll over the audience like billows of steam in a Turkish bath.

Almost immediately a low murmur arose along the aisles of the delegate sections, as those who had decided to listen to the speech thought better of it and started whispered conversations with their neighbors. When Terhune finally roared through his peroration a half hour later, they fired off one noisy volley of applause and quickly trooped to the exits.

The delegates went back to their hotels, where endless streams of curious people wandered through the great lobbies in search of a face that would match one they had seen in the newspapers. The curious laughed, shrieked, guffawed and pointed as they would on the sawdust paths of a carnival midway, unsure of what might happen next but sure that something would. Round and round they milled, inspecting everything and seeing nothing. They peeked into gloomy, unlighted banquet rooms, lifted the covers off trays borne by harassed waiters, stole ashtrays for souvenirs, and congregated in cheerful knots around the little booths where spangled girls gave out literature and campaign buttons.

This aimless elation reached its peak at the Sheraton-Blackstone, headquarters of Governor Bryan Roberts and his workers. The stone steps leading from the sidewalk to the lobby were jammed with the curious, many of them waving at the

TV cameras focused on the entrance under arc lights. A commentator, microphone in hand and voice full of portent, was elucidating the obvious for his world beyond the camera.

"Victory," he said, "has a smell of its own. The convention crowds can scent it, even as the trackers can sniff out a lion's trail on a big game hunt. And here at the Blackstone, the headquarters of Governor Roberts, there's the smell of victory tonight. The balloting is still two days away, but these people think they smell a winner."

On the ninth floor the target of this olfactory fervor, Governor Bryan Roberts, pushed his way through a solid mass of people in the narrow corridor. Sweat ran freely in the creases of his neck and his full face glowed with satisfaction. His shirt was soggy and his tie had somehow been hauled askew across his chest. People pumped his meaty hands, plucked at his sleeves, thumped him on the back.

The ninth floor was crammed to capacity, but two elevators nevertheless disgorged a dozen members of a girls' golden band. They shoved into a semblance of a file and inched their way forward with trumpets and trombones blaring.

> *California, Here We Come,*
> *Bryan Roberts, He's the One . . .*

A cheer punctuated the music and a half dozen signs waved over the crowd. "Enough's Enough—Go Roberts" . . . "I Am Not a Delegate: Pres. Stuart" . . . "Win With Bin" . . . "Daphne Sí, Manchester No" . . . "Don't Bet a Gnat's Eye on Manchester." One sign bobbed steadily in front of a TV camera, provoking the inevitable cascade of curses. When these proved ineffective, the enraged cameramen lunged at the signholder who toppled into the bosom of a fat woman who fell back on the arches of a thin youngster who yelped with pain. The chain reaction spilled a dozen people against the wall like falling dominoes.

A husky hireling of the "Midnight" television show was delving into history, less for educational purposes than because he had run out of current material.

"This scene of jubilation by the Roberts people is on the ninth floor of the Blackstone," he was saying into his microphone, "just four floors above that famous 'smoke-filled room' where Republican leaders selected Warren G. Harding in 1920. The fifth floor also housed the convention headquarters staff of General Eisenhower in 1952 . . ."

The "Midnight" man spotted Carl Fleischer's smoked glasses and he tunneled through the crowd, talking as he went, until he reached Fleischer's side. He pointed out the Roberts manager to his cameraman with a sweeping overarm gesture and thrust the mike forward.

"This is Carl Fleischer, Governor Roberts' manager," he explained triumphantly to his audience. "Carl, this looks like pandemonium for your man. How do you size things up at 10:47 P.M. here in Chicago?"

Fleischer put his cigar behind his back and with the other hand fingered the pill case in his coat pocket. "Ordinarily," he said into the microphone, "I'm not much impressed by crowds, but this demonstration tonight is different. The delegates can sense a winner, and they know it's Governor Roberts."

"What's your estimate now, Carl, on the voting?"

"Roberts will be nominated, period."

"First ballot?"

"As my old friend Obie O'Connell says, you always win on the last ballot."

"Now, there's something you won't hear very often," said the interviewer, turning to face the camera while he took the listening audience into the mysterious world of first-name, big-time politics, "a campaign manager quoting the other side. Obie O'Connell is Manchester's manager." He turned back to Fleischer and lowered his voice confidentially, in the manner of a race-track tout. "Speaking of O'Connell, there's a rumor he's out. What about it, Carl?"

Fleischer shook his head and the lights glimmered on his dark glasses. "Don't know a thing about the opposition. I've got enough problems of my own."

"What about the report that Boise Floberg, the Senate Republican leader, may switch to Roberts?"

"Could be," said Fleischer. "Everybody's switching to Roberts."

The interviewer grinned like a man sharing a jest with an old friend. "Thank you, Carl. That was Carl Fleischer, Governor Bryan Roberts' manager, and as you can see he's a happy man tonight."

A slim blonde, wearing a huge golden Roberts button and a look of pained fascination, elbowed her way to Fleischer's side. "Gus Maguire wants you on the phone," she whispered.

It took Fleischer five minutes to negotiate the few yards to his room. A single bed had been shoved against the wall. The rest of the room was a jumble of telephones, stray pieces of clothing, newspapers and sheets of paper covered with penciled names and tabulations.

"Yeah, Gus. This is Carl."

"My thirty-three Missile Worker delegates just caucused and went unanimously for Roberts," said Maguire over the phone. "You want to make an announcement of it, or would you rather keep it quiet for a while?"

"No, no, let it go. I want to keep that bandwagon rolling. Any break you hear of, fire it in here. On this one, get one of the delegates to put it out. That's better than having us do it. Tell him what to do."

"Okay, Carl, I'll keep in touch."

Fleischer looked at his watch. Eleven o'clock. He sighed, poured a modest splash of bourbon into a glass, and filled it with ice and water. Opening the little pill case, he selected the right rack and picked off a green capsule. He popped it into his mouth and washed it down with the whisky.

Roger Abbott and Art Segunda, the floor manager and the computer wizard, arrived for the nightly position count. Abbott brought more good news. Hawaii, one of a dozen completely uncommitted delegations, had just caucused at the LaSalle and decided to vote unanimously for Roberts. Eight more votes. The three men took out their lists and compared totals. Abbott, from his contacts, and Segunda, from his latest bout with his computer, each came up with about 420 certain votes for Roberts. Fleischer, more cautious, believed the base of sure votes to be about 400 out of the 655 needed to nominate.

"We ought to charge Mark Davidson rental time on the computer," said Segunda. In the quiet decor of the Blackstone, his red hair shone like a torch. "About every hour he calls for something new. We ought to call Oscar the 'Mark D'."

"For God's sake," said Fleischer, "don't tell anybody we're letting Davidson use that machine, Art."

"Don't worry," Segunda assured him. "Nobody even knows about Oscar except your floor managers." An expression of longing, as for a faraway tropical island, came over his face. "I wish we could give Oscar some new input," he said. "With his data storage, he could keep a book on every delegate. I've got some good ideas for the next convention."

"If we win this one," snapped Fleischer, "we won't need to worry about delegates next time."

The phone rang. Fleischer listened and made a note on a pad. "How do you spell that? . . . Oh, with a K . . . Kolsak. John Kolsak, New York. Yeah, I got it now." The manager printed the name and handed it to Segunda.

"Back to the salt mine, Art," he said. "Davidson wants everything we've got on a John Kolsak, a delegate from New York. Manhattan, I think. He needs it right away. Call him at the Executive House number."

"After midnight I get double time," said Segunda. But he left happily enough, waving a salute off his crown of carrot-red hair.

"Are we all set on those gallery tickets, Roger?" asked Fleischer.

The floor manager nodded. "We get them tomorrow night from the printer. I don't want any of that stuff floating around until we need it. We'll hand 'em out Thursday morning."

As the two men talked on, Tuesday became Wednesday and a kind of fever gripped the whole ninth-floor Roberts headquarters. In the suite of offices where the volunteers labored, the jangling of telephones became a symphony of discords.

Coffee cartons and sandwich wrappers covered the desks like picnic lunches in a public park. The girls squealed at the news coming over the phones—it was all good for Roberts—and hurried about with eager, flushed faces, carrying bits of paper from one room to another.

The hall outside Roberts' own suite bulged with people waiting to see him. Many wore expressions of harassed determination, as if willing to wait until breakfast, if necessary, to see the candidate. Every five minutes or so, as he ushered his latest caller out, Roberts himself would appear at the door. An exclamation of pleased recognition would flash through the crowd, accented with cries of "Atta baby, Bin," or "Yea, Roberts!" The Governor grinned and waved a heavy arm aloft each time.

The ninth-floor lobby, into which the elevators opened, was still a welter of people, most of them beginning to look rumpled and seedy. The carpeting was littered with the day's debris—cigarette stubs, newspapers, matches, and scraps of exposed movie film. Against the wall sat a half dozen reporters, one lucky one on a chair, the others on the floor.

The newspapermen scrambled to their feet when the center elevator door slid open to reveal a new visitor. It was Grace Orcott, and her appearance seemed to brighten and freshen the dingy post-midnight air of the lobby. Her silver-white hair, swept upward from her forehead, glistened under the floodlights. Her beige dress, neatly tucked and pressed, seemed as fresh as the morning that was still hours away. The reporters, welcoming the touch of elegance, surrounded her. A television man pushed a hand mike toward her.

"What brings you up here at this hour, Mrs. Orcott?"

She smiled in dismissal of the question. "Just a routine appointment with the Governor, gentlemen. I've been trying all evening, and this was the earliest he could see me."

"Do you agree there's a bandwagon going for Roberts?"

"The Governor is doing very, very well," she said. Waving the microphone away, she walked down the hall leading to Roberts' suite. The reporters trailed behind her. She waited a few minutes in the crowd at the candidate's door; then Bryan Roberts appeared with his latest caller. The California Governor beamed at her.

"Grace!" he said. "As beautiful as ever!"

Grace Orcott stayed in suite 901 almost half an hour. When she left, her smile for the newspapermen was as gracious as ever, but she declined comment. Alone in the elevator, she sat on the little upholstered bench and chewed at her lower lip.

16

In the row of offices adjacent to the Conrad Hilton's Royal Skyway suite, lights burned over empty desks. Papers littered the floors and one corner of a long wall poster—"The Man Who? Manchester!"—had been torn away from its thumbtacks. It drooped like a flag in a dead calm. Only the occasional ring of a telephone marred the small-hours stillness, and the lone girl on duty easily handled the infrequent calls by moving from desk to desk. Two scrubwomen had started work, several hours ahead of their usual mopping-up time. One of them retrieved a poster picture of Manchester from the floor, wiped off the heel marks and held it up in front of her for a moment. Then she crumpled the portrait and stuffed it in her trash basket.

Archie DuPage sat in a swivel chair in the room immediately adjoining the candidate's suite. His feet were propped on the desk, his tie was loosened, and a stubble of beard made little dark patches around his jawbone. He felt half drugged, yearning for sleep but unwilling to make the effort to walk to his bedroom a few yards down the hall.

Kay Orcott sat on a corner of the desk, her legs crossed and her eyes fixed on Archie with amusement. She tapped cigarette ash into a paper cup.

"Well, now you know what it's like to be a manager," she said.

"Manager!" Archie snorted. "Some manager. And all he knows is what it's like to lose."

Kay ran her free hand through her close-cropped hair. "Things can't be that bad, Archie. You're looking at a flesh-and-blood example of the 'Switch-to-Manchester' movement."

"It's an interesting example, all right," he said, eying her legs, "but unfortunately it doesn't mean one vote in this convention."

Kay shook her head. "Honestly, Archie, I just don't believe things are as bad as you think."

"Name me one single little encouraging sign in this whole long lousy day," he said glumly.

"Well, I may not know anything about politics, but I can listen, and I hear people saying lots of nice things about Manchester."

"Oh, sure. Everybody pities the guy about to be trampled by the stampede going thataway." He swept his arm around. "Okay, name me one person who's saying 'nice things' about Manchester—one delegate, that is."

"There are plenty of them." She dropped her cigarette in the paper cup. It hissed in the dregs of cold coffee. "And some people are . . . well, sort of upset."

"Like who, for instance?" Archie refused to be encouraged.

"Well, like Mother, for instance. I mean, she—" Kay stopped. Wait a minute, she thought, you talked too much once and Archie's had nothing but trouble since. But Mother *did* sound upset, as if she was beginning to have some pretty serious doubts. . . . Kay looked at Archie and wondered how she really felt about him, and suddenly felt a rush of emotion —was it only pity?—for this bedraggled, overwhelmed guy. He's in such a mess. I think I like him a lot.

Kay made up her mind and leaned forward, snapping her fingers under his nose to rouse him. "Mother's *upset*," she repeated.

"She is? That's too bad." He stretched and yawned.

"Yes, she is. I mean, she called up Governor Roberts tonight and insisted that he see her. About Oscar."

"That so?" He showed only mild interest. "Who's Oscar?"

"Oscar keeps track of all the delegates, and I bet you didn't know *that*, Mr. Manager."

"Well, if Oscar can keep track of thirteen hundred delegates, he's a good man," said Archie sleepily. "All by himself? We have four or five girls running our card file."

"Oscar isn't a man." She said it a trifle impatiently.

"Oh?"

"No. Oscar is a computer."

"A what?"

"A *computer*. That's right. You know, one of those electronic things with a memory and a typewriter that writes out the answers by itself, and everything. The Roberts people keep it hidden in an old place over on Clark Street."

"Are you kidding, Kay?" He said it as if he were sure that she was.

"Cross my heart"—she did—"and hope to die. They have a computer that stores up all kinds of facts about the delegates. When they want to find out everything about Mr. So-and-so, they just push a button. A man named Segunda, with red hair, runs it."

Archie pulled his feet off the desk and grasped Kay's thighs to swing her around so that she faced him directly.

"All right, honey," he said. "I'm listening now. Tell me some more."

"I'm not sure I should." Kay paused. "I don't know if Mother—"

Archie interrupted. "Kay, anything about your mother goes no further than this room, but this computer thing could be big stuff."

"Well," she said uncertainly, "the computer and Mother, they're kind of mixed up together. I mean, I'm not sure . . ."

Archie stood and spread his hands, palms open. "Trust me to sort it out, Kay. Please, give me a break."

Under his prodding, Kay related several conversations with her mother about Oscar. At first, Grace Orcott was intrigued by the machine, even though she didn't like some of the things it had stored away about her. But the more she thought about it—especially the fact that it not only knew all about her husband's income, and their mortgage, but also about Kay's baby brother who died of a birth injury when he was only four days old—the less she liked it. Then she found out somehow that Mark Davidson of Uniforge was using the computer to get information on delegates he wanted to approach on behalf of Roberts.

Archie listened with increasing intensity. His body, though still exhausted, began to come awake again and his scalp started to itch. He scratched at his head.

"My God, honey," he asked, "why didn't you tell me all this a long time ago?"

"Well, I couldn't. I mean, it didn't make any sense to me until tonight when I heard Mother phoning Roberts, trying to get in to see him," she said. "They finally told her she could see him about midnight. So I got curious. So would any girl, when her mother goes across town in the middle of the night to see a man."

"What did she want from him?"

Kay laid a finger along her thin nose and squinted in speculation. "I'm not sure. But she was pretty mad. I think she wanted him to promise to quit using that machine."

"Where did you say this 'Oscar' thing is supposed to be?" asked Archie.

"It's right near here, over on Clark Street, I think. Mother said there's a funny beat-up doorway, next to a place called the Tropic Isle. Then you go upstairs to the first landing. At least, I think that's it. I mean, I haven't seen it, but that's what Mother said."

"Honey," said Archie, "you're the sweetest little spy this side of the CIA."

He stood up and hugged her and she shut her eyes and clasped the back of his head as they kissed. When her perch on the edge of the desk became too precarious they parted, both a little shaken, and she fussed in her purse until she found a handkerchief to wipe the smear of lipstick from his lips.

"Am I forgiven now," she asked, looking up at him, "for telling Mother about the gnat's eye?"

They talked no more politics as they walked, arm in arm, to the elevators. In front of the hotel, Archie put her in a cab, paid the driver and watched as she rode away. Nicest convention I've ever been to, he thought, even if it is my first. Three raucous drunks lurched by, one of them trying to sing: "Chicago, Chicago, that toddlin' town . . ." Archie began to hum the melody. The night air was cool and he realized that he had no coat. He buttoned his shirt collar, tightened his tie, rolled down his sleeves and walked rapidly down the block. He turned the corner and headed west, toward Clark Street.

The Tropic Isle was running full blast. The sound of a small orchestra—perhaps three or four pieces, the insistent beat underlined by the thud of a string bass—came through the open door. Smoke drifted out under the flashing neon signs. A short, fat man stood on the sidewalk clinking half-dollars in his hand. "Kashmir's just going on, Mac," he said. "Still time to see the whole show." The barker's eyes measured Archie as though weighing his wallet.

Archie shook his head and walked through the patch of light to a door from which grimy gray paint was peeling. He tried the doorknob tentatively and found that it turned. The stairway inside was lighted by a lonely, dust-covered bulb, and the linoleum-covered steps creaked under his weight. At the head of the stairs he saw a galvanized-iron door. There was the sign: "No Admittance." The door was locked. Archie knocked and waited, then knocked again. No answer. Then he saw a doorbell and pressed it.

Soon the door opened a few inches. A red-haired man looked out.

"Yes?" the man asked.

"Mr. Segunda?"

"What do you want?"

"I came to take a look at Oscar," Archie said.

"Well, this is one hell of a time to come calling. Who are you?"

"Bill Angell," Archie lied. "A delegate from Maryland."

"Who sent you up here at this time of night?" The voice was friendly, but guarded.

"I got a message from Mark Davidson. He wants me to bring back the print-out on a fellow." Archie inwardly congratulated himself on his glibness, but he wished he'd given it a little more thought on his walk from the hotel.

"Well, just a minute," said the red-haired man. "I'll have to check on that."

The door closed and Archie heard the lock snap. He stood for a moment, wondering what his next move should be. He realized that he had none, so he turned and trotted down the stairs to the street.

Once back in his office, Archie settled into his swivel chair. What should he do? Kay's story checked out: the galvanized-iron door, the black-painted sign on it, the red-haired man who didn't disavow the names of Segunda and Mark Davidson. The acceptance of the word "print-out." Archie smiled. Pretty fast thinking, that one—it was the only piece of computer slang he could remember, but apparently it passed muster.

Should he tell the newspapers? The Associated Press? Cal-

vin Burroughs? Or should he wait until morning and tell
Manchester first? Dammit, if only Obie were around. He'd
know how to milk this thing for all it was worth. And it's
worth a lot, Archie thought. Thank God. We sure need a
break of some kind. What a miserable, lousy, stinking day.
The President gone, Senator Floberg gone, Obie gone. . . .

Archie pulled out a sheet of names and studied it, trying to
focus his weary eyes. Tomorrow—today—was the final strategy meeting of the state leaders for Manchester to plan for
the nominating speeches and the floor demonstration. Good
God, who was supposed to run the demonstration? What was
that guy's name? That was another thing Obie had set up.
Archie began searching feverishly through the pile of papers
on his desk. His stomach ached, his scalp itched, and his eyelids felt heavy as lead.

And this was the way Julia Manchester found her hus-
band's young campaign manager when she arrived at 2:30
A.M. after a charter flight to Boston, a commercial jet to
O'Hare Airport, and a fast taxi ride on the expressway into the
Loop. She tipped the bellboy and told him to leave her two
pieces of luggage.

Mrs. Manchester offered her cheek to Archie for a kiss,
then looked around the little office.

"This place looks like a pigpen," she said. "Archie, tell me.
How is he doing?"

"He's asleep, Mrs. Manchester."

"Julia, please, Archie."

"He's asleep, Julia, or at least he should be. He felt pretty
low and he canceled a couple of state delegation meetings.
It's just as well. He needed the rest."

She stripped off her brown traveling gloves, lifted off her

hat and shook out her hair, casually smoothing the short curls. She was tanned, healthy and competent-looking, and Archie was very glad she was there.

"I gather from the papers that we're going to lose." She said it matter-of-factly.

"I wouldn't go quite that far," said Archie. "But we couldn't stand another day like the one we just went through."

"Tell me about it." She tapped a cigarette on the desk and waited for a light. She listened quietly while Archie sketched recent events, including the dismissal of Obie O'Connell.

"That's bad," she commented. "Charlie made a mistake. He's a babe in the woods without Obie."

Archie nodded, not at all cheerfully. "So am I, Julia."

"Well, that's the way it is." She got up briskly and then went next door and into the living room of suite 2306. Archie put her bags down next to the door of Manchester's bedroom.

When Archie left, she looked around the room, then automatically began picking up papers and magazines, fluffing pillows on the sofas and pushing chairs a few inches this way or that. She saw the deep black headlines on the afternoon papers—"Manchester Drive Crumbles" . . . "President Dumps Manchester." She sniffed and stuffed them into a wastebasket.

Then she selected the smaller of her bags, opened the door to the bedroom and carried it quietly inside. The curtains ballooned at the open window and a pale patch of moonlight fell on the big double bed. Julia Manchester smiled. Her husband lay diagonally across the bed, his right arm thrown over his head. He sprawled full length, snoring softly. Some people might sleep curled up, subconsciously seeking the form of the womb they left many years before, but not Charles

Bedford Manchester. He slept as he lived—with confidence. He shared and laughed and worked with others, but he seldom needed them. Julia felt better, looking at him, to know that he still felt that way.

There was more giving than taking to this man, even in the love-making that had bound them together through the years, not only as husband and wife, but as man and woman. She thought of Martha and Jake, and of how amazed the children would be to think of their father as a lover. But they could not know, as she did, the tenderness or the passion or the occasional ferocity of the man. . . . Julia smiled once again, recalling the night at the lake before he flew to Chicago and destiny. Destiny? Now his fate might be to return beaten to Washington, then fade back to Cincinnati.

As she slid out of her clothes and hung them carefully in the closet, she tried to imagine her husband defeated. It was almost impossible. He had never really lost—not anything big, never anything he had determined to win. How would he take it? Jake always said nobody could guess what would happen to his father in such an event, simply because Charles Manchester would never concede the possibility of defeat in anything. Did he now? It certainly looked as if it was all over but the shouting—the Roberts shouting. At least Charlie can go down fighting, she thought.

Julia slipped on a simple nightgown, a lightweight shift, pretty but without frills. Not a bow or a ribbon on it. She went to the window and tied back the curtains, then pushed her husband's legs to one side of the bed and crawled in.

When she kissed his cheek, feeling the bristle of his new beard, he stirred and shifted. His eyes came open slowly, and when he recognized her, there was no surprise in his greeting.

"Well, hello," he said sleepily. "Are you the Red Cross lady with the rescue expedition?"

"How did you guess? That brain of yours—it's terrific."

He smiled slowly. "I thought I told Archie not to let any more women into this bed tonight."

"It does feel a little mussed over on this side."

He reached over and pulled her head against his shoulder. She nestled down against his chest and said no more.

When she raised her head and looked at him a minute later, he was again sound asleep—this time with a smile on his face. She lay there and looked out at the moonlit sky, and her mind wandered back over the unnumbered nights when they had lain close and content. Then Julia Manchester was asleep herself, and despite the distant drums of defeat, she too slept content once more.

17

Archie felt fragile and unsteady as he stood before the thirty-five Manchester leaders who had squeezed into a room down the hall from the Royal Skyway suite. The lack of sleep—for the fourth straight night he'd been in bed barely four hours—gave him a lightheaded, floating sensation. A tickle low in his throat signaled the beginning of a summer head cold.

But it was the gnawing doubt about his own position that made him most uneasy. Almost all of the men sitting before him, chewing on cigars or flipping through the morning newspapers, were many years his seniors. Most were old hands at the convention game and up-from-the-ranks veterans of precinct politics, about which Archie knew nothing. Now Charles Manchester had thrust him into the manager's position so abruptly vacated by Obie O'Connell—the man who had carefully selected and recruited the men now sitting before Archie. They had gathered for the final strategy conference, one man from each of the states where Manchester had any substantial strength.

"You know as well as I do that I don't belong here," Archie began. He rolled a pencil between his moist palms and tried to keep his voice as confident as possible. "Obie's sudden illness has been a tough blow to take, and I hope you gentlemen will give me all the help and advice you can. I'll need plenty."

He hesitated, then went on. "There's no point kidding ourselves about the last couple of days. They've been bad. But we can still win this nomination if we work and fight right on through until the roll call. Now, just to start things off, I want you to meet a fighting lady—Mrs. Julia Manchester."

Archie pointed toward the rear. Julia Manchester, wearing a trim blue suit, walked forward. The gray streaks in her hair swirled over her forehead, her tanned face was rested and cheerful, and there was jauntiness in her step. Julia Manchester was a female obviously ready to do battle for her man. At the front of the room, she turned and faced the leaders.

"The only thing I know about politics," she said, "is that my grandfather went out and got blind drunk the night women got the vote." They chuckled as she went on. "I guess we've been a nuisance to you ever since. Personally, I have only two rules in politics. I always vote Republican—and I always vote as many times as they'll let me."

The men laughed again, and Archie could feel some of the tension lift from the room. It was obvious the leaders liked this forthright little woman.

"I'll be frank, gentlemen," she continued. "I'm here to help my husband in any way I can. If I were Mrs. Roberts, I'd be doing the same thing for Bin—and the first thing I'd do to help him would be to cut his helpings in half."

There was a roar this time. She's off and running, Archie thought.

"I know why Archie wanted to show me off here," she said. "It's so you can see that I don't have two heads, don't drink in the morning, and don't wear orange lipstick. Charlie and I have been married for twenty-eight years, happily married, mainly because I let him win all the arguments that don't concern money, housing, clothes, children, furniture or vacations." The men applauded, but Julia Manchester quickly changed her tone. "Seriously, gentlemen, I think my husband has raised an issue here that deeply concerns—or should concern— everybody. And while I'm no expert, I know that if you nominate Charles Manchester, the people of this country will thank you for it."

They stood and clapped as she left, and there was admiration in the eyes that followed the pert figure and purposeful stride of the candidate's wife. "Say, that's a real pro," whispered one man to his neighbor.

"Archie," said one of them when the door had closed, "if you don't show that little lady to the convention tonight, you're off your rocker."

"She'll be in the first box off the platform," Archie said, "and I want every state standard brought by to salute her during the demonstration."

The group got down to business. Discussion centered on the floor tactics for that night's nominating speeches and the balloting the next afternoon. Louis Cohen, as darkly anxious as ever, announced that he would be on hand at headquarters to help with last-minute changes in the nominating and seconding speeches in case the opposition threw in some new charges. A technician from the telephone company explained the mechanics of the private circuit which linked state leaders with Archie's seat on the platform and Manchester's suite in the hotel. The names of all delegates still known to be uncommitted were read off and assigned to various floor leaders. Archie listed their speakers for that night: the Governor of Ohio would have fifteen minutes to nominate Manchester; the seconders, limited to five minutes each, would be another governor, a national committeewoman, and a senior member of the House of Representatives.

One of the older leaders asked if any precautions had been taken against gallery-packing. The ten thousand spectator seats, all reserved, had been divided meticulously between Manchester and Roberts; but there was always a chance that counterfeit tickets would be printed and distributed. The memory of 1940, when holders of fake tickets packed the galleries in Philadelphia and howled for Wendell Willkie, was still strong. Archie replied that Joe Terhune had promised to crack down on any violators, and that he trusted Terhune. The others agreed.

"Our big problem" offered one leader, "is this terrific pressure from the missile people. Frankly, it's pretty rough in my state. I just don't know how to handle it."

"What we need is some solid evidence that we could feed to the papers," suggested another man.

"Listen," said Archie, holding up a hand. "All we need is one good specific case. I've heard a bale of these stories, too, but I can't pin any of them down. Does anybody have anything definite?"

One man raised a huge, freckled hand. His sandy mustache, twirled into incongruous waxed spikes at each end, wiggled as he spoke in his Tennessee drawl.

"Well, I got a call yesterday from my banker in Chattanooga," he said, "askin' me to go for Roberts. I said, 'Why, Zelmo'—I've known ol' Zelmo since we was kids together on Missionary Ridge—'how come you messin' in politics?' So he said it's a free country and he's free, white and twenty-one. I said I hadn't noticed that bein' white was doin' anyone much good lately, and ol' Zelmo, he laughed and said, well, he'd just taken a shine to Roberts and he wanted me to know it.

"I thanked him kindly and asked what he got against Manchester, and he says, well, it seems to him like Manchester is actin' kinda strange for a banker. So I says 'Thanks, Zelmo ol' buddy,' and that's all he said.

"Now, what ol' Zelmo didn't say, but what I'm tellin' you, is that he's got a lot of stock in a new electronics plant down our way that makes gadgets for missiles. And another thing he didn't say is that the son of a bitch charged me five and a half per cent on the last loan he made me, and come to find out I could have got it for five at the bank across the street. So, you're lookin' at a man who's a hundred and five and a half per cent for Manchester."

Archie joined the laughter as the big Tennessean sat down, but he hunched his shoulders and held out his hands, palms up. "See what I mean?" he asked. "They tried to put pressure on Hank, here, but if Hank made a public charge, his banker would deny it—and maybe sue him for slander."

"No, he won't be doin' that," said the delegate. "I got more on ol' Zelmo than a hound dog has fleas. Roberts, he says. Humph!"

Hubert Germaine, the cool, effective Manchester leader in Missouri, rose to his feet.

"I'd like to add my version of the Zelmo story," he said, "but it proves what Archie says. This stuff is murder, but it's almost impossible to combat. Now, what I'm going to tell you has got to stay right in this room.

"Monday morning I got a call before breakfast, from Mark Davidson of Uniforge. He's staying at the Executive House. Now, I don't know Davidson. I've never met him. He began pleasantly enough, mentioning some mutual friends. Then he said he was 'disturbed' about Manchester's press conference and its implications for the whole missile industry. He said he knew I was for Manchester, but he wished he could have a few experts sit down with me and explain things from the industry viewpoint. I said I was pretty well briefed already and thought I understood the situation. He said he thought it was important to nominate Roberts and hoped I'd give it a lot of thought. I said I would, and that was all. He didn't say any more.

"But here's the point, gentlemen. I am sales manager for a company called Vitrionics, in St. Louis, and three quarters of our business right now is in one big subcontract for Uniforge —and Davidson damn well knows it. I don't need to tell you the kind of spot that puts me in. I'm sticking with Manchester, but it's rough."

"I think it's obvious why we can't put that story out," said Archie, "and I also want to say for all of us that I admire Mr. Germaine's guts."

There were more stories, all tinted with the same coloration of pressure, some of it direct, some quite sophisticated in execution. But all were second- or third-hand stories. The meeting ended with orders from Archie to keep the floor telephone system manned that night for quick changes in tactics. Archie took the Tennessee and Missouri leaders with him when he headed for the candidate's suite.

He had not seen Manchester since the night before when a tired, depressed candidate canceled his evening appointments and went to his bedroom. His first glance today was at least partially reassuring. Manchester stood in the center of the sitting room, his summer-weight blue suit freshly pressed and his shirt showing the soft sheen of new white linen. He seized Archie's hand and tilted his head slightly, as he always did when he shook hands with someone he liked. The Manchester buoyancy, if not quite all his usual confidence, was back in his voice.

"Good morning, Archie," he said. "How's my manager?"

Archie introduced the Missouri and Tennessee leaders and Manchester greeted both by their first names. He gripped each hand hard.

"Boss," Archie said, "I want these fellows to tell you just what we're up against."

They recounted the incidents much as they had at the strategy meeting, except that the Tennessean went into sulphurous detail on some of his past dealings with "Zelmo ol' buddy." Manchester laughed so hard he had to dab at his eyes with a handkerchief, and Archie decided that the tonic to the candidate's spirits was worth the time whether or not any counterstrategy developed from the session.

Listening to Germaine, Manchester pulled at his ear as he grew more serious.

"Of course," he said at the end of the story, "I'm dismayed that this kind of pressure tactic is being used in a Republican convention. You might expect it with the Democrats, because of the unions and some of those tight minority pressure blocs, but it's hard to believe that Bin Roberts would countenance that kind of thing."

"Not for me, it isn't," Germaine protested. "You can't tell me that Fleischer and Roberts don't know what Uniforge and the union are doing."

"I agree," said Archie. "As a matter of fact, I have some pretty fair evidence of it." He was on the verge of revealing Kay's report about the computer and his own visit to Clark Street, but decided he'd better check that through with Manchester first. "At least, I hope I can nail something down before the day is over."

They were seated around the coffee table now, and Manchester leaned toward them with his elbows on his knees. "It seems to me that we might make some use of this," he said, "without compromising you gentlemen in the slightest. What would you say to this: Suppose I get Cal Burroughs up here under a pledge that he won't use any names. Then you tell him exactly what happened. With him printing the story under his own name—perhaps disguising the circumstances somewhat—it would have quite an impact. Burroughs carries a lot of weight."

Archie shook his head. The floating sensation was still with him, as though he were a puff of cotton about to be blown away. "We can do that," he said, "but it's not enough. Cal Burroughs couldn't get into print until tomorrow morning, and how many delegates would see the story before they voted? What we need is some quick way to build a backfire in the country."

"There's no question about that," said Manchester, "but we've got to work with what we've got."

"How about one of those television fellows?" asked the man from Tennessee. "They could have it all over the air tonight."

"Nope," said Germaine firmly. "I'm not telling my story to anybody I don't know. If any names got out in this thing, it could ruin Vitrionics—to say nothing of Mr. and Mrs. Germaine and the three little Germaines."

As they discussed Manchester's proposal, the new-born enthusiasm ebbed. They were fighting the clock, the relentless sweep of the minute hand. Time, time, time: There was so little left. Less than twenty-four hours to go. From the sidewalk, far below, came a faint snatch of the Roberts convention song, the jubilant accompaniment to the opposition bandwagon. It was rolling, and the delegates were clamoring to get aboard for the final victory ride. In the end, Manchester called Calvin Burroughs. There was nothing else to do.

*   *   *

It was two hours earlier in Tiburon, California, as Jake Manchester drank a second cup of coffee before leaving for work in San Francisco. The morning sun streamed through the big picture window and shimmered on Patsy's tiny silver earrings.

Jake leafed through the last pages of the *Chronicle* without speaking. There had been few words exchanged in the apartment since Monday night's eruption. Patsy's flood of tears had doused the fire, but the coals of resentment still smouldered in both husband and wife.

"Sugar?" she asked. She eyed him as she might a mackerel

that had lain too long in the sun.

"Sugar." His voice grated. "I haven't used sugar in my coffee in five years. Is that your idea of a joke?"

"My, aren't we poisonous this morning." Patsy jerked at the corners of her stiff shirtwaist collar, then got up—too fast— for an imaginary errand in the kitchen.

Silence. Then, from the kitchen: "You never said, but you called Jim Steadall the other night, of course."

"Yes, I called him." Jake offered no further information.

She came back to the table. "I think it was *terrible* of the President to throw C.B. overboard the way he did. And those delegates! All running like disgusting little ants to fat old Bin Roberts. Somebody ought to tell them how the people feel."

"And you know how the people feel, Mrs. Gallup?" He said it with exaggerated slowness, as though he were the teacher in a backward class.

"You bet I do," she flared. "Yesterday I talked to just about every woman in the neighborhood. They're *all* for your father."

Jake got up and put on his topcoat, for the August air in San Francisco had a bite to it. He walked to the door without offering the customary good-by kiss.

"Jake Manchester," Patsy said bitterly, "I should think you'd at least call somebody and do *something*. You must have some friends in politics besides Jim Steadall."

He turned with his hand on the doorknob. "Listen. If you're so hot and bothered about everything, why don't you call *your* friends?"

"I just might do that," she said. He went out, closing the door with a bang. She stared at it, thinking hard. "Yes, sir, Mr. Smart-Aleck Jake Manchester, I just might do that."

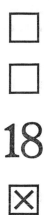

18

Calvin Burroughs tapped his wrist watch to emphasize his point. "Your trouble is that time's running out on you."

The publisher sat with Manchester and Archie in the candidate's suite. Julia Manchester was across the room, listening intently but not taking part in the discussion. The delegates from Tennessee and Missouri had told their stories for the third time and then departed, leaving uncertainty and frustration in the room.

"I believe those stories," Burroughs went on, "and we'll print them in the morning. But without names, they won't really help you much. We get a good story, but that won't solve your problem."

Archie looked inquiringly at Manchester, and the Secretary of the Treasury nodded.

"There *is* something else, Mr. Burroughs," Archie said. "Have you heard anything about 'Oscar' around the convention?"

"Oscar?" Burroughs shook his head.

"Oscar is the name of a computer," Archie explained. "The Roberts people are using it to keep track of the delegates."

Burroughs looked at him quizzically. "Well, that's a new wrinkle, all right. But I don't think you can beat Roberts just because he used punch cards for his delegate file."

Manchester waved his hands impatiently. "It's not that, Cal. We're not talking about a slightly improved version of something that every candidate has. This is entirely different."

"How?"

Archie leaned forward. "In two ways, Mr. Burroughs. First off, they apparently dug up a great deal more than the usual information—much more personal stuff on the delegates' lives and families and financial problems—and put it all on magnetic tape so they can break down the delegate list in any number of ways and pull out what they need. And, second, and I think this is the real point, there's circumstantial evidence, at least, that they've turned the machine over to Davidson and Gus Maguire. They're letting Uniforge and the Missile Workers have all this private information to use in putting the heat on delegates."

Burroughs was obviously impressed now, but he still seemed skeptical. Archie launched into a more complete explanation. Without using Kay Orcott's name, he told of her report and of his own after-midnight visit to the old building on Clark Street.

"If half of that is true," Burroughs said, "it's the best story of the convention. I'd like to put a couple of reporters on it right away to check it out. Okay, C.B.?"

"It's yours, Cal," said Manchester. He hesitated. "But try to go easy on Bin Roberts. I just don't believe he's aware of what's being done."

"Boss!" Archie chided him. "You're giving him too much of a break. The evidence is pretty strong. We all think so. Look what Hubert Germaine said."

"I know," said Manchester, "but I'm not sure you fellows realize. . . ."

He cocked his head and smiled at Archie. Then he walked to the writing desk and selected a thin cigar from the silver case lying there. He fussed with lighting preparations, settled into the big armchair and blew a ring of smoke at the ceiling. The others watched him in silence. Archie wondered vaguely what Manchester was aiming at, for the ceiling was bare.

Manchester was thinking: It's all going too fast. Too much commotion, too much talk, too many people. He thought of a deep, quiet pool on a river in northern Michigan and of his hope to be fishing there next week with Jake. The woods and the distant, muffled croak of a crow . . . a place where a man could think, a place where no cackle of voices intruded. Did Bin Roberts yearn for such a retreat? He didn't know Roberts too well. He had to go on instinct and his instinct told him . . .

"I'm not sure you fellows quite realize the situation," he said aloud. "Bin Roberts isn't running for county commissioner. He's running for President. There's a vast difference and it does something to a man. I know it and Hendrickson knows it and Roberts knows it. A man imposes his own restraints on himself. I just don't think Bin really knows what's going on over there on Clark Street."

"You mean he doesn't know Davidson and Maguire are using the computer?" asked Archie.

"Perhaps he does." Manchester blew another smoke ring.

"But I'm sure he doesn't realize the kind of personal information that's stored there, the stuff that could be used to blackmail a delegate."

"You're drawing a pretty thin moral line, C.B.," said Burroughs, "much as I respect your effort to see Roberts in the best light."

There was that moral line again, thought Manchester. How many times had he drawn it since Saturday? Rohrbaugh and Obie and Floberg. Did right and wrong always merge at the fringes in the pressure of a convention?

"No," he said, "it's a pretty broad line, Cal. Look, we know from . . ." He paused awkwardly for a moment. "Well, from Obie, that Roberts wouldn't let his people use that *Pravda* editorial against us. Fleischer was going to distribute handbills or something of the sort. Bin put his foot down. He wouldn't have it."

"That could be plain shrewdness," said Archie. "Something like that could have boomeranged."

"Possibly," said Manchester, "but I think the motive wasn't quite that selfish. At any rate, Cal, please don't let your story imply that Roberts is the villain in the plot."

Burroughs nodded. "I'll check it myself before it goes on the wire."

"Good." Manchester got up and stalked across the room, the cigar trailing smoke. He's like a locomotive, Archie was thinking, with a full head of steam and no track to run on.

"The thing that really bothers me," said Manchester, "is that not one single responsible voice has spoken out on my side of the argument. I know I'm right on this missile thing, Cal. So do you. And so do a lot of other people, maybe millions. But what real *leader* thinks so? Apparently none."

"That's not so, boss," protested Archie. "You've got quite a few delegates and state leaders going to bat for you. How about Germaine? He's really sticking his neck out."

Manchester gestured impatiently. "They're all fine people, but I'm talking about national leaders, men the people know and respect. Somebody outside of politics, somebody whose opinion counts with the whole country. Nobody like that has spoken up. The silence is deafening."

"Time, time," Archie said moodily. "If we had a couple of weeks to let opinion jell, I bet there'd be dozens."

Burroughs snapped his fingers and pointed at the candidate. "Hey, wait a minute, I know somebody," he said. "Wes Shaw. Everybody over five years old knows who *he* is."

"You mean General Wesley Shaw?" Manchester asked.

"That's right. You know him, don't you, C.B.?"

"Sure. We were on the same committee on the balance of payments problem when I was undersecretary and he was just out of the Air Force. But what makes you think . . ."

"I talked to him Sunday morning," explained Burroughs, "just to get his reaction to your press conference. He's an old friend of mine. He was right with you—said the Daphne wouldn't help our defense much. If you could get him to say something now . . ."

"But, good God," Archie protested, "isn't General Shaw an officer of Uniforge?"

"No, he's just one of their directors," Burroughs said. "He holds a little stock, sure, but he's not really involved in management full time, or anything like that. Anyway, that's just the point." He crossed the room and pointed out the window. "Can you imagine the impact in McCormick Place if a director of Uniforge came out for your candidate?"

"It seems pretty far out to me," Archie objected, "to think that a director would go against the interests of his company."

Now Manchester protested. "But, Archie, as I told that delegation up here yesterday, the Daphne contract isn't a life-or-death thing for Uniforge. They've got a huge backlog of other orders."

Burroughs nodded agreement. "At any rate, I think it's worth a try. Wes Shaw has more integrity in his little finger than most men have altogether. And he's a blunt old rascal. If he believes something, he'd just as soon say it out loud."

The publisher walked to the end table which held three phones. "Shall I try?"

Manchester nodded.

Burroughs looked at his watch. "He's probably still at home. I think we can catch him before he leaves for the golf course." The publisher asked the long-distance operator to connect him with Shaw's home in Santa Barbara.

"This is Cal Burroughs in Chicago again, Wes."

"You got me at breakfast," said Shaw. "You're going to work early these days."

"There's a convention on, Wes. Or haven't you heard?"

"I've heard nothing else for five days," said the retired general. "But what's that got to do with a publisher? You've got your slaves to do the work for you. The way I hear it, you publishers just stand around and get in the way of your reporters."

"In a convention, everybody gets in everybody's way," said Burroughs. He laughed. "Even a publisher can't get anything to eat without standing in line."

"You calling to discuss food, Cal?"

"No, I'm calling to tell you that Secretary Manchester is getting beaten to death on this missile issue I talked to you about Sunday."

"So I see by the papers," said Shaw. "Too bad. Manchester is a pretty good citizen. He's getting a bum rap."

"Look, Wes, I'm up here in the Secretary's room, as a matter of fact. I told him about our talk, and he'd like to speak to you about it. Would you mind?"

"Charlie Manchester? Hell, no. Put him on."

Manchester took the phone. The candidate and the general exchanged greetings in the hearty but slightly formal manner of men who knew and respected each other, but had never fraternized over a drink.

"Cal tells me you're on my side in this missile argument, General," said Manchester.

"I'm glad you're giving it a public airing," Shaw said. "It's about time." He grunted. "Of course, it's too bad our Daphne has to be the whipping boy. It's going to be a pretty good bird. But that's all right. You got to start somewhere."

"Frankly, General, if the decision were yours as a public official, would you put ten billion into Daphne?"

Shaw thought a moment. "I'd put a good-sized chunk into R and D, maybe, something on the order of a few hundred million. But production? No, not unless the boys come up with a lot more than it looks like now. Mr. Secretary, let's face it— hell, you *have* faced it—we've got these things coming out of our ears."

"General," said Manchester, "my selfish interest in what I'm about to ask is too obvious to be mentioned, but would you be willing to make a public statement of your views?"

Shaw's mind, tuned to political implications during his two terms as Air Force Chief of Staff in Washington, worked swiftly. He had decided long ago that Manchester was his choice for President. Though he never thought of Bin Roberts without a feeling of warmth and affection, Roberts just didn't have the stature for the job. Neither did Hendrickson, the Democratic candidate. Besides, Hendrickson's views weren't his—not by a long shot. But to jump into politics cold, in this kind of situation? The general hesitated.

"Well, Mr. Secretary, I certainly do agree with you on the missiles. But I don't know about making a public statement right now. Politics has never been exactly my line, after all."

Manchester gripped the phone more tightly. "General, I don't think this is just a matter of politics. I think the issue I have raised here is far above politics—and I think you'd agree with me on that. But if I don't win this political fight, I'll never have a chance to do anything about the missiles either."

There was a moment's silence. When Shaw replied, his tone as well as his words provided evidence that he had made up his mind.

"Okay, Mr. Secretary, you're right on that one. I guess if I agree with you on the issue I ought to be willing to go along the rest of the way. And we agree on a lot of other things, anyway. What do you want me to do?"

"If you could write out a statement supporting me—limit it strictly to the missile issue if you prefer—that would be a big help," Manchester said. "We could put it out here, of course."

"All right, if you don't mind my language. I'm pretty blunt sometimes," Shaw said. "I never could learn that diplomatic double-talk."

"Neither could I, General—which seems to be my main trouble right now. You just say exactly what you feel."

"All right," Shaw said. "Now you fellows decide how you want to handle it."

"Hold on a minute," said Manchester. He turned to Archie and Burroughs. "He's willing to make a statement. Shouldn't we have him phone it back so we can release it here?"

Burroughs grinned and reached for the phone. "Here, let me talk to him. If he's going to get his feet wet, he might as well dive all the way in. . . . Wes, this is Cal again. Look, we might as well do it right. The way things stand this morning, our man is going to get licked. About our only chance is something dramatic. Why don't you fly in here right away and let us set up a press conference for you? That way we'd get maximum coverage, television and everything."

"My God, you fellows work pretty fast," said Shaw. "I haven't even had my second cup of coffee." He was silent for a moment, and when he spoke again his tone was serious. "No, Cal, I can't do that. A statement is one thing, but a TV appearance, no. I've had enough press conferences in my day. I'm out of touch now. Some wise guy would trip me up."

"No danger of that, Wes. We'd brief you first," said Burroughs. "Besides, you know this missile thing inside out."

"Quit while you're ahead, Cal," ordered Shaw. "I'll make a statement, but an appearance in Chicago is out. Definitely. Now, shall I phone you back when I've finished drafting the thing?"

"That'll be fine, Wes. Then we'll put it out here. Of course, you can expect to be called right away by newspapermen wanting verification."

"I can handle that all right," said Shaw. "Now, give me about half an hour to write the damn thing."

Burroughs' face was slack with disappointment when he hung up.

"A statement is as far as he'll go," he said.

Manchester brooded over his cigar. Archie, his hands jammed in his pockets, walked to the window and stood there, slouched against the window frame.

"I tried," said Burroughs. He sat down and began rapping his ivory cigarette holder on an arm of the chair. There was a long period without conversation. Julia Manchester eyed first one man, then another.

"The happiness boys at work and play," she said.

They failed to smile.

"Nobody pays this executive fifty thousand a year to think," she went on, "but I've got an idea. Any of you joy birds like to hear it?"

Manchester forced a grin. "We're all ears, Julie."

She patted at her pepper-and-salt hair. "Maybe it's crazy, but I was thinking. Why can't you get General Shaw to go before the convention tonight and make one of those seconding speeches?"

"A speech?" asked Burroughs. "When he won't even stand for a press conference?"

"I've got an idea about how to do that too," said Julia, "but what about the seconding thing?"

Archie's reply was glum. "Even if he'd do it, we're only allowed three seconders and they're all lined up."

"Of course," said Manchester, "we could substitute him for one of the five-minute seconding speeches, but . . ."

"Never mind the buts," said Julia. "First, I just want to know if it's possible."

"Anything's possible in a convention," said Burroughs. "You could let him substitute for all three seconders. Give him fifteen minutes."

"How about the convention rules?" asked Archie. His tone

lacked interest. "I'm not sure Terhune would allow one long seconding speech. Anyway, it's all academic."

"Can you imagine anyone trying to stop General Wesley Shaw from speaking to that convention?" scoffed Burroughs.

"Archie's right," said Manchester. "It's all academic. What are you driving at, Julia?"

"You leave that to me, gentlemen." She rose from her chair and walked briskly to the bedroom. "Now, you just go about your business. I want to use the phone in here for about fifteen minutes."

The minutes crawled by amid desultory conversation. Manchester fixed briefly on a floor-lamp tassel as a target for his smoke rings, but after one hit and two misses, his attention flagged and he tapped out the cigar. Archie tried to make his brain focus on strategy, but found his thoughts evaporating like water in a boiling kettle. Burroughs did not add to the cheer when he remarked that none of the Manchester speeches scheduled for that night promised to be inspiring. It was almost half an hour later when Julia Manchester re-entered the room.

She arranged herself elaborately in a chair, folded her hands in her lap and smiled brightly.

"Well?" asked Manchester.

"Wait," she said.

Again the crawl of the minutes began. "Great time for jokes," grumbled Archie. Burroughs looked as though he'd like to echo the sentiment, but said nothing.

The phone rang. "You get it, Cal," said Julia Manchester.

The publisher picked up the instrument, then quickly covered the mouthpiece end.

"It's Wes Shaw," he said. "I suppose with the statement."

"Damn all politicians," said the general cheerfully. "You're a bunch of connivers, the whole lot of you. That includes you, too, Burroughs."

"Thanks for the compliment. What produced it?"

"What produced it, he asks!" The general was barking into the phone now, but his tone was good-natured enough. "Do you think it's fair to turn a woman loose on a helpless old man?"

"I know some old men who'd consider it a favor," said Burroughs. He tried to banter, but his face was blank.

"So you sick one on a guy whose defenses against women were never too good to start with," Shaw went on. "I managed to get through your piteous pleas without crumbling, but then that female voice so filled with innocence and love . . . My God, you guys are cruel!"

Burroughs glanced inquiringly at Julia Manchester, but her only answer was a smile as sweet and enigmatic as the Mona Lisa's.

"For Christ's sake, Cal," Shaw sputtered, "how rough can you pirates get? First you talk me into making a statement. Then you want me to go on television, and when I say no to that, you get a woman to plead with me to make a speech to the whole convention!"

Burroughs slid smoothly into the general's line of thought without disclosing his own surprise. "Oh, come on, Wes," he coddled. "You're old enough to know you can't be partly pregnant. If you're going to do something, you might as well do it right. I don't recall that you ever suggested giving a bomber pilot a plane that would go seven hundred miles an hour and then telling him he couldn't fly it faster than five hundred."

"That's not the point, Cal, and you know it. Look, I'm willing to do what's right because I think Manchester's right and it's important. But I *am* a director of Uniforge, after all.

I think making a seconding speech would be overdoing it."

Burroughs covered the mouthpiece of the phone. "He's weakening—and for a seconding speech to boot. If you want him to do it, I'll have to give him the whole story. Okay?"

Manchester nodded quickly, his face showing surprise and elation. Burroughs spoke to Shaw again.

"Wes, if you're worried about the company and the propriety of doing this, there's something else you ought to know, too. Your man Davidson has been here since Sunday, and he's been twisting arms ever since he landed. And you know who's helping him? Gus Maguire. . . . That's right, the fellow who wasn't going to shake hands with him for four years. They've been playing plenty rough, too. I've heard some stories—good solid stories—that would curl your hair."

"What do you mean?" Shaw demanded. "Don't talk riddles, Cal."

Burroughs told him about Davidson's pressures on Hubert Germaine, the sales manager of the Uniforge subcontractor in St. Louis. "And what's more," he added, "the Roberts people have been using some kind of electronic brain to store up information on the delegates, and Davidson has been its best customer all week."

"That doesn't sound so good," Shaw said. "Still, I don't know."

"Look, Wes. If you're questioning the ethics of the thing, it seems to me the president of your own company has answered that one. If he's not worried about out-and-out blackmail—and that's what it is, believe me—you ought not to worry much about doing something to help a man you know is right on a hell of a big issue."

"Well . . ."

"Wes, I'm leveling with you. Unless you do this, Charlie Manchester doesn't have a snowball's chance in hell to be nominated. Even if you do it, it's going to be tough. But with you, it's possible. Without you, it's impossible. It's as simple as that."

Shaw hesitated again. The four people in the hotel room waited in silence. The far-off sounds of traffic, twenty-three stories below, came clearly through the open window.

"Well, all right." Shaw's answer was delivered so crisply that Archie and the Manchesters could hear it distinctly. "I'll do it—if you promise to help me with the speech."

"Sure, sure," said Burroughs. "But you write out a draft on the plane, too. We don't need anything about Manchester. Just a good, frank talk about this missile thing and what it means."

"All right, Cal. I'll do that."

"Just come to the Secretary's suite here at the Hilton," Burroughs said. "We'll find a bed for you."

"Okay. I still don't know, though, Cal. I wonder whether it's right for me to—"

"Never mind that now, Wes. Think about it on the plane. Just get going."

"Okay, but can one of you Machiavellis tell me how I'm supposed to get there? I'll have to get from Santa Barbara to L.A. to catch the jet. I don't suppose you just happen to have an airline schedule in your pocket?"

"Charter," ordered Burroughs, "and charter again in L.A., if you have to. This outfit ought to have some campaign money left for transportation. Just get here in a hurry and let us worry about the cost."

"All right. I'm on my way as soon as I pack my toothbrush."

Burroughs faced Julia Manchester as he hung up. He bowed deeply.

"Mrs. Machiavelli, it seems."

Manchester's face was radiant. The three men converged on Julia and stood in a ring about her. She tried to keep her smile coy, but there was triumph in it.

"Well, after he turned you all down, I figured a woman might as well give it a try," she said. "I called him and I reasoned with him. No dice. So I pleaded with him. I really almost cried, but I managed to hold it back. That would have been too much. He still said no, but I was pretty sure he'd change his mind. So I sat down and waited, and . . ."

"And he surrendered!" exclaimed Manchester.

"Good God," murmured Archie, "maybe we're running the wrong Manchester."

"That's the best break you've had in this convention," Burroughs said.

"It's the *only* break I've had," replied Manchester. "I think maybe the good Lord owes me one."

"Look," said Archie. The flush of reborn hope was on his cheeks. "I've got another idea. Suppose when the general gets here I take him over to Clark Street and let him—"

"Say no more," interrupted Burroughs. "If he'll do it, it'll make him so mad he'll say anything you want him to."

"Let's just be sure we don't smear Bin Roberts in anything that's said tonight," Manchester cautioned. Then he strode over to his wife and gave her a powerful hug. "Maybe you changed my luck, Julia. They may have us licked, but by God we'll fight right down to the wire."

"To the last ballot," Archie corrected.

Manchester looked hard at Archie, then grinned and threw him a mock salute. "The last ballot," he agreed. "Thank you, Mr. Manager."

19

"The convention will come to order!"

Joe Terhune brought his arm up and down like a pump handle, but the crack of his gavel was lost in the din of the convention hall. McCormick Place growled with the throaty turbulence of twenty thousand excited people. Delegates and spectators alike refused to heed the commands of the chairman. Terhune's face was flushed and his white hair shone under the lights which hung from the roof like beads on a string.

A delegate grabbed his state's microphone and yelled: "Tell 'em enough's enough, Joe!"

The crowd laughed, and Terhune took quick advantage of the following lull to slam his gavel once more.

"The gracious secretary of the convention, Mrs. DeWitt

Sprague of Michigan," he cried, "will now call the roll of the states to obtain nominations for the office of President of the United States."

Mrs. Sprague, a choker of pearls adorning her throat above her pink dress, walked down the long runway of the platform to the rostrum as the crowd applauded. In a corner box, between the delegates and the raised tiers where the spectators sat, Mrs. Julia Manchester found herself being swept by a television camera from the hanging platform in the center of the hall. A few boxes away sat Mrs. Bryan Roberts, a younger, fashionably dressed woman, flanked by the three teen-aged Roberts children.

Noting the little Roberts nest, Julia Manchester wondered whether her husband had been right in his insistence that Jake, Patsy and Martha should not appear until and unless he was nominated. He would not use his children for political advantage, he said. Just a little too stuffy and old-fashioned, Charlie, thought Julia. People want to see a candidate's family. She was beginning to wonder whether politics wasn't too deft an art to be left to the men.

On the platform Archie DuPage sat at a small table, nervously fingering a green metal phone box with keys that could be flipped to connect him with a score of Manchester lieutenants on the floor. Other keys opened direct lines to the Hilton headquarters and to the suite of the candidate himself. Despite the briefing by the telephone expert at the meeting of the Manchester leaders that morning, Archie felt uneasy with the system and had come to the hall a half hour early to practice on it. He still felt uncertain, and a ripple of panic flowed through him. What if the device failed at a crucial moment?

Across the aisle from him, Carl Fleischer sat confidently at a similar keyboard. Fleischer turned his smoked glasses toward Archie and smiled—a little too patronizingly, thought Archie.

The audience was quieter now as the slender woman from Michigan rapped the gavel once and laid a long printed roll-call sheet on the lectern.

"Al-a-ba-ma!" Her voice came shrill and thin through the loudspeakers.

A man stood ready by the Alabama microphone on the floor. "Madam Secretary," he drawled, "Alabama, by a vote of fourteen to six, yields to California."

A roar welled up from all sides of the hall.

"A-las-ka!"

"Alaska," said a voice from the floor, "considers it a rare privilege to yield also to her little sister to the south, the golden state of California."

Another roar of approval came from the crowd.

"Arizona!"

"Madam Secretary, Arizona passes."

"Ar-kan-sas!"

"Arkansas," came the response, "wishes to inform our very gracious and beautiful secretary that it yields to the state of Ohio—for the purpose of nominating the greatest Secretary of the Treasury in this nation's history."

Cheers and applause greeted this not entirely impartial statement, but they could not match the volume of the earlier outbursts.

"California!"

"California," said the state chairman, "presents the name of Dr. Hugh Rollins, chancellor of the University of Southern California and a former Olympic decathlon champion, to nominate the next President of the United States."

The call of the states continued. Ohio offered the name of its governor to place Manchester in nomination. Pennsylvania announced that it would nominate Governor Benjamin Wilcox. The roll continued through the rest of the fifty states, the District of Columbia, Puerto Rico and the Virgin Islands.

The lady from Michigan retired from her brief reign in the glory circle and Terhune resumed his patriarchal stance at the head of the runway long enough to introduce the chancellor of the University of Southern California.

Hugh Rollins, lean, tanned and handsome, spoke in the well-modulated, almost conversational tone which he used with such effect at university convocations. His diction was clear, his phrasing compact, his gestures limited. This was a no-nonsense speech that somehow invested the heavy bulk of Bryan Roberts with an aura of trim efficiency and academic sophistication. Only in the last minute did Rollins permit his voice to soar and his words to take wing.

"My candidate," he shouted, "is a man of warmth, a man of vision, and a man of compassion. He is the very essence of the virtues which built this mighty nation. He will lead with wisdom. He will decide with maturity. He will execute with justice. And he will defend his country with every fiber of his being. But more important for this month of August, fellow Republicans, he is a man who will campaign with the soul of a warrior, armed with the conviction that his cause —our cause—America's cause—is right. Ladies and gentlemen, I nominate for President of the United States on the Republican ticket a winner—Governor Bryan Roberts!"

A roar of approval rolled through McCormick Place and Rollins raised his arms in an answering salute. Down the center aisle came a girls' golden band, the brassy instruments seeking valiantly to coexist with the thunderous notes pealing forth from the hidden organ. The noise was shattering.

California, Here we come!
Bryan Roberts, He's the one!

Thousands of voices took up the cadence. As the band moved slowly down the crowded aisle, two hundred organized "spontaneous" demonstrators were released through the rear door to join the parade. Each time a state standard was reached, hands shot out to pull it from its place. Occasionally —but only occasionally—the effort was resisted, and a few tussles ensued. At the place reserved for the Ohio delegation, a young demonstrator sought to wrest the standard loose, but a dozen hands clutched the staff to keep it anchored. The paraders laughed and moved on, leaving Ohio's placard a lonely Manchester island in a Roberts sea. Hundreds of Roberts signs, brought into the hall for this show, waved in the crowd. Bells jangled, horns blew, men and women jumped up and down in the aisles. A cheerleader hoisted a golden girl to his shoulders and she blew kisses at one and all. When the head of the parade reached the box where Mrs. Roberts sat, the girls' band switched tunes and the organ, by prearranged signal, joined in:

A pretty girl
Is like a mel-o-dy . . .

Delegates and guests sang the familiar words until Mrs. Roberts stood up and waved.

Soon the parade became mired in its tracks, unable to move forward, unwilling to retreat. So many people had left their seats that locomotion in the aisles was impossible. The Roberts demonstrators merely shouted and waved where they stood, as though a huge caterpillar had taken root, its back and sides squirming in protest. Joe Terhune advanced to the rostrum and eyed the writhing mass of people wearily, frequently glancing at his watch. Terhune had organized a few demonstrations himself over the years, and he was not impressed. Finally he began banging his gavel. He had to hammer away steadily for almost ten minutes before the aisles were clear enough to satisfy him.

"Under the rules," Terhune announced, "three seconding speeches will be permitted, each to be limited to no more than five minutes. I now present to the convention . . ."

The first two orators struggled bravely to scale new peaks of forensics, but they failed to cross the timber line. Bryan Roberts had been saluted, applauded and worshiped in the best convention tradition, and the crowd was ready for new adventures. Only the third seconding speaker was worth the time to the Roberts forces: he was a swarthy delegate from New York named John Kolsak, head of a building trades local. He had created a ripple of interest earlier in the day by announcing he was switching from Manchester to Roberts, a circumstance which now monopolized his fulsome and obviously ghost-written prose. In the end, thousands cheered and he concluded in sweat-soaked triumph, three and a half lines behind the teleprompter.

The speech by the Governor of Ohio, placing Manchester in nomination, included no surprises and evoked little enthusiasm. The Governor handled his oratory as he handled his state administration—like a bookkeeper. He toted up Manchester's assets, indicated that a lengthy search had turned up no liabilities, and left the impression that his words had been edited by an accountant. Archie shifted uneasily during the speech. He knew that Louis Cohen had pleaded with the Governor to insert a few inspirational paeans, but he stubbornly resisted all efforts to fling his message skyward. Still, Archie felt the speech had not hurt Manchester's cause. The Governor said what the delegates expected him to say, and many were grateful that he refused to lead them up new avenues of thought at this late hour.

Archie flipped a key connecting him to a station at the rear of the hall and gave a cue to the cheerleaders waiting there. Somewhat to his surprise, the intercom functioned perfectly and provided a channel for instant pandemonium. The organ roared into the Ohio State University marching song and the banjo band from Cincinnati led the parade down the center aisle. Bells, horns and whistles raised a shrill canopy of sound over the demonstrators, while thousands of gaily colored megaphones were pulled from under chairs to serve as amplifiers for friendly delegates and spectators. Balloons, marked with a big "M," floated from the upper tiers and climbed lazily toward the roof. A miniature calliope, small enough to fit into the aisles, added to the medley of noise. Its effect, however, was dissipated when one delegate shouted to his neighbor, "It looks like the Manchester bandwagon is shrinking!" The witticism could not be heard five feet away, but it soon raced around the hall from mouth to mouth like a lighted fuse. In general, however, the demonstration went off as planned, and the TV cameras showed the nation a tangle of state standards waving before the box where Julia Manchester stood and threw kisses to the demonstrators. After exactly twenty minutes, Joe Terhune began work with his gavel. The aisles cleared more quickly this time, and Archie had to console himself with the thought that the second firecracker never sounds as loud as the first.

Back in his suite at the Conrad Hilton, Manchester looked away from the television set and observed to Calvin Burroughs, who sat with him: "Not much steam in that one, Cal." Burroughs nodded, but replied: "Wait. Maybe it's better that way."

As the demonstration sputtered out, delegates began to be aware of an argument on the platform. Terhune stood with his hand over the rostrum microphone listening to Carl Fleischer and Archie DuPage, both of whom appeared to be talking at once. Fleischer, his face set in angry protest, shook his finger at Archie. Terhune beckoned to a sallow-faced man, known to a few in the audience as the convention's parliamentarian, who joined the little group at the rostrum. Archie seemed to be pleading earnestly with the newcomer, while Fleischer clenched his fists and shook his head emphatically. Terhune whispered to both managers and then waved them back to their seats. Archie looked pleased; Fleischer stomped angrily back to his little table and began speaking to someone over his intercom.

A hush had fallen as thousands of eyes tried to interpret the platform scene. This time, the sound of Terhune's gavel rang out in a hall that was already quiet.

"The chair," he said, "was informed earlier that Secretary Manchester would have but one seconding speaker. The request was made that he be allotted the entire fifteen minutes that would ordinarily have been divided among three seconding speeches. The chair ruled that this was entirely within the rules. However, objection was made by a representative of an opposing candidate. The chair consulted the parliamentarian and the parliamentarian informs the chair that nothing in the rules precludes such an arrangement. The chair therefore recognizes, for fifteen minutes, a distinguished servant of his country, the holder of the Purple Heart in two wars, the former chief of staff of the United States Air Force, General Wesley F. Shaw."

Shouts of approval and dissent from the floor were smothered in a swelling hum, as though thousands of bees were flying about a hive. Delegates and spectators were trading excited fragments of speculation. The Kansas standard waved demandingly and Terhune pointed his gavel toward it. A voice boomed from the Kansas floor microphone.

"Mr. Chairman," it said, "this is Roger Abbott, chairman of the Kansas delegation. With all due deference to the wartime bravery and the distinguished career of General Shaw, I must make the point of order that it is not in order for him to speak. Only a delegate or alternate to this convention may make or second a nomination, and I submit that General Shaw is neither a delegate nor an alternate."

Cheers mingled with boos. Terhune beckoned the parliamentarian back to the rostrum and both men pored over a pamphlet which the parliamentarian placed on the lectern. Fleischer and DuPage hurried to join them again. This time Terhune could be seen pointing to a section of the pamphlet and arguing with DuPage. Again he pushed the two managers back to their posts and leaned toward the microphone. His long white hair had become disarranged and a wisp trailed over one ear.

Fleischer settled into his seat with a smug look. Archie flicked an intercom switch and spoke rapidly to Hubert Germaine, who sat on the floor with the Missouri delegation.

"The chair is ready to rule," said Terhune. "Under section four, paragraph two of the permanent rules of the convention, adopted Monday, only delegates or their duly designated alternates may conduct the business of this convention. The chair is forced to rule that a seconding speech does constitute convention business and that therefore—and I say this with deep regret—the distinguished general does not qualify since he is not a delegate."

The great hall was quickly engulfed in a confused roar of protest and approval. Terhune raised his hands for silence.

"But the chair should point out that the rules may be suspended by a two-thirds vote of the delegates," he said.

"Mr. Chairman!" Hubert Germaine shouted his appeal almost simultaneously with Terhune's last syllable.

"For what purpose does the gentleman from Missouri seek recognition?"

"I move, Mr. Chairman," said Germaine, "that the rules be suspended with regard to General Shaw—in deference to his long and patriotic service to his country."

"Second the motion!" The shouted declaration came from the Tennessee delegation, where a big man with a sandy, spiked mustache held the microphone.

"A motion to suspend the rules is made and seconded," said Terhune. "All those in favor say 'aye.' "

A thunder of voices responded.

"Opposed 'no.' "

The second outburst could not match the first in volume.

"In the opinion of the chair," said Terhune, "the ayes appear to have it."

Abbott shouted a protest into the Kansas microphone, but his words were unrecognizable in the din.

"The ayes have it." Terhune whacked his gavel doggedly.

The medley of cheers and boos turned slowly to laughter, then leveled off into excited chatter. It was obvious that the convention, regardless of personal preferences, was intrigued by this new development and anxious to hear the general. Fleischer's smug look had turned sour. Archie raised a circled thumb and forefinger toward the Missouri delegation. Germaine saw the signal and waved back happily.

"I now present to the convention General Wesley Shaw," Terhune said.

The stillness which occasionally fastens on a huge crowd is always awesome. Not a voice could be heard now as the general walked down the long platform to the rostrum. His bald head shone like a beacon under the massed lights. His rough, oval face above the too-large jaw, the network of old pilot's wrinkles around his eyes, the homely smile—all were familiar landmarks to millions who had seen his picture in newspapers and magazines since his fighter-ace days in World War II. Tonight he was dressed in a trim blue suit, but for many the mind's eye still saw him in the coveralls and faded baseball cap that were his usual costume in his flying days.

The applause for him was brief, and the strange quiet again settled on McCormick Place. Shaw's midwestern accent gave his opening words a flat, matter-of-fact tone.

I come before you tonight, not as a delegate, not as a Republican, not as a political partisan, but as a citizen of the United States. I have never made a political speech in my life.

I have been in this city only a few hours. I came because it was my duty to come. I won't mince words with you. I wouldn't know how if I wanted to.

Delegates and fellow Americans, I am deeply concerned over

developments in this convention since last Saturday, when a great American, a man of honor and conviction, stated his beliefs on a crucial issue of national policy—an issue which troubles the minds and hearts of all mankind.

First, let me make my own position clear, so that you may understand why I am here tonight. I am a director of the Universal Forge Corporation, which is the government's prime contractor for the development and construction of the Daphne missile. I own two hundred and thirty-five shares of common stock in that company, and I consider it to be one of the finest and best-managed industries in the country. Furthermore, I can assure you, from my own personal and detailed knowledge, that the company is in an excellent financial position. It has the resources to take on hundreds of jobs available to it. Any person who tells you that my company's future, or that of the aerospace industry in general, is dependent on the Daphne missile is guilty of gross distortion, to say the very least—and I don't care whether that statement applies to any person connected with Uniforge. If the shoe fits, let him put it on.

In the back of the hall, Gus Maguire turned to a Missile Worker member standing beside him and muttered: "The man's nuts. He's eating his own lunch and everybody else's too." In his suite at the Executive House, Mark Davidson stared at the TV screen with growing alarm. If Shaw had been a snake charmer, Davidson couldn't have watched his performance with more reluctant fascination.

Delegates, Secretary Manchester has asked us all a question that goes to the heart of national strength and survival. I agree completely with him—if I did not, I would not be here. Like Charles Manchester, I believe in a mighty defense for this nation. I have devoted my life to that cause. Like Charles Manchester, I believe we should spend whatever is needed to preserve this nation, whether it be tax dollars today or flesh and blood some other day. But I do not believe—and I will never believe—that we should ever perpetuate the arms industry for the sake of the arms industry itself. This nation is too proud, too ingenious, too inventive, ever to let its economy become anchored to the manufacture of unnecessary armaments. And I say that as a man who has followed the profession of arms all his life.

Are these new armaments necessary? I would answer: no. We are already strong enough to deter any enemy from attacking us. I say this with the deepest conviction. I have seen what we have —the stockpiles of nuclear warheads, more than we will ever need, God willing, and certainly enough to wipe any aggressor from the earth. I have seen our missile bases on the Dakota plains, in the Rockies, in the Southwest. All of us have seen, and many of us have counted, the Polaris submarines going down to the sea to form their own indestructible deterrent. Anyone who bothers to look up into the sky can see the vapor trails of our strategic bombers as they fly a constant alert above us.

Fellow Americans, we *do* have enough. Every citizen of this country will realize that if he stops to think about it. We must maintain this strength—we must keep it modern, strong, alert— but we are strong enough now and will be strong enough—with what we already have—in the years ahead.

Shaw paused to take a drink of water. Only the sound of typewriters, clicking swiftly in the press benches on each side of the platform, disturbed the eerie stillness. In glassed-in booths behind the platform, television and radio commentators took advantage of the break to chatter excitedly. "No one has the vaguest idea what General Shaw is leading up to," said one, "but right now, he's got this convention in the palm of his hand. Let's listen."

So it is not a question of need. We do not need this new weapon, and perhaps that is all that has to be said. But I cannot leave it at that tonight, for there are other things more important still—more important to the very basis of our free society— more important to the success of this wonderful continuing experiment we call Democracy. You may think it strange that a professional soldier, supposedly raised in the tradition of absolute obedience to authority, should feel so strongly about that. But that is what professional soldiers offer their lives to preserve, so perhaps you won't mind if I talk about it—and about your part in it.

Delegates to this convention, you are here for only one reason: to exercise your own best judgment—the collective sum of your own individual best judgments—to select the next Republican nominee for President of the United States. You have been chosen by your neighbors to do that. They have a right to expect that each of you will search your own individual conscience, will make up your own mind without regard to the pleadings or pressures of those who seek the office, and then cast your own vote as you alone see fit.

Obie O'Connell's fat little body was dumped in a big easy chair in his room at the Hilton. Above his waist he wore only a T-shirt, and he clutched a glass of Scotch and water on the little end table beside him. *The old guy has really got 'em in his hand,* he thought. *Wonder if Archie thought this one up? That's a good kid, even if he is a hopeless amateur. At least he knows how to deliver in the clutch. Give him time and maybe we'll make a politician out of him yet.* Obie grinned, somewhat sourly, and let some more of his drink trickle down his throat.

You are given a great privilege for this one week. You are, for this brief time, the chosen instruments of this wonderful society we have built and are still building. And on you, for this brief time, rests a great responsibility—to act in a way that will keep this society one that is never quite satisfied with what it has achieved, but is forever seeking ways to improve itself and help others who want to improve themselves.

It has always been this way: the greater the privilege the greater the responsibility. There is no greater privilege, in our political life, than to have a deciding hand in choosing a President of the United States; and so there is no greater responsibility. You do have a deciding hand, for you will choose one of only two men who may be the next President.

So you must vote as free citizens, putting aside any thought of personal gain or loss, of fortune or misfortune. Do not listen to those who would influence you for their own selfish benefit. Do not act through fear, for nothing built on fear can stand up against the truth.

Delegates to this convention, you know that the forces of fear and selfishness have been at work here this week. I do not claim to know precisely how they work; but I do know that they have made good and wise men lose their courage and perspective. These forces have gone to great pains to learn about you. I know that to be a fact. They know your family histories and they know your financial histories. They know your wealth and your problems. They know your income, your mortgage, your credit rating, your total indebtedness, the names of your creditors.

Patsy Manchester uncurled herself from the sofa in the cliffside apartment in Tiburon and hooted with glee. "Give it to 'em, General!" she exulted at the television screen. "You're a great, big, ugly livin' doll!" Jake Manchester sat in his corner of the sofa; husband and wife were still maintaining a policy of apartheid, although the barrier showed signs of crumbling. "If Dad and Roberts don't look out," Jake observed, "that bunch is likely to wind up nominating Shaw."

How is this highly personal information about you being used? I charge that officials of outside groups—specifically, management and unions in the missile industry—have been given it to help them bring pressure on as many of you as they can reach.

They call this "politics." That is not the name I would choose for it. I myself would look for some word in the dictionary of tyranny—or perhaps in the records of the Gestapo. That would be more appropriate, for to my mind this is an alien thing, ugly and repellent, and it has no business within a thousand miles of this convention.

Cheers burst from the Manchester sections of the spectator tiers, but there was little sound on the convention floor. Archie could see a look of bewilderment on many delegates' faces. They obviously had not yet absorbed what the general was saying.

Delegates to this convention, I plead with you, when you cast your vote tomorrow, remember what I have said tonight. Remember it when someone—perhaps your banker or your best customer—calls you and asks you to vote for a particular candidate. Remember it if you are a workingman, and the head of your union tries to tell you how to cast that vote. Remember it —and remember that the President of the United States himself has said you are "free and independent" delegates. Remember it—and remember that the Republican party has never believed in "machine" politics of any kind.

It is no secret where I stand. I stand for Charles Manchester. He has all the qualities that make great Presidents. You will be proud to have him in the White House. You will be proud of his dignity, proud of his integrity and his intellect and his humanity. But above all, you will be proud of his courage.

And in seconding Charles Manchester's nomination, I offer you a slogan that has been used here in scorn and jest, but which should be the battle cry of free and independent men and women. Delegates, ladies and gentlemen, Americans: Enough is enough!

A torrent of voices broke over the hall like a river rushing through a suddenly opened spillway. Shaw waved two outstretched arms, then quickly left the platform. A fist fight erupted in a spectator section and police shoved through to stop it. Newspapermen stood on press benches, trying to gauge the crowd's reaction. Typewriters beat furiously; a dozen television and radio commentators let go with a flood of words into their microphones.

The Ohio delegation poured into the aisle and tried to start another demonstration. Joe Terhune flailed at the lectern with his gavel, trying in vain to restore order. Delegates and spectators began pushing toward the exits, unwilling to wait through the anticlimax of Benjamin Wilcox's nominating speeches. Kay Orcott climbed over the railing of the box where she had been sitting and tried to fight her way to the platform, where Archie was waving at her. The organ surprisingly began bellowing forth the Air Force song, and an angry Carl Fleischer rushed to the rostrum to demand that Terhune stop it. McCormick Place wallowed in sheer sound.

In his suite at the Hilton, Manchester caught a brief glimpse of his wife as a TV camera panned past her face. She wore an expression of mingled surprise and happiness.

"I hope she gets out of there in one piece," Manchester said. He turned and studied Calvin Burroughs' face. "Well, what do you think, Cal?"

Burroughs held up a hand, his fingers crossed. "With luck," he said, "you've got a chance. It'll take an awful lot of luck —but you're alive again, C.B."

20

Archie ran his thumb idly over the raised gold lettering on the big red ticket he had taken from the stack on his desk. He looked at Kay Orcott inquiringly.

"I don't get it," he said. "Who gave them to her?"

It was 2:30 A.M. The last delegate had long since left McCormick Place after the final seconding speech for Benjamin Wilcox. Archie and Kay were seated at the desk in his little office in the Hilton. Fatigue had settled on Archie like a gray mantle: his eyes were bloodshot, his stomach quivered in protest against the long hours of wakefulness, a black stubble of beard covered the lower part of his face, and his nerve ends felt like running sores. Archie had had a total of only sixteen hours of sleep in five nights.

Kay's freshness, enhanced by an afternoon nap before the convention session, did nothing to appease his own yearning for slumber. She smiled brightly, and Archie found himself counting the freckles on her thin nose and wondering how her head would feel nestled in the hollow of his shoulder. He felt a surge of affection for her, and longed for time to sort out his feelings. All he knew now was that he felt both comfortable and happy when she was nearby, vaguely restive when she was elsewhere. She was a strange little thing who wore her emotions and desires on the outside, like buttons on a dress. Her flashes of candor startled him. If he could go away with her, away from politicians and telephones and crowds and adding machines . . . He thought of the way the sunset looked from the Lake of the Clouds hut on Mount Washington, and he felt the warm press of a girl's body beside him and the sting of the evening wind on his cheeks. If only there were time.

Then he noticed the cardboard tickets again. Those damn tickets. He rubbed the heel of his hand against the whiskers on his jaw. Back to the business he didn't understand.

"What was your mother supposed to do with them?"

"Honey," said Kay, "those tickets are fakes. Somebody working for Carl Fleischer—search me who—got a whole bunch of them printed and a little man brought five hundred of them up to our room. Mom was supposed to hand them out. I guess the other floor leaders must have gotten packages of them, too."

"So what are they doing here?"

"Mom got mad. First that computer thing, and now this. I guess she popped off to Governor Roberts last night. She complained about the kind of information the computer had stored up on the delegates, and the Governor said she must be mistaken—"

"I know," he interrupted. "You told me all about that. But I don't get the deal on these tickets."

Kay shook her head. "I don't know either, except that Mother got mad and tossed the bundle of tickets on the dresser and said she wouldn't have anything to do with them." She grinned. "So I brought them over here. You know me—Little Miss Double Agent."

Archie studied the numbers on the tickets, then burrowed into the stack of papers on his desk. He extracted a long sheet labeled "Allotment of Gallery Admission Cards."

"Here's the thing," he explained. "The arrangements committee divided up the ten thousand spectator seats by states. So naturally the states that are for Manchester, like Ohio and Arkansas and the rest, will have Manchester rooters getting their tickets. The same goes for the Roberts people. The California seats will all have Roberts fans in them this afternoon for the balloting."

"Well," she speculated, "I suppose the fake tickets would all be handed out to people who are for Roberts, and they'd be told to get there early, before the regular ticket holders show up."

"Sure, but it wouldn't make much sense to throw out one Roberts backer and put another one in. There must be some other gimmick." Archie was comparing the numbers on the counterfeit tickets with his long sheet. "Hey, wait a minute. I think I'm getting the idea."

He took a batch of tickets and fanned them out on the desk. "Now, here's a whole section, rows E, F and G, North

Tier, Seats 1 through 20 in each row." He consulted the list. "On the table made out by the arrangements committee, those seats are allotted to Idaho. And Idaho . . . Yeah, that's it."

Kay leaned closer and scrutinized the tickets.

"See," said Archie, pointing at the list, "Idaho is an uncommitted state. Nobody knows for sure yet who's going to get those fourteen votes. So Fleischer was going to stack the Idaho gallery section with Roberts people, and they'd whoop and holler for Roberts. The delegates would be bound to notice it, and anyway if you multiply that fifteen or sixteen times to cover all the uncommitted states, you've got an awful lot of noise in the galleries for Roberts to add to the states that are for him anyway."

Kay screwed up her face in disapproval. "That's not playing fair, is it?"

Archie sighed wearily. "Fleischer and Roger Abbott play to win."

"I think it's dirty," she said. "And Mother does too."

"Isn't your mother cooled off on Roberts by now?"

"Lord knows she ought to be." Kay dunked another cigarette in a coffee cup and it hissed at them. "I don't think Mother knows what to think right now. She's so proud, and she's given her word to Roberts. She's a great one for never going back on her word. But General Shaw's speech really shook her up. And she knows Manchester is right about those bombs and all. She just won't admit it."

Archie felt his eyelids drooping, and he wondered how much longer he could stay awake. "If you could only bring her around," he said sleepily, "we'd give you a medal or something."

Kay leaned across the desk and brushed his lips with a kiss. "You look worse than the city dump," she said. "I'm leaving —and you're going right straight to bed."

He walked her to the elevator, then across the almost deserted lobby. Two porters pushed wide brooms through the nightly debris of the convention: torn banners, discarded buttons and posters, wooden noisemakers, shredded balloons, crumpled newspapers. A fat man, carrying a pennant with the legend "I Like Everybody," teetered indecisively near the Michigan Avenue door. He stared at his hotel-room key, apparently uncertain whether to go to bed or go out again. Archie helped Kay into a cab and watched until she drove off.

In his own room, he peeled off his shirt. It smelled of tobacco and sweat—and perfume. Only about eleven more hours to go, he thought. Does Manchester have a chance? Not much. And what did I do for him today? Not much. The Shaw speech was great, but it probably came too late. Everything seems to be too late. A hot shower. That's what the country needs right now. A hot shower to soothe the nerves and comfort the itching skin. He tugged at his shoelace and swore at the inevitable knot. The phone rang.

Archie picked it up as he sat on the edge of his bed, staring dolefully at the balky shoelace. Who the hell is calling at three o'clock in the morning? And who cares?

"All right," he said.

"Archie?" He had heard that inflection hundreds of times, most recently this—yesterday—afternoon. It was Obie O'Connell.

"Yeah, Obie." Archie was not interested. He was so tired it would have been an effort even to lift his eyes from his shoes.

"Archie, I got a hot item for you."

Archie could hear the tinkle of a piano and a clatter of voices in the background. It took little imagination to smell the whisky on O'Connell's breath.

"Where are you?"

"At a joint on North Clark called the Purple Paddock."

"Well, let the horses have the rest of the rye and go home to bed," said Archie. "That's where I'm going, if you'll get off the goddam phone."

O'Connell's voice sank to the conspiratorial level he favored for the transaction of important business. "Easy, kid. When do I call people at this hour without a good reason?"

"Right now. I thought you were the one who told me to stay off the sauce until the last ballot."

O'Connell kept his voice in low key. "The last ballot, kid, that's what I'm thinking about. You want Manchester to win, don't you?"

Archie didn't bother to answer.

"So if you want to win," continued O'Connell, "you'll get off your duff and get over here toot-sweet to the Purple Paddock. I got something'll knock your eyes out."

"Blonde or brunette?"

"Archie, don't kiss this one off." There was no levity in O'Connell's tone—and Archie had to admit he could detect no trace of a blur in his speech.

"What is it?"

"You got to see it, and you got to talk to a guy. Listen, kid, this could be the biggest break the Manchesters get in this whole crummy convention. I don't say you win with what I got, but it gives you a chance."

"Obie, are you leveling?"

"Kid, when I give my word I give my word."

Archie was still skeptical. "Why do you care, Obie? A guy who gets . . . well, canned . . . usually doesn't want to help the man who fired him."

"Always the psychiatrist, huh, kid?" asked O'Connell gruffly. "Let's just say I put a year of my life into this deal and I don't like to see hard work thrown away."

A year? Archie thought. More like ten years in one. Scenes from the trips he and O'Connell had made together flickered through his fatigue. The night Obie argued until dawn in a Montpelier hotel room, trying to persuade two Vermont delegates who leaned to Roberts. The morning during the Wisconsin primary campaign when they landed at Eau Claire in a snowstorm to keep an appointment. The pilot had wanted to turn back to Milwaukee, but Obie doubled the charter price and they waggled down to the runway, snow pelting the cockpit windshield from a 100-foot ceiling. Yes, Obie had committed his professional pride—and perhaps more of his emotions than he realized.

"Obie," said Archie. "I think you've forgiven Manchester."

"Maybe yes, maybe no. Now, for Christ's sake, kid, can the psychology and get over here quick."

"Okay."

O'Connell supplied the address and Archie, almost mechanically, pulled a fresh shirt from his drawer and buttoned it on, then went to the bathroom and ran the electric razor over his jaw. He looked longingly at the shower nozzle. Later, maybe.

He was almost to the elevator when he remembered. He

walked back through the empty headquarters to his desk and wrapped up the stack of counterfeit tickets, using the brown paper in which Kay had delivered them. The package weighed only two or three pounds, but to Archie it felt like twenty.

The Purple Paddock consisted of two long rows of booths, upholstered in black leather with crimson buttons. Wreaths of smoke lay in the air and human sounds came in the spasms which characterize a bar in its final half hour before closing. A Negro fingered the piano keys lazily while a blonde in a low-cut evening gown sat on the end of the bar and crooned throatily of illicit love.

O'Connell was in a back booth with a thin, hollow-cheeked man whom Archie recognized as Bones Cramer, the party mercenary currently in the employ of the Rocky Mountain Conference. O'Connell moved over to make room for Archie.

"You know Bones Cramer, don't you, Archie?"

Archie nodded. "Sure. How are you, Mr. Cramer?"

Cramer said nothing. He merely showed a twisted grin as he fingered the little metal box at the end of the wire which led to his hearing aid.

"He's tuning you in," said O'Connell. "Bones does me a big favor tonight, Archie, but as far as you're concerned, you never saw him and you never saw me either. Okay?"

"Okay." Archie knew that Obie was never happier than when whetting the appetite for intrigue. He eyed the glass on the table before the fallen manager. O'Connell, noticing, shook his head.

"Lemonade," he said. "Plain, straight, lousy lemonade. In this place it costs me a buck-fifty. And for once, Bones isn't picking up the check."

"Scotch and water," Archie said to the waitress who was standing at his elbow.

O'Connell's pudgy face wore a small, almost secret, smile. He had shoved his dumpy body deep into the black upholstery, and his double chin showed more prominently than usual because of the slouch. Bones Cramer, his wasted cheeks almost funereal in the gloom of the Purple Paddock, said nothing.

"Bones," said O'Connell, "thinks I got a bum rap from the Secretary of the Treasury, so he came to visit me." He winked slyly. "In my hospital room. He brought me a very nice gift."

O'Connell reached into his coat and brought out a sheet of paper. It was of more than ordinary weight, and it crackled when he unfolded it. The former manager held it slightly away from Archie.

"You remember the name Kolsak?" he asked.

Archie tried to remember. "I've heard it somewhere," he answered, "but it doesn't ring any bells right off."

"If you're going to be a pro in this business, kid, you've got to work on that memory of yours. It stinks."

"Wait a minute," Archie said. "Kolsak. Wasn't he one of the guys who seconded Roberts tonight?"

"That's the stuff," O'Connell said. "John Kolsak came to Chicago for Manchester. He was on my list. But yesterday he switches to Roberts and tonight he makes a seconding speech for him. Kolsak is head of a building trades local in New York. Now read this."

Archie took the stiff sheet of paper and tried to read it. It was too dark, and O'Connell snapped his cigarette lighter on and held it beside the paper. It was a typewritten document:

August 16
Chicago, Illinois
Voluntary Statement of Henry Yobst

I, Henry Yobst, swear under oath to the following facts:

That I am a delegate to the Republican National Convention from New York City, duly elected in a party primary. That John Kolsak is also a delegate to the same convention from New York City, and was also duly elected and qualified.

That on August 15, in the city of Chicago, at about 3:15 o'clock p.m., Kolsak and I were in my room, room 512 in the Drake hotel, where we were visited at that time by one Jacob Sheffelin, known to me to be an employe of the Missile and Aerospace Workers union, with headquarters in Los Angeles, California.

That Mr. Kolsak and I were known to Mr. Sheffelin to be delegates to the said convention and to have announced our intention of voting for Charles B. Manchester of Ohio for the Republican nomination for President of the United States.

That Mr. Sheffelin did present various and sundry arguments in behalf of the candidacy of Governor Bryan Roberts of California and that he departed from my room in the Drake hotel at about 5 o'clock p.m., after placing two envelopes on the top of the dresser, one envelope marked "K" and one envelope marked "Y."

That I opened the envelope marked "Y" and found therein one thousand dollars ($1,000) in cash, in twenty-dollar ($20) bills, and that Mr. Kolsak opened the envelope marked "K" and found therein one thousand dollars ($1,000) in twenty-dollar ($20) bills.

That Mr. Kolsak thereupon observed that Mr. Sheffelin was a generous man and that he, Mr. Kolsak, believed that such generosity should be rewarded, or words to that effect, and that Mr. Kolsak left my room at about 5:15 o'clock p.m., and that he carried the envelope containing the money in his inner suit coat pocket.

That after about one hour, during which time I thought about the circumstances and concluded that I had been offered a bribe in violation of federal laws, I left the room and went to the Roman Catholic Church of the Blessed Redeemer.

That at the Church of the Blessed Redeemer, I described the above events to Father Kelly, the priest, and that I gave the one thousand dollars ($1,000) to him for the church or for such good works as Father Kelly might deem fitting.

That the above facts are true and complete to the best of my knowledge and recollection.

Signed:
Henry Yobst

State of Illinois
Cook County

I hearby certify that on this day personally appeared before me, an officer duly authorized to administer oaths and take acknowledgments, *Henry Yobst,* to me well known and known to me to be the person described in and who executed the foregoing affidavit; and he acknowledged before me that he executed the same for the purposes therein expressed.

Witness my hand and official seal at Chicago, Cook County, state of Illinois, this *16th* day of *August.*

Signed:
Galen Moriarty
Notary Public

Archie reread parts of the statement, stared at the paper for a minute, then handed it back to O'Connell. The little Irishman shook his head.

"That's for you, kid," he said. "I wouldn't show it to any newspapermen if I was you, but from now until they finish voting, I'd show it to every delegate I could find who's wobbling between Roberts and Manchester."

"My God, what a break," said Archie. He folded the sheet

carefully and tucked it into his breast pocket. "How in hell did you get hold of that, Obie?"

O'Connell toyed with his glass without looking up. "Let's not be too curious," he said. "Let's just say that my old friend Bones is a man with pity in his soul and righteousness in his heart." Cramer coughed hoarsely and his gloomy face cracked in a grin. "And Bones has a lot of friends in this convention who are under—shall we say—some little obligation to him."

Archie looked inquiringly at Cramer, but the mercenary merely chewed on a swizzle stick and cast a brooding eye on his own drink. If Cramer's hearing aid was turned on, there was no outward sign of it.

"But you said you wanted me to talk to somebody here." Archie looked inquiringly at O'Connell.

"I did. I wanted you to ask Bones, who is a man of his word, if that affidavit is on the level, just so you'd satisfy yourself."

After a pause, Archie spoke to Cramer. "Well, is it? I mean, are you sure Kolsak was bribed?"

"Yep." It was the first word Cramer had uttered since Archie arrived, and though he waited for further enlightenment, Cramer offered nothing more.

"You got your answer, kid," said O'Connell. "And you can bet ten grand on anything Bones says."

Archie put his arm around O'Connell and gave him a hug. "You're a goddam cutthroat, Obie, and if I were the candidate you'd still be my top pirate."

"Bones and I may not look so pretty, but we know where a lot of the bodies are buried. Right, Bones?"

"Right," said Cramer, showing the twisted grin again.

"So look, kid, don't ask too many questions," said O'Connell. "Just go your way, work hard, keep your nose clean, and if your man makes it, don't forget your friends."

Archie wondered whether the wetness he felt on his eyelids was merely one more symptom of his lack of sleep. At any rate, he turned his head, lest O'Connell misunderstand, and he started to slide out of the booth.

As he moved, he felt the paper package resting against his thigh. He lifted it onto the table, then looked uncertainly from O'Connell to Cramer.

"Don't worry," said O'Connell. "Bones is neutral—for me. Anything you want to show me, kid, Bones never sees it. Right, Bones?"

Cramer nodded. Archie unwrapped the package and handed each man a sample ticket. He explained where Kay Orcott had got them and how he thought the Roberts people planned to use them. O'Connell compared the bogus tickets with a pair of genuine ones he had in his pocket.

"It's a perfect copy," he said, "right down to the name of the printing company and the union bug. But you can bet your last cent that Roger Abbott—he's the guy, for my dough— didn't get them printed by the same people that made the real ones. It's a smooth job, though."

The two men studied the counterfeit tickets with admiration. Cramer caressed the raised gold lettering. O'Connell tapped the table with a ticket.

"What are you going to do with these, Archie?"

"I was going to take them down to the hotel incinerator and burn them, but on second thought I decided to bring them along and show them to you."

"That was not a clean thought," said O'Connell. "You came to tempt me, didn't you? The Secretary would not like that."

Archie sighed and smiled.

"The Secretary doesn't have to know everything that his friends talk about, does he?"

O'Connell laughed and his tubby body jiggled. "Kid," he said, "I like you better every day. Now, I'm just thinking out loud, you understand, but if you're up against a bunch of sharpies, and you get a chance to fix the game so you wind up conning the con men, well . . ."

"Well?"

"Well, if Mrs. Orcott got five hundred of these phonies, Abbott must be putting out three-four thousand of them, and wouldn't he be surprised if somebody else found a nice printing plant right after breakfast that could do another fast job?"

"He would be," said Archie.

"Of course," O'Connell cautioned, "a rush job like that would cost maybe a couple of grand. Now, if I knew where a fellow might get reimbursed for an enterprising endeavor like that, I might . . ."

"Fortunately," Archie pointed out, "Louis Cohen writes the checks for the convention expenses."

"And Louis's a reasonable man, huh? Even if he does act like the world's going up in smoke every day before dinner."

Archie nodded and extended his hand. O'Connell shook it. Cramer took care to keep his eyes on his glass, as befits a man who does not care to be in the position of having to testify about what he saw.

"I can get hold of a seating chart, all right," O'Connell said thoughtfully. "But I'm going to need an awful lot of strong young college kids with big lungs who'll be willing to get to McCormick Place about three hours ahead of time."

"The lobbies are full of 'em and they'll do anything for a

seat in the gallery," Archie said. "And most of them like Manchester too."

"So who doesn't?" asked O'Connell.

Archie tried to sleep in the cab taking him back to the Hilton, but he failed. His mind was on Bones Cramer. A neutral, Obie had said. . . . But the gossip around the convention was that Cramer did some undercover errands for O'Connell. . . . And Cramer's reputation in the party was linked to money, not all of which went through checking accounts. . . . What was his role and why would he turn such an affidavit over to Obie? . . . Where did he get it?

On a hunch, Archie stopped off at the headquarters office, switched on a light and went to Louis Cohen's cubicle. The top filing cabinet drawer, Archie knew, held the record of the convention expenses. Cohen and his assistant for finances were meticulous in keeping track of expenditures. Archie looked behind "C" in the cardboard index and pulled out a sheaf of papers . . . carpenters, Cohen, cab fares, communications, classified ads, cowbells. . . . He replaced the papers and thought a minute, then looked under "S" for a folder marked "Special Expenditures." A simple typewritten note on a sheet in the folder said: "Paid to O. B. O'Connell, Friday, August 11, $3,000. For disbursement to Wilfred Cramer for special services during convention."

Archie replaced the folder. Special services? Mr. Bones Cramer, he thought, has been about as neutral in this convention as Julia Manchester. Archie looked at the affidavit again. It seemed genuine enough, but he made a mental note to have Cohen check both the delegate and the notary public in the morning.

Archie made his way to his room like a sleepwalker, and fumbled for his key. As he swung the door open, he noticed an envelope on the floor. It was addressed to him in Cohen's handwriting. He read the note under the bedside lamp:

Archie:
My count, as of 4 a.m., shows us with only 470 sure votes. I make it between 600 and 610 sure for Roberts. I understand Fleischer is claiming 665 now, or 10 more than he needs to win.
How we're going to pick up 185 by this afternoon I don't know. Hate to send you to bed like this, but knew you'd want it straight.

Louis.

Archie slowly tore the paper up and dropped it in the waste-basket. There just wasn't enough time left, and if there had been, he was too tired to use it. He undressed numbly, completely forgot about the shower and wilted into bed without even pulling on his pajamas. With his head on the pillow, he reached for the telephone.

"Seven o'clock call for this room, please," he told the operator.

"But, sir, it's already almost five."

"I know."

A montage of convention halls, tickets, girls with freckled noses, Bones Cramers, drunks, and trampled placards whirled though his head. He could see Bryan Roberts, his arms outstretched to the multitudes. He could see Julia Manchester with tears in her eyes, and he could hear the roar of thousands of voices like a wild wind funneling through a mountain pass. Then he heard and saw nothing more. Archie DuPage was snoring.

21

He should have been thinking of Manchester, McCormick Place and the afternoon balloting, but all that really concerned Archie at the moment was whether he would live through the day. It was 7:30 A.M. and he had the cab window wide open to let the freshness of the morning envelop him. The streets were still clean and cool; the rising August sun had not yet bleached the tang out of the air. Over the Chicago River two rival terns plunged at an unseen fish and the loser shrilled his dismay.

Archie should have felt refreshed as he rode north, but in fact his head pounded, his eyes ached, and his feet were sweating inside his clean socks. He sneezed and then let out a melancholy sigh. A summer cold was inevitable: his resistance was down to zero. He could envision himself, the responsible manager of a candidate for President, snuffling and hacking through the coming combat in McCormick Place.

The lobby of the Ambassador East was almost as vacant as Archie had anticipated, but he was somewhat surprised to see a Western Union boy, carrying a big bundle of telegrams, at the information desk, while a second messenger came toward him from the elevators. The second boy grinned at Archie.

"Back for another armload," he said.

Archie was surprised again when Kay Orcott answered her phone after the first ring.

"You disobeyed me," she said. "You were supposed to sleep till eight-thirty."

"How did *you* get out of bed so fast?"

Kay laughed. There was no sleepy mist in her voice. "Bed? We've been up since six. Isn't it fascinating?"

"Fascinating?" He sneezed again. "Kay, are you and your mother decent? I want to see her right away. I'm in the lobby."

"Sure, handsome, come on up. But you won't see me—not until I get rid of this hair net and robe."

Grace Orcott opened the door to the small sitting room of her suite and offered her hand to Archie. Despite the hour, she was faultlessly attired in a gray linen dress and her hair was swept up as smoothly as though she had just left the beauty parlor.

"Business or pleasure, Archie?" she asked. Her smile was easy and warm. "Me or Kay?"

"Politics, Mrs. Orcott. It's you I want to see."

"Grace, please."

"All right, Grace," he said, "I've got something I want to show you in confidence. You're the first person I thought

ought to see it this morning."

"Not another telegram, I hope," She pointed to a large easy chair. It almost overflowed with telegrams, most of them still in their small yellow envelopes. "I've got about five hundred already."

"Birthday?" he asked.

She laughed at his puzzled look. "Not mine, and it sure isn't Bryan Roberts', either."

"I want you to read this," said Archie. He handed her the affidavit O'Connell had given him in the Purple Paddock.

Mrs. Orcott took the paper, then pulled her reading glasses from the purse on her writing desk. The pale, pearl-studded frames gave her a piquant harlequin appearance when she fitted the spectacles over her ears.

"You can be reading the wires," she said, but Archie kept his eyes on her as she read. She scanned the paper, fingered it as if assuring herself of its authenticity, then reread parts of the affidavit.

"Where did you get this?" she asked.

"I can't tell you, Grace. But you have my word that it's genuine."

That is, Archie thought, you have my word that I trust Obie O'Connell. And Louis Cohen should be trying to find Henry Yobst and that notary right now.

Mrs. Orcott tapped the paper against her finger nails.

"That's the last straw," she said.

Archie suppressed his urge to cheer. "I hoped you'd say that."

"I mean, it really is. First that frightful—no, ridiculous is the word—computer. Then Roger Abbott having the gall to ask me to distribute fake gallery tickets. And now this."

Mrs. Orcott folded her arms and looked Archie in the eye. I'm glad, he thought, that I'm not the guy who crossed her.

"Archie, I think Secretary Manchester made a dreadful mistake in raising that missile issue," she said. "His timing was horrible, even though I'm beginning to think I agree with him. But I just can't tolerate the tactics that Bin Roberts is letting his people get away with. I told him so to his face. I think it's bad for the party. Just imagine what people around the country must have thought about Republicans during General Shaw's speech last night—even if they weren't sure just what he was driving at."

"The Secretary wouldn't let us tie anything to Governor Roberts," Archie said. "He thinks Roberts doesn't know what's going on."

"I must say the Governor was convincing when he denied knowing anything about that personal stuff in the computer," she said, "but he admitted he let Mark Davidson use the room on Clark Street. For my money, it adds up to the same thing."

"Mrs. Orcott," said Archie, "I think you ought to vote for Manchester."

"Don't worry," she said. Her cheeks were flushed and she looked every inch the regal politician. "I'm going to."

"Can I quote you on that, Grace? It would be a big break for us, and we can sure use one. We're still short a lot of votes and there's only about five hours to go."

She gave a brisk nod. "You can tell anybody and everybody. I'm ashamed of what we've been doing out of Bin's head-quarters—and anyway it looks like the people like Man-chester."

She pointed at the telegrams in the chair. At the same time, Kay stepped from the bedroom and there was a loud knock on the hall door. Kay planted a small kiss on Archie's cheek while her mother answered the door. It was a Western Union boy with another bundle of telegrams.

"My God," said Mrs. Orcott, "I don't think anybody in the country went to bed last night."

She dropped the yellow envelopes in the chair. It was now so full that several wires fell over the arms and fluttered to the floor. Mrs. Orcott picked one at random, tore open the envelope and read aloud:

" 'My husband and I implore you to vote for Charles Manchester stop He is a great man stop America needs him stop Mrs. Evelyn Foley 122 Fourth Avenue Odessa Texas.' "

She opened another envelope. "This one is from Houston, someone named Otto Schoenfelder. 'I am a high school junior and I can't vote but please nominate Manchester so I can vote for him next time stop Our whole family wants Manchester.' "

Archie was stunned. He stood by numbly as Mrs. Orcott opened telegram after telegram, announcing only the points of origin. "Dallas, El Paso, San Antonio, Pecos, Midland, Dallas, Austin, Houston, Houston, Corpus Christi, Galveston, Dallas again, Houston, Uvalde, Tyler, Bonham, Austin, Dallas.

"I don't know about the rest of the country," she said, "but somebody set Texas on fire for Manchester."

Archie groped for an answer. He found it hard to believe —let alone evaluate—what he was hearing. He sneezed again and when he wiped his nose, he found his handkerchief was getting soggy. "I don't get it," he said.

"It's just plain people," crowed Kay. "They're talking up, Archie. I told you they would. Maybe it was General Shaw's speech."

Grace Orcott held three wires in her hands and studied the

wording. "It doesn't seem to be organized at all," she said. "You don't get the same phrases."

The three people in the room were linked now as though by an electric current. Archie could feel his fatigue scattering as if he had suddenly undergone shock treatment on his scalp. When Kay poured coffee for them from a big silver pot, her hand trembled.

"Let's put in a call," said Mrs. Orcott. She picked up one of the opened wires. "I'll try this Mrs. Foley in Odessa. I'd just like to check. Something's going on, but I'm not sure what."

Kay sat on the floor by the coffee table while her mother telephoned. Archie remained standing, shuffling his feet restlessly. Mrs. Orcott had trouble getting through and asked the operator the reason for the delay. She put her hand over the mouthpiece. "The Odessa operator says half the town is placing or getting long-distance calls and it isn't even seven o'clock there yet."

"Mrs. Foley?" she spoke into the phone. "This is Grace Orcott, Mrs. Orcott, in Chicago. I'm the Republican national committeewoman from Texas and you sent me a wire. Would you mind telling me how you happened to do it?"

She listened intently. Archie and Kay could hear the babble of a woman's voice in the phone. Mrs. Foley seemed to be excited; her words ran together in a swift chain. Grace Orcott thanked her and hung up. Her face showed surprise and she patted nervously at her hair.

"Young Mrs. Foley, and she did sound young, says she was called about three A.M. by an old friend in Denver, another woman," Mrs. Orcott explained. "She was asked to send a wire to a delegate—any delegate—on behalf of Manchester, and then to call ten friends and ask them to do the same. I was the only delegate whose name she knew. I'm at-large, so it figures. She didn't know the name of the delegate from Odessa."

"Good Lord," said Archie, "do you suppose it's one of those chain-letter things, only on the telephone?"

"Mom, try another one," Kay said.

Mrs. Orcott dug into the pile of telegrams on the chair and pulled one up from the bottom. "Here's one of the early ones. From a Frank Eyerly in Corpus Christi. It was sent at eleven-fifteen last night."

She picked up the phone again and called the man at the address he had given. She introduced herself, asked what had prompted the telegram and listened closely again. Her eyes were wide when she turned back to Kay and Archie.

"The speech didn't start it," she said. "Mr. Eyerly has a florist shop and last night, while he was watching Shaw on television, he was called by another florist he knows in Houston. The man said he'd been called himself an hour or so earlier, and asked Eyerly to send a wire and then call ten friends and ask them to do the same."

Archie pulled a notebook from his pocket and began scribbling figures. "Holy Moses! . . . If one person calls ten and then ten call ten and then a hundred call . . . Why, that's a million people on the sixth round. And ten million on the seventh. You don't suppose that's really happening?"

"I'll tell you one thing," Mrs. Orcott said. "As a professional, I'll guarantee you couldn't organize anything like that. It's been tried and it doesn't work. It'd have to be some kind of spontaneous thing. And from the way those two I talked to sounded, people might be just excited enough to do it."

Kay tucked up her knees as she sat on the floor. Her eyes were bright. "Of course," she said, "you'd never get all ten to call. You have to figure it's only seven or eight each time, or maybe less."

"Even so," Archie said, "even if only five called each time, you'd have an awful big swarm of people inside of twelve hours." He grabbed Kay's hand and pulled her to her feet. "Come on," he said. "Let's go find out what the hell is happening."

"I haven't had breakfast yet," she complained. "Only coffee."

"Who has?" He had to let go of her hand to muffle a sneeze. "Lend me some Kleenex and let's go."

Kay stuffed some tissues in his pocket, took his hand and walked to the door with him. She wore a starched green cotton dress, its collar held by a little gold pin. The freckles on her nose were countable this morning, her hair was a soft brown cap, and Archie knew he'd never seen a girl who looked so appealing. He waggled his finger at Mrs. Orcott from the doorway.

"No backsliding to Roberts, now, ma'am," he said.

"Don't lose my daughter," she replied. "Her dad is a right big man and he's got a temper."

In the hallway, Archie and Kay passed another Western Union boy. He had a bundle of telegrams tied with string.

"Orcott again?" asked Archie.

"Nope," said the boy, "some guy named Fuller in 612. It's his second batch."

In the lobby, Archie looked up the address of the main downtown Western Union office in the city phone book. Kay chattered gaily during the cab ride. Archie felt a surge of elation. His stomach was tense again, but this time it didn't seem to bother him. Unfortunately, he sneezed three times en route and arrived with his eyes watering helplessly.

The Western Union office was a bedlam of noise and activity. Phones rang, teleprinters beat rhythmically, signal bells jingled, and workers shouted at one another over the mechanical sounds. A man in shirt-sleeves hurried across the room, trailing three long strips of printer tape. Messenger boys, some without uniforms, crowded the front desk to pick up bundles of yellow envelopes from harassed, unsmiling clerks. Archie guessed that at least fifty people were at work in the big room. He asked for the manager and was directed to the second floor.

"Never seen anything like it," said the manager in response to Archie's questions. "The whole country must be going nuts over this fellow Manchester. We're getting wires from every state in the Union and from a lot of towns I never heard of before—and I've been handling traffic for thirty years."

"Many for Roberts?" asked Archie.

The manager shook his head. "Not one out of twenty, if that." He swept his hand around the second-floor room, where operators struggled to cut and paste the ribbons of printer tape pouring from the machines. "Some of these people have been working fifteen hours now. The rush started before my shifts changed last night and I just kept 'em on. I've called out every operator on my sub list and now I'm having to borrow them from the brokerage houses."

"Any idea how many telegrams you've handled?"

The manager squinted and looked at the ceiling for a moment. Archie noticed that the man's eyes were flecked with red lines. Had sleep been repealed all over? "It would just be a wild guess," said the manager. "Maybe a hundred thousand so far, maybe more. But they keep coming in all the time. My circuits are jammed and we've had to set up a lot of crazy routings to get these things in here. Some of them are going to be hours late."

Archie propelled Kay out of the building at a half run. They drove back to the Hilton, where Archie found half a dozen of his college-girl volunteers already at work and bubbling like fountains. One girl threw her arms around his neck and kissed him, leaving two crimson stains on his chin. "Isn't it wonderful?" she cried. "They're burning up the wires for Manchester!"

Archie thought of going down to the basement press room to alert the dayside reporters to the story, but a glance at his ticker told him it was already out. The first item of the day was just coming in on the convention wire. Archie ripped off the copy and he and Kay huddled over it.

UPI Convention 1
          (Wires)
          Chicago—A yellow tide of "vote-for-Manchester" telegrams poured in upon still-sleeping Republican delegates in this convention city early today.
          Western Union city manager Peter Donahue estimated that 100,000 pro-Manchester wires already had been delivered to the 1,308 delegates and that another 50,000 might be delivered by noon.
          The flood of telegrams threatened to overwhelm Western

Union facilities. Donahue called 100 extra operators and messenger boys for emergency duty.

No comparable traffic load could be recalled by Donahue, a 30-year veteran in the company's Chicago office. On a nation-wide basis, the deluge far exceeded the telegraphic demonstration in the 1952 campaign for Richard M. Nixon, then the Republican nominee for vice-president. The 1952 telegram flow was provoked by Nixon's famous televised speech on his campaign finances.

Meanwhile telephone officials said the nation's phone circuits were carrying what appeared to be one of the heaviest loads in years. The calls, apparently almost all urging the nomination of Manchester, seemed to be the result of a "call-ten" chain phenomenon in which each person receiving a telephone call for Manchester is asked to send a wire to a convention delegate in Chicago and then call ten other persons on behalf of the Treasury Secretary.

Officials were at a loss to explain the tremendous communications surge, but doubted it could be traced entirely to General Wesley Shaw's explosive convention speech last night. The upturn in traffic apparently began on the West Coast Wednesday some hours before Shaw's evening speech.

EDW—830ACDT

Archie was about to take the ticker copy to Manchester's suite when his own phone rang. It was the city editor of the Los Angeles *Herald-Examiner*.

"Mr. DuPage," the newsman said, "we've got a tip out here that this chain telephone thing started somewhere in California. Can you help us any?"

"Gee, no," said Archie. "I haven't got the foggiest notion. I just got out of bed. The whole business surprises me as much as anybody."

"You're surprised?" The newsman's question was laced with cynicism. "Come on, Mr. DuPage. Somebody in your outfit had to plan this."

"So help me," protested Archie, "nobody around here was smart enough to think of it. I wish we had been. But whoever started it, you've got to admit it couldn't keep going unless there was an awful lot of basic sentiment for Manchester."

"I'll buy that," said the editor. "Still, somebody had to start it."

"Well, I'm not covering up anything. I'd be glad to tell you if I knew. Is there a lot of telephoning out there?"

"Are you kidding? People have been calling each other all night. Women, mostly. Every dame and her sister has been on the horn. The whole state of California is going crazy."

"That's news?" asked Archie, and the editor laughed with him.

Tugging Kay with one hand and carrying the sheet of ticker copy in the other, Archie went to the Royal Skyway suite. Charles and Julia Manchester were eating breakfast in the dinette. Archie introduced Kay.

"And you're getting a big break, C.B.," he said. "Kay's mother—Grace Orcott, you know, the committeewoman from Texas—is switching from Roberts to you. We'll get an announcement out right away."

Manchester beamed. "Grace Orcott is one of the most astute women I know. But what's going on this morning, Archie? The waiter told us there was a lot of excitement."

Archie handed him the ticker copy. Manchester's eyes swept rapidly through the story, and he grinned as he passed it to his wife. "Maybe we're not dead yet, Julie," he said.

"The whole thing is fantastic," said Archie. "It's hard to believe."

He described the scene at the Western Union office.

"Honestly, Mr. Secretary, the whole country's going goofy," said Kay.

Manchester laughed and cocked his head at Kay. "Well, now, Kay, I hardly thought when I started this campaign that people would have to be goofy before they supported me."

"I didn't mean it like it sounded, Mr. Secretary." She smiled in embarrassment.

"If you ask me," said Julia Manchester, "at this stage, we'd better take anything we can get—from soup to nuts."

Manchester began pacing the floor. He was a walking exhibition of pent-up energy.

"Where did it all start?" he asked.

"Nobody knows," said Archie. "I got a call from a Los Angeles paper. They think it started out there. But who cares? It's the biggest thing on the phone lines since Orson Welles and his Men-from-Mars program."

Archie drew Manchester aside and showed him the Henry Yobst affidavit. "We're going to make a lot of time with this, boss," he said.

Manchester read the document through slowly. His face clouded. "Where did you get it?" he asked.

Archie hesitated. Should he tell the whole story? He quickly decided in the negative. A candidate, as Obie said, didn't have to know everything that was done for him.

"Obie O'Connell got it for us," he said.

"Obie?"

"Yeah. Knowing Obie, I'm sure it's genuine, but I've got

Louis Cohen checking it out right now, just to be safe."

"I hate to think of that kind of thing in a Republican convention," said Manchester. "You don't intend to give this to the newspapers?"

"No, no," said Archie. "We're just going to show it to key people in private. People who are still wavering."

"Be careful," said Manchester. "We don't want to blacken the whole party just to win a nomination."

"Right," said Archie, though inwardly he was far less concerned about that aspect than his tone indicated.

A headquarters typist, her young face dappled with joy, came into the suite carrying a bundle of telegrams. She giggled as she handed them to Julia Manchester.

"A lot of people want you to vote for your husband, Mrs. Manchester," she said. "They must think you're a delegate or something."

"That's the plain people again, Mr. Secretary," said Kay Orcott. "They've been for you all along, but they're speaking out now."

But others were speaking out too. From the sidewalk far below wafted the strains of a band playing the Roberts song. Archie flinched. Time, time, time, he thought unhappily. People across the country were voicing their support for Manchester—finally—but had they waited too long? Once more Archie sneezed, and this time he cursed.

22

A loud hum, not unlike the sound of an angry swarm of bees, filled McCormick Place. Delegates, messengers, miscellaneous officials and various interlopers who had stolen floor passes or simply crashed the gates moved through the aisles in endless slow motion. All over the convention hall people spread tally sheets on their laps, unwilling to rely on the big screen behind the platform where the running vote totals would be maintained as the balloting proceeded.

Now for the first time the press benches flanking the platform were filled to their thousand-man capacity. Hundreds of typewriters clacked and reporters waved sheets of copy at waiting messengers.

In the raised tiers at the sides and rear of the hall, built to accommodate ten thousand spectators, knots of people argued furiously over seats and ushers struggled to settle skirmishes over duplicate tickets. In one far corner a woman screamed when a fat man, struck full in the face by a foe, fell across her lap and sent both of them sprawling into the aisle.

Chairman Joe Terhune, his face flushed and angry under his shock of white hair, eyed the galleries balefully and looked again at his watch. It was 1:40 P.M.; he had been pounding vainly for order for the past ten minutes. One of the several dozen television cameras covering the scene was aimed at Terhune from a corner box reserved for ranking guests. A roving newspaperman leaned across the box railing to speak to someone. The cameraman yelled and cursed at him. "My picture! My picture! Get your lousy head out of my goddam picture!" The reporter, not moving, turned his head and asked: "You own this convention, Fatso?"

Abandoning all efforts to reduce the chaos to some form of manageable confusion, Terhune signaled the organist with a special button and the introductory bars of "The Star-Spangled Banner" thundered forth. To the rostrum microphone stepped Lily Angelica, a soprano whose high notes cut the smoky haze like a knife. Miss Angelica completed the casting call of the nation's big minorities; the national anthem had now been sung by a Negro, a Jew, a Pole and an Italian.

In the relative quiet following her rendition, Joe Terhune moved swiftly to cap the volcano before it could erupt again. He thrust a waiting minister into the breach, actually giving the man a little push on his last step to the lectern. It was the Rev. Jonathan Corleigh Kirkpatrick, the best-known Episcopal divine in the nation. As he prayed for spiritual insight for the surprisingly hushed congregation, Bones Cramer crouched in the aisle beside the Minnesota standard. He fingered the control mechanism of his hearing aid and whispered to his friend Montcalm Andersen.

"Trust Joe," he said. "He lets a Catholic and a Jew and a Baptist pray at the other sessions, but when the party gets down to business, Joe wants to talk to the Lord in the Lord's own language—Episcopalian."

With the Rev. Mr. Kirkpatrick's final sonorous "Amen," an explosion of human sounds burst once more in the great hall. The struggles broke out again in the spectator sections. Into the aisles from the rear poured a score of Western Union boys, each carrying an armful of bundled telegrams. The messengers fought their way through the clogged pathways to the state standards, then cried out the names of the delegates for whom they were searching. Terhune flailed the stout wooden sounding board on the rostrum.

"The chair will repeat that all delivery of telegrams to delegates must cease at once," he shouted.

A chorus of boos welled from the spectator galleries. Many delegates looked up in surprise. At the Kansas standard, Roger Abbott stood up on his chair to get a better look. The prolonged sounds of protest seemed to be coming from all sections of the visitors' tiers.

At a little table on the platform ramp, Louis Cohen's normally unhappy face was lighted with a smile as he reached over to shake Archie DuPage's hand. "For a couple of new boys," he whispered, "we didn't do too bad with those galleries." Archie's answering grin was split by a violent sneeze. "Thank God for Obie," he said, swabbing his itching nose with his fourth handkerchief of the day.

Carl Fleischer slammed down the intercom phone at his little table across the platform from Archie and rushed to the rostrum. He grabbed Terhune's arm and spun the chairman around. Fleischer's dark glasses shimmered under the arc lights and his face was knotted in anger.

"Joe, those galleries are being packed for Manchester," he shouted. "I demand a recess."

Terhune shook his head. "I talked to the sergeant at arms," he said. "He says it's impossible to tell one ticket from another."

Fleischer jabbed at the chairman's chest with his finger. Archie hurried to the head of the platform to join the argument. A medley of cheers and boos shook the auditorium. The two managers faced the chairman like mutineers on the bow of a storm-tossed ship.

"Are you responsible for any counterfeit tickets, Mr. DuPage?" asked Terhune.

"No!" Archie's answer was almost a shout. He shook his finger at Fleischer. "But his people printed thousands of phonies."

"Prove it!" yelled Fleischer.

"I saw them!"

"Then why are the galleries yelling for Manchester?" Fleischer spit out the words.

Terhune poked his gavel between the two men and ordered them to step back. Under the rostrum a man with hands cupped to his mouth was shouting up to Terhune. It was Boise Floberg, the Senate leader, who had fought his way down the aisle from the Iowa delegation.

"Joe, Joe," he yelled, "for God's sake, cover up those microphones. The whole country's listening in!"

Terhune heard him at last and flung an arm across the row of microphones which bristled on the rostrum like iron roses.

Sweat stood on his forehead and he looked imploringly at Fleischer and Archie.

"Go back to your seats, please," he said.

"I want a fair shake," growled Fleischer. "It's your duty, Joe."

"I'm doing my best," said Terhune wearily.

The opposing managers retreated slowly, like circus animals threatened with the whip. Terhune turned, uncovering the microphones, and began hammering steadily with his gavel. The roar of the crowd dwindled to a hum again.

Roger Abbott was shouting from the floor mike at the Kansas standard. "Mr. Chairman. Mr. Chairman. Mr. Chairman!"

"For what purpose does the gentleman from Kansas rise?" asked Terhune.

The crowd stilled. "Mr. Chairman," said Abbott, his yellow bow tie bobbing with his Adam's apple, "there is now clear and irrefutable evidence that thousands of spectators have been admitted to the visitors' galleries on forged tickets. Therefore I move that the convention do now recess until three o'clock, and that the chair appoint a committee to investigate and determine which tickets are valid and which are counterfeit."

A chorus of boos—mostly from the spectator seats— clashed with loud cheers from the floor. Terhune brushed back his white hair and beat the lectern with his gavel.

"The chair will state that he has already made such an inquiry in his own right, with inconclusive results. However, the gentleman's motion is in order. Do I hear a second?"

"Second the motion." It was Joseph Rohrbaugh at the Pennsylvania microphone.

"You have heard the motion and second," intoned Terhune. "All those in favor signify by saying aye."

"Aye!" The shout came as from one voice.

"Those opposed, no."

"No-oo-oo!" A massive cry resounded and hundreds of throats held the vowel to a long, mournful finale.

"The noes appear to have it." Terhune paused only a second. "The noes have it, and the motion is defeated. The clerk will call—"

Now the noise from delegates, alternates and spectators climbed to new peaks. Newsmen swelled the din around the platform by standing on their press benches and shouting to one another.

A rolling chant began in the spectator tiers: "Enough's enough! Enough's enough! Enough's enough!" It faded, but a new chant emerged: "Vote! Vote! Vote! Vote!"

Terhune shook his gavel at the spectators. The noise abated not a bit. On the platform, Archie tried to make himself understood to Louis Cohen as he handed him a stiff sheet of paper.

"Take this Yobst affidavit," he said, almost shouting. "Here's the names of six more leaders I want you to show it to, the ones I didn't get to this morning. For God's sake, don't let anyone get it away from you. I don't want this thing out of our possession."

Cohen nodded and stuffed the paper into an inner pocket before standing up to survey the mass of people on the floor. Archie had to grin; Cohen looked like an unarmed and lonely traveler about to venture into trackless jungles. The little professor squared his shoulders and left by the rear of the platform.

Archie swung around and sought out the V.I.P. box where Kay was sitting. She was ducking to avoid having her head bumped by a cardboard sign which read "Vote Roberts." Their eyes met and Kay fluttered a hand at him in a

half salute. Archie sneezed and thought of a cool, white bed
with Kay standing beside him with a pitcher of lemonade.

Terhune stood helpless at the rostrum. He had given up the
gavel; nobody could hear it. At last, mopping his face, he
strode down the ramp to the place where Archie and Fleischer
sat opposite each other. He beckoned the two managers to
his side. Their heads formed a tight semicircle, which Terhune
hoped would prove to be an island of reason in this sea of
insanity.

"This nonsense has got to stop," the chairman said. "We
can't proceed in that inferno."

"Recess the convention, Joe," said Fleischer quickly, "and
let's try to work something out."

Terhune shook his head. "That wouldn't help. We'd never
get to the bottom of this thing in a dozen years. Anyway,
they just voted down a recess."

"Yeah, with half the no votes coming out of the galleries,"
Fleischer snapped.

"Never mind that now," Terhune said. "I've got a compromise for you two fellows."

Both Fleischer and Archie were wary. They said nothing.

"It's obvious," the chairman said, "that most of those people
in the spectator seats are on Manchester's side."

"That's what I've been telling you," Fleischer said. "The
joint is stacked."

"Now, wait a minute, Carl. Listen to what I'm proposing.
The convention will proceed with the balloting, with spectators
now holding seats staying in their places. But I'll order visitors
to be quiet, and at the first breach of the peace I'll clear the
galleries."

"It'll never work," said Fleischer sourly.

Archie thought fast. If he agreed, Manchester would lose some of the reborn momentum of the day, for his cheerleaders in the galleries would be silenced. But if he refused, Terhune might order the spectator sections emptied right now. The chairman could be pushed only so far. And anyway, Fleischer was right—it wouldn't work, at least not well enough to really silence his people in the gallery.

"It's all right with us," he said.

"No deal," said Fleischer.

Terhune prodded the Roberts manager with the handle of his gavel. "Don't forget, Carl, that I've forbidden any more delivery of telegrams. You know that ninety-nine per cent of them are for Manchester. I could lift that ruling and let the Western Union boys keep bringing their bundles in right through the voting. Do you want that?"

"You're blackmailing me, Joe," protested Fleischer.

"I'm trying to reach a sensible compromise," Terhune countered. "Now, how about it?"

"Okay, go ahead." Fleischer bit off the words and turned back to his seat.

Terhune returned to the rostrum and threw his arms wide. The noise flowed over him like a river in flood. He pressed his signal button. A thunderous blast came from the organ; then another; then a third. The crowd subsided enough for Terhune to return to the gavel. This time he beat it without stopping, his arm rising and falling like a pump handle. Joe Terhune was determined to be heard and finally the throng surrendered to the inevitable and fell silent.

"Thank you, ladies and gentlemen," Terhune said, "for your reluctant return to civilization."

He followed up the laugh with his new orders: "And at the

first sound from the galleries, the sergeant at arms will be instructed to clear every seat. Visitors are here at the sufferance of the delegates, who have business to transact."

A small collective groan came from one spectator section and Terhune waggled his gavel in that direction. "That will be the last out of you," he scolded, "or the sergeant at arms will go to work."

In the unexpected hush that had fallen on McCormick Place a scraping of chairs could be heard. The Pennsylvania delegation had risen and was filing up the aisle toward the exit.

"Don't worry, Mr. Chairman," said Joseph Rohrbaugh at the floor microphone. "We're not mad at anybody. We're just going out to caucus."

All over the floor little mounds were growing as delegates opened the telegrams that had been delivered before Terhune shut off the flow. Governor Jim Bob Cole of Kentucky seemed to be sitting in a yellow swamp. He tore open one envelope after another, glanced knowingly at the point of origin and skimmed the message. "If this is organized," he said to his neighbor, "I'll eat my Uncle Paul's shirt. Why, even the folks in Big Swallow are wiring me to vote for Manchester." At the Iowa standard, Senator Floberg angrily shoved away a Western Union boy who had brought him a stack of messages in defiance of Terhune's earlier orders. Terhune spotted the incident and banged his gavel again.

"The sergeant at arms," he said, "will take those messenger boys out by the scruff of the neck if he has to. No more telegrams of any variety will be delivered to anybody in this hall."

Louis Cohen was kneeling in the aisle beside Montcalm Andersen, showing the Yobst affidavit to the Minnesota leader. "My God," said Andersen, "you're not going to make this public, are you?" Cohen shook his head. "We don't want to hurt the party," he answered. "We just want the leaders to know what's been going on."

"How do I know it's straight?" Andersen asked.

Cohen whispered in his ear: "We got it through Bones Cramer. You're welcome to check it with him." Andersen looked puzzled as he handed the paper back to the little professor.

At the Illinois standard, Mark Davidson, wearing an official messenger's badge which had got him onto the floor, leaned across two delegates to whisper to Stanton Colby, the ruddy-faced national finance chairman.

"Stanton," Davidson said, "those wires are all organized by the Manchester people. We've run a check on them."

Colby nodded. "I assumed so," he replied. "I never pay any attention to that kind of thing."

Joe Terhune's arms were outstretched again, seeking to prolong the quiet which had settled over the hall for almost a full minute. He glanced behind him to make sure the big electric tally screen was ready, then beckoned to a man who sat just behind him. The man, dressed in a spotless white suit, stood up with an enormous sheet of paper in his hand. Two other clerks with similar sheets moved up to sit at a table nearby.

"The Thirtieth Republican National Convention," announced Terhune, "will now ballot for a candidate for President of the United States. The clerk will call the roll of the states!"

The only sound in McCormick Place was the rustling of thousands of paper tally sheets.

23

"A-la-ba-ma!" The clerk's high, reedy voice gave each syllable exactly the same emphasis. "Twenty votes."

"Mr. Chairman," came the answer, "the sovereign state of Alabama casts 19 votes for Governor Bryan Roberts, 1 vote for Charles B. Manchester."

A cheer went up, tentatively, as if the delegates were trying out their voices. There were also some boos from the spectator seats, and Joe Terhune spoke fiercely: "The galleries will not participate. That's a final warning." The big screen behind the platform flashed its first announcement:

ROBERTS 19
MANCHESTER 1

"Alabama," repeated the clerk, "19 votes for Roberts, 1 vote for Manchester." He made appropriate pencil marks on the long tally sheet he had draped over the lectern.

"Alaska! Twelve votes."

"Alaska," came the response, "the largest state in the Union, unanimously casts its 12 votes for the next President of the United States, Governor Bryan Roberts."

California waved its standard up and down as another cheer echoed in the hall. Terhune studied the spectator seats carefully, but appeared satisfied. The tally screen flashed:

ROBERTS 31
MANCHESTER 1

"Alaska," intoned the clerk, "12 votes for Roberts."

In front of a television set in the Hilton's Royal Skyway suite Julia Manchester squeezed her husband's hand.

"Never could make a dent in Alaska," he mused. In nearby chairs, Calvin Burroughs and Wesley Shaw busied themselves with their own score cards.

"Arizona! 16 votes."

"Arizona, Mr. Chairman, the fastest-growing state in the Union, votes 11 for Bryan Roberts and 5 for Manchester."

Again the numbers changed on the big screen:

ROBERTS 42
MANCHESTER 6

The phone rang in Manchester's suite. "I've been trying to reach you since breakfast, Dad." It was Jake.

"Hi there, Son. I hoped you'd call."

"Good luck, Dad. You'll get one vote from Massachusetts you didn't expect. Jim Steadall promised me he'd switch to you."

"Good boy!" Manchester's *voice had its usual hearty, confident ring.* "Win or lose, we've got a fishing date next week up in Michigan. Right?"

"Right, Dad."

"Kiss Patsy for both of us. If—and it's a pretty big if right now—if I'm nominated, I'm expecting both of you here for the acceptance speech."

"Sure, Dad. You couldn't keep Patsy away with the National Guard."

Manchester turned back to his wife as he hung up. "You can't lose with a boy like that."

Julia Manchester felt a sudden dampness in her eyes. She smiled and clasped the candidate's hand harder.

"Arkansas! Twelve votes."

"Arkansas," replied its chairman from his place on the floor, "responding to the obvious wishes of the American people, casts 11 votes for Manchester, 1 vote for Roberts."

The tally screen flashed:

ROBERTS 43
MANCHESTER 17

A cheer from the spectator tiers rolled down to mingle with cries on the floor. Terhune slammed his gavel. "The sergeant at arms will remove every spectator who demonstrated," he commanded. The crowd fell silent, stunned that the chairman would actually enforce his threat. In the silence, a voice boomed from a rear row: "Give us one more chance, Joe." Terhune joined the laughter. "It is so ordered," he agreed. "Just one more chance. One."

"Arkansas," repeated the clerk, "1 vote for Roberts, 11 votes for Manchester."

Obie O'Connell sat alone in his hotel room, watching the television set. His feet were propped on a stool and his shirt was unbuttoned to the navel. He marked his private score pad, which already carried a series of esoteric footnotes, and he thought of the back booth of the all-night restaurant in Little Rock where he had dickered for hours with the state's leading Republican. When they finally parted, he had his pledge—a Manchester delegation. In return, he . . . What had he given? Not much, really. A promise that all patronage for the state would funnel through his benefactor. And why not? Both senators and all the congressmen were Democrats. Obie made a note to remind Archie of the man's name and the nature of the promise.

"California! Ninety-two votes." Again there was complete quiet. Every person in the hall knew that the convention's biggest delegation would yield a crushing majority for its governor. McCormick Place waited in silence for the blow to fall.

"California," said its chairman in an even, conversational tone, "the Golden State and the most populous in the nation, casts 91 votes for the next President of the United States, Governor Bryan Roberts. For Secretary Manchester, 1 vote."

The last announcement was drowned in noise. The California delegation stood up, waving and cheering. The tally screen showed:

ROBERTS 134
MANCHESTER 18

In his suite at the Blackstone, Bryan Roberts did not reflect the enthusiasm of his backers in McCormick Place. He heaved himself out of his armchair, wiping at the sweat on the side of his neck, and picked up the phone which linked him with key delegations on the floor. "California," he told the operator. The state chairman answered. "Who did we lose?"

"That was Mrs. Paulson from Marin County," the chairman replied.

"Why? What happened?" asked Roberts.

"Those damn telegrams, Governor. She's gotten nine hundred of them and the boy was trying to bring her more when Terhune cracked down. She's all broken up, crying right here on the floor. She says she wanted to stick by you, but she couldn't buck the people."

"Any more losses if we go to a second ballot?"

"No, I think we're solid the rest of the way." Then the chairman added: "But who knows? This thing is getting kind of nutty."

"Colorado! Eighteen votes."

"Colorado," said its spokesman, "the state of unparalleled vistas and apparently uncertain mind, casts 9 votes for Manchester, 8 votes for Roberts, and 1 for Moon."

"Colorado," echoed the clerk, "9 votes for Manchester, 8

votes for Roberts, 1 vote for—uh—Moon."

A titter ran through the hall and Joe Terhune brushed the clerk away from the microphone. "Now just a minute," he said. "How do you spell that third name?"

"Moon. M-o-o-n," spelled the Colorado spokesman. "Like astronauts on the moon."

Terhune disliked foolishness at a Republican convention. He gaveled twice to break up the laughter. "And who, please, for the benefit of the tally clerk, is Mr. Moon?"

"It isn't Mr. Moon," replied the voice from the floor. "It's Mrs. Moon."

"All right," said Terhune testily. "Who is Mrs. Moon?"

A voice from the spectator tiers answered him: "Mr. Moon's wife!" The laughter convulsed the audience and anger rushed over Terhune's cheeks like a flame. He whacked his gavel again.

"That is correct," said the Colorado spokesman. "Mrs. Moon is married to Mr. Moon, one of the leading citizens of Colorado Springs, Colorado."

"Well," spluttered Terhune, "could we have her first name for the record, please?"

There was a whispered conference at the Colorado standard as a woman leaned across to talk to the delegation chairman.

"Mrs. Moon," said the chairman, "who is a delegate to this convention, requests that her name be withdrawn as a candidate. She thinks someone must have voted for her as a joke."

Terhune glowered from his rostrum like a wrathful judge. "Voting for a President is no joke. The rules prohibit any changing of votes until the roll call is completed. May we have Mrs. Moon's first name, please?"

The man at the Colorado microphone hesitated. "Her first name," he said slowly, "is Dawn. Mrs. Dawn Moon."

This time the laughter rolled over the hall in waves. Terhune stood erect, irritated but patient, and waited for it to subside.

"The clerk," he said, "will record one vote for Mrs. Dawn Moon."

The voice from Colorado spoke again. "As long as this is going into the record of the convention, Mrs. Moon asks that her vote be recorded with her husband's name. We would like it to read Mrs. Chester Moon."

Terhune had passed the point of vexation. He let the laughter die out this time, then said: "The clerk will delete one vote for Mrs. Dawn Moon and substitute one vote for Mrs. Chester Moon. Are there any further nominations from Colorado? If not, the clerk will proceed." The tally screen flashed its announcement:

ROBERTS 142

MANCHESTER 27

MOON 1

On the platform, Archie picked up his phone as it buzzed. He was not greatly surprised to hear Obie O'Connell's voice.

"Listen, kid, it's none of my business, but if it was me I'd do all I could to keep that Pennsylvania delegation out of the hall until the first ballot is over. If they come back now, they ain't gonna come back for your guy. Stall 'em somehow, huh?"

Archie reached for another button on his phone box even as he replied. "Thanks, Obie. I'll try to get word to that Mrs. Potter." He sneezed violently. "Oh, damn it to hell!"

"Connecticut! Sixteen votes," announced the clerk.

"Connecticut," cried its chairman, "votes 14 for Manchester, 2 for Roberts."

ROBERTS 144
MANCHESTER 41
MOON 1

In his suite at the Congress Hotel Gus Maguire glanced up from the TV set and spoke to an aide sitting by the telephone. "Neither Mark nor I could make much headway with that bunch," he said. There was a knock at the door. The aide answered, then handed Maguire a telegram. It was addressed to him, care of the hotel, and it read: "The nation needs Manchester. Please cast one vote for common sense. Ann Schmidt, Denver, Colorado." The Missile Workers' president crumpled the wire and tossed it at a wastebasket. "How did she get my name?" he wondered aloud. "The country's going nuts. Who started this crazy stuff, anyway?" The aide merely shook his head.

"Delaware! Twelve votes."

"Delaware," replied the delegation spokesman, "has hearkened to the speech of a great American. General Shaw didn't send us a telegram—but we got the message. Delaware casts its 12 votes for Charles B. Manchester."

The jangle of a cow bell in the Texas delegation could be heard above the cheers and protests.

ROBERTS 144
MANCHESTER 53
MOON 1

Terhune whispered to the tally clerk, who paused for a drink of water while the chairman summoned a young man from the back of the platform.

"Tell the fellow running that screen to leave off that vote for Moon," he said. "It looks ridiculous."

The youngster scurried away and Terhune held up the proceedings until he received a signal from the screen operator. The tally clerk cleared his throat.

"Florida! Thirty-four votes."

Florida split—20 for Roberts, 14 for Manchester—but the next three states gave a majority of their votes to Manchester. Thus, after Georgia, Hawaii and Idaho, the cumulative total read:

ROBERTS 181
MANCHESTER 96

"Illinois! Fifty-eight votes."

Two men argued heatedly at the Illinois standard. Stanton Colby, the broker and national finance chairman, waved a slip of paper in the face of the delegation chairman, a United States senator. The senator shook his head, finally thrust Colby bodily into his seat. The broker's coat caught on the back of the chair and a panning TV camera caught him looking for a moment like a fashionable scarecrow.

"Illinois!" the clerk repeated.

"Illinois casts 35—no, 36 votes for Roberts, 22 votes for Manchester," said the senator. This time, both Roberts and Manchester claques loosed competing cheers.

ROBERTS 217
MANCHESTER 118

"How about Moon?" yelled a man in the galleries. Terhune ignored him.

Manchester managed to regain the Illinois slippage in Indiana, which gave him 21 votes to 11 for Roberts.

"Iowa! Twenty-four votes."

All eyes were on the delegation chairman, Senator Boise Floberg, as he rose to report. The switch of the Senate Republican leader from Manchester to Roberts had been big convention news, second only to President Stuart's change of heart.

"Iowa casts 14 votes for Roberts," said Floberg, pushing back his dangling lock of sandy hair, "and 10 votes for Manchester."

ROBERTS 242
MANCHESTER 149

As the figures flashed onto the screen, a surprised "ooooh" rose from the crowd.

In their hotel suite, Julia Manchester looked inquiringly at her husband. But before she could say anything, the phone linking the candidate with the convention platform rang. It was Archie.

"That was a real break for us in Iowa," he said softly. "I figured—"

"I know," interrupted Manchester. "I thought Floberg would take the whole delegation to Roberts." The candidate grinned as he turned back to his wife.

"My," she said, "you lose a state and you positively gloat over it."

"That's politics," he said cheerfully. "We didn't lose as much in Iowa as we thought we would. And the convention sensed it too. That's why you heard the big 'ooh.' "

Mrs. Manchester, obviously unconvinced, returned her gaze to the television set with all the fascination of a playgoer watching a Greek drama in which certain doom has already cast its shadow.

"Kansas! Twenty votes."

Roger Abbott almost crooned over the state's microphone. "Kansas," he said with silk in his voice, "casts all of its 20 votes for our next President, Governor Bryan Roberts." The roar of the crowd was heavier now, as tension built up with the call of each state. The screen showed:

ROBERTS 262
MANCHESTER 149

And now a new figure was added:

NEEDED TO NOMINATE 655

At the back of the hall, Bones Cramer was chewing a hot dog at a refreshment stand. His sepulchral face showed no overt concern over the contest on the floor. A wire-service reporter was standing beside him.

"What's your guess, Mr. Cramer?" the newspaperman asked.

"I never guess, son," Cramer said. He shook his head. "But you got to hand it to Roger Abbott. I never liked the son-of-a-bitch, but he delivers in the clutch. All twenty for Roberts— and in a peace state, too." There was admiration in his tone.

Kentucky, Louisiana, Maine and Maryland yielded a small net gain for Manchester. Kentucky provided the biggest margin for Manchester and the TV cameramen delighted in the picture of Governor Jim Bob Cole, for the keynoter made his state's announcement while standing in a puddle of yellow telegrams that covered his feet and ankles.

A kind of mass hypnosis settled on the crowd. Thousands of eyes were fixed on the front of the hall and there was little movement during the state announcements. It was almost as if each band of partisans felt that the wrong gesture or twist of the head might provoke the hand of vengeance against its candidate. The cries of approval or displeasure were almost automatic now. The ten thousand spectators in the upper tiers remained quiet, tamed by Terhune's menacing glare. The score stood:

ROBERTS 294
MANCHESTER 195
NEEDED TO NOMINATE 655

"Massachusetts! Thirty-four votes!"

"Vice-chairman James Steadall reporting," came the reply. "The Bay State has caucused on the floor with these results: Manchester 18 votes . . ." Steadall delivered the Manchester vote in a booming voice, then dropped an octave: ". . . and Roberts 16 votes."

Crack! went Terhune's gavel. "Delegation spokesmen," he declared, "will refrain from announcing the vote in a tone designed to prejudice the cause of one candidate or another."

"Massachusetts," intoned the clerk, "16 for Roberts, 18 for Manchester."

ROBERTS 310
MANCHESTER 213
NEEDED TO NOMINATE 655

In the apartment in Tiburon, Patsy Manchester threw her arms around her husband. "You got Jim Steadall, you lovely lug, you," she said. Then she planted herself in front of the TV set again, clenched her fists and waved them up and down. "He's got to win," she said. "I'll die if he doesn't."

"Maybe I'm jinxing him by watching," said Jake. He looked unhappy. "Roberts seems to stay about a hundred votes ahead. I don't like it."

Chairman Terhune's brooding face appeared on the TV screen and Patsy stuck out her tongue at the image. "If he'd only let those Western Union boys bring in the telegrams," she said, "we'd drown Bin Roberts in them."

"Michigan! Forty-eight votes."

"Michigan casts 27 votes for Roberts, 21 votes for Manchester."

The figures on the big screen flickered, then came up:

ROBERTS 337
MANCHESTER 234
NEEDED TO NOMINATE 655

"Minn-e-so-ta! Twenty-six votes."

Montcalm Andersen, standing ready at the Minnesota microphone, almost yelled. "Minnesota casts 15 votes for a man of conviction, Charles Manchester." He dropped his voice to a lower key. "And 11 votes for Roberts."

Terhune roared: "That type of announcement is specifically forbidden."

Louis Cohen rang Archie on the intercom from a rear position in the hall.

"You must have got to Andersen with that affidavit," said Archie.

The professor grunted. "Yeah, but there's another thing. Obie saw him this morning and told him that he'd lied about Manchester not meaning it. And Andersen was almost buried in telegrams before Terhune choked them off. He's voting the way he thinks his people want him to vote."

"How many delegates have you shown that paper to, Louis?"

"Only four guys who count," said Cohen. "It's a mess trying to move on this floor. I've been trying, but I think I ought to go check on that Pennsylvania caucus now."

"Yeah," Archie said. He passed on Obie's advice. "Try to get word to Helena Potter, will you? She's about our only friend in that gang."

The clerk droned on. "Mississippi! Thirteen votes."

Mississippi yielded no surprises. It split 7 to 6 in favor of Roberts, following the O'Connell-Fleischer agreement precisely. The screen flickered:

ROBERTS 355
MANCHESTER 255
NEEDED TO NOMINATE 655

Missouri proved a disappointment to Manchester. Despite Hubert Germaine's efforts and an earlier caucus favorable to Manchester, Roberts got a majority of the votes. Montana,

Nebraska, Nevada and New Hampshire redressed the balance somewhat.

ROBERTS 393
MANCHESTER 291
NEEDED TO NOMINATE 655

"New Jersey! Forty votes."

"New Jersey," reported its chairman, "casts 26 votes for Roberts and 14 votes for Manchester." Shouts of glee erupted from Roberts' backers around the hall and elsewhere there was a swelling murmur, uncertain and confused, as the score went up:

ROBERTS 419
MANCHESTER 305
NEEDED TO NOMINATE 655

Kay Orcott, almost frozen with excitement in her chair in a front-row box, could hear a radio commentator in the aisle below chattering into his portable microphone.

"That may be the start of the Roberts bandwagon, folks," he said. "New Jersey may be the turning point. Roberts has been running about a hundred votes ahead, but now he's lengthening his lead. Big New York State, coming up, may tell the story."

Kay leaned over the rail. "That's nothing but propaganda," she yelled at him.

The broadcaster finished his stint, appraised her sadly and said: "It's way past the hour for propaganda, baby. Besides, if it means anything, I like Manchester too."

New Mexico gave Roberts another boost with 9 of its 14 votes, and the crowd tensed again.

"New York! Eighty-six votes."

"New York casts 50 votes for Roberts, 36 for Manchester."

A roar convulsed the hall and a nest of balloons rose slowly from the California delegation. A song began in the rear and spread through the delegates: "California, here we come . . ."

ROBERTS 478
MANCHESTER 346
NEEDED TO NOMINATE 655

Carl Fleischer was not happy, however. Cupping his hand to his mouth, he barked into the intercom at Roger Abbott.

"What the hell happened there, Roger? We had more than sixty votes in New York this morning."

"It's something about some goddam affidavit," said Abbott. "It involves Johnny Kolsak, who seconded for us last night."

"Well, Gus Maguire got him to switch to Roberts. Hell, Kolsak isn't changing again, is he?"

"No, no," said Abbott, "but there's some kind of paper charging that Kolsak took some money, I think. I've only heard secondhand. Louis Cohen is supposed to be showing it around."

Fleischer's voice was frayed. "Well, is it true?"

"I don't know, Carl. Frankly, I thought you'd know."

Fleischer snapped off the phone key and summoned an aide from farther back on the platform. "Take over here," he ordered. "I have to go down and bird-dog Pennsylvania."

North Carolina and North Dakota gave Manchester a slight majority of their votes over Roberts.

"Ohio! Fifty-eight votes."

"Ohio, the mother of Presidents, a great Republican state," boomed the voice at the state standard, "casts all 58 votes for its favorite son, the favorite son of all America today, Charles Bedford Manchester."

This time the galleries roared. Terhune brandished his gavel, but without effect. The noise rolled from above in a rising swell.

> ROBERTS 496
> MANCHESTER 426
> NEEDED TO NOMINATE 655

In the overhead television booths, fiercely gabbling announcers noted that for the first time since the early balloting, the gap between Roberts and Manchester was considerably less than a hundred votes. But the joy of the Manchester rooters was short-lived; Oklahoma and Oregon both gave majorities to Roberts.

"Pennsylvania! Sixty-four votes."

The sixty-four Pennsylvania seats were vacant, a bare patch in the forest of faces. A lone man stood at the state standard.

"The Pennsylvania delegation is still caucusing," he reported. "Pennsylvania passes."

"Pennsylvania passes," repeated the clerk. A scattering of jeers greeted the announcement.

Two state troopers stood guard at the door of the conference room outside the auditorium where the Pennsylvania delegation was locked in secret session. Newspapermen milled about helplessly; this time there was no unguarded back door.

Carl Fleischer, pacing opposite a sad-faced Louis Cohen, had his hands jammed in his coat pockets. His smoked glasses failed to mask smears of sweat around his eyes, and his usually faultlessly knotted tie hung loose from his collar. Fleischer scribbled a note and gave it to a state trooper. The policeman shook his head.

"Dammit, it's for Speaker Rohrbaugh," barked Fleischer. "All you have to do is knock on the door, for God's sake."

The trooper reluctantly opened the door and handed the note to a man inside. But when Fleischer stood on tiptoe to peer in, the officer shoved him away.

Not to be outdone, Cohen wrote out a message for Mrs. Helena Potter and got it passed in. "All right, that's all," the trooper ordered. "No more notes."

Roberts gained slightly in the next four states—Rhode Island, South Carolina, South Dakota and Tennessee. The screen now showed:

> ROBERTS 564
> MANCHESTER 470
> NEEDED TO NOMINATE 655

The hall became quiet again and heads bent over tally sheets. The figures told the story: If Roberts could get a sizable majority from the big Texas delegation he would pass the 600 mark and have the nomination within his grasp. There was not a sound from the spectator tiers, save for the uneasy rustle of papers. Joe Terhune mopped his forehead and stood aside for the clerk.

"Texas! Fifty-six votes."

"Mr. Chairman," came the slow drawl in reply, "Texas casts 32 votes for Roberts, 24 votes for Manchester."

Amid the roar which exploded from the floor, a woman in a gray linen dress could be seen struggling past the knees and legs of other Texas delegates. She seized the microphone while still several feet away, and almost fell against it.

"Mr. Chairman," she said, "I am Grace Orcott, a delegate-at-large from Texas, and I request a poll of the Texas delegation."

"Does the gentlewoman contend that the vote of the state has been incorrectly stated?" Terhune asked.

"The vote, Mr. Chairman, was correctly stated as approved by this delegation yesterday morning in caucus," Mrs. Orcott said, "but since that time, a number of votes have changed. I know mine has."

A long, low murmur rose from the convention floor, as if a vast chorus were sounding its pitch. The delegates—unlike most of the spectators—knew that Mrs. Orcott was an official leader of the Roberts forces. A bubble of conversation, excited in the Manchester regions and apprehensive in the Roberts groups, broke and fractured into little gossiping huddles. Terhune rapped his gavel.

"Under the rule, any delegate may request a poll of his state, and the poll is ordered. But also, under the rules, the poll will be taken privately while the call of the states proceeds."

"Mr. Chairman," said Grace Orcott quickly, "the standing of Texas is crucial to this nomination and of concern to the entire nation. I therefore ask unanimous consent that the poll be conducted openly for all to hear."

Roger Abbott was just as quick. He grabbed the Kansas

microphone and shouted: "Mr. Chairman, I object."

"Objection is heard," noted Terhune. "The call of the states will proceed."

The galleries loosed a collective, plaintive protest, but Mrs. Orcott was speaking again as soon as it died away.

"In that case, Mr. Chairman," she said, "I request, in the interest of fair play, that the remaining states pass until Texas has completed its poll."

An indignant shout from California and other Roberts sectors followed her plea. Again Terhune had to pound for order.

"The lady has made her request," he said. "The clerk will call the roll."

"Utah!" cried the clerk. "Fourteen votes."

"In deference to the gallant lady from Texas," said the portly Utah chairman, "a gentlewoman who has served this party's national committee faithfully and well, Utah passes."

An Associated Press reporter stood on a press bench just below Archie's seat on the platform and waved a sheet of paper at him. Archie leaned down to take it. The paper had been torn from the AP running teleprinter of convention news. It read:

CHICAGO, Aug. 17 (AP)—A near-riot occurred today on the front steps of McCormick Place as delegates inside balloted for the G.O.P. presidential candidate in a close two-man contest.

More than 100 Western Union messengers, carrying heavy bags of wires imploring delegates to vote for Treasury Secretary Charles B. Manchester, milled about outside the big doors, which had been barred to them by permanent chairman Joseph Terhune.

Manchester supporters tried to crash the police lines in front of the doors to open a path for the messengers. Chicago police threw them back, and a number of persons went sprawling.

One woman, who gave her name as Margaret St. Clair, was placed in a police ambulance after suffering a broken arm in the fracas. She said she was a University of Michigan student and a "volunteer worker" for Manchester.

Archie flicked an intercom key and got a floor lieutenant in the Virginia delegation. He read the AP dispatch hurriedly to him and asked, "See if you can't give it a little public airing, will you?"

Vermont, like Utah, passed—with more flattering references to Grace Orcott.

"Virginia! Thirty votes."

"Mr. Chairman," said the Virginia spokesman. "A parliamentary inquiry."

"The delegate will state it," said Terhune, stepping forward.

"Mr. Chairman, Virginia is informed that the Chicago city police are preventing more than a hundred Western Union messengers from entering this building to deliver telegrams addressed to delegates. Mr. Chairman, my parliamentary inquiry is this: under what authority are the city police acting to prevent persons from entering this building?"

"That is not a proper parliamentary inquiry," barked Terhune. His face was splotched with temper. "The police are acting under my orders. If one more person enters this building, it will become a fire hazard."

The galleries groaned in protest. Terhune swept his eyes grimly over the spectators, but refrained from rebuking them. He wanted to avoid two rulings in succession which would be interpreted as hostile to the Manchester forces. Joe Terhune had his own private preference, but he was trying to do his duty as he saw it.

"Virginia!" repeated the clerk. "Thirty votes."

"Virginia, always gallant to a lady," said the spokesman, "also passes."

That set the pattern. With Fleischer away from his command post on the platform, the Roberts forces were unable to get any of the remaining delegations to cast a vote. Washington, West Virginia, Wisconsin, Wyoming, the District of Columbia, Puerto Rico—all passed.

"Virgin Islands! Three votes."

"The Virgin Islands," came the answer, "passes—not because of Mrs. Orcott, but because we don't know yet who's going to win, and the Virgin Islands is always with the winner."

Terhune joined the laughter, which died swiftly as all heads in the hall turned toward the Texas standard. But the call reverted to the first state which had failed to vote.

"Pennsylvania! Sixty-four votes."

There was still only one man at the Pennsylvania standard. "Mr. Chairman," he said unhappily, "Pennsylvania still passes."

At the door of the caucus room, Carl Fleischer had Speaker Joseph Rohrbaugh against the wall a few feet from the state troopers. Sweat streaked his whole face now and his hands trembled as he placed them on Rohrbaugh's chest in an imploring gesture.

"Jesus, Joe, make the Governor come to his senses." Fleischer's voice was almost gone. He spoke in a scratchy whisper. "For God's sake, he doesn't have a chance to be nominated. This convention is going for either Roberts or Manchester—in about five minutes."

"I know." Rohrbaugh's mouth was grim as he shook his

head. *"I know, Carl, but he's in a trance. He won't let the caucus come to a vote."*

"Tell him, tell him," said Fleischer, the veins standing in his neck with the effort to push sound through his vocal chords. *"If Pennsylvania goes for Roberts, it's all over—and Ben Wilcox can have anything he wants. Anything!"*

"I'll try again," said the Speaker.

Fleischer almost shoved him to the door. "Get in there, then," he croaked, *"there's only about four-five minutes left."*

Rohrbaugh re-entered the caucus room and Fleischer slumped against the wall. A few feet away, Louis Cohen studied a note passed out of the room for him. It was from Mrs. Potter: "Louis, I've only got 11 votes for Manchester, and I don't know how long we can stall a vote. But we'll keep trying."

Cohen hurried off to the nearest intercom phone to call Archie.

"Texas! Fifty-six votes."

"Mr. Chairman," said the man at the state standard, "Texas has completed its poll and is ready to vote. Texas now casts 17 votes for Roberts—" he had to pause while the roar swept across the hall and subsided—"and 39 votes for Charles B. Manchester!"

The sound was overpowering. It swept down in a cascade from the spectator galleries and rolled over the delegates. In the rear, hundreds of alternates stood and cheered. In her V.I.P. box, Kay Orcott tried to wave at her mother and Archie at the same time. Her mother was lost in the sea of faces, but Archie stood on his chair and thrust his hand toward

Kay in a V-for-victory sign. Three lights blinked on his phone box, but he failed to see them. In the press section, a wooden bench cracked under the weight of those standing on it, and two typewriters crashed to the floor. A chant began in the galleries: "The Man . . . The Man . . . The Man . . . The Man . . . The Man . . . The Man . . ." The operator of the tally screen punched his keys to change the totals:

ROBERTS 581
MANCHESTER 509
MOON 1
NEEDED TO NOMINATE 655

Terhune shook his gavel at the operator. "Get that damn Moon out of there!" he shouted.

"Utah!" The clerk's voice was smothered by noise. He pointed at the state standard to convey his call. "Fourteen votes."

"Utah," came the reply, and the hall quieted. "Utah casts 3 votes for Roberts, 11 votes for Manchester."

The roar was steady now, like the sea wind in a rising gale.

ROBERTS 584
MANCHESTER 520
NEEDED TO NOMINATE 655

"Vermont! Twelve votes."

"Vermont . . . please, please." The sound lessened by a fraction. "Vermont casts 2 votes for Roberts, 10 votes for Manchester."

The clamor mounted again and spectators began to pour down from their seats into the boxes. Police struggled to hold back the surge. A half dozen fistfights broke out. Above the clamor came a bull voice through an electrically amplified megaphone: "Enough's enough! Enough's enough! Enough's enough! . . ."

"Virginia! Thirty votes."

The response came calm and steady, as though from far away. "Virginia, the Old Dominion state, unanimously casts all 30 of its votes for a great fighter, Charles B. Manchester."

> ROBERTS 586
> MANCHESTER 560
> NEEDED TO NOMINATE 655

The uproar had no peaks or valleys now. McCormick Place was all sound, and nobody in it could be heard by his neighbor unless he screamed in his ear. The clerk was giving his cues to the delegations by hand signals, his voice completely lost beyond the first few rows.

"Washington! Twenty-four votes."

"Washington, committed by primary and proud of it, casts . . ." The rest was lost in sound. The clerk turned to Terhune helplessly, and the chairman summoned his voice for one more blast.

"The balloting will not continue until the clerk can hear the responses," he shouted. "The convention will be in order!" There was a slight slackening in the din. Terhune waited. Another slight drop in the roar, and Terhune nodded to the clerk.

"Washington!"

"Washington, committed by primary and proud of it, casts all 24 votes for Charles B. Manchester."

ROBERTS 586
MANCHESTER 584
NEEDED TO NOMINATE 655

"West Virginia! Fourteen votes."

"West Virginia . . ." The state spokesman put his lips against his microphone to be heard. "West Virginia casts 6 votes for Roberts—and 8 votes for Manchester."

In his hotel room, Obie O'Connell scratched his little round belly and brooded over his score card. Up and down those West Virginia hills and hollows, driving the hairpin turns at midnight, beating from Beckley to Wheeling—and still the best he could do was eight out of fourteen. He sighed for the lost days of spring and cursed, for the hundredth time, all nonbinding primaries.

ROBERTS 592
MANCHESTER 592
NEEDED TO NOMINATE 655

"Wisconsin! Thirty votes."

"Wisconsin, following the results of its primary"—the dig at West Virginia was overlooked in the uproar—"casts 5 votes for Roberts, 25 votes for Manchester."

The sound could not have increased any further, but it did. A nest of "M" balloons soared upward from the Ohio delegation to signal Manchester's capture of the lead.

ROBERTS 597
MANCHESTER 617
NEEDED TO NOMINATE 655

Alone in his big office at the White House, President Frederick Stuart watched his TV set as the camera swept the turbulent crowd. Only four years, and yet a lifetime ago, his had been the convention triumph, his the dreams—dreams unfulfilled and now never to be fulfilled. So this is the way it looks from here, he thought. God help him, whichever one it is, and give him time and luck when he gets here . . .

"Wyoming! Twelve votes."

"Wyoming casts 3 votes for Roberts, 9 votes for Manchester."

"District of Columbia! Nine votes."

"The nation's capital," came the cry, "casts 2 votes for Roberts, 7 for Manchester."

> ROBERTS 602
> MANCHESTER 633
> NEEDED TO NOMINATE 655

"Puerto Rico! Five votes."

"Puerto Rico," the response came back, giving the name its Spanish inflection, "casts 5 votes for Manchester."

"Virgin Islands! Three votes."

"The Virgin Islands, now quite sure how it's going, casts all of its votes for Manchester."

Now noisemakers, trumpets and megaphones were added to the din as the last delegation completed its report. The galleries stretched out their cadence: "The Man, the Man, the Man, the Man, the Man . . ." Terhune looked over the mob and smiled for the first time that day.

"The clerk will call the names of the states that passed," he ordered.

"Pennsylvania!" called the clerk for the third time. "Sixty-four votes."

"Pennsylvania passes." The state's seats were still empty.

Terhune whacked once with his gavel, hard. "The clerk will announce the results of the first ballot."

The clerk turned to his two assistants at their little table nearby to check the official tally, though the big screen behind the platform already showed it:

> ROBERTS 602
> MANCHESTER 641
> MOON 1
> NEEDED TO NOMINATE 655

In the surging bedlam on the floor, the shining hair of Mrs. Grace Orcott could be seen bobbing along a row of seats in the Texas delegation. She was pointing a finger first here, then there. At last she reached the standard and the state chairman. She grabbed his coat by both lapels and shouted at him. He nodded emphatically and pushed her in front of his microphone.

"Mr. Chairman!" she called shrilly. "Mr. Chairman! Texas wishes to change its vote!"

"No! No! No!" It was the bull-like voice of Governor Ben Wilcox as he charged into the center aisle, shoving and pushing at the crowds clogging it. "Pennsylvania! Pennsylvania is ready to vote!"

Carl Fleischer was at his elbow, trying to clear a way for Wilcox and at the same time get Terhune's attention. "Joe! Joe!" he cried hoarsely. He bumped into a man waving a Roberts sign and his dark glasses were jarred off. "You son-of-a-bitch," he croaked. "Get outta my way! Pennsylvania's going for us 53 to 11! We're in!"

Boise Floberg of Iowa, the Senate Republican leader, saw Wilcox coming and shoved to the foot of the rostrum to shout at Terhune. "Joe! Joe! Pennsylvania!"

"Mr. Chairman! Mr. Chairman! Mr. Chairman!" Grace Orcott shouted in a frenzied chant, not once losing her grip on the Texas microphone. Her once-trim gray linen dress was rumpled now.

The two big delegations, Texas and Pennsylvania, held seats across the aisle from each other midway in the hall. The Pennsylvanians struggled down the aisle behind their governor, striving to reach the oasis of vacant chairs and their state's microphone—the only place from which they could cast their vote.

Governor Wilcox crunched ahead through the press of bodies.

"We're for Roberts, 53 to 11!" he shouted. In the din, he couldn't be heard ten feet away.

Under his dark brows, Wilcox's face glowed crimson and trickles of sweat ran down his cheeks. Manchester supporters surged into the aisle to block his progress. The Governor flailed his arms like semaphores in an effort to clear a path. One man was caught full on the jaw by the back of Wilcox's hand. He toppled over, snapping off the Utah standard in his fall.

"Roberts," roared Wilcox as he bulled forward. "Roberts is nominated!"

"Mr. Chairman. Mr. Chairman!" Grace Orcott's chant was shrill, insistent, rising above the pounding roar of the crowd which now had a new, strangely sullen quality.

In the center aisle with the Pennsylvanians, Fleischer

croaked in a voice that sounded almost insane: "Pennsylvania! Pennsylvania! We got the votes to nominate!" His cries were drowned in the swamp of sweating flesh surrounding him.

Archie DuPage cupped his hands and yelled at Terhune's back: "Texas, Joe! Texas! Recognize Texas!"

The party would debate for years whether old Joe Terhune heard the anguished pleas of Wilcox, Fleischer and Floberg. Whether he did or not, his eyes were on the Texas standard. Texas was ready; Pennsylvania was still not in its proper place.

Terhune pointed his gavel at Grace Orcott. "The chair recognizes the gentlewoman from Texas to change the vote of that state," he cried.

"Texas . . ." The high-pitched female voice cut across the crowd's unheeding roar. "Texas casts all of its 56 votes for Charles Manchester!"

"Texas," began the clerk, "casts 56 votes . . ." The rest was lost forever. The big screen flashed:

ROBERTS 585
MANCHESTER 658
MOON 1

Then the screen went blank for a second before proclaiming:

MANCHESTER NOMINATED

"Mr. Chairman, Mr. Chairman!" Wilcox had finally reached his microphone. But the organ was playing the Ohio State marching song and the aisles were choked with leaping, clamoring, delirious Republicans.

Epilogue

Between the hours of 4 P.M. and 7 P.M. on Thursday, August 17, the following stories rated priority on the Associated Press news wire in Chicago:

156
Roberts

Chicago (AP)—Gov. Bryan Roberts left his suite at the Blackstone Hotel this afternoon to call on Republican presidential nominee Charles B. Manchester.

Roberts, who only a half-hour before had lost the nomination to Manchester by a razor-thin margin in a tumultuous first-ballot contest, declined to say whether Manchester had telephoned him.

The burly 240-pound governor, showing the strain of the hectic five-day battle, was accompanied on his short journey across Balbo Street to the Hilton by his convention manager, Carl Fleischer.

"I thought I ought to go over and offer my congratulations to a great candidate," said Roberts as he left for Manchester's headquarters. "That's all there is to it."

The governor was asked by reporters whether he believed convention chairman Joseph Terhune had erred in recognizing Texas instead of Pennsylvania at the close of the first ballot. The action in effect tipped the outcome in Manchester's favor, since Pennsylvania was prepared to deliver a hefty majority to Roberts.

"That's all ancient history," said Roberts. "What we want to do now is elect Manchester president."

The governor's comment was in sharp contrast to an earlier remark by Fleischer, who was reported to have bitterly criticized Terhune in a heated discussion with Louis Cohen, a Manchester aide, as they left the convention hall.

EDW405PCD 8/17

187
Stuart

Washington (AP)—President Stuart late today congratulated Charles B. Manchester on his selection as Republican presidential nominee and pledged his "full support and assistance" in the coming campaign.

Stuart called White House newsmen to his office to read his statement. He said he had talked by telephone to both Manchester and Gov. Bryan Roberts of California after the photo-finish balloting that nominated Manchester. The chief executive said both men pledged to work harmoniously for a G.O.P. victory in November.

The President, who withdrew his earlier support of Manchester midway through the convention because of a dispute over defense policies, said the Treasury Secretary had "won the hard way—on his own."

"That was the best way—for him and for the party," Stuart said. He added that he would be willing to make any public appearances that Manchester requested during the campaign.

As for the hold-down on new nuclear warhead and missile contracts advocated by Manchester, the President said there had never been "any meaningful difference" between himself and the Treasury chief on the issue.

EDW443PCD 8/17

Correspondents:

Manchester headquarters advises the Republican nominee will make his first public appearance before the convention tonight. His daughter is flying in from Lake Winnipesaukee and his son and daughter-in-law from San Francisco. The family is expected at McCormick Place about 10 p.m. (CDT) after the balloting for vice-president.

EDW/GR455PCD 8/17

192
Convention

Chicago (AP)—The Republican convention recessed at 4:57 p.m. until 8:30 p.m. tonight.

GR458PCD 8/17

195
Hendrickson

Washington (AP)—Democratic presidential nominee Glen G. Hendrickson said today he does not plan to make defense policy an issue in his campaign against G.O.P. candidate Charles B. Manchester.

Hendrickson told a reporter after Manchester's nomination that "the issue was knocked out of the campaign today." He said the telegraphic outpouring backing Manchester's position on new missile contracts "is obvious evidence of popular support."

"Actually, Mr. Manchester has taken the same position I have always held on the matter," Hendrickson said. "I'm glad he has spoken out frankly. There are plenty of other issues on which we disagree, and I am sure the country will choose to go forward with the Democratic party in November instead of standing still with the Republicans."

Hendrickson said he had already called Manchester to congratulate him on his nomination. He declined to discuss details of the conversation.

Ironically, the chain-telephone-and-telegram phenomenon caused irritation among Hendrickson's Senate aides. About fifty telegrams imploring the senator to vote for Manchester were delivered to his Senate office building suite today.

GR511PCD 8/17

196
Convention

Chicago (AP)—Republican convention chairman Joseph Terhune said today he "had no choice" under the rules but to recognize Texas in the blazing G.O.P. nomination finale.

Terhune's decision to recognize Mrs. Grace Orcott of Texas gave the nomination to Secretary of the Treasury Charles B. Manchester by a scant three votes. Had he recognized Pennsylvania, Gov. Bryan Roberts would have won the nomination by a hair.

"Under the rules," Terhune said, "any state may switch its vote until results of the ballot are announced. But the announcement may not be delayed 'unreasonably.'

"Texas was the only state ready to act under the rules. Pennsylvania was not at its place on the floor. It was as simple as that."

(Convention clerks had not finished compiling the official first-ballot count when Texas was recognized to change its vote, even though the unofficial tally screen had flashed the result.)

The veteran party official, interviewed as he left the convention hall after the convention recessed, declined to reveal his personal preference for the nomination, but said he would "of course" support Manchester "to the hilt."

EDW514PCD 8/17

199
Convention

Chicago (AP)—Charles B. Manchester, newly nominated presidential candidate, today summoned G.O.P. leaders to a conference to discuss selection of a vice-presidential candidate.

Archibald DuPage, press secretary for Manchester, said the meeting would take place at the nominee's Hilton Hotel suite beginning at 6:30 p.m. (CDT). DuPage said representatives of "all the groups in the party" would participate. Among them, he said, would be the following:

Gov. Bryan Roberts of California, the defeated challenger; Carl Fleischer, Roberts' convention manager; Roger Abbott, Roberts' floor manager; Joseph Rohrbaugh, Speaker of the Pennsylvania House of Representatives; Louis Cohen, a Manchester aide; Hubert Germaine, a Manchester floor leader from Missouri.

Also Graham Reddig, White House special counsel; Joseph Terhune, Republican national chairman; Gov. Jim Bob Cole of Kentucky; Stanton Colby, G.O.P. national finance chairman; and Sen. Boise Floberg of Iowa, Senate Republican leader.

DuPage declined to discuss the names of possible running mates for Manchester, who won the presidential nomination on a cliff-hanging first-ballot vote.

One of those invited to the meeting, Gov. Roberts, was already in the Manchester suite. He arrived less than a half hour after the balloting and posed for pictures with the candidate. Roberts said he had "absolutely no interest" in the vice-presidential nomination.

EDW521PCD 8/17

206
Telegrams

San Francisco (AP)—The "call-ten" telephone and telegram campaign which swept the nation and helped power Charles B. Manchester to the Republican presidential nomination was started by his son and daughter-in-law, it was learned today.

Mrs. John G. Manchester, wife of the candidate's son, told an AP reporter that she had called "about a dozen" women Wednesday morning and asked them to send wires to the California delegation, and then to call ten other people with the same request.

"But I never thought it would catch on like it did," she added.

The vivacious blonde, who was wearing blue jeans when interviewed at her home in Tiburon across the bay from San Francisco, said she "just got mad" at developments in Chicago and "decided to do something to help Jake's dad."

Mrs. Manchester said she believed that the telephone-telegram chain would not have acquired the momentum it did without Gen. Wesley Shaw's seconding speech for Manchester.

"I think it was going pretty good through the day yesterday," she said, "but after that terrific speech last night—wow!"

She refused to discuss what role her husband played in the stratagem, which led to tens of thousands of wires from all over the nation by the time voting began today.

"He says he wants me to have all the credit," she explained.

Young Manchester, a junior bank executive, declined to comment beyond saying that "I have a date to go fishing with the next President of the United States next week."

(In Chicago, Manchester headquarters said it had no knowledge of the origin of the spectacular phone-and-wire campaign until young Manchester and his wife called the candidate after his nomination. Press Secretary Archibald DuPage confirmed that Manchester planned to go fishing with his son next week in northern Michigan, a favorite vacation area of the Treasury Secretary.)

JGS545PCD 8/17

Correspondents:

Reporters and photographers planning to accompany Manchester on the Michigan fishing trip next week are advised to submit their names to Louis Cohen at Manchester headquarters before 5 p.m. Friday.

Cohen will act as press secretary during the trip in place of Archibald DuPage, who will be in Texas next week. DuPage said he plans to spend several days in Dallas on "purely personal business."

EDW548PCD 8/17

214
Convention—Mrs. Manchester
Chicago (AP)—Mrs. Julia Manchester, wife of the

Republican presidential nominee, said tonight that her husband
had "already won the only thing that counts."

"Whether he wins in November is immaterial, really,"
she said, "much as we want him to become President. The people have decided that 'enough is enough' on nuclear weapons
and I thank God that my husband had the courage to lead that
fight."

Mrs. Manchester revealed in an interview that Senator
Glen G. Hendrickson, the Democratic candidate, called soon
after her husband's nomination and personally assured Manchester that he would not contest the missile issue in the fall
campaign.

EDW615PCD 8/17

Note to Editors:

The AP wire for Sunday will carry 1,000 words from

Washington on Hendrickson's past statements on the missile

issue, including quotes from his Senate speech last year urging

construction of the Daphne missile. This is in response to Hous-

ton's request.

EDW623PCD 8/17

232
Convention

Chicago (AP)—Charles B. Manchester announced tonight that O. B. O'Connell, manager of his preconvention
drive for the Republican presidential nomination, will direct his
campaign for election this fall.

Manchester appeared outside his hotel room here to
make the announcement personally with O'Connell standing beside him.

"I am proud to be able to tell you that Obie O'Connell

has agreed to continue as my campaign manager," Manchester said. "He will have full direction of my campaign between now and election day."

There was no indication why Manchester chose to make a personal announcement of the appointment, which had been expected as a matter of course. It was speculated the move was intended to spike rumors, circulating here for two days, that O'Connell was seriously ill and would drop out of the Manchester-for-President drive.

O'Connell, a veteran of Republican convention maneuvering, was asked whether he had accurately predicted today's outcome.

"Sure," he said. "You always win on the last ballot."
JGS641PCD 8/17

ABOUT THE AUTHORS

FLETCHER KNEBEL and CHARLES W. BAILEY II are internationally known as the co-authors of the novel *Seven Days in May,* published in 1962. *Seven Days in May* was not only a smash hit on the best-seller lists for more than a year in the United States, but was also extremely high in popularity in foreign-language editions throughout the world and was made into a major motion picture. Along with their fame as novelists, Mr. Knebel and Mr. Bailey are important and highly respected political journalists. They are both with the Washington Bureau of Cowles Publications, and Mr. Knebel's daily political column, *Potomac Fever,* is carried in more than ninety major newspapers.

A graduate of Miami University in Oxford, Ohio, Mr. Knebel was a reporter in Pennsylvania, Ohio, and Tennessee before going to Washington. After graduating from Phillips Exeter Academy and Harvard College, Mr. Bailey worked as a reporter for the *Minneapolis Star and Tribune* and came to the Cowles Washington Bureau in 1954.

Besides *Seven Days in May,* the authors' works include a nonfiction book about the Hiroshima bomb, entitled *No High Ground,* and contributions to *Candidates 1960,* edited by Eric Sevareid.